Twice In One Lifetime

Twice In One Lifetime, Volume 1

Jonathan Hubbard

Published by Flying Titanic Press, 2025.

TWICE IN ONE LIFETIME

This is a work of fiction. Similarities to real people, places, or events are entirely coincidental.

TWICE IN ONE LIFETIME

First edition. October 3, 2025.

Copyright © 2025 Jonathan Hubbard.

ISBN: 979-8998836602

Written by Jonathan Hubbard.

TWICE IN ONE LIFETIME
This is a work of fiction. Names, characters, organizations, places, events, and incidents are products of the author's imagination. Any resemblance to actual persons, living or dead, or actual events is purely coincidental. No part of this book may be reproduced, stored in retrieval system, or transmitted in any form or by any means, electronic, mechanical, photocopying, recording, or otherwise, without the express written permission of the author.

TWICE IN ONE LIFETIME

First edition. October 3, 2025.

ISBN: 979-8998836602

Written by Jonathan Hubbard.

Table of Contents

For Robbie

The Cold Wait

Misty November rain and a gusting north wind drive the chill close to a 1923 record low. Baptist Hospital—tied to Wake Forest's School of Medicine—has led regional cardiac and cancer care for fifteen years, a thought that steadies Michael as he waits.

Hidden in the hospital's labyrinth is a small exam room. Nurse Reyes enters, wheeling a computer cart, and checks his wristband and compares to the chart.

"Emergency contact?" she asks.

"Nobody." Michael growls.

"Spouse?"

Michael stares at the ceiling. "Caroline—my ex. But don't bother; she'd probably celebrate."

"Confirm your age, fifty-eight?" Tapping the keys.

Michael nods. "Yes, ma'am."

Reyes doesn't look up. "Children?"

His throat tightens. "Two daughters—Gabby and Leigh. Gabby's the last one who answers."

The nurse sighs. "Siblings?"

He exhales. "Brother—Mark Carson. He moved out West."

With a heavy sigh, Reyes rolls the cart away. The overwhelming sensation of being abandoned eats away at Michael.

The door opens again. Michael glances into the next room. He looks back at the ceiling tiles. "I doubt I'll fit in that..."

The technician's smile is warm beneath a heavy country drawl. "First time in the tunnel? Don't worry—I've never lost anyone in here."

Michael flexes his fingers on the cold table. "Lucky you. I've lost everything."

The tech's brow furrows, hesitates. "You ready?"

"Yeah, get it over with..."

The machine hums to life, its vibration as hollow as an empty house—no Caroline, no Gabby, no Leigh.

With the technician's assistance, he struggles off the table. Examining the new open-ended MRI machine that dominates the immense room with curiosity—anything to divert his focus from the purpose of his visit this morning, annoyed that the flimsy hospital gown barely fits around him. An irritation that is brewing just under Michael's calm demeanor.

The room feels freezing, and although he usually shrugs off low temperatures, today, he can't ignore it. The absence of anyone with him intensifies his loneliness, a solitude rooted in history. Despite understanding the reasons, the pain persisted. Sitting patiently in the wheelchair, Michael grows irritated at being wheeled around. His legs are perfectly fine, and the feeling of being treated like an invalid bothers him.

"Hospital rules, my ass!" Michael growls.

Time seemingly slows to a standstill as he is alone for an hour, although he has no way of knowing. There is no clock in the room, and Michael followed the rules, as he was instructed to remove any metal from his body in the examination room. Not even a watch could be worn during the MRI scan. The old man fights the intense urge to complain vigorously. He thinks *this is no way to treat a human being.*

"Hmph, you barely qualify as a human being," Michael mutters in disgust, shaking his head.

Michael anticipates the orderly returning to the room. He waits in the cold room, listening to the quiet humming of the intricate medical equipment. This isolation is all that he has left. It isn't like the technicians and orderlies care about him; they are just doing a thankless job that is often overlooked, he knows, but it is of no comfort to him.

"I'm sorry, Mr. Carson," the young orderly apologizes as he swiftly waltzes into the room. The orderly flips the brake handles on both wheels.

"Finally!" Michael tries to protest. "I've been left here over an..."

As the orderly whips the wheelchair around, he effortlessly drapes a thin blanket over Michael. He doesn't seem to hear the statement, let alone react. After settling Mr. Carson, the orderly spins the wheelchair around in a different direction and exits the room. They rapidly move down the corridor.

"...hour!" Michael hangs on to the armrests, gasping as he yells, "Hey! Where's the fire, kid?"

"That's a good one, sir." Rolling his eyes, the young man replies politely. "Just need to get you back to Doctor Silva's office."

"Will he have an answer today?" Michael inquires, hoping his situation is not as dire as he fears. He tries not to be unsettled by the wheelchair's reckless maneuvering.

"Doctor Silva will discuss that with you, but I think it usually takes a week to get and review the results. Oh, watch your feet, sir," The orderly explains, spinning the wheelchair around. "Hold the elevator door, please!"

The orderly steps backward with the wheelchair into the large elevator car. Michael shivers under the sad excuse of a blanket. Michael decides the elevator is colder than the MRI room. This is humiliating, and he wants to scream at the staff. He knew that was not going to help. It would not make him feel better. He sighs.

The orderly leans against the control panel, "Say, I haven't seen you around. What's your name?"

The young nurse giggles, a flash of redness to her cheeks. "Beth..."

As the doors close, Michael can see across the hallway through the large glass windows that the cold November rain has turned to snow.

"Perfect..." Michael quietly snaps. The tone is draped in sarcasm as the young orderly engages in a conversation with a pretty nurse as if Michael isn't there.

Storm of Regret

The streetlamp's light splinters and scatters as snow whips through its beam, casting a chaotic dance of shadows on the large drifts. Inside Terry's Bar, the warmth hits Michael like a wall—cotton-thick air, low hum of generators, amber glow flickering off brass rails. He slips off his coat, snow melting in puddles at his boots.

It's January 29, 2022, and a heavy snowstorm blankets the East Coast, covering the small town of Denton, Rhode Island, in a layer of pristine white snow–it has fallen for twelve hours, leaving most of the town without power. Michael Willis Carson III, now in his late fifties, sits alone in Terry's Bar—a place he's frequents on many lonely nights. The bar is unusually crowded tonight; it's one of the few businesses left with a working generator. Still, to Michael, the room full of people is just another backdrop to his isolation. He's seated at the end of the bar on his usual stool, a spot the regulars leave open out of unspoken respect—or perhaps avoidance.

Terry slides a Jack and Coke onto the scarred wood. "Rough night, Carson?"

Michael doesn't look up. He lifts the glass by the rim, knuckles whitening around the cold metal. "No more than the usual Cat 5 disaster."

Gabby's words crack through his mind: "I don't want to see you ever again."

His fist tightens on the glass— it rattles against the coaster. A shard cuts his palm; blood beads along a crease. He presses fingers to his lips, tasting metal.

Terry sets a napkin under Michael's hand. "Shelter run tomorrow?"

Michael flexes frost-nipped fingers. He traces a circle on the condensation, then shakes his head. "Not in my plan."

"Storm like this, they'll be packed to capacity, those kids will need you."

"That's because they don't know me."

"Maybe, but does it matter?" Terry asks, wiping the bar. "That shelter coordinator is a regular, she brags on you."

"I'm good at what I do, doesn't make me the best."

"Aren't the kids the reason you took all that training and help out?" Terry asked, cautiously. "You once told me that it wasn't about you, it was about **them**."

"OK, Terry, you win." Michael sighs. "Tonight, I want to crawl in a bottle and forget the world."

Terry nods and goes away as Michael stands and peers through frost-streaked windows at drifts piling against the door. Empty stools line the bar—he's the only patron watching the storm bury the street. The generator's drone fills his ears. He takes a slow breath, the sharp sting of regret in every inhale.

Encouraged by a local pastor, he's reached out to those from his past, confronting the painful truth of his selfishness, control, and ingrained narcissism. For years, he believed he was one of the *"good guys,"* only to realize how deeply he's hurt the people closest to him.

Michael shakes off the noise of the other people in the bar. He focuses on how he ended up here. Michael has taken steps to make amends, though many of those he wronged are no longer alive.

"Several friends have passed away, some tragically lost to suicide." Michael whispers as he downs the remainder of his drink.

His parents are long gone, and he regrets never apologizing to his mother for not being the son she deserved. He thinks of his father, knowing they were cut from the same cloth, but he wonders if he'd ask forgiveness if he could see him one last time.

Michael's extended family is a similar story of regret. He was never close to his cousins, except Scott, who struggled through a difficult childhood only to fall into addiction. Their relationship soured over a pointless political argument, and they haven't spoken since 2010. He wishes he'd been there for Scott. It's one of many regrets he carries, a reminder of his selfishness.

"Stop beating yourself up, Michael," The man whispers to his shot glass.

Then there's his Uncle John, the last of his mother's siblings, who passed away in 2018. They'd tried to reconnect, but Michael suspected his uncle's avoidance was tied to Michael's many years of negative comments. John, a kind man who had quietly lived with his partner long before it was socially accepted, had been his mother's favorite sibling. Another bridge burned, another painful memory of his own ignorance.

"So many have left me..."

The thought of his estranged brother, Mark, who moved to the West Coast to escape Michael's toxic presence, weighs heavily on him as well. Some relationships are beyond saving. He pulls out his iPhone, looking at an old photo of Gabby and Leigh. The fond memory is spoiled by Gabby's anger on the phone call still echoes in his mind, and the drink in front of him does little to numb the sting. Gabby had spoken the truth. Despite all his attempts at change, he knows he has failed his daughters.

"Terry, another round?" Michael yells out, rapping on the hard wood counter.

Terry walks over with another glass. "Hittin' it kinda heavy tonight. You OK?"

"Well, I figure I've fallen off the wagon, might was well go for broke." He nods, taking the new glass.

Taking another drink of Jack and Coke, Michael searches for relief, but tonight, nothing seems to dull the pain of his past.

It is coming to the point that Michael is ready to die, though he has no choice. There is nothing left. His fear that an insensitive man is still in his heart, a selfish, immature child, and that is the underlying truth he can't escape. Michael has to expend every ounce of his will not to be that man. It is a tiring endeavor. The monster will come back with the right trigger in his life. Tonight, Michael is exhausted from trying to keep his inner monster at bay. Disgusted, he took another drink from the glass but found it was merely ice.

Waving the empty glass, Michael demands another drink, "Terry!"

He sits alone in the bar, though the place is packed. Isolated, there is no polite chit-chat. Michael assumes it must be because he has been an ass to everyone for weeks. The news from Doctor Silva has spoiled any goodness he may have had left. Michael hates himself. He hates everyone. Even though he has made progress on being a better person, there isn't anyone left for it to matter. Time has become his enemy. Michael buries his face in his hands.

"Uh, Mister Carson?" A young woman interrupts his thoughts.

Michael prepares to snap back bitterly but sees it is the young newlywed couple who lives in the townhouse beside his. "Yeah?"

"We don't mean to intrude, sir," The younger man answers.

"Oh...uh, Joseph, my apologies. You'll have to excuse me, I don't think I'd be good company tonight. Thank you, but it's best if I remain in solitude," Michael replies, sipping his drink.

"Is everything ok, Mister Carson?" She asks, compassion flowing easily from her heart.

"Yes, Sarah. Only spending quality time with my only friend," Michael slurs in response as he holds his glass for them to see.

"You shouldn't be alone, Mr. Carson," Sarah replies, hesitating with a touch to his arm.

"We received a text," Joseph motions with his phone. "Power company fixed the lines..."

"Yes, sir, we wanted to offer you a ride home," Sarah adds with a nervous smile.

"Sarah..." A tear forms in Michael's eye, "Hm...that is most kind, but I'm not ready to be ferried home..." He fears being alone tonight.

Sarah looks at her husband with an urgent compassion. Joseph smiles, "Yes, sir, of course. No need to rush. Sarah and I are going to order sandwiches anyway; we can wait."

Sarah smiles. "Just find us when you're ready to go."

"Would you..." Michael answers. "You would do that for me?"

"Absolutely, Mister Carson," Sarah laughs in relief. "We will be over there." Pointing at the corner booth.

Michael is speechless as he watches the couple walk away. He should have been in a better mood. His latest therapist commented that he is so proud of their last session. For forty-six years, Michael lived a life with a self-loathing that smothered everything else. He felt that something had to be wrong with him. Some mental diseases that had to be cured.

As a teenager, he began spiraling out of control. He lost interest in everything. He was well-known in high school as a student who didn't care. He started hanging with the wrong crowd. Those new friends were people who also made bad choices, which added poisonous fuel to Michael's toxic tendencies.

Michael could feel alone in a room crowded with people. Battling depression and hopelessness, he tried alcohol and pot at nineteen, disastrous choices leading to life as an alcoholic.

Bouncing around from one empty relationship to another, he eventually succeeded in finding a steady girlfriend. Their connection was simple. It was good sex. A heterosexual relationship that his father and the world would approve of. Eventually, Michael dove blindly into a marriage doomed to fail.

He was determined not to be an absent father like Willis Carson, Jr. was. His father had been distant and unloving to Michael and his brother. Decades have come with so many failures piling up. It was inevitable, considering that Michael did not have a good role model for how to be a dad. Michael's choices became mistake after mistake, coupled with a selfish desire. Michael ended up being a carbon copy of his dad. Perhaps, by comparison, Michael was even worse.

So many years wasted. It wasn't until Michael started going to the last therapist that he was able to have a breakthrough. A highly regarded mental health expert in Providence, Doctor Ezekiel Elmhurst, a specialist in helping patients reconcile their past. Terry, of all people, recommended him. The young Michael had no one to talk to about this. However, in retrospect, Michael's mother was someone he should have trusted.

The call did not go the way I wanted, nothing has lately. Michael consoles himself. *The monster has never left.* Gabby had forced it out. *It isn't her fault;* Michael knew he brought everything upon himself. The phone call left a familiar ache, a sour taste of regret and words that should never have been said.

"Uh...Terry," Michael yells. "I need another!"

Terry walks over and places the glass on the counter in front of him. Michael lost track of how much he had consumed that day, but he doesn't care. Gabby is his last chance to steer away from damnation.

"If you want any more, Carson, gotta give me your keys." Terry demanded.

Michael digs in his pocket, ready to toss the keys across the room–anger rages in his heart. But he sees that Terry is asking as a friend. Defeated, Michael lays the keys on the counter and gently slides them over. Terry slides the drink across the bar to Michael.

"Thanks, Terry...Hey, cheers, bud," Michael lifts the glass, spilling a few drops amongst the drunken laughs.

"The good doctor would not approve," A polite Englishman declares.

Startled by the comment, Michael looks around. Sitting beside him is an older gentleman with a full head of graying hair. He is nicely adorned in a pressed white linen suit. He has dark blue eyes that command respect but offer empathy. Michael smiles. A new patron would rarely stumble into his web. But Michael is not looking for a sparring partner tonight; he doesn't want to be alone. The alcohol helping him forget about Joseph and Sarah, and Terry is not being friendly this evening.

"What doctor do you mean, old man?" Michael slurs, looking at the man suspiciously.

"Doctor Elmhurst. I have seen you in his lobby," The man's voice is strangely calming. "I often bring the lost to see the good doctor. He sincerely cares about all of his patients."

"Elmhurst?" Michael clumsily answers, his body swaying. "Oh, yeah... the new shrink. Listen up, bub, he may care, but he hasn't done shit to help me..." Pointing his finger back to the kind gentleman's chest.

"Come now, Michael." The older man smiles. "You underestimate the positive changes you've made since becoming his patient."

Michael tries to stand but can't. He almost falls to the ground, but the stranger steadies and sits him back down. Gabriel is strong for an older man, and Michael didn't expect that. The old man guides Michael back to the stool and helps him get situated.

Stunned, Michael asks, "Thanks, uh...did you tell me your name?"

"My name is Gabriel," he warmly answers. "Come, Michael, tell me what is bothering you tonight."

Despite Michael's prickly demeanor, Gabriel is very polite and does not lose his composure. Michael is about to chase the old man away, but he realizes that Gabriel is offering to listen to him. Tonight, Michael only wants to be heard. He longs not to be alone.

"Ok, I just might," Michael slurs. "But I only talk with people I share drinks with. Terry!"

Terry slowly approaches, "Are you needing something?"

"Terry," Michael stutters. "I would die for a screwdriver. Hold the OJ, my good man. Oh, and my friend here; uh, this fine mate would like..."

Gabriel smiles, "Water and ice, Michael."

"Oh, the hard stuff!" Michael laughs, slapping the wooden bar with his free hand. "Water on the rocks for this fine English gentleman!"

Terry grimaces, looking at Michael with curiosity. Without saying anything, he goes to the other end of the bar. Micahael glances at Gabriel with a goofy grin as Terry returns with two glasses. He sets them both in front of Michael. Terry lets out a huff and walks away.

"A toast, my good sir?" Michael starts laughing.

"How about we toast you, Michael? I would like to hear your story." Gabriel speaks softly.

Michael raises his glass and taps the other, "Cheers, my good mate. May fortune be kind to me before I die."

"Why are you so grim, Michael?" Gabriel asks with a comforting appeal in his voice. "Haven't you had a blessed life?"

"Blessed?" Michael grunts, his laughter bitter. "I'm a terrible person. The only person I've ever cared about was myself."

"I most assuredly doubt that, Michael." Gabriel leans close. Studying Michael's face. "Why would you say that?"

Michael watches himself in the mirror behind the bar. "I deceived myself into thinking I was a better person than I truly am. Like a colossal tornado, I've left a trail of destruction everywhere I've been. I've hurt the people I claimed to love... if I ever even truly felt love. I don't know what I did to them, but I understand it's all my fault."

Gabriel sits patiently, absorbing Michael's confession. "No one bears the full weight of responsibility in the complexities of life. Human beings are interconnected in ways that often elude their perception. Every action can potentially alter another person's life, often without their awareness or consent. Yet, Michael, you must still take accountability for your good and bad choices."

"That doesn't make me feel any better." A tear rolls down Michael's cheek as he responds, "I want to be a better person, Gabe. I *do*. But I keep messing it up! It takes every ounce of my being to resist becoming the monster that I am. But, I can't do it anymore. There's no one left to care about me." Michael sighs deeply, gazing at his glass of alcohol.

"You would be surprised, Michael," Gabriel smiles, standing close to Michael's shoulder.

"Nothing would surprise me, Gabe," Michael utters in disgust, taking a significant taste of his drink. "The only thing I have to look forward to is death…"

"Perhaps, Michael. That's a step in the journey that everyone must confront inevitability," Gabriel remarks, placing a comforting hand on Michael's shoulder. "Yet, in my extensive experiences, I've observed that humans often fear the challenges of life more than the prospect of death."

"Yeah? Even if their life is nothing but pain?" Michael asks with sorrow.

Gabriel laughs warmly, his eyes glistening in the light, "Probably more so when that is the case. But death isn't the center of your pain tonight."

Michael looks back at him, confusion running wild. "Uh…what?"

"Are you worried about the call with your daughter? I suspect that deep in her heart, she wants you to succeed." Gabriel's voice is strong, commanding, yet comforting. "Leigh wants the same thing. To gain forgiveness, you first have to forgive yourself, Mike."

"Forgiveness?" Michael starts a drunken laugh, "You sound like a slimy preacher off TV beggin' for money to get saved."

"I am *not* here to save you, Mike," Gabriel replies resolutely, folding his arms while observing Michael as he speaks.

"Or...uh...I bet you're a speaker from a Dale Carnegie class. Are you trying to sell me something?" Michael laughs hard; his eyes dance with a faint spark. "Uh...wait. Did you call me Mike?"

"I did." Gabriel tilts his head slightly to the left, and a small smile grows. "That is what your friends called you, wasn't it?"

Michael's getting a headache. He gulps down the rest of his drink. It doesn't help. He shifts his weight on the stool. His right leg grows numb, as always. Years of being overweight have long past made the simple things complicated.

He stares at Gabriel. The old man is smiling. He has a pleasant way to him. After a few moments, Michael does not feel the least bit hostile. The longer they talk, the more at peace Mike feels.

"I haven't gone by Mike since I dropped out of high school," Mike clarifies, realizing he slipped up; he quickly counters. "But being a dropout doesn't make me stupid!"

"Absolutely, Mike." Gabriel pridefully boasts, "You drove yourself hard to be a monetary success. Despite not being a college graduate, you pull in a six-figure income. You are better at analysis than the younger software engineers with all the degrees."

"Damn, Gabe. You been spying on me?" Mike slurs and leans forward, forcing portions of his drink to spill over the rim.

"No, but I have seen your file." Gabriel chuckles, "In my line of work, I must have full knowledge of the people I help. Otherwise, I could make things worse."

"My life couldn't get any worse..."

Gabriel scratches his chin, carefully planning his next words. "You still have not told me why you are in such pain tonight. I know that Gabby upset you, but her anger is nothing new. Was it the MRI? No, that was over a month ago, and you knew full well the outcome. Tell me, what has brought you to this particular bar tonight?" The older gentleman thoughtfully watches Michael.

"Simple, it is the past; there is no future," Mike lets out a tired sigh. "I was not joking about leaving a path of destruction. I have hurt everyone—loved ones, acquaintances, and strangers alike. I was oblivious to the fact that I'm a bad person."

"Mike." Gabriel rests his hand on Mike's arm.

Tears rolled down his cheeks as he continued, his voice thick with the weight of it all. "I've tried to reach out to everyone still alive to apologize. I've been forgiven, I've been cursed out, I've been hung up on. Most never reply at all. And while every rejection hurt, none of them were the source of the void in my heart."

"Interesting. Who did that to your heart, Mike?" Gabriel probes, looking into Mike's eyes.

"The one person I'm speaking of is Robert Davis," Mike sniffles, fighting back the tears. "He was my best friend in high school. He and I were close for many years."

"Best friends can be very important. Tell me what happened with Robbie."

Staring at the mirror, Mike coldly answers. "I think my soul died on February 17th, 1981."

"That was a bad day for us all, Mike," Gabriel consoles him, resting his hand on Mike's shoulder.

Not listening, Mike continues, "I gave up. I stopped going to school. Stopped seeing my friends. I met Catherine and thought I was in love. It was just sex. Great sex! But empty. I let all that come between me and Robbie. I tried to locate him through the years..."-

Absorbing everything Mike is saying, Gabriel concludes, "I take it Robbie is significant to you."

"Robbie was the once-in-a-lifetime kind of best friend, and I lost him," Mike sobs. "...years ago, I had given up trying to find him."

"Was he truly lost, thought?" Gabriel shifts on the stool.

"I always assumed he'd moved away and would never be found again. About three weeks ago, I was doing a job search on xFerma, a dedicated website for anyone on the Certified Analytics Board. It connects people with a technical background. The forum often suggests members with whom you can connect. That day, Robbie appeared on my list. Just like that, out of the blue. After years of searching with no results, some algorithm finds him one day and puts him on my list. Maybe fate was being kind? I sent an instant message to him on the forum. I did not hear anything back. At least I tried, right?"

"You tried, but it wasn't what you expected?" Gabriel asks. "Humans always want more."

"A few days ago, I returned to the website to check on one of my job applications," Mike cries.

"And you didn't like what you found?"

Mike nods, hanging his head down. "No, I figured out that he had blocked my profile. It is one thing to see that I messaged him and chose to ignore it. He blocked me... He had to take the time to set up a blocking filter. He must really *hate* me."

"Maybe he thought you were from Dale Carnegie and was trying to sell him something?" Gabriel jokes.

"If that was the case, he could have just ignored the IM. The CAB Forum isn't like other social media sites; I don't know anyone who checks it regularly. Blocking me was a message," Mike takes a deep breath, downing more of the liquor. "The pain was deeper than that. I did not get the chance to apologize to him. More than any of the other people I reached out to, not talking to him hurt the most. I hurt deep within my heart, Gabe..."

"Did you tell Doctor Elmhurst?" Gabriel suggests. "Perhaps the doctor could act as a liaison between you?"

"Gabe, are you *crazy*? That's internet stalker talk!" Mike exclaims. "Besides, I'm afraid of what could happen."

"Fear is a powerful force."

"I know I deserve this. Robbie's reason for closing me off could be because of any one of a thousand thoughtless comments or selfish actions I have done. I hoped that maybe we could be friends again. I was, uh, I am...so unworthy of his friendship. I was a fool to think my life could end happily. The reality is that I just wanted to have closure with him." Michael buries his face in his hands as the pain returns. He sobs quietly.

"I suspect there is more, Mike. Let me help you."

Taking a deep breath, Mike answers, choking on his tears. "I wanted Robbie to be my *twice-in-one-lifetime* best friend. I was a fool for thinking such things.

"Hmm," Gabriel said with a smile of satisfaction, lost in deep thought. "Twice in one lifetime. That is a great idea, Mike. Another toast?"

With much excitement, Mike reaches for his glass, "Always ready for more booze, Gabe!"

Mike picks up his glass. He is confused; it is still full. He wonders *when did Terry refill the drink*. It didn't matter; Mike proudly held the glass high. He smiles at Gabriel. Oddly, Mike is feeling at peace. The headache is gone. This impromptu therapy session has helped. Michael thinks *Gabriel is much cheaper than the psychiatrist I have been seeing...*

"OK, Gabriel. Here's to Twice in One Lifetime!" Mike yells out...

Neither Purgatory nor Hell

The darkness of the void is all around him. Mike feels his existence spinning around in an uncontrolled fashion. He has nothing to focus on. There is no sound. There is no sense of being. However, Mike is falling like a stone thrown from a mountain cliff. He knows that this fall will end; it would have to!

Michael spins in the void.

A distant roar—wind or memory—rips at his eardrums.

No light. No end.

Mike remembers his life. It seemed oddly distant to him but incredibly clear at the moment. Mike thinks that he is hollow. In an undeniable sense, he is not a man anymore. Just a shell of a man in the emptiness. He has no visual reference but guesses he is falling at incredible speed. He could see the effects of the wind passing over him but not the sound or the feeling of reality.

Michael tumbles through an endless black.

A rushing hiss fills his ears—colder than any wind he's known.

He thrashes, but the effort is pointless. His fingertips scrape against nothing.

He tries to speak—voice fractures in his throat. Silence presses in, heavier than stone. His limbs jerk; phantom gravity clenches his chest. He coughs, breath ragged.

Somewhere beyond, a snap: like a breaking branch or the crack of his own spine. Cold seeps up his arms, though no breeze stirs. His skin prickles with ice and dread.

He tastes metal—fear bleeding across his tongue. He presses sweaty palms to his ribs, hunting for a heartbeat.

"Am I dead?" Confused, an uncertain Mike asks. But there is no one with him.

His voice is distorted. He thinks it is someone else speaking but using his voice. *This must be some bizarre dream that I'm having.* Yet it does not feel like a dream to him, and it does not feel like reality either. Mike screams in frustration and terror from the unknown.

"Dammit, answer me! Am I dead?" Mike pleads to the emptiness.

He is answered by silence. The idea that hell is a place of pain and torment is a commonly held belief. Mike instantly worries. Is his eternity going to be this? Alone and forever falling to some dreadful ending. There isn't even a demon here to torture and keep him company.

"But is this purgatory where I can be redeemed?" Michael asks. "Or Hell and my final damnation?"

Michael Willis Carson, the third, is alone. Uniquely alone. The only object within this prison without bars, only infinite emptiness. It would be fitting if this is the verdict of the universe being served after a trial. The Judge rules Mike Carson guilty, and the sentencing is harsh. Eternity in solitude...

"I do not want to die alone!" Mike yells at the top of his lungs, believing he must still be in the bar. "Gabriel! Joshua! Help! Terry! Anybody!"

The sound is the same. It is disconnected and is not him. Mike is afraid. Being alone is the worst fate he could have faced. He knew it was too late to beg for forgiveness. No one would have listened to him. Tears begin to well up in his eyes. There is no one with him. The void is empty, except for himself. He has no idea how long he has been here. Time has no meaning to Mike.

Then, his memories begin to flow in his mind. With flashes of vivid images of his life, he experiences each moment with an intensity, such realism that he cannot ignore. He is five. Michael has just stolen his older brother's favorite toy. Michael has no excuse. He is in pain. Their parents are arguing non-stop; if he could get them to stop and focus on something else! He wants to hug them both, but it is all in his mind. He is alone. Memory after memory appears in his mind, completely recounting his life. Michael sobs uncontrollably. He does not need this reminder of the bitterness in his life. But it worsens as the memories morph into a new perspective.

He can hear the thoughts of those he has hurt. A loud chorus of condemnation. *Indeed, this was the work of the devil,* Mike fears. Time has felt like this experience has been countless days of constant guilt. Yet time has no meaning in the void.

Michael exists in nonexistence. He has not slept. He is not tired. Michael does not want to sleep. His body could not sleep. This is his reality now. He is fully aware of every second. Being forced to experience their feelings, there is no way to hide from his past, from their pain. Michael sees his parents. Every disappointment he gave them. His grandparents. He can hear his grandmother's daily prayers. He can feel how much Anne Marie Dalton loves him and the hurt she feels as he wastes his life.

"Stop!" Michael screams as the memories flow.

The pain worsens, and he can hear Gabby and Leigh's prayers. Their sadness burns like acid covering his heart. His body shakes from crying uncontrollably. There is no comfort, no relief, only the endless void, nothing in every direction. Mercy is nowhere close in this emptiness. Michael wants it to end.

In desperation, Mike yells out, "Please! Just fuckin' stop. Forgive me, I beg of you..."

Second Chances

Mike suddenly jerks and gasps deeply for air. His body aches as if he's been falling for days, slamming down into his own past. A textbook tumbles off his desk, and he looks around, dazed, feeling every eye in the room on him. Mike sits upright, terror coursing through him.

Mrs. Austin, her expression a blend of frustration and pity, fixes her gaze on him and steps away from the blackboard. He feels exposed. He takes a breath and feels the air filling his lungs. He closes his eyes and draws in another. Mike surveys the classroom as Mrs. Austin places her hands on her hips.

"*Mr. Carson*, can you please..." Mrs. Austin barks.

"Sorry, ma'am. I didn't mean to disrupt class—I must've fallen asleep," Mike says, meeting his classmates' eyes. "I apologize. It won't happen again."

He runs a hand along the rough desk surface—real, solid. *This isn't another memory; this is real.* Mike raps his knuckles on the wood. The scent of chalk dust and the faint murmur of a locker slamming in the hallway bring him back—this is 1980, Pinewood High School, unmistakable. The hum of the fluorescent lights echoes overhead.

The shocked expression on Mrs. Austin's face highlights her deep concern. She has given up trying to solve whatever is troubling this student. In her fifteen years of teaching, she has never seen anyone give up so completely as Mike Carson has. She even got to the point of not caring if he slept in her class. Nothing has worked with him before. Reluctantly, she had written him off some time ago.

Mike looks around the room as if he needs to recognize where he is. His hands shake as he reaches for his glasses, eyes wide with the realization: *this is a second chance.* He surveys the classroom.

The clothes, the decor, everything suddenly feels right to Mike. He notices the school's clock on the wall has stopped, frozen at 8:42 AM. He removes his glasses, as if that is why he sees these things. Michael remembers having corrective eye surgery in 2004, *Wearing glasses feels unnatural.* He looks around the room in awe.

For a moment, Mrs. Austin suspects drugs. She will mention this to the guidance counselor. She decides to let Mr. Hammond handle this young man. Mrs. Austin does not care any longer. She returns to the lecture as if nothing has happened. She doesn't let him steal any more time from her hardworking students.

"Now, as I was saying. Charles Dickens writes of personal transformation in this classic novel," the teacher resumes her lecture.

"Mrs. Austin, is Ebeneezer really meeting ghosts?" Asks a girl named Francine, who sits in the front row.

"Well, literary art gives the author a platform to speak through the characters on the importance of confronting his past mistakes with the help of supernatural guides, facing both his regrets and the lives he hurt," Mrs. Austin explains, smiling. "The story's themes of redemption and transformation should resonate with all of us, hinting that we, too, have a chance to reshape our future by acknowledging and taking responsibility for the past."

Mike listens to her speak about literature as if she is quoting the sacred gospels. It is clear to Mike that she profoundly loves teaching. She always took the time to answer the questions, even if it stopped her lecture.

He is here, but it is like Mike still does not exist. He smiles—truly smiling—for the first time in years. He'd forgotten how it felt to hope even though everyone chose to ignore what happened. The end of the period arrives, and the school bell rings.

The students quietly gather their books and head to their next class. Mike slowly stands. He cautiously walks to Mrs. Austin's desk. Mike knew one thing, *I can fix my life!* He takes a chance on her love of teaching. She glances up at him with a look of irritation.

"Mrs. Austin?" Mike timidly asks, "I know I have no right to ask this of you..."

"Ask me what, Mike?" She snaps back, casually tossing aside the papers she is reviewing.

With labored breathing, Mike glances back at the desk he was sitting at. He isn't sure what to say and then looks back at his teacher, "I had a nightmare. I was falling...uh, going in the wrong direction. Mrs. Austin, please. Is there anything I can do to get caught up with the class? I will do whatever you ask..."

"Mike, you are way behind." Leaning back in her chair and folding her arms, Mrs. Austin is stunned, "It would take a lot of hard work."

"I realize that. I am a failure," Mike said, glancing fearfully from his desk to her face. "It wasn't just a nightmare, it felt so real. Even now, I don't know what reality is. I saw a life—*my life*—where I was alone, and I'd hurt everyone who ever mattered. If I stay on this path, it'll end in nothing. I don't want that anymore."

Mrs. Austin uncrossed her arms, eyes narrowing slightly. "Mike, this is... unexpected," she replies, scrutinizing his gaze. "You're far behind... but if you're willing to do the work..."

"Please, Mrs. Austin, I don't want to fail again." His voice cracks. "I'll do whatever it takes. I don't want my life to be meaningless."

As his pleas reach her heart, Mrs. Austin feels a flicker of hope mingling with her surprise. She thought of Dickens, today's lecture on redemption and second chances. Was it just a coincidence? She knew Mike would be problematic from the first day of this school year. She'd given up on him—until today. *Today, something in his eyes is...different...*

"Are you truly serious, Mike?" she asks, her voice softer now, still searching for the sincerity in his expression.

In all her discussions with Mike Carson, he never acted like he cared. Though she is skeptical of his intentions. Today, this is a different young man standing before her. She is no longer worried that he is on drugs or even making up this wild story. She can see that his fear is real. Erika Austin watches him closely, weighing his sincerity. She wants to believe him—a force urging her to consider that truth. And then she nods, a note of hope entering her voice.

"I will draw up a reading list," Mrs. Austin relents. "You can write a report on each one. But to allow that, I want you to write a paper about what your nightmare was about."

"Yes, ma'am. Thank you." Mike's heart begins to race; his voice is sincere and excited. "Would it be okay if you wrote me a note so I can talk to Mr. Hammond?"

"I was going to suggest it anyway." Mrs. Austin replies, writing out the permission slip.

She hopes that she has made the correct decision. She smiles at him as he leaves the room in excitement. Mike runs down the hallway. He had forgotten how ratty this old bookbag had been. It is hard to keep balance and not drop any of its contents.

Looking around while running, he eyes the door to the boys' bathroom and dashes inside. Mike needs a quiet moment to wrap his mind around what happened. He coughs with irritation. He could tell someone was in the last stall smoking a cigarette.

Mike laughs in amusement, *"The things we did as kids."*

Cautiously, Mike slowly approaches the mirror. His heart races as he peers into it. The face staring back is younger—a boy's face, his face, with light brown hair and eyes full of life. He removes his glasses slowly, barely breathing. *This is real.* He touches his cheek, marveling at the softness of youth. *The possibilities are endless!*

Still gazing at the mirror, the reflection is his sixteen-year-old face, youthful and wide-eyed. A grin spread across his face as he muttered to himself, "1980. And hair!"

Still disoriented about what has happened, Mike takes a couple of times to find the proper hall to head down. Luckily, he is able to find Oliver Hammond's office. Hammond is only a few years out of college, but that does not prevent him from doing a good job. Though Mike has spoken to Hammond before, today he wants counseling on making things right.

"Wait!" Mike stops and asks himself. "I wonder how long I have?"

Mike warns himself: *I don't know why this was granted to me. Fate, the Universe, or God! Whoever has allowed this to happen and granted this second chance would have conditions or rules! What changes can I do?*

Mike realizes that he may have limited time. *"I can't waste a minute."* He is correct about the possibilities, but it would not be fun and games. Mike's heart speeds up; anxiety drives the change and the fear of missing this opportunity. He has to come up with a plan and stick to it. Mike gently raps on the door and waits to enter.

"Please come in," A man with a deep voice calls out.

The latest person on the school staff is a trustworthy guidance counselor, and he immediately garnered a reputation as someone the kids could rely on. Oliver Hammond is 28. He stands at 6 feet 5 inches. He is a gentle giant. By comparison, Mike Carson is about average height for a sixteen-year-old. Hammond has a slender build. His thick brown hair is parted to the side. Mr. Hammond's own life had been shaped by a teacher who cared enough to make a difference, and now Oliver is doing what he can to plant that seed in some of his students.

"Uh...morning, Mr. Hammond." Mike nervously takes a few steps in.

Mr. Hammond's warm eyes met his, studying him intently as if seeing something more than a troubled student. It takes Oliver a moment to recognize the young man standing in his office.

"Hey. It's Michael Carson, right?" Oliver asks, scratching his chin. "Haven't seen much of you lately. Some of your teachers are very concerned..."

"Yes, sir." With a long sigh, Mike answers, "I know. I just had a long talk with Mrs. Austin. She's going to give me a chance to get caught up. Could you help me with my other teachers? I don't want to be a dropout and a failure."

"Hmm, well, Michael. I need to know why I should help," Hammond explains, folding his arms.

"Uh...sir?" Michael is confused but quickly realizes his old self is known to be the 'give up' type...

"Though, if you could get Mrs. Austin to agree to help you, I could not turn you away!" Hammond jokes, gently tapping Mike on the shoulder and motioning him to sit. Hammond is glad the vice principal canceled their conference.

They both share a laugh. Mike drops the remnants of his bookbag on the floor, and some contents slide out the sides. Mike decides *that thing has to go.* He smiles and sits down. He clears his throat. This will be challenging; Mike carefully thinks about what to say.

Mr. Hammond sits patiently in his chair and crosses his long legs. He has a disarming smile. Oliver Hammond is a good listener and always has been. He has the gift of getting people to open up. He is glad that he is finally getting the opportunity with Michael Carson.

"I was asleep in her class," Mike sheepishly admits.

"You have been the only one, Michael," Oliver shrugs as he begins taking notes.

"I know," Mike starts. "This morning, I had a bad dream—not a dream, a *nightmare*! It was intense and vivid. I was going down the wrong path. I will eventually be a failure—a lonely old failure that no one wants to be around. That isn't a life worth living... I woke up and realized I have this chance to right those wrongs—a second chance to keep my best friend..."

Glancing up from his notepad, Mr. Hammond comments, "Michael, I know it can seem real to you, but it could only have been a dream." His eyes study Mike as he carefully jots down his notes.

"Dream... or a reality to unfold in the years to come? Who can say? *Does it even matter*? It scared me..." Mike pleads as he leans forward. "That is the important takeaway from this happening, sir..." With a sigh, Mike slumps back in the chair, feeling hopeless realizing not everyone will believe he wants to be a better person.

"Enough to change?" Mr. Hammond studies Mike carefully, surprised by the intensity of his gaze. This isn't the disinterested student he remembers.

Do not give up! Mike leans forward and taps the coffee table between them, "The sadness, that sense of loneliness, *it* is real. It hasn't gone away. I can still feel it." Placing his hand on his heart. "I need to change! I can't give up. I've had forty-six years to come to the realization of who I am. I want to change the bad parts of my life before it poisons everything in my future."

Mr. Hammond's warm eyes soften, and he crosses his arms thoughtfully. Michael's sincerity is unmistakable. Oliver decides to help him, but he'd also hold Michael Carson accountable.

"Forty-six years?" Oliver Hammond laughs; the cinder block walls echo the joyful noise. "I know it can feel that long sometimes, Michael."

"You don't know how true that is..." Mike whispers.

"You have the strangest sense of humor I've ever encountered," Mr. Hammond nods, his gaze softening. "Alright, but you'll meet with me every week. I want to make sure you're following through."

"Every week?" " Mike replies, hope sparking in his eyes. "I can do that."

Mr. Hammond chuckles, leaning back. "I know you can. Michael, we're going to make sure you don't let yourself down, uh again."

Mike nods, feeling a wave of relief, "Mr. Hammond, my friends call me Mike."

"I'm glad you stopped by," Oliver Hammond smiles; the joy of being able to communicate with Mike is overwhelming.

As they wrap up, Mike gathers his things and nervously smiles. "Uh, sir... could I also get my class schedule and locker number?"

Mr. Hammond raises an eyebrow. "Your schedule? We're halfway through the semester."

"Yeah... and the combination, too. It has been almost forty years..." Mike mutters with a sheepish grin. Mr. Hammond laughs, shaking his head and heading out to get the information.

"Alright, Mike," he calls over his shoulder. "Wait here."

The rest of the morning goes quietly. He could hear some of his classmates whispering about the incident in Mrs. Austin's class. News travels fast in this small high school. Many people are gawking in every class.

He is beginning to feel like a goldfish in a tiny bowl. Suddenly, his life is exposed to the entire school. Some students claim Mike is doing hard drugs. The others are treating this morning like it is some prophetic sign. For Michael Willis Carson, it is prophetic. But no one else could know; they would never understand. Mike is living it, and he doesn't understand. He does not want to understand; he has to make the changes while he can. Mike takes the time to orient himself with the layout of the school. Forty years is a long time.

Glancing at the class schedule he received from Mr. Hammond, Mike quietly thinks, "I need to find these last two classrooms. I can't continue to wander around like a space cadet."

He begins to formulate his plan—the new Mike will be a model student, and a better friend. He rehearses his apology in his mind, bracing himself to set things right. When the last bell rings, he makes his way outside, hoping to see his old car. Near the main doors, he spots some friends loitering in their usual spot, the same "nerd" group he'd known since elementary school. And he misses them more than he realizes.

"Hey, Peter!" Mike yells, jogging over.

Mike smiles as he approaches Peter Kraft, who may look like a simple boy from the country but he is quite the opposite. Mike remembers Peter as the group's unofficial leader with an eye for details. They will be the first to get the apology; Mike swallows hard from nervousness.

Peter looks up, grinning. "Damn, it's Mike Carson! The prodigal son returns."

"Prodigal son, Peter?" Mike chuckles, feeling the warmth of familiarity he hasn't felt in a long time. "Close enough. But yeah, I'm back—and I'm gonna make things right this time."

Larry Richter comes over and slaps Mike on the back. Larry is big enough to be a football player but detests sports. With a deep voice and a strong personality, he has been the group's protector.

Larry frowns, looking concerned. "Is everything okay, Mike? You seem... different."

"Yeah, Mike, what's up?" Peter asks.

Steve Wolfe steps closer. Shorter than the others and slightly overweight, Steve is an academic—the smartest of the pack.

Everyone here has received a tutoring session or two for him. Mike takes a deep breath, feeling his heart pound.

Mike clears his throat nervously, "Hey, guys, I just wanted to apologize. I've been a jerk lately, uh, well, I've always been a jerk, and I know it. I'm sorry if I hurt any of you."

Mike's stomach knotted as he waited, scanning their faces for any sign of acceptance. The initial silence seems to last minutes. Mike does not want to fail on his first attempt.

Steve smiles at Mike. Peter folds his arms and winks. Mike hesitates, relieved to see his friends nodding in understanding.

"You're not a jerk," Steve said with a smile, and the others murmured in agreement.

Jonah King joins the conversation. Mike smiles. They were never close, but he always liked Jonah, the jokester, always quick with a teasing comment. Games were the one thing he was serious about.

"He's only a jerk when he beats me in chess!" Jonah teases, laughing with a high pitch.

Mike grins, shaking his head. "You telegraph every move, Jonah. But thanks, guys. I want to do better. I'm glad we're still friends."

"Have you slain the evil twin, then?" Jonah inquires, scratching his chin with a dramatic flair. "Or is this an ongoing quest?"

"Ahh!" Peter nods, smiling. "Classic inner battle. We should write all this down."

"Best-selling book, then a movie!" Steve jokes, giving Mike a light punch on the shoulder.

"Well, if you're gonna be the 'good twin' now, you need a new name," Larry said, nodding thoughtfully. "You can't just be 'Mike' or 'Michael'—those are way too boring."

"Right, keepin' your old name is totally against the rules," Steve adds, crossing his arms.

With a sarcastic head bob, Jonah yells, "It's a rule, man—every hero needs a new name."

"What did your mom say she'd name you?" Peter asks, grinning. "Tripp, right? Well, sounds like the perfect name for a guy on a journey with a second chance."

"Uh... my mom wanted to call me Tripp back when I was a baby," Mike admits, a little embarrassed.

"Perfect!" Steve declares the resolution. "You're starting fresh. It's like a second birth. All hail Tripp Carson!"

"Tripp it is," Jonah agrees, laughing. "With a name like that, you'll never win another chess game."

"Tripp it is," Mike replies with a broad smile, humbled by their affection. "But remember, Jonah, it's still me. My chess game hasn't changed one bit. Hey, I gotta run, but see you guys tomorrow?"

"Anytime, Captain!" Peter salutes as Mike jogs off, feeling lighter than he had in years. They are still his friends, still there for him. Maybe he really could change, one step at a time.

Old Friends, New Paths

Mike smiles as he walks away, excited to have reconnected with his friends. Heading out the main double doors, he jogs up the hill toward his car, feeling fantastic and satisfied that he succeeded with Steve and the guys. This is only the beginning, and though he knows the journey ahead won't be easy, he is determined.

As usual, his '67 Mustang is on the side street near the school, where he often parks. Today, he spots Lauren waiting by the car, but there is no sign of Robbie or Porter. Mike squints in the afternoon sunlight, pushing his glasses up his nose, and jogs over, tossing his worn-out backpack into the trunk. A few books spill out through the torn sides, and he sighs, making a mental note to fix that later.

Lauren stands by the car, tall and blonde with shoulder-length hair feathered out—a style Mike always admired. Athletic, naturally beautiful, and a loyal friend, she looks as if she'd stepped out of one of his best memories. Taking a deep breath, he reminds himself of his mission. It is for everyone he connects with. Mike believes that the future will change for the better.

"Hey, Lauren," he said, giving her a timid wave. She chuckles, smiling at him.

"I hear you scared the crap out of Mrs. Austin this morning?" Lauren teases. "If you were stoned, you should have found me. I'm always up for good weed."

Mike laughs, scratching the back of his neck. "Next time, I promise. But I wasn't stoned. It's just... hard to explain, you know?"

"Paranoia? Confusion?" Lauren smirks, crossing her arms as she looks him over. "Sounds like the good stuff. You holding out on me?"

"No, really," Mike said with a nervous laugh. "I had a nightmare, and it... it kind of shook me up. It made me realize I need to change things. I know this sounds silly, but... can I ask you a favor?"

She arches an eyebrow. "Depends. Are you gonna share those imaginary drugs?"

"I swear, no drugs," he chuckles. "But... can I get a hug? Just a friendly one?"

Lauren pauses, noticing something new in his expression—a kind of openness, a softness she'd never seen before. He looks vulnerable, almost like that lost puppy, yet a stranger. But she shrugs off her doubts, stepping forward, wrapping her arms around him. Mike leans in and wraps his arms around her. He wants to cry, but tears of happiness.

"Sure, Mike." She answers.

He thinks about Lauren, the woman he remembers; they were good friends and kept in touch until Greg went to federal prison in 1986. For the first time in years, he felt grounded, anchored in something real. After a moment, he stepped back, smiling.

"Thanks. You've always been a good friend; I should've told you that long ago," Mike said gently. "Like I said, my dream scared me."

"You're being serious?" Lauren asks, looking deep into his eyes. A sly smile creeps on her face. "You sure there aren't any drugs left, Mike?"

"Nope. Just thinking about my future... I realized my life wasn't what it should be, what I wanted it to be," he said quietly. "I'm thinking of going by Tripp. My mom always liked that name, and it feels right. But you can call me Mike if you think it's stupid."

She laughs, shaking her head. "Tripp, huh? Fine, I'll call you Tripp. But it's still gonna take more than a new name to get rid of your old habits, you know."

Mike grins and gently nods, "It will take a good friend to help me..."

As he watches her walk to the passenger side, Mike feels lighter, as if a piece of his past has started letting go.

Lauren smirks and replies before getting into the car, "No problem, Tripp. Hey, here comes your dorky friend..."

Mike turns and freezes, seeing his friend. His heart skips a beat as a familiar, bittersweet feeling washes over him. Robbie Davis, his best friend, walks up the street, looking exactly as he remembered. Taller now, close to six feet, with jet-black hair parted down the middle and a baseball-style shirt that hung just a bit too high, Robbie flashes him a big smile. His bright blue eyes are striking even without his glasses, and his expression is pure joy. Mike wants to run up and hug his old friend, but he stops himself. Here, in 1980, they are just kids who'd known each other for three years.

"Robbie," Mike calls out, unable to keep the excitement from his voice.

Robbie grins, tossing his book bag into the trunk. "I'm coming, Mike!" He laughs as he joins them by the car. Mike can hardly contain his happiness—it has been thirty-nine years since he'd last seen his friend. He takes a few steadying breaths, fighting back tears.

"It's been so long, my old friend. I've missed you, Robbie," he said, voice thick with emotion.

Robbie blinks in confusion. "Since first period?" he asks, clearly amused.

Mike laughs, closing his eyes briefly. "Yeah, Rob. But it felt like a lifetime."

"I guess it would have been a long day after that freak show in English Lit..." Robbie starts laughing hard.

"Is there anyone who hasn't heard about that?" Mike asks, his cheeks reddening as he scratches the back of his neck.

"Probably not; it is all Mrs. Austin could discuss in every class. Evidently, she is giving you a second chance," Robbie adds.

"She told people that?" Mike is astonished. "I was fortunate to convince her..."

"Well, you know she used to talk about how you were the only kid she couldn't help. You were the student that no one should try to be. Everyone knows that you sleep through her class, and she doesn't care anymore," Robbie sounds concerned. "She said that today was different. Mrs. Austin offers extra credit to anyone who can help you catch up. I may need to take her up on that myself."

"She did that?" Mike gasps.

"Like I told you, Tripp," Lauren replies as she sits in the passenger seat. "You scared the shit out of her..."

Mike opens the driver's side door, leaning the seat forward as Robbie climbs awkwardly into the back of the Mustang, his long legs cramped in the narrow space. It's routine for Robbie to sit behind Mike when Lauren rides along, though he never felt entirely comfortable around her. Robbie shifts in the back seat, glancing at Lauren. He didn't trust her boyfriend, Greg—trouble seemed to follow him. Robbie has always wanted to warn Mike about him, but he'd never had the courage.

"So... what did Lauren call you?" Robbie asks as Mike slides into the driver's seat.

"She called me Tripp. Remember, I told you once that Momma wanted to call me that? If I'm changing into a new person, I might as well have a new name, right?" Mike jokes.

"A new name for a new you?" Robbie asks, puzzled.

"Yeah. This morning just made me realize I've gotta turn things around. Apologizing to people, making up for stuff... I'm trying to be a better version of myself. Going by a new name feels like a fresh start." Mike explains his life's new mission.

"Makes sense, but why the change all of a sudden?" Robbie leans forward.

"I need to turn my life around. Going by that name is symbolic of me being a new person. Tripp Carson!"

Robbie scratches his head, frowning. "I dunno, man. You've been Mike since we met. It'd be hard to think of you as someone else."

"You can keep calling me by my name. I guess Tripp kinda sounds stupid," Mike says, digging the key out of his jeans pocket and stopping.

"No, it's *not* stupid," Lauren chimes in. "You're on a journey, right? The name suits you."

"Yeah, I didn't mean it was stupid, just... y'know, habit. " Robbie adds apologetically.

Suddenly, Mike's face tenses up. "Wait—was anyone else in the car this morning?"

Robbie and Lauren both laugh, and Mike reluctantly joins in, though he feels a pang. The morning had been just a few hours ago for them, but it was over forty years for him. As Robbie leans forward between the seats, Mike takes a steadying breath, glad to have his friends with him for this second chance.

"Nope, remember Porter went to Florida." Robbie keeps laughing. "Dork!"

"No drugs, my ass. Come on, Tripp, I want to call Greg before my parents get home..."

T ripp turns up the volume, letting the music fill the car. Robbie gazes out the window, head bobbing to the beat. Lauren starts filing her fingernails. She watches as Tripp takes several wrong turns. She's sure that Tripp must be high. There is no other explanation.

Tripp silently curses under his breath. He knows where Robbie Davis lives but determining the exact location or route to take to drop Lauren off is aggravating him. He misses the conveniences of driving in 2022. But even if he did have a GPS, he didn't have her address.

"Tripp?" She asks.

"Hmm?" Tripp responds.

"I guess your new name fits," Lauren eyes him suspiciously. "Are we taking a *trip* around town?" Lauren emphasizes the word trip.

"Huh? No, just listening to Boston."

Lauren glances sideways at Mike, her suspicion growing. "Are we going somewhere specific, or are you just lost?' she asks, eyebrow raised.

"Not lost! Really, I love this song. Wasn't paying attention," Mike answers with a nervous laugh. "So, how do we get there from here?"

Lauren sighs in frustration, shaking her head, "Goober, take the next right."

Mike Carson knows he recognize the house once they're close. He's grateful that no one has made an issue of his bad memory. Tripp decides he needs to come up with a plan. He can only play off his disorientation for a short time. Then, Tripp spots Daisy's home. He knows they are close. They go farther down the street. He pulls into the driveway of Lauren's family home.

"Are you going to be okay, Tripp?" Lauren asks, gathering her things. "I'm proud you want to improve, but you seem off."

"Yeah, it was a rough day. Thanks, Lauren." Tripp smiles.

"OK, now you will remember where to come in the morning, right?" Lauren inquires with a skeptical expression, though it is a gentle tease rather than a serious question.

"I will keep the space cadet on track," Robbie jokes, leaning forward between the front seats.

Lauren laughs and leaves the door open for Robbie. He climbs out of the back. Robbie stretches, and then he sits up front. They wave goodbye to Lauren as Tripp backs his car out of the driveway. Tripp revs the motor, and they take off. He is afraid to admit that he hasn't driven a straight drive in a long time.

"Mike, now that the princess has been dropped off, you want to tell me what really happened?" Robbie is concerned, looking at Mike's face. "I know I joked about it, but Doug said you acted like you had never been in that room before. By the end of the class, you looked like a caged animal that knew it was in a zoo."

Mike sighs, thankful for how good a friend Robbie is. He knows that the truth- well, the truth, as Michael Carson understands it- will sound insane. Mike wonders if it has been a dream, though the memories in his mind are too real. The regret and emptiness Mike had felt after his call with Gabby were real and still looming in his mind.

Mike hesitates, "I...uh, it is complicated."

"I have all day, Mike," Robbie smiles, leaning back in the passenger seat.

Surrendering, he admits, "Well, Robbie, I didn't sleep well last night. I haven't been sleeping well for a while. Today, I was sound asleep in her class. Guess I was exhausted."

"You seemed fine this morning," Robbie notes. "Well, maybe a little pissed and distant." Robbie pauses, having a flash memory of the morning's ride to school. "Uh...but this afternoon, you do seem different, Mike."

"Sorry," Mike explains. "I had a dream, a nightmare, you could say."

Robbie is confused, "Couldn't have been that long. Doug said it was only ten minutes into class when you jumped."

"It felt like an eternity, Rob," Mike explains with a heavy sigh. He honestly did not know how long he was in the timeless void. "I know I haven't been that good of a friend. I'm sorry I ever let you down. Can you forgive me?"

Robbie is dumbfounded, having never thought that of his friend. "Nonsense, Mike. You're my best friend."

"Yes, Robbie, we are best friends. That still doesn't mean I can't be wrong. I'm truly sorry. I have been going through a lot. I guess my mind dealt with it by giving me a bad dream," Mike tries carefully not to speak like an adult of fifty-eight years. "I hate to admit it, but my dream has terrified me."

"How much of the dream do you remember......Tripp?" Robbie asks, shaking his head. "Okay, that just felt weird, Mike."

"You can keep calling me Mike; I don't want you to feel forced. I remember most of it, though—it wasn't a single moment, it was an entire lifetime. My next forty-two years filled, stained with bad decisions and loneliness, all starting from February seventeenth, 1981. That future... terrified me. I don't know why I'd given up, but living through it—well, even in a dream—it made me realize I was heading down the wrong path. Second chances like this don't come often."

"Second chances?" Robbie asks.

"Yes..."

"An entire lifetime in one dream? Hmm. That sounds like a plot in one of the old TV shows you like to watch," Robbie laughs.

"But I can see a difference in you. You aren't the same guy from this morning..."

"I do not like him, Robbie. He will become a heartless monster that only cares about himself." Mike replies in a somber tone, avoiding eye contact.

"He...uh..." Robbie laughs nervously. "...that does not sound like anyone I want to be around."

Mike thinks, *and that is precisely what happened! But not this time...*

Robbie continues, "If you want to be a better person, you can count on me. Just tell me what you need, Mike."

Mike pulls up to the stop sign and waits, glancing at Robbie. A warm smile graces Mike's face as he searches for the right words to convey the significance of this moment with his best friend. This second chance at reclaiming his life cannot afford any missteps.

Mike speaks very seriously, "Robbie, you have been the best of all my best friends that I've had in my life..."

"All sixteen years of it?" Robbie interjects with a laugh.

"Yes, all sixteen years, you smart ass." Mike chuckles, rolling his eyes, "It's not about how long we've had this friendship but the strength that friendship holds. I have immense respect for you. At the risk of sounding a bit dramatic, I'd give my life for you. You're the most honorable and incredible man I know."

Robbie grows silent momentarily and looks away, rubbing the back of his neck. 'I had no idea, Mike. But... thanks. That means a lot.'

"It's the only truth I've known," Mike confesses, hanging his head down. "I should have told you a long time ago."

"But you've told me now, Mike Carson," Robbie reassures, trying to address the heartfelt declaration. "I have always believed in you."

Tripp nods, looking at Robie directly in the eyes, "I want to be a better person and be worthy of having you as my friend."

Robbie is about to reply, but the pickup truck behind them starts honking its horn. Tripp glances at the rear-view mirror and sees several cars waiting for him to move. The two friends laugh as Tripp revs up the motor and takes off. Robbie turns up the volume on the radio as several Led Zeppelin songs play. Tripp can see that Robbie is thinking. He guesses it is about the things they have been discussing. Tripp is certain he has said all the right things. He wants to get everything right. The silence continues as Tripp turns onto Pleasant View Drive. He sees the driveway to the Davis home just ahead. Tripp pulls in and parks beside the '69 Pontiac GTO.

Mama Davis and Robbie's stepdad had surprised him with the car on his birthday. They only paid $600, though it didn't run at first. Since then, Robbie had been working on his "GOAT" every day, determined to restore it to full muscle-car glory. The GTO was running now but still needed work before it could earn a tag.

Though he wasn't mechanically inclined, Tripp usually keeps Robbie company as he worked. Oil changes were about as far as Mike's knowledge went, and he winced at the thought of grease under his nails. Tripp steps out of the car, popping the trunk for Robbie, who grabs his bag with a grunt and slings it over his shoulder.

"Hey, Mike. I don't have homework today. Want help with Mrs. Austin's stuff?" Robbie offers.

Mike shakes his head, closing the trunk. "She's putting a list together, so nothing to work on yet. But the GTO here... I'm guessing it needs a few hours?" Mike flashes a big grin.

Robbie laughs. "Try more like a few weeks."

"It's amazing how much you've accomplished," Mike praises Robbie's mechanical prowess. "She'll be roadworthy soon!"

Robbie laughs. "Yeah, the goat is getting there. Let me grab a Coke. Do you want anything?"

Mike sheepishly nods, "No thanks, Rob."

Mike resists the lure of the soda, thinking of how different his life will be if he starts with small, consistent changes. He wants to prove, even to himself, that he can stay on track. The sixteen-year-old Mike is around 170 pounds but can carry it well. He stands a total of five feet and eight inches. Mike is determined to avoid gaining weight in the first place. Mike laughs, thinking how proud Doctor Elmhurst would be of his choice for a healthier body.

Robbie disappears into the garage, returning with the coke and a lawn chair for Mike. Robbie grabs a few tools and heads over to the hot rod, where Mike sets up the chair. The GTO's engine purred under Robbie's careful attention, though he still dreamed of upgrading it to full muscle-car glory. The new rocker arms and valve covers were next, stamped with the GTO logo. Robbie's stepdad has purchased the new parts. Robbie wants to install them today. An ambitious task is ahead of him.

Mike walks up beside him, watching Robbie's hands work deftly around the bolts. A shiver runs down his spine at the thought of getting greasy, but seeing Robbie's excitement, he smiles.

"Looks complicated..." Mike remarks, gesturing at the engine.

"Not really," Robbie chuckles, sipping his soda. He likes having Mike around to keep him company. It was rare to feel alone when his best friend was by his side. And Mike has been a great friend for the last three years. He is happy that Mike wants to improve, though Robbie loves him the way he is.

"So, where's your starting point?" Robbie asks, glancing over his shoulder as he focuses on the engine. "Have you worked out this whole 'better man' plan yet?"

Mike takes a deep breath. "No plan for tonight, Robbie," He said, leaning into the engine bay. "Thought I would help you with the goat until I need to go home."

"Help?" Robbie responds with excitement. "You mean *real* help? The 'get dirty' kind of help?"

"Yep, real help," Mike laughs, knowing this was uncharted territory. "You always have my back. The least I can do is lend you a hand—even if it means getting oily."

His heart races; Robbie leans on the car, grinning wide. "Mike Carson, you *are* full of surprises! Alright, let's see what you got."

Mike holds his hands up defensively. "You'll have to guide me through it, but I'll give it my best shot."

Robbie beams and dashes back into the garage, returning with an extra ratchet set. He motions for Mike to join him on the right side of the car, handing over the tools and pointing to the valve covers.

"Okay, just loosen these 7/16 bolts. Once you're done, we'll pull the cover together." Robbie's excitement is contagious. "You do realize it's going to get messy, right?"

"Just shut up, Rob. Let's get to it," Mike replies, psyching himself up.

Mike goes right to work. Robbie returns to the driver's side and picks up where he left off. Robbie can't help but glance over at his friend. At one point, Robbie watches Mike examine the bolts, as he'd never seen anything like them. Robbie focuses on his task but finds that his gaze keeps settling on Mike Carson. Robbie spots a small glob of grease on Mike's left cheek. Robbie thinks *I hardly recognize my friend. Apologies, fixing cars, grease... Mike was acting like a stranger—but one I don't mind getting to know.*

"Say, Mike," Robbie says quietly.

Mike looks at Rob and smiles, "Yeah, Robbie, I'm being careful."

"No, not that..." Robbie chuckles softly. "I don't want to pry..."

Mike stops working and stands tall, "You're curious. I get it. I...uh."

"I don't want to discourage you, but today, it's just that you seem like a stranger."

"That's fair, Robbie. I want to think this is who I am," Mike sighs, gently laying the ratchet on the fender. "The truth is yesterday, I was lost. I felt condemned and cast out into purgatory. It was a fate I *deserved*. Waking up in Mrs. Austin's class was...a second chance. Perhaps my only chance. I found my way out because I need to make amends to the important people in my life."

"Michael Carson, a good person *is who you are!*" Robbie looks at him closely as though seeing a side of Mike he'd never known.

"Thanks, Rob. You can always count on me."

Robbie considers his words before breaking into a grin. "Well, as long as you don't scratch the Goat!"

"Yes, sir," Mike smiles, looking down. He takes the ratchet and finishes his job. A few chuckles of relief break the silence.

After a few hours, Robbie stands back, admiring their work on the GTO. Despite his initial hesitation, Mike has been a surprisingly quick learner, and they've managed to switch out the rocker arms and valve covers. Robbie tosses Mike a rag as they wipe down their hands, watching his friend attempt to clean off the remaining grime. Mike thinks about what has happened. *Today was different—a reminder of how much I've taken for granted. This is a first step I won't forget.*

Robbie's face is proud—not just for his car, but for Mike's determination to change. Upon catching the look in his friend's eyes, Mike feels a similar surge of satisfaction, realizing he's taken the first step in showing up for someone who matters.

Mike quietly admits to himself, *"If I were to wake up in Denton tomorrow morning, this one day would've been worth it."*

"What?"

"Nothing, Rob..." Mike replies with a smirk, accidentally smearing some of the oil onto his forearm.

"I have some stuff in the garage to help get the grease off," Robbie directs his friend to the back of the garage. "I couldn't have finished this quickly without the help. But, Mike, you know I would have been happy if you just stayed and talked to me."

Mike smiles; it warms his heart. He could never lose Robbie again. "I know you would've been, my old friend."

"Old? What are we, senior citizens?" Robbie jokes as he collects the tools. "Say, Mike. Was it what you thought it would be like?"

"Well, it was more grease than I expected. But I'm glad my help made a difference," Mike said with gratitude. "We need your goat on the road so I can be the passenger."

"A-ha! Your real motives finally come to light," Robbie laughs and points at his friend. "You will regret letting me drive, and you know it!"

"I'm looking forward to every terrifying moment," Mike replies with a hearty laugh.

Coming Home

At 5:30, the gray clouds move in, and the early darkness builds a feeling of October settling in as Tripp drives home, feeling a mix of anticipation and anxiety. Today, he will see his mother again. It is just another day for sixteen-year-old Mike—but for the fifty-eight-year-old inside him, it's a miracle he did not expect.

As he approaches the house, its familiar yellow exterior walls and worn shutters look comforting and bittersweet. The house is smaller than he remembers, or maybe he sees it with new awareness. He knows he will face memories and emotions he hasn't anticipated.

"Many people depend on me to make all the right choices, and I cannot fail them!" Tripp proclaims loudly.

Tripp switches off the radio. He needs the silence to think. He rationalizes; *I am fifty-eight, after all.* Tripp pulls his Mustang into the short driveway. Mark's '71 Olds Cutlass 442 is there. Tripp stares at the old house with a fond smile.

He takes a deep breath, steeling himself, and opens the door. The old living room, with its mint-green walls and tacky 70s couch, envelope him in memories. Sitting down, he lets the feeling wash over him—he is home.

Even if Mike Carson successfully changes his life now, his choices will always be complicated because of the old lifetime of memories. Tripp wants to change and be a better person, but that old man is still part of his identity. He knows he can never let his guard down regarding how he treats people. He is OK with that if that is the price for this second chance.

It suddenly hits him much to his shock, "I could make changes that worsen the future." He closes his eyes and exhales deeply.

"Stay focused, can't think of those prospects..." Tripp consoles himself.

"Hey twerp, you home for once?" His older brother snaps as he walks through to the kitchen.

"Mark?" Startled, Tripp sits up and sees his brother.

Mark Carson is twenty. He has short blonde hair. It is parted in the middle and always looks perfect. Tripp was in awe of his older brother ever since they were young–his hero. It is at this moment, he realizes that Mark was the closest thing to a father figure that Mike Carson's ever had in his life. Tripp follows his brother as Mark walks through the dining room. The kitchen on Glade Avenue is a narrow hall with cabinets; counters line both sides. The walls are covered in bright yellow wallpaper with weird-looking flowers. His momma loved that kitchen.

An old refrigerator is on the left, and the stove is on the opposite end. The sink is in the middle on the right side, just below a single window. Cabinets are attached to the walls on either side. On the end of the kitchen is the back porch door. Tripp had forgotten how this house was such an architectural nightmare.

Tripp smiles and walks through the swinging door of the kitchen. Mark is mixing some powdered chocolate milk in a tall glass. The familiar scent starts a cascade of memories within Mike; tender moments of his youth spent with his older brother. Mark turns to see his younger brother staring at him. Tripp slowly smiles. Mark grins, shaking his head as he focuses on making the drink without creating a mess.

"Uh...Mark," Tripp quietly asks, his voice shaky, holding in his tears. "Is there enough for two?"

"Yeah," Mark answers, grabbing another glass from the cabinet beside the sink. "What's up, Michael?"

"Nothing, Mark. I just had a bad dream this morning. I guess I can't shake the feeling it gave me," Tripp starts. "Can I tell you something?"

"Sure," Mark answers as he mixes the second chocolate milk.

Tripp suddenly can't find the words. The love for his brother is all that he could feel. He runs over, hugging his brother. Mark is surprised but hugs back. Mark has a gentle laugh and gives Mike one last big squeezing hug.

"It's just milk, stupid..." Mark smiles, speaking softly. "But you're welcome."

"I know," Tripp replies, voice choked, "but...it's good to be home."

"Good to be home?" Mark repeats, curious about Mike's intentions.

"I've missed being around you." Tripp answers.

"That is what family does..."

"Thanks, Mark," Tripp answers, not letting go. "I know I don't tell you enough, but I'm so thankful to have you as my brother. It's just you, me, and momma against the world."

Mark messes up Mike's hair as they end the heartfelt embrace. He smiles big, handing Mike the glass. Mark leans back against the opposite counter. His legs are extended forward at a slight diagonal from the wall. This creates a wide, stable base that suggests he's settled in and isn't planning on going anywhere—Mark's giving his younger brother his full attention. He laughs again. *What is he up to this time?* Mark thinks as he sips his drink.

"It will always be us, Michael," his brother said. "Always, but I need to go study for a test."

"Thanks, Mark," Tripp replies. As Mark walks away, Mike silently mouths, "I love you..."

Tripp takes another swallow of his milk as Mark leaves for his bedroom. This is more challenging than he expected. In 1980, his brother was struggling at community college. High school was just a long, continuous party for Mark Carson. It was by a slim miracle that he graduated at all.

Michael's older brother is brilliant, but without a father figure, both Carson boys had a difficult time in their teenage years. Mark wants to be a nurse. Meeting the financial demands of Mark's education poses a considerable challenge for both him and their mother.

Mark, characterized by his tenacity, is not one to surrender easily; this resilient trait consistently defines his approach to overcoming obstacles.

Tripp walks back into the living room. He stops abruptly; glancing through the front window. He can see his mother is coming up the walkway. It is six o'clock. The city bus runs the next street over. Tripp remembers that she'd given him the car and relied on public transportation.

She is a wonderful mom. Anne Carson sacrifices everything for her sons. She is an angel on Earth. More of a parent than Mike Carson deserves. She is returning from the office. Dressed in a navy-blue skirt and matching blazer. Anne is barely five feet tall. Her short brunette hair is nicely feathered back. She is in her early forties but still full of life.

He stands there, frozen, as she approaches the door. He is getting overwhelmed. In seconds, he will speak with his mother for the first time in over a decade. Michael panics; *I don't know what to say!*

She enters and puts her purse on the end table by the door. Then she places the carry bag beside the door. She looks up and is startled to see her son standing there.

"Oh, Michael. I did not expect to see you, honey." It surprises her as she gasps. "Weren't you staying with Robbie tonight?

"I was...plans changed," He could not speak, shaking his head. Michael runs over to his momma. He wraps his arms around her and holds her tight.

She is alive. Tripp thinks warmly. *She is right here with me.*

The tears start running. He begins to sob uncontrollably. He never thought he would see her again.

"Michael, baby, are you ok?" His mother is concerned.

"Don't let go..." Tripp pleads. "Please...

"Michael, honey, what's wrong?" Her voice softened, a growing concern replacing the surprise.

"I am fine, momma," Tripp struggles to say between the sobs. "Please don't let go..."

Tripp's pain consumes the silence in the small living room. He struggles not to cry but cannot stop. His face is buried against her shoulder. Tripp thought seeing Robbie was difficult, but he realizes those feelings pale in comparison to a mother's love.

"Please don't let go..." He pleads.

She pulls him close, instinctively stroking his hair. "Michael, I'm right here, sweetheart. I'm not going anywhere."A few minutes pass as she holds her son; Tripp continues to plead, "Please don't let go..."

Anne Carson has never heard him cry this way. In fact, she has never heard anyone break down and cry in this fashion. It is a deep sound, its origins wrapped in years of pain and regret. The chorus of his cries echoes in the small room.

The kind of crying that comes from the soul. The hint of a deep sadness and emptiness echoes in the small room. She does as he asks. She holds her baby boy. She knows that Michael has been going through tough times this year. Actually, the past few years. She doesn't know how to help her son.

Her ex-husband, Willis Carson, is no help as a part-time dad. Mark has his demons to fight. Anne tries to enlist her brother to help, but he can only do so much from another state. She feels like she isn't good enough to raise two men.

Tripp repeats the phrase 'Don't let go' several times as he weeps. His mother embraces him close as the tears continue.

Mark returns; the commotion from the living room summons him. He witnesses his brother hugging their mom tight. Thinking back to how his brother acted earlier, Mark realizes something is up with Michael. Their conversation in the kitchen slowly makes more sense to Mark.

He stands by silently, fighting his urge to cry. Several minutes pass when Tripp finally stops the tears and steps back. He takes a deep breath, gathering his thoughts and wipes his face with the back of his hand. He can't help but sniffle. Tripp's never cried like that in his entire life.

Just seeing Anne Dalton Carson has helped him release all the destructive emotions. Five decades of pain. It will be a struggle, but he knows his momma will be there. He does not doubt that his mission is to better his life and everyone he loves...

"I am sorry, Momma; it has just been so long since I've seen you..." His voice is scratchy.

"Michael Carson, I saw you this morning." She giggles with a smile.

"I know, it has just felt like a lifetime to me," Tripp explains as it is true. "I need to tell you something. Well, both of you. I'm sorry. I've been selfish and self-centered. *A spoiled little shit!* I have taken you both for granted, and I am wrong."

"Shh! I've never thought that." Anne comforts her son.

"Michael, we are family," Mark said, coming closer. "We all make mistakes."

"I love you, Mark," Tripp says, and the tears fight to come back. "I love you, Momma. I decided I didn't like who I was or who I would become. I want to change; I *have* to change..."

"Michael, I love you the way you are," His mother hugs him, smoothing his hair.

"I know; I've always known that your love is real. I want to be better to you and to everyone else. That is why I want to change.

I'm starting over. I want you to start calling me Tripp," He said. "I want you to hold me responsible for my bad decisions and help me make the good ones."

Mark comes over and gives his brother a big hug. Their mother smiles as she fights the tears of joy. Tripp starts crying again as Mark holds him tight.

"It is going to be alright, baby brother!" Mark declares. "I will always be here for you, Tripp."

"Thanks." Tripp whispers amongst his sniffles.

"Tripp... You know that name was my idea."

"You were always a bad liar, Mark..." Tripp laughs as he cries. Mark joins in the laughter, not letting go.

"Well, Tripp," Mrs. Carson said. "You know your father hated the idea of calling you that."

"I remember that," Tripp doesn't let go as he answers his mother. "Unless Dad changes as well, his opinion won't matter. This is what I want."

"I am so proud of you—both of you," their mother said. "You're the heart of my life, and I want you to be happy."

Tripp spent the rest of the night speaking with his mom. He gave her the simple version of his nightmare. Recounting all the bad in his fifty-eight year lifetime, though he carefully took a long time to explain. Tripp had to share as many details as possible and paint a picture of how miserable his future life could be. He explained that it is so real to him that he could not ignore it. It is a warning, and now is his second chance. Maybe his last and only chance.

Tripp's momma knows of her son's shortcomings, but as a parent, you must look beyond what is there and see what your child can be. Tripp told her about the things that have been going on in school.

"That's certainly a powerful reason to change." Anne answers. "How are you going to fix what's happening at school?"

Tripp takes his mother's hands. "I'll catch up with the help of Mr. Hammond and Mrs. Austin. This year may not be the best, but the years to come will be better. I promise."

Anne Carson smiles, hugging him tight. Tripp promised his mother that night. She's so proud of her son. Even if he's not the best, he's trying.

Second Home

Tripp wakes up early. For several minutes, he remains still, hiding beneath his covers. He wants to stay in 1980. He has only begun to right the wrongs he has done.

"Today **is** October eighth." Tripp declares.

Everything that has occurred since he arrived in class almost twenty-four hours ago could have been a drunken hallucination, and Tripp knows it. He is happy that his body feels the same as it did yesterday.

The sunlight is peaking through the window, forcing Tripp to summon courage; Tripp slowly opens his eyes to find himself still in his former room. He lets out a joyful chuckle. Glancing down to the foot of his bed, a delighted smile burst across his face as he marvels at the sight of his feet. He can't resist wiggle them.

"Hello, toes!" Tripp laughs joyfully.

Having battled weight issues for most of his former adult life, the sheer fulfillment of seeing both of his feet brought forth genuine happiness, and he couldn't help but laugh at the simple yet profound moment.

"Get in gear!"

He jumps out of bed and showers before school. He makes breakfast for his brother. Tripp asks Mark if he could use one of his spare bookbags for school. Tripp transferred his books and papers into the new bag and tossed what was left of his old one in the trash.

Still having enough time to spare, Tripp heads out to his car. He has to pick up Robbie and Lauren before heading to school. As he heads down the road to Robbie's, Tripp thinks about what has happened. He has been making significant changes.

"But will these changes stay in place should fate pull me back to where I belong?" he asks himself. "And if that does happen, will these few changes be enough to erase the terrible future I desperately wish to avoid?" He wrestles with the idea that all this could be meaningless.

"Fate can't be that cruel!" Tripp tells himself. "It just can't!"

He knows he cannot focus on what might happen; it would drive him insane. Tripp decides to live each day to the fullest. Make everything count.

"One day at a time, Mike, one day at a time..."

Make a significant impact in the lives of the people he loves one day at a time. Tripp turns left onto Pleasant View Drive. He parks and runs to the front door, a happy spring in his steps. Tripp walks in. This is like a second home to him. The Davis family treats him like one of their own. Tripp sees Robbie's mother in the kitchen. She is preparing for work.

"Morning, Mama Davis!" Tripp calls out fondly, gently pulling the door closed behind him.

"Morning, Mike," she replies, her smile warm and welcoming. "I hear you're quite the grease monkey now."

He lets out a bashful laugh. "Well, a little bit. I didn't know what I was doing," Tripp admits, his laughter growing as he walks over to her. "But it felt great to help out."

Mama Davis smiles broadly. "Must've been a big help, then. Robbie talked about you all night."

"He did all the real work; I just followed his directions," Tripp says with a playful grin.

"Well, you know, Robbie's happiest when you two are together," she says, her tone affectionate.

Tripp nods, the satisfaction clear on his face. "Yes, ma'am. I think I'm starting to understand that more every day."

"He really appreciated the help," she confides. "He worried he wouldn't get those parts installed on his own."

"Of course! He's my best friend—helping is what you do," Tripp replies, feeling a quiet pride. Mama Davis affectionately pats Mike on the arm.

Just then, Robbie's voice calls from upstairs, "Hey, Mike! Be down in a minute."

"OK!" Tripp answers, heading to the kitchen with a satisfied grin. As he pours himself a bowl of cereal, Mama Davis watches him move about the kitchen, her expression warm. She's always been fond of Mike Carson, knowing his quirky humor but recognizing his loyalty and kindness to her son. Though Robbie never had trouble making friends, his bond with Mike is something special. But this morning, something feels different.

Last night, Robbie had been full of excitement, talking about how much fun they'd had working on the car together. Recently, she'd noticed a shadow of depression around Mike, something that had worried her. But now, seeing him here, it's as if that shadow has lifted. She smiles, walking over to the counter as he finishes putting things away, and gives him a warm nod of approval.

"Thanks, Mama Davis," Tripp says, catching her look, feeling like he's truly part of this family.

"I bet if you keep helping Robbie, the GTO will be road-ready in no time," Mama Davis says with a smile. "No pressure on you, of course!"

They laugh, and Tripp replies, "As long as he's supervising, I'm all in."

At that moment, Robbie comes down the stairs, still adjusting his shirt. "Sorry I'm late, Mike."

"No rush! I made your cereal, just in case," Tripp says, handing his friend the bowl with a proud grin.

Mama Davis raises an eyebrow, surprised. She hadn't realized Tripp was making breakfast for Robbie, and the gesture brings an approving smile to her face.

Robbie stops, taking the bowl with a warm smile. "Thanks, Mike. Uh, I mean—thanks, Tripp," he corrects himself, giving Tripp a playful shake of the head.

Noticing the exchange, Mama Davis looks at them with curiosity, feeling as though they share a language of their own. "Tripp?" she asks, intrigued.

"Mike's new name," Robbie answers with a mouthful, already halfway through his cereal.

"New name?" she repeats, a bit confused.

Tripp nods, offering a gentle explanation. "I've decided to be a better person, Mama Davis, and I wanted a fresh start—something symbolic. My mom wanted to call me 'Tripp' when I was born since I'm the third. So, I figured it's the right time to use it."

"Oh, I see! Well, I might need some practice," she laughs, her tone kind. "I've always known you as Mike."

Tripp nods, smiling. "No worries if it doesn't stick, Mama Davis. Robbie's still adjusting too."

Robbie chuckles, finishing up his breakfast. "Yeah, it's taking some getting used to. You'll always be Mike to me, but I'll give it my best shot." Glancing at the clock, he adds with a grin, "We'd better go—the princess won't be too happy if you forget where her house is located again."

Robbie gulps down the last of his cereal and places the empty bowl in the sink.

"I just made a couple of wrong turns, that's all!" Tripp snaps back, trying to hide a grin as Robbie laughs.

"Have a good day, boys!" Mama Davis calls as they head to the car.

Running a bit late, Tripp drives to Lauren's house as quickly as he can. She's waiting on the front steps and stands with a wave when she hears the Mustang's familiar roar. Robbie hops into the back seat to give her space up front, though Tripp notices his friend's slight wince as he settles into the cramped back.

Lauren sprints over, gets in, and gives them both a curious look. "Tripp, you two look like you're up to something," she laughs. "What's going on?"

"We made a lot of progress on my goat yesterday," Robbie boasts. "Mike even helped out!"

"Goat?" Lauren asks, feigning confusion as she glances between them.

"GTO. It's his 'Goat'—a muscle car by Pontiac. Very fast!" Tripp jumps in, missing her teasing look. "And yes, I actually helped."

Robbie bursts into laughter. "There was grease everywhere! You wouldn't believe it."

"Mike Carson with grease on his hands? Now *that's* a shocker," Lauren teases, eyeing him playfully. "Tell me the truth!"

"Okay, fine...maybe a little on my hands," Tripp admits with a sheepish grin. "And my arms...and, well, my face too."

Lauren touches his arm, clearly amused. "So you really are changing," she says warmly. "I think that's great, Tripp."

"Hopefully, we'll get Robbie's GTO on the road soon. I'm getting tired of always driving," Tripp says with a laugh.

Robbie leans forward between the seats, grinning. "Don't worry, Lauren. When the GTO's ready, you're riding shotgun in *my* car. Mike can have the back seat for a change."

"Really?" Lauren's eyes light up. "I'd love that, Robbie. Thanks."

"Settled, then," Tripp declares, smiling at the thought of their plans. Then, shifting gears, he asks, "By the way, Lauren, did you talk to Greg last night?"

"Yes. I even told him about your plans," Lauren replies with a warm smile. "He said to tell 'Tripp' he's got your back. He cares about you like a brother."

Tripp nods, touched. "Deep down, he's a good guy. Some people don't see that side of him, caring about people. They just see the tough guy," he adds with a hint of sadness.

"Maybe you can help him, too?" Lauren suggests, placing a gentle hand on Tripp's knee. "I love him just the way he is, but he seems to keep his anger in check more when you're around. Maybe your changes will inspire him..."

Tripp looks at her, thoughtful. "His anger...well, it's the kind that sent him to prison, Lauren," he says without thinking. "Trouble enough to warrant felony charges. But with your help, maybe we can keep him on a better path."

Lauren meets his eyes with a soft, encouraging smile, giving his hand a quick squeeze. Behind them, Robbie bobs his head to the rock music on the cassette. Lauren, recalling her comment to Robbie yesterday, feels a twinge of guilt. She realizes she can be a bit condescending at times without meaning to.

Turning around, she looks at Robbie. "Hey, Robbie, I'm sorry for calling you dorky yesterday," she says sincerely.

"It's fine, Lauren," Robbie chuckles. "I am dorky."

Tripp laughs, chiming in. "And that's why he's my best friend."

Lauren grins, rolling her eyes as she turns forward again. "Hate to break it to you, Tripp, but you're dorky, too!" she teases, letting out a laugh.

"Ouch! Good thing I don't have any feelings left," Tripp jokes, pretending to be hurt as he watches the road.

Lauren laughs, then leans forward. "Hey, just a heads-up, guys. I need to stay after class for about twenty minutes to talk with my teacher."

Tripp glances over at Robbie, who shrugs and gives an easy nod. Catching Lauren's gaze, Tripp flashes a big smile. Lauren giggles, appreciating his reaction.

"Sure, Lauren. No problem," Tripp replies with a grin.

The sky is slightly overcast as they arrive. Robbie heads off to his locker, dashing toward the east wing, while Tripp and Lauren walk together to the main entrance. Typically, Lauren would go her own way by now, but today she sticks by him. Tripp doesn't know why, but he welcomes the company. They weave through the line of students getting off the buses, and Tripp reaches forward, grabbing the door and holding it open for her.

"Well, thank you, Tripp!" Lauren says with a grin. "Didn't know manners were part of your whole 'better person' plan."

Tripp laughs. "Yep, they were! I'm even getting a haircut this weekend. And Mark and I are spending time helping Mom around the house."

Lauren's smile widens. "I bet your mom's proud, Tripp."

Morning Routine

"I want her to be proud of me, not just for myself, but because she gives Mark and me so much without hesitation. I want her to know how much we appreciate her..." Tripp answers sincerely.

"That's really sweet..." Lauren replies, though her attention shifts as she hears a voice from nearby.

"Hey, here comes Tripp!" Peter calls out.

Tripp spots his small group of friends waiting near the office doorway, noting that Steve isn't with them. He waves, heading over, and Lauren follows, noticing for the first time that this group of boys, whom she'd seen by the main doors, were Tripp's friends.

"Hey, guys!" Tripp greets them. "Where's Steve?"

"Missed the bus," Peter laughs, shaking his head. "He's probably getting an earful on his way here."

"I bet he's beating himself up about it," Tripp chuckles.

Jonah grins, casting a flirting look at Lauren. "So, Tripp, I see why you don't hang out with us as much these days. How about an introduction?"

"This is Lauren," Tripp says, giving her a nod. "We're just friends—she's dating my buddy, Greg."

"Greg?!" Larry exclaims, his eyes going wide with surprise.

"Oh—sorry!" Jonah stammers, taking a step back. "Didn't mean any disrespect!"

Lauren laughs, "Don't worry. It's okay! I took it as a compliment."

The boys let out a collective sigh of relief, and Larry starts laughing at Jonah's embarrassment. Tripp chuckles along, enjoying the lighthearted moment. Jonah, still red-faced, tries to play it cool, but his friends keep up the teasing.

Just then, Steve hurries in through the side door, joining the group. He pauses, noticing Lauren and Tripp together.

"Oh, hey, Lauren," Steve says, slightly surprised.

"Hi, Steve!" she replies warmly.

Jonah seizes the moment. "Okay, so now you, too, Steve? Holding out on us?" he teases, folding his arms with mock indignation.

"First Tripp, now you?" Larry adds, grinning.

Lauren laughs. "Wow, you guys are brutal! I was friends with Steve's sister in middle school, actually."

Steve nods, a hint of sadness crossing his face. "Yeah, she lives with our mom now. I'll tell her you said hi next time I see her."

"That would be nice," Lauren says, glancing at Tripp. "Maybe Tripp and I could visit when she's in town?"

Steve's eyes light up. "You and Tripp? Are you two...?"

"No, Steve," Tripp interjects with a grin. "We're just friends. She's dating my buddy Greg."

"I don't have a car," Lauren teases, nudging Tripp's arm. "So Tripp is my knight on a white horse."

"Cool. I don't think my dad would mind, but I'll ask," Steve says with a shrug.

Lauren observes Tripp's easy rapport with his friends, noticing how he's been opening up to them and how genuine their support is in response. She can tell that these are friends he genuinely values, and from their reactions, she senses that his recent efforts to apologize to people aren't needed here. Watching Tripp joke and banter with them, Lauren feels a quiet happiness for him, realizing she cares about his well-being—and she's happy to see him find joy in reconnecting.

As the first bell approaches, the group begins to disperse for their classes, but Lauren lingers beside Tripp as they turn into the north wing hallway. Tripp stops abruptly, his gaze fixed on a group of three students near the door of his second class on the left. He spots a tall black guy in a bright shirt and purple parachute pants, a tall white girl with thick glasses and an Einstein t-shirt, and a shorter white guy with stylish, cropped blond hair in a blue t-shirt and jeans. Lauren notices Tripp's reaction and studies the trio closely, recognizing the shorter guy but not recalling any personal connection.

"Tripp?" she asks gently, sensing his distraction.

"Huh?" Tripp replies, sounding distant, his attention still focused on the three students. "Oh, yeah. What is it, Lauren?"

She follows his gaze. "Are they people you want to apologize to?" She nods toward the group. "Is one of them Jeff?"

He hesitates, glancing at her before looking back at the trio. "...Yeah. Just Jeff."

"You know him?" she asks carefully.

"Yeah," he says quietly. "Jeff Tyler. We were close friends in middle school. I don't really know the other two."

Lauren leans in, speaking softly, "Want me to distract the others so you can talk to him alone?"

Tripp looks at her, surprised. "You'd do that?"

"We're friends, right?" She shrugs with a warm smile. "Just doing what Robbie would've done."

Tripp's eyes soften. "Thanks, Lauren. That...really means a lot. But I don't think I'm ready to talk to Jeff. Not yet."

She gives his shoulder a reassuring rub. "The offer stands, but you'd better hurry—you don't want to be late."

Tripp glances over his shoulder, grateful for her support. He takes a deep breath and heads to class, sneaking a quick look back to see where she's gone, but Lauren has already disappeared down the main hallway. He runs past Jeff and the others without stopping, determined to wait until he's better prepared. This conversation, he knows, will require the right timing, and he needs to be ready if things don't go as planned. The last thing he wants is to feel trapped.

Anne's Phone Call

That night, the house settled into uneasy quiet, though Anne Carson found no rest in it. October the 12th has been a long day.

Spending the afternoon with her sister was emotionally draining. *As if I don't have enough to worry about,* she sighs. Anne sets the receiver back into the cradle twice before she finally dials. The line hums faintly, then clicks, and a man's steady voice answers.

"John Dalton speaking."

Anne lets out the breath she'd been holding. "It's me. Anne."

A pause, then warmth. "Annie. It's been too long."

She forces a tired laugh. "Everything feels too long these days." She glances toward the dark hallway, where Michael's bedroom door is shut tight. "I don't mean to bother you. I just...needed to hear a voice that knows this family."

"What's happened?" John's tone sharpens, a thread of worry beneath it.

"It's Michael." The words are heavier than she expects. "He's—different. For weeks he's been withdrawn one moment, angry the next. Sometimes it feels like he's looking right through me. I don't know if it's something Willis said, or if I've just missed too much, but..." Her voice falters.

John is quiet a long moment. "You're not imagining it, Annie?"

"I wish I were. Mark helps where he can, but he's only a boy himself." She presses a hand against her temple. "I lie awake wondering if I'm failing both my sons."

"You're not failing anyone," John says firmly. "You've carried enough for three lives already. Maybe what Michael needs most is time. And someone he trusts outside the house."

Anne swallows. "Someone like you."

"Has something changed?" John asks, just as another line clicked alive.

"Hello, Anne." Jake has picked up on the extension.

"I miss you, both." Anne holds in the tears.

"You sound upset." Jake asks.

"It's nothing, I'm worried about Michael."

Silence for a moment, the John speaks up. "He's spiraling out of control."

"Well...not exactly." Anne hesitates. "I don't want to jinx it, but Tuesday, something happened."

"Did he get expelled?" Jake asks.

"It's nothing, really. I want to believe it's a glimmer of hope." Tears trace down her cheek. "He says he wants to change, he wants to be a better person."

John exhales through the line. "I'm always here for you. Is this urgent? Should I come down next week? Things are quiet at the firm."

"No," she says quickly, almost too quickly. "Not yet. You've got responsibilities in D.C., and I won't drag you into our chaos unless it's life or death."

"Annie... I mean it. If you call, I'll be there."

Jake cut in, firm and insistent. "Don't let him hedge. I'll put John on the next plane."

"Family is too important, Anne." John whispers, sounding much like their father.

"I know," she whispers. "Just knowing you'd say that—it helps."

For the first time in days, her shoulders ease a fraction. "I'll keep you posted. If things worsen, you'll hear from me first."

"You're never alone in this, Annie," John replies. "Remember that."

She blinks back the sting of tears. "Goodnight, John."

"Goodnight, sister."

Anne hangs up, staring at the silent phone. In the hallway, Michael's door remains closed. She presses her hand against the wood grain as if she could reach through. Sadness fills her eyes as she rests her head on the door.

She whispers. "Please, God...help me understand my son."

The words replay in her mind: Michael's plea to be called Tripp, his promise to Mark, his apology to her. If he truly wanted to change, maybe God had answered already.

Seeking Redemption

Tripp pushes his earlier encounters from his mind as he settles in the first period. The teacher's lecture takes up the entire period, so he doesn't get a chance to talk with Robbie. His next class, though, holds significance—his English Lit meeting with Mrs. Austin. He's written a fourteen-page paper, all by hand, a difficult task he hadn't anticipated. It's a brief biography of his fifty-eight-year-old self, rewritten several times to tone down the more detailed, adult elements, framing it as a nightmare experienced by a sixteen-year-old. To add depth, Tripp included personal reflections on the events, inspired by the kind of commentary Doctor Elmhurst encouraged in their sessions. Mrs. Austin seems moved by the section about Gabby, even reading part of it aloud, her voice soft with emotion, a tear welling in her eyes.

"I have to say, Mike, I'm impressed," Mrs. Austin says, carefully flipping through the pages. "Your handwriting could use some work, but the content here... it's remarkable." She pauses, considering him. "Was all this truly in your dream?"

"Yes, ma'am. It felt incredibly real," Tripp replies, his gratitude evident. "That's why it scared me so much. I don't want to end up like that man."

She nods, holding up the paper. "Mike, look beyond who he seemed to be on the surface," she says, encouragingly. "Even in this account, he's not all bad. Raising two daughters alone isn't easy. He kept trying, even at the end. That takes strength."

Tripp frowns slightly. "I can be stubborn, yes. I just don't want to end up like that...like I will, in the dream, I meant," he says, catching himself.

Mrs. Austin's gaze softens. "And this date here," she says, pointing to a passage, "what was its significance?"

"It was...the day his spirit died. After that, everything felt meaningless," Tripp replies, his voice tinged with sadness.

"You describe a mental breakdown with such vividness. It reads like a firsthand account. Remarkable work, Mike," she adds, studying him thoughtfully.

Tripp looks away, embarrassed. "I wish it was just a description."

Mrs. Austin places a gentle hand on his arm. "Thank you for trusting me with this. It was brave of you, Mike. And remember, he did come back from it on his own. He showed regret and resilience, both qualities you're embracing. Perhaps, given a real chance, he'd change too. But remember, it was only a dream."

Tripp hesitates. "Maybe you're right, maybe he wasn't a monster. But I can't take that risk. I only see the pain he caused everyone."

She nods understandingly. "I can see you believe it to be real. And, Mike, it's a remarkable story. If it were an actual assignment, I'd give it the highest marks." She gives him an encouraging smile. "Whether real or imagined, it clearly inspired you. And I'm proud of the steps you're taking. Mr. Hammond mentioned you're getting help with your other classes too. That's truly commendable."

"I'm only sixteen, Mrs. Austin. I know that the man in the dream isn't me—not yet, anyway. I don't know why I woke up in your class, but I'm thankful for it." Tripp's voice softens. "My friend Robbie said you're offering extra credit to people who help me. I don't know what to say except...I won't disappoint you." His voice catches, emotion breaking through his resolve.

Mrs. Austin holds up a finger, gently. "I don't want others doing the work for you, Mike."

"Believe me, I won't allow that. That's what the man in my nightmare would do," he replies, conviction hardening his tone. "I can't be him, not anymore."

She nods, visibly touched by his sincerity. "I believe you, Mike. Maybe this second chance of yours will give others a second chance as well. Just keep me in the loop about who's helping on each assignment. They deserve credit too."

"Yes, ma'am," Tripp replies respectfully.

The rest of the school day is a blur. Tripp finds himself drifting into daydreams, caught in thoughts of his next steps. After the final bell, he rushes to his car. With Robbie riding the bus with Doug Barrett, he's free to drop off Lauren quickly before heading to see his cousin, Scott. As they drive, Lauren engages him in light conversation. Tripp answers her questions briefly, sensing she's subtly fishing for details he's not yet ready to share. He's focused, running over what he'll say to Scott, preparing himself for what might be a messy conversation.

When they pull into her driveway, Lauren leans over, offering him a quick, warm hug. She pulls back with a gentle smile, and Tripp finds himself genuinely moved by her support—something he'd once taken for granted.

"Not sure where your mind was, Tripp, but thanks for the ride," she says, touching his arm.

"Sorry, Lauren. I was thinking about what I need to say to my cousin..." His response is almost automatic, his mind still preoccupied.

"Another apology?" Lauren raises an eyebrow, her concern apparent. "Aren't you worried you're going overboard with all this?"

"Maybe," Tripp admits in a whisper. "But in that nightmare...there were so many people...so so many people that I hurt, I didn't even think twice about. I feel like if I apologize to the people who mean something to me, it'll keep me grounded. Keep me from making those same mistakes."

She studies him, her expression softened with understanding. "It's like you're a completely different person. A few weeks ago, I was worried you were drifting. It was like nothing mattered to you. And now..."

"Now it seems like everything matters. Even the smallest detail." Tripp lets out a deep breath. "I don't know what to call that kid I used to be, but I hate who he was. And I hate the man he would have become."

Lauren leans in, her voice soft but steady. "That kid wasn't all bad, Tripp. It was you, and you're here, choosing to be better. That takes a lot of courage. If you ever need someone to talk to, I'm here for you."

Tripp nods, gratitude evident. "Thanks, Lauren. I'll see you tomorrow."

"Yes, goodbye, Tripp," Lauren replies, offering him one last supportive look before stepping out of the car. She stands by the street, watching him drive away, sensing that there's more to Mike Carson's transformation than he's letting on.

Tripp shifts his Mustang into reverse, backing out of the driveway. His mother's younger sister, Linda Graves, lives a few blocks away with her two children. The oldest, Regina, is a bit of a drama queen and distant, four years older than him. Scott, however, is three years younger than Tripp and a different story altogether. The old Mike rarely treated him well—some actions bordering on outright bullying. The thought of it fills Tripp with shame, knowing this will be one of the truest tests of his resolve to change.

Will Scott forgive me? The question lingers, heavy with doubt.

The drive to the West Side Condominiums doesn't take long. His aunt's unit, a three-bedroom in the older section of the complex, was once the source of jealousy for the younger Mike, who saw it as a symbol of stability he craved. But today isn't about those old feelings; it's about new beginnings. Tripp sits in the car for several minutes, running through different scenarios, each one tinged with the fear of Scott's rejection. Scott had always been quick-tempered, and their last encounter three weeks ago had ended with Mike's sharp words. *How could I have been so cruel?* he wonders, though he knows he has no excuse.

Taking a deep breath, Tripp steels himself, steps out of the car, and heads toward the condo entrance. He knows he has to make things right, no matter how difficult the path may be.

Rhythms of Reconciliation

He gets to the porch and presses the doorbell. He knows they are home; his aunt was the proud owner of a Pontiac Bonneville, slumbering in the parking space in front of unit 2D. The old Mike called that car the QE2 because it was as big as a cruise ship. Tripp's aunt is the one to open the door. She greets him with a big hug. Tripp follows her into the small living room. She takes a sip of wine that she has been drinking.

"Hey, Aunt Linda, how have you been?" Tripp greets her.

"Oh, I have been better, Michael," His aunt replies with a sigh. "I am still working two jobs. I can't sleep worth a damn. But I'm sure that you didn't come by to hear my troubles."

"It's okay; I can listen. I care about you, Aunt Linda. I know I can be a jerk sometimes, but I love you. I'm sorry if I have done anything to upset you," Tripp said, hugging her.

Linda accepts the hug and pats her nephew, "Michael, honey. That is just a figure of speech. Pay it no mind."

"I won't, but I was being serious," Tripp smiles. "I really am sorry. I'm making an effort to change the way I treat people—apologizing to everyone that I care about."

"That is lovely, honey. I wish you all the success in the world," Aunt Linda gives him another hug. "So, what is the reason you came by?"

"Uh...Scott," Tripp cautiously begins. "Is he around? I just wanted a few minutes with him."

"He's downstairs. Just a warning. He is in a *mood*," She emphasizes and nods towards the stairs. "They had a big argument three days ago while he stayed with his father. It was a big fight and has eaten away at Scott ever since."

"What happened?" Tripp steps forward with concern.

"So, now it appears that Scott does not like to bathe when he stays with his father. He refused even to change clothes while he was there. Your uncle called me to talk sense to *my son*," Aunt Linda huffs. "Like that man had nothing to do with it..."

Tripp feels bad for his cousin; Scott's hatred for his father is strong. "I'm sorry, Aunt Linda. I want to help."

"Scott was screaming when I arrived to pick him up," she said, taking another sip of wine. "Broke my heart..."

"Maybe I should wait to speak to him," Looking at the stairs, Tripp is worried.

"Michael Carson, I think this is the perfect time to share your new outlook on life," Linda Graves said, finishing the glass of wine. "He needs to know there are people that still care about him. Especially from you."

"OK," Tripp reluctantly responds, heading downstairs.

The basement of unit 2D was converted into a bedroom. It is very large and crammed full of all sorts of toys. Scott's drum set topped it off. Tripp slowly comes to the bottom step. He can see Scott sitting in a slump at the base of his bed. Scott looks so unhappy. His face exhibits bitterness and disgust. He is surrounded by an army of Star Wars action figures, elaborately arranged in formation as if they are protecting Scott from an attack. Tripp sees Scott glance at him but does not react. Tripp takes a deep breath.

Tripp timidly asks, "Uh...hey, Scott. Can I come into your room? Something I want to talk to you about."

Expressionless, Scott replies, "Sure. Hello, Michael."

"It's been a while since we spoke..." Tripp said as he carefully approached.

"I know," His reply stings of anger. "Three weekends, Michael..."

Scott glares as Tripp slides down the side of the bed to sit beside his cousin. Scott is sporting a new haircut, a style that is more like a buzz cut. His father is pushing to send Scott to a military-style school for boys. No one is happy about that, especially Scott. The young cousin is more carefree than his uncle wants to allow. He feels Scott should be serious about school. Scott loves his music. That is his passion. Scott has a scowl on his face. Looking like a small dog ready to pounce. There is so much anger beneath the surface. Tripp is worried that he may have chosen the wrong day to come here.

Tripp timidly asks, "I take it that your new haircut is in preparation for heading to Asheland Academy?"

Scott grunts and nods yes, "I'm hoping Grandpa Dalton will get Father to change his mind."

"Papa Dalton will fight hard for you," Tripp reassures his younger cousin. "Before we talk about that, I want to tell you why I am here."

Scott's glare is unyielding, but Tripp takes a steadying breath. He reminds himself to stick to what he needs to say, despite his nerves. This apology feels crucial.

"Scott, I'm sorry," Tripp begins, voice quiet but firm. "I treated you worse than I'd ever treat a stranger. I was selfish and thoughtless, only ever thinking of myself. I was wrong—so very wrong. Family is supposed to mean something." He starts looking down, but as he finishes, he lifts his gaze, meeting Scott's eyes.

Scott's posture shifts, the scowl softening as he straightens and watches his cousin with a curiosity that Tripp hasn't seen in a long time. Despite everything, Scott always looked up to him, and this revelation seems to catch him off guard.

"I cried all day after you said those things," Scott's voice is quieter, the bitterness fading as he kneels to face Tripp. The hurt behind his words is clear.

Tripp feels the weight of guilt pressing down on him. "I know, Scott. I don't have an excuse. I was thoughtless and inconsiderate. If you can find it in your heart to forgive me…" His voice trails off.

Without hesitation, Scott leans forward and wraps his arms around Tripp. He begins to cry softly, and Tripp holds him close, feeling his own eyes grow wet. Scott has carried so much pain, and Tripp knows how deeply his cousin needed this apology.

"I promise, Scott. The person I was is gone, hopefully for good. I'll always be your cousin, and I'll be here for you this time," Tripp vows, holding him tightly. "I'm working to apologize to everyone important to me. I don't want to end up as a person who only ever hurts others."

"I love you, Michael," Scott says, his words muffled through soft sob

"I love you, kid. Since I'm changing, I want to be called Tripp," He explains. "To symbolize I'm a new person."

"Tripp?" Scott is genuinely confused.

"Yeah, you know how you're a junior named after your dad," Tripp explains as Scott nods, saying he is following. "I'm named after my dad and his dad, so makes me the third.."

"Like a triple scoop of ice cream?" Scott yells out.

Tripp laughs hard, "Tripp, like three, so yeah. That OK?"

"I don't like it as a name, Michael," Scott makes a face of displeasure. "I just want to be around you, that's all."

"That will change, Scott. I will make time for you and me every week. I'm struggling in school and have a lot of hard work ahead of me," Tripp comforts his cousin, who cannot prevent a smile and feels connected with Scott. "But I won't let that stand in the way. OK?"

Scott nods with a happy smile. He takes a few more minutes of crying. Scott eventually stops, moving to sit down beside Tripp. The thirteen-year-old boy is not sure why his cousin has come on this day, but he is glad. He forgives Michael; Scott knows he also said some pretty nasty things. He's always upset with his dad and lets that anger spill over to everyone.

"You want to talk about your dad, Scott?" Tripp asks.

"No...I hate that big jerk. He just wants me to suffer and not enjoy life. He was born an old man, I think!" Scott yells out. "I don't think he knows what it is like to be a normal kid. I hate him."

"I'm here for you, Scott," Tripp replies calmly. "I told you that family is important. I meant that."

Scott speaks softly, leaning close, "I believe you, Michael. It meant a lot that you asked me to forgive you. It was brave. However, my ass of a dad..."

"Scott," Tripp stops him. "You know who taught me that family was important?"

"Aunt Annie?"

"No, Scott. Though my momma believes that it is, it was my father. And I know he is right," Tripp explains. "Yes, he left us, just like your dad left y'all. But they will always be our dads. We won't get another one. We don't have to like who they are, but we must respect that our parents can make mistakes too. I know it doesn't make sense."

"I don't understand, Michael..." Scott has a perplexed look.

"I respect my dad. He will always be a part of me. I just do not let him have that much power over me," Tripp tells him, folding his arms. "Let me ask you something."

Eager to hear what his cousin has to say, "Anything, Michael."

"Have you been sulking in your room for days, just hating him?" Tripp asks, nodding at the army of toys protecting Scott.

"Yeah, wouldn't you? I do hate him. He does not care about us. He wants me to be some boring nobody..." Scott folds his arms with a vulgar scowl on his face.

"I bet that he has not once thought about it," Tripp concludes with a shrug of his shoulders. "If he's like my dad, I can guarantee that he hasn't"

Scott growls, "That just makes me hate him more..."

"Maybe, but this hatred is eating you up," Tripp rests his hand on Scott's arm. "Soon, there will be nothing left. You hating him does not change him. I am not saying you can't dislike the way he is, but you have to let go of this bitterness. It will only get worse. Do not let him make you miserable."

Scott thinks for a minute, "I guess that makes sense. How did you get so smart?"

Tripp laughs, "It took me forty-six years to figure out who I was..."

"Michael, you're so funny!" Scott blurts out with a round of giggles.

Scott laughs. He wrestles with his cousin. Tripp tries to tickle his cousin, but Scott is immune. They start laughing. Scott finally gives up. Both cousins sit down on the bed. Tripp looks over to the drum set with a large grin.

"Hey, Scott," Tripp playfully asks. "Can I ask you for one more thing?"

"Yeah."

"Can you do that drum solo from the Kiss song? You play it so well." The old Mike always liked to watch Scott play.

"Sure, let me start the record..." Scott yells out as he rolls over and darts to his stereo.

As Scott moves around, Tripp has an intriguing thought, "Hey Scott, do you think you can teach me to play the drums?"

"Yeah," Scott answers with a tease. "But we need to start with something easier!"

"Meh, you are a good teacher; you can do it!" Tripp jokes.

Tripp watches his cousin light up. He bounces around, getting the music ready. Scott grabs his drumsticks and sits behind the big bass drum. The music starts, and the young drummer plays hard. Tripp thinks that this is the happiest he can remember his cousin ever being. He smiles proudly as Scott begins to play. He is in awe; Scott is an extremely talented musician. If he misses a note, Tripp is not able to tell. They spend the next hour on the drums.

Echoes of the Lunchroom

The following day, Tripp is still trying to make sense of the course before him. He hasn't spoken with Robbie since the first period. His friend wanted to spend some time with Doug, *Probably to discuss their projects for shop class,* Tripp thinks. It is a welcome breather from the day; he should be planning the mission. Tripp knows he has taken the correct first steps. Now, it is up to him. This will be a long process to ensure he gets to everyone who matters.

Tripp slides into his usual spot at the table, his seat from last year, the clamor of the lunchroom enveloping him like a familiar, cacophonous blanket. The nerd group has already assembled, their trays forming a mosaic of the school's culinary offerings. With so much chaos erupting around him, Tripp feels at odds with a large room of teenagers. *My last birthday was my fifty-eighth, yet I'm sixteen today? Indeed, I'm a teenager myself, right?* Tripp ponders: *Why did I get this second chance?*

Jonah asks Larry, "Since you are the bigger fan of the show, how much did O.S.I. spend to make the bionic woman?".

"Morning, captain!" Peter calls out from the far end of the table.

Steve laughs, waving his hands, "Save your breath; either the good twin is deep in philosophical thought, or the evil twin is most certainly plotting our demise..."

Hearing his name captures Tripp's attention. "Huh? Oh, yeah. Hey guys," Tripp answers robotically. "Didn't sleep last night..."

"Jonah, why is that even important?" Larry asks, shrugging his shoulders. "She has the same abilities."

"Uh-oh, evil never sleeps!" Steve burst out in laughter.

Tripp shakes his head, quietly masking a gentle laugh at his friends. He does not consider that this would be something he missed. He has fond memories with them, but now he could make things better. His attention is drawn away as he spots a girl several tables away. *She will eventually become one of Gabby's teachers; what the hell was her name?* Tripp struggles to remember as his friends continue their day.

"Correct, Larry, but see, that's my point. Her bionics were smaller," Jonah explains earnestly.

"Jonah..." Larry replies, secretly annoyed; this conversation has been running for a while.

Jonah stands, briskly walking over to Larry's chair, "Now hear me out, I've done some research..."

"Research? Jonah, it's just a TV show!" Larry laughs.

Jonah looks frustrated; Steve jumps to his rescue, "See, here's the thing: Colonel Austin was the prototype; she gets the bionics with the improvements..."

"Of course, I never thought of that!" Larry exclaims. Jonah has a big smile. "But, then again, it's just a TV show."

Tripp chuckles as he tunes them out. He watches his friends' lively debates and easy camaraderie with a bittersweet tang of envy. They are unburdened by the knowledge of what the future holds; each day is a blank canvas of possibilities. Tripp, however, is haunted by the shadows of what has been and the daunting task of steering his future away from his past mistakes.

Larry excitedly describes his latest model car project. At the same time, Peter and his sister, who'd decided to grace them with her presence today, debating the merits of classic literature over contemporary works. Peter, ever the elder statesman of the group, listens with a patient smile, occasionally interjecting with a wisecrack that sends ripples of laughter through the table.

Having the satisfaction of getting Larry to relinquish his refusal to talk about the show, Jonah shuffles a deck of cards, a new game always ready. Still, Tripp finds himself unusually detached from the conversation. Instead, his gaze drifts across the lunchroom, taking in the sea of faces, each a story, a history that he felt compelled to understand. *That is Bobby, yeah, I think it is...* He tries to remember their names, piecing together fragments of interactions and whispered stories that floated through the halls like ghosts. Tripp glances as Peter's sister departs. It was 1980; this table is not where a preppy girl wants to be seen. *Give my boys a few years; they'll have good jobs...* Tripp laughs at his private joke. The conversation at the table slowly blends into the noise that surrounds them. Tripp finishes off his drink in one swallow. He strolls over to the trash and tosses the empty container nonchalantly.

"Hello, Mike," a short-haired brunette greets him, tearing his focus away from his thoughts.

She is short. Her pale face has a hint of makeup, and Tripp thinks she may still be learning how to apply the enhancements. Her designer jeans tightly cling to her shapely body. She is wearing a lovely pink t-shirt with a picture of some heartthrob of the day; Tripp doesn't recognize the image.

"Oh, hey..." Tripp answers automatically, flashing a pleasant smile. The girl responds with a flirtatious grin and walks back to her table.

"Do I know her?" Tripp asks aloud. He tries to remember as he returns to the table. He stops, looking back over his shoulder towards the girl. Evidently, she has moved on and engaged in a whispered conversation with a tall blonde girl.

"Tripp, you think so?" Larry's voice pulls him back, a question hanging in the air, awaiting his verdict.

"Sure," Tripp mutters, his response automatic, his mind still adrift.

He watches as Robbie and Doug share a table across the room, their heads bent in close conversation. Memories of their shared past flicker in his mind, a reminder of the intricate web of relationships that define this microcosm of the world. It strikes him then how much they all carry, the weight of their stories and secrets intertwining like the roots of an ancient forest. Tripp looks around the cafeteria, a multitude of different souls living their lives.

"Tripp's out of it today, huh?" Steve's voice breaks through his trance, accompanied by the light touch of his hand on Tripp's shoulder, a gesture of concern.

Tripp offers a half-smile, an acknowledgment, yet his mind remains preoccupied. Steve quietly returns to the conversation, leaving Tripp in his solitude. Mike Carson wonders about the histories that each person at the table carries, the silent battles, the triumphs and defeats that are etched into the very fabric of their being. It is a rich and complex tapestry of human experience, and Tripp feels a sudden urge to understand it all, to see the world through their eyes, if only for a moment.

"I envy them..." Tripp mutters aloud, his words not directed at his friends.

"Envy who, Tripp?" Steve asks, pausing from his trivial debate with Jonah.

"Them..." Tripp replies, still focusing on the other table, and then he turns to Steve. "You, well, all of you. Your innocence. Each day is fresh, a restart of your existence. You move through life, not knowing what the future holds..."

"Oh, and I guess you are a time traveler or a wizard with a crystal ball," Larry jokes. "You must have been foretold of your future; how it's all planned out, huh?"

"No...not a crystal ball," Tripp lets out a distressed sigh. "I only know the future that I don't want..."

Steve hesitates, unsure if he needs to inquire deeper into Tripp's comments. The bell rings, signaling the end of lunch, the sudden shift jarring. Tripp lingers as the group disperses, watching the empty lunchroom, the echoes of laughter and conversation fading into silence. He realizes then, perhaps for the first time, the profound beauty in the simplicity of this daily gathering, a momentary reprieve from the solitude of existence, a connection to the myriad stories unfolding around him.

With a deep breath, Tripp stands, the weight of his thoughts grounding him yet also freeing him in a way he couldn't quite articulate. He steps into the flow of students, a silent observer, a guardian of their stories, ready to face the remainder of the day with a newfound appreciation for the intricate dance of human connection.

Report Card

Mark sits on the couch. He and his mother have made a plan to sell Mark's guitar. October 22 is tomorrow, and the remaining balance of his tuition is due.

"I'm sorry, Mark. I know your grandfather gave that to you, but we're still struggling." Anne tries to console her son.

Mark takes her hand. "I meant it when I said I wasn't going to burden you with my school. I'm a man — I should stand on my own two feet."

"Mark Patrick Carson." Anne's tone sharpens, a stern rebuke. "You will always be my son. I have never thought of you as a burden."

Mark holds back his tears. He knows a mother will always care for her children, but right now he believes Tripp should be her only focus.

"There isn't any other way. I'll take it to the music shop in the morning..."

The phone rings, ending the debate. Mark is thankful for the interruption — he can see how much the matter has already stressed his mother. Tripp's progress report is still weighing heavy in the back of his mind, a bad omen.

Anne picks up. "Hello?"

"Good evening," comes the steady, familiar voice of John Dalton Jr.

"Hello, John! How are you?" Anne asks warmly, her tone lifting with genuine happiness.

Mark smiles. "Tell Uncle John hi for me." He points toward his room, indicating he has to get ready for work.

Anne continues, "You sound happy?"

"Maybe. Jake and I have a new client — could mean a huge boost for the company."

The line rustles, and a younger, warmer voice chimes in. "Hello, Annie. Keep an eye out for the mail — I sent you a check, to help cover groceries and things."

Before Anne can protest, John comes back on. "I had no idea about that, Anne."

She hears Jake's joyful laugh in the background. "Guess it's too late to say no?"

John chuckles. "He loves you just like a sister. The matter's settled. And the initial purchase orders from the new client have already come through."

"That's such good news. I have a little good news for you, too. Mark is helping Michael get a job at Maddox."

"That is good news."

"John, you know I don't want to be a burden. You and Jake are so wonderful. Since he sent that check, I might need to use some of it for Mark."

"Everything okay?" John asks.

"His last tuition payment is due tomorrow. He plans on selling the guitar Dad gave him for Christmas."

John covers the receiver, muffling his voice as he speaks to Jake. "Mark's still at the community college?"

"Yes. He's doing well. It's a struggle, but he's not giving up."

"Jake says his check is only for groceries. I don't want him mad at me, but I'll call the school in the morning."

Anne's tears fall. "John, I wasn't meaning for you to do that."

"Anne Dalton Carson," John says firmly. "Listen here. Jake and I don't have kids. We consider our nephews our children."

"You're sure? It's a lot to ask of you... you and Jake." Anne wipes her eyes.

"It'll give me a little less to worry about. I spoke to Mother last week. She mentioned the plan to ship Scott off to boot camp. Dad's trying to stop it."

Anne sighs, frustration bubbling up. "Yeah, I've heard. Linda's not doing Scott any favors. I don't understand her... she just lets her ex-husband walk all over them."

"I spent time with Scott last month. I tried to reach that barrier he has," John says, disappointment heavy in his voice. "He's so full of anger, Anne. It's like trying to talk to a wall."

"Then this news will brighten your day," Anne replies, pride softening her voice. "I think Tripp has gotten through to him. You wouldn't recognize Scott today."

"Tripp?" John sounds puzzled.

"My son — Michael. He's been going by Tripp," Anne chuckles. "My baby boy..."

John laughs. "What brought that on?"

"Michael's been going through some things," Anne admits softly. "He said he wanted to change. Said a nightmare showed him the kind of person he didn't want to become. Since then, he's been... amazing."

"Just like that?" John asks, skeptical.

"I came home two weeks ago on Tuesday," Anne says, her throat tightening at the memory, "and he met me at the door. He broke down, sobbing — held me so tight, like he hadn't seen me in years. Begged me not to let go."

John is silent for a moment, absorbing it. "That doesn't sound like the Michael I remember."

"Exactly." Anne smiles through the emotion. "That's why he wants to go by a new name. He's not that boy anymore."

"I remember Willis didn't want him called Tripp," John says knowingly.

Anne chuckles. "Of course not. Willis thought it wasn't 'respectable.' But when did Willis Carson ever know anything about respect?"

John laughs loudly on the other end.

Anne shakes her head, chuckling with him, though sadness lurks beneath. "Heaven's, listen to me. That's the past. I've let it go. I have my sons — and that's what matters."

"It sounds like Michael — Tripp — is doing better," John says kindly.

"He is. He's lost about twenty pounds. He's eating better, taking care of himself, even trying to do better in school." She laughs lightly. "He's working so hard, John. Really hard."

John's voice turns reflective. "He really does sound like a different person."

"He keeps surprising me," Anne beams, unable to hide her pride. "He's trying to be a man, John."

"That's worth celebrating," John says, pausing as someone speaks in the background. "Keep me posted on how it's going with Scott. I can't tell you how much that means to us."

"I love you both," Anne calls warmly. "Tell Jake I miss him."

"You know, Anne," John says after a moment, "North Carolina's too far away."

Anne smiles sadly. "It is. But it makes our reunions even sweeter."

She hung up, staring at the receiver. For once, the house felt a little lighter.

The Power of Understanding

Wednesday has blurred into the other days of the week. it's been several days since Tripp and his friends shared a table at lunch. He can't ignore the fact that Steve seems troubled, even though he hasn't figured out what's bothering him. Tripp spent some time with him that morning but could tell Steve wasn't ready to open up.

In first period, he and Robbie chatted excitedly about the next addition to "the goat." Robbie's beloved GTO would be getting a new carburetor—or at least, one that's new to the car. Tripp grinned as Robbie talked about it like a kid getting a new toy, explaining how he'd roped Doug into helping with the installation. Of course, Tripp's official title would be "tool monkey," a role he'd gladly fill if it meant being part of the project. They laughed together, already envisioning the weekend they'd spend in Robbie's garage.

As he heads to English Lit, Tripp feels a lightness that's becoming familiar. Where the old Mike had dreaded Mrs. Austin's class, Tripp is now grateful for the second chance she's given him to catch up on the work he'd neglected. His plan to make amends and focus on improvement is moving forward, though it's taking longer than he expected. He's determined, though, and the progress he's making with family and friends keeps him going.

When he walks into class, he quickly notices Mrs. Austin isn't there. An old memory surfaces—*her husband had battled cancer around this time, a battle he thankfully survived.* In her place is Mr. Summers, a substitute teacher that Tripp vaguely remembers from years later. As he spots Mr. Summers's name written on the blackboard, an odd flash of recognition strikes him. Mike would eventually marry into Mr. Summers's family through Caroline. Tripp recalls meeting him only once, but he'd heard more at Mr.

Summers's funeral back in 1985. Seeing him now, young and full of life, Tripp feels an urge to do something kind for him. "Everyone deserves a second chance," he reminds himself.

Several students are still talking when the bell rings. Mr. Summers, a shorter man but weighing close to 295 pounds, clears his throat to get their attention, his nerves evident.

"Okay, class. Uh..." Mr. Summers begins hesitantly, his voice soft, wavering against the noise. "The lesson plan...uh, excuse me, everyone. Can I have your attention, please?"

"We normally just get a free period when Mrs. Austin is out..." Bobby jokes. Several other students nod in agreement while several others laugh.

"Mrs. Austin left instructions, and, well... the free period isn't today. Uh, guys, please be quiet," he pleads with the class.

"Shhhhhhh!" Several girls from the front of the class loudly demand. Finally, the students are quiet for the teacher. Tripp watches with an intrigued curiosity.

"Thanks. So, now you need to read the pages written on the board. You'll have ten minutes. After that, Mrs. Austin wants you to write a poem. It will be graded," he instructs as the class groans. "When she returns to class, everyone must read their poem aloud. However, she said that would be for extra credit."

Tripp wastes no time, reading through the material quickly. He thinks this assignment is exciting. He decides to write his poem about the timeless void. *Maybe it will impress Mrs. Austin.* Most of the other students are still reading. Several of the athletes haven't stopped talking.

Tripp takes out some paper and begins to write out his thoughts. From the corner of his eye, Tripp spots Jerry Riggins struggling. Tripp stops writing and looks at the boy. Jerry looks pale. In addition, Jerry looks like he has a cold sweat on his forehead. Jerry coughs a couple of times and raises his hand.

"Mr. Summers?" He weakly asks.

The substitute teacher quickly references the seating chart, "Yes, Mr. Riggins?"

"I think...I need to see the nurse," Jerry forces himself to speak. "I don't feel well."

"Well, you do look pale. I will take you down there myself. Class, continue to do the reading and begin on your writing assignment," Mr. Summers motions for Jerry to go with him.

After they exit the room, several of the popular girls start chatting. Tripp is a little aggravated. The girls take their lives for granted, and Tripp knows all too well the price of not doing well. He shakes his head and goes back to writing.

Ryan Grant walks over and checks the door. " I'm glad he took Jerry; the man needs some exercise!"

Many of the kids break into laughter. Ryan pretends to waddle back to his seat, and more kids join in the laughter. Tripp disapproves of this. It was not that long ago; Michael Carson was a large man like that. Secondly, Tripp has the benefit of knowing the history behind Mr. Summers' condition.

Bobby adds, "He really mooo-ved out the door; maybe he will stop at the vending machine and not come back!"

The class erupts in laughter again, but Tripp feels a wave of disgust. Not everyone is laughing, though. He notices a few students, including one of Robbie's friends, looking visibly uncomfortable. Some of the girls at the front seem equally disturbed by the mockery. Deciding he's had enough, Tripp clears his throat and speaks up.

"It's easy to go for the cheap laughs, Ryan. But, you know, he's a person too," Tripp says, his voice steady and forceful. "Don't you think you're being a little hard on someone you barely know?"

Ryan scoffs, rolling his eyes. "The man is a cow."

"What do you actually know about him?" Tripp asks, his tone sharpening, his gaze steady on Ryan. "All of our teachers were just like us at some point—figuring things out, probably making mistakes too."

Ryan rolls his eyes again, shrugging. "I know he's gotta be lazy and stupid. Every fat person is."

The room falls into silence, the laughter fading. Tripp stands, slamming his pencil down on the desk. A few gasps ripple through the class as he steps out from his seat, his eyes locked on Ryan.

"Well, you couldn't be more wrong," Tripp says, voice rising as he stands tall. "Let me clue you in: Mr. Summers was on his high school track team, and he was good. Freshman year, he ran the 100-meter in 10.42 seconds—he won the state championship. How fast can you run, Ryan?"

Ryan stammers, looking around for support, but most of the class is now watching Tripp with quiet respect.

Tripp steps closer, voice low but clear, "And that's not all. He was on the road to win in his sophomore year but had a terrible accident."

"What kind of accident, Mike?" Bobby interjects, as if to defend Ryan.

Tripp's eyes don't leave Ryan's. "Mr. Summers raced motorcycles. There was a tough race and one of the motorcyclists was driving aggressively. Summers was forced off the track in a race, hit a concrete barrier, and broke his back in three places. The doctors told him he'd never walk again."

Ryan looks down, visibly embarrassed. "I...I didn't know. How was I supposed to know?"

Tripp raises his hands in a frustrated gesture, shaking his head. "Exactly, Ryan. You didn't know, because you didn't take the time to think. Summers didn't give up. Two years later, he was walking. That isn't someone that quits."

Ryan blinks, unable to respond. Tripp takes a deep breath, calming his tone but keeping his voice firm. "Mr. Summers is anything but *lazy or stupid*, Ryan. Next time, maybe try a little empathy before you speak."

Knowing he's made his point, Tripp returns to his seat, hoping his words have resonated. The room remains quiet, and even Ryan looks pensive, clearly reflecting on the exchange. Ten minutes later, Mr. Summers returns, surprised to find a calm, focused class.

"OK, everyone," he announces, still a bit puzzled. "You can talk quietly until the bell; the period's nearly over." He heads back to the teacher's desk, glancing around the unusually attentive room.

Sitting near the front, Betty Kinsey raises her hand with a curious smile. "Mr. Summers, what were you like as a kid?"

Caught off guard, Mr. Summers blinks glancing at the seating chart, then smiles, trying to make sure he heard her right.

"Yeah, sometimes it's nice to know our teachers were like us once," Frederick chimes in from the back row.

Tripp watches with interest, his curiosity piqued. He can't help but wonder if his defense of Mr. Summers encouraged this shift in the room's atmosphere.

With a slight chuckle, Mr. Summers finally responds, "Well, Ms. Kinsey, thanks for asking. I, uh, grew up on a farm just outside Durham, North Carolina. We worked hard, but it was a good life. I went to college in Wilmington."

"Did you have any brothers or sisters?" Tracey asks, leaning forward.

"Oh, yeah. I was the youngest of three boys. My oldest brother was the quarterback for the State of North Carolina University for two years," He grins, his pride evident. "Stephen, he was a gifted athlete. And Thomas, my other brother, he joined the Marines and still serves."

The class nods approvingly, clearly interested. Tripp notices the shift in energy and can't help but smile as the conversation unfolds.

Bobby raises his hand. "What about track? You like it?"

Mr. Summers stands up a bit straighter, his smile growing. "Track and field? My brothers and I all did sports. My parents encouraged it, but we still had to do farm chores every day," he chuckles, clearly enjoying the memory.

Seizing a chance to redeem himself, Ryan asks, "Mr. Summers, did you ever compete in sports?"

Mr. Summers laughs, "Oh, just track. I loved to run."

Hoping for his approval, Ryan nods. Tripp acknowledges with smile, noticing a subtle change in Ryan's attitude.

With newfound confidence, Mr. Summers adds, "My favorite was the relay events, but I was best at the 100-meter race. It was my thing back then."

Henry chimes in, "When I stay with my grandparents, I ride my dirt bike around their farm!"

Mr. Summers smiles warmly. "Farms are great for that! I used to race motorcycles competitively. Dangerous sport, but there's nothing quite like it."

The bell rings, interrupting the lively discussion. Mr. Summers collects himself, smiling at the class. "I'll be here for a few more days. Tomorrow, we'll keep going with the assignments."

Several students approach Mr. Summers, offering quiet thanks and nods of respect. He lights up, visibly moved by the change in their attitudes. Tripp watches from his seat, a warm smile crossing his face as he notices how much this small act has lifted Mr. Summers. He feels a quiet satisfaction, knowing he's helped the class see the teacher differently, if only for today. He understands all too well the silent judgments people pass on someone's appearance, and he's glad to have shifted the focus to the man behind the weight.

As Tripp places his books into his bag, Robbie's friend Doug navigates through the departing students and stops by Tripp's desk.

"That was pretty brave of you, Mike," Doug says, patting Tripp's arm in a show of support.

Tripp shrugs and smiles. "It just felt like the right thing to do. Judging someone based on their looks alone—it's unfair. We all carry a story, and sometimes, people forget to consider that."

Doug nods, a bit taken aback by Tripp's sincerity. "Yeah... we could all use a little more kindness." Then, with a curious expression, he adds, "So, how did you know all that stuff about Mr. Summers, Mike?"

Tripp hesitates, quickly thinking up a plausible response. He can't exactly tell Doug he learned those details at a funeral that won't happen for another five years. "Oh, uh, my older brother Mark," Tripp improvises. "He had Mr. Summers as a substitute once and got to know him a bit. Mark always had a knack for caring about people. He wants to be a nurse."

Musical Bonds

I t's been nearly a week since Tripp last visited, and Scott waits eagerly, hoping his cousin will keep his promise. Scott sits on the small loveseat in the condo's cozy living room, craning his neck every few minutes to check the parking lot for the Mustang. He tries to keep himself positive.

"Michael did apologize," Scott mutters to himself, trying not to feel let down. "I shouldn't be upset. Nope, not going to be..."

The silence gnaws at him, and he lets out a frustrated groan. Scott jumps up at the sound of a car approaching, but it's only a repair truck for the unit next door. He lets out a disappointed sigh and heads to the kitchen to distract himself. He opens the fridge, debating what to drink, before grabbing the milk jug. Scott unscrews the cap and takes a big gulp straight from the jug, letting out a loud burp that makes him laugh.

"If only Regina had seen that," Scott snickers to himself. "Never fails to annoy her."

In a final attempt to shake off his impatience, he decides to play his drums, hoping the sound might draw Michael over somehow. With renewed energy, he heads downstairs, but as he reaches the bottom step, the doorbell rings. His heart leaps.

"Michael!" Scott yells, racing to the door, taking the steps two at a time. He opens it breathlessly, beaming as he sees his cousin.

"I knew you'd come!" he exclaims.

Tripp smiles warmly. "I meant what I said, Scott. We're family, and I'm here. Always."

Scott laughs, pulling him into a quick hug. "Thanks, Michael. I was trying not to worry...but still."

Tripp grins, motioning to the driveway. "How about a trip to the record store?"

Scott's face lights up, and he yells in excitement, "Yay! I love music, Michael!"

"Wait a second. We should leave Aunt Linda a note," Tripp says, pausing Scott's celebration. "Wouldn't want her to worry."

Scott pauses mid-exit. "Oh, yeah. Good idea, Michael. I'll be right back," he says before darting back inside.

Tripp waits by the Mustang, leaning on the door with a smile. His thick hair, parted down the middle, falls to his shoulders in true 1980 style. He's wearing his favorite red Boston concert T-shirt, gray cargo pants, and a pair of well-worn white sneakers. Watching Scott run around with so much excitement reminds Tripp of his resolve not to let his cousin down again.

"All done, Michael!" Scott calls out as he runs back outside, stopping abruptly to double-check that the door is closed behind him. He scrunches his nose in slight irritation but is grinning by the time he reaches the car. They both climb in, and Tripp cranks up the engine, pulling out of the parking lot and heading toward the record store.

"Scott, it's okay if you thought I wouldn't come," Tripp says after a moment. "I've given you plenty of reasons..."

Scott interrupts him with a loud shushing sound, "But, Michael, you apologized! You don't have to talk about it anymore!"

"Really?" Tripp says, a little surprised. "Just like that?"

Scott folds his arms, clearly serious. "Yep. My mom says you can 'will' things into existence just by saying them. So we're only going to talk about being 'bestest buds' now, 'cause we're cousins." He nods firmly, then adds, "I'm gonna will it that my cousin is my hero!"

Tripp feels his throat tighten, not wanting to let the emotion show. No one, least of all Scott, has ever said anything like that to him. He looks over and sees his cousin grinning back, the moment so sincere and touching that it brings a laugh to both of them. Scott bursts into giggles, trying to hold a serious face, but quickly loses his composure.

Tripp chuckles, savoring the moment. "Well then, I'll will it into existence that my cousin is the coolest drummer around. He's a total *rockstar!*"

Scott's smile softens, his eyes brimming with pride. "Really, Michael?" he asks, leaning in closer with a small, hopeful grin.

"Absolutely. Some things are too important to joke about. And you, Scott—you're very important."

Scott, obviously touched by the statement, places his hand on Tripp's arm. "Then it's official! So, what are we getting at the record store, Michael?"

Tripp laughs, "Well, I stayed up late talking to Mark last night. We had one of those heart-to-heart conversations, you know? He was really happy to hear that you and I are 'bestest buds' now."

Scott's eyes widen. "Mark is so cool!" he blurts out, admiration clear in his voice.

Tripp smiles, thinking of his brother. "Yeah, he is. So, while we were talking, this song came on the radio that I hadn't heard before. I mentioned I liked it, and Mark gave me eight bucks to get the album."

"Eight dollars!" Scott exclaims, bouncing in his seat. "You could buy the whole store with that!"

"Not quite, but it was a pretty generous offer. Maybe we can learn the drum sequences together?"

Scott's face lights up with a wide grin. "I'd love that, Michael, but..." He puts on an exaggerated wise expression. "You still have a long way to go, grasshopper."

Tripp chuckles at Scott's reference to *Kung Fu*, the TV show they'd both watched. He's impressed by this side of his cousin—quick-witted and enthusiastic. Tripp feels a wave of contentment, recognizing that these are moments he wouldn't have appreciated before. The old Mike wouldn't have taken the time for Scott like this. *But that Mike is gone*, he reminds himself. *Make today count.*

Scott, barely able to contain his excitement, watches eagerly as they pass by his school and head into a strip mall. Their destination: *The Record Changer*. This local shop specializes in the latest hits and buys and resells older records, making even the best albums affordable on a teenager's budget.

"I've never been to this shop, Michael!" Scott says, straining to see over the dashboard.

"It's been a while for me, but this place has all the best music," Tripp grins as he parks. "Plus, they've got unbeatable prices."

They step into the store, which is scattered with about seven other customers browsing the racks. Behind the counter is a young guy Tripp doesn't recognize. Tripp waves, receiving a friendly nod in return, then heads to the new releases and begins flipping through records behind the "G-H" tab. Scott dashes over to an end cap display, eyes wide, visibly star-struck at the sheer volume of music.

Tripp laughs at Scott's enthusiasm as he continues searching, savoring the carefree joy of the moment. Being here with Scott makes him feel like a regular kid, just enjoying music with his cousin. Within moments, he spots the album he was looking for.

"And Then There Were Three..." Tripp murmurs, reading the title aloud as he pulls the album from the shelf, flipping it over to examine the back cover.

"Michael, Michael!" Scott comes bounding over, practically shouting with excitement.

"What's up? Is the building on fire?" Tripp teases, looking up with a grin.

"No, silly! There'd be sirens and you'd see smoke if it were! Look at this!" Scott says, holding up an album with reverence. "It's a promo disc from *Kiss*! Only a handful were made. Can you get it? I want it so bad! I'll teach you the drums...oh, and that band's drummer is like a god. I want to be like him someday!"

Tripp knows that this type of promo disk was common, most record companies sent them to radio stations as a way to get the songs air time. Still, he can see Scott's eyes light up. Tripp would find a way to get the record.

The clerk behind the counter, a man in his early twenties with sandy blonde hair, a goatee, and a muscular build, has been watching the two with interest. He sees his opportunity, grabs the price gun, and approaches with a smile.

Tripp glances at Scott, then at the album, feeling a pang of guilt. "I know eight dollars sounds like a lot, Scott, but it isn't. Let's see if they have a used copy of the one I want. Maybe that way we can get both." He nudges Scott encouragingly. "Help me look?"

"Really? Really?" Scott's eyes widen as he nods eagerly, bouncing up and down.

"Excuse me, guys, need a hand?" the clerk offers.

"Actually, yeah. Thanks!" Tripp replies. "I was looking to get this one," he says, holding up the album. "But my cousin found a promo disc he really wants. If there's a used copy of *And Then There Were Three...*, maybe I can get both since I've only got eight dollars."

The clerk glances between them with a pleasant smile. "Ah, so you two are cousins?" he says, glancing at Scott. "Would've guessed brothers."

Scott laughs. "Bestest buds, that's even closer than brothers!"

"Bestest buds, huh?" The clerk replies, smiling big. "That's a strong bond, indeed!"

Tripp chuckles, nodding. "I'm Michael, but my friends call me Tripp. It's a name for the 'new me.' And this is Scott, drummer extraordinaire."

"Tripp. I like it," the clerk, Geoffrey, says with a nod, winking at Scott. "And I bet you're a great drummer, Scott."

Scott beams as he replies, "I'll be as good as Neil Peart one day. You'll see."

Geoffrey grins. "I don't doubt it. Hey, Tripp, let me see that album for a second. Looks like it might be on sale."

"On sale?" Tripp raises an eyebrow as he hands it over.

Geoffrey adjusts the price gun and clicks a new tag onto the album before handing it back, grinning. "There we go. Looks like it just made your budget," he says, patting Tripp on the shoulder.

Tripp glances at the adjusted price, feeling a surge of gratitude. He looks back at Geoffrey, catching his eye. "Thank you," he mouths silently, smiling.

Geoffrey gives a small nod. "Happy to help, Tripp. I'll be here when you're ready to check out."

"Michael, can I get the *Kiss* record?" Scott asks, bouncing with excitement.

Tripp chuckles, giving his cousin a warm look. "Yep, the new price makes it just right. I'm glad we came here today."

"Me too, Michael!" Scott exclaims, his face lighting up.

As they walk to the counter, Tripp catches Geoffrey looking at him with a friendly, curious smile. Scott, noticing this as well, takes Tripp's hand, giving it a squeeze. When they reach the counter, Tripp places the albums down.

"Scott's teaching me the drums," Tripp says playfully. "And he's great."

"Sounds like you're a lucky student, then," Geoffrey replies with a grin. He brushes Tripp's hand as he takes the albums. "And it looks like all that practice is building your upper body, Tripp."

Tripp feels his face flush as he hands over the $8. Geoffrey counts back some change, placing a couple of dimes and a penny in Tripp's hand with a lingering smile.

"You know both of us, now, but I didn't catch your name." Tripp answers playfully.

"Goeffery, we're friends now?"

Tripp nods with a soft giggle. Holding up the albums, he conveys his gratitude one last time.

As they exit, Scott glances back, noticing Geoffrey's gaze still on Tripp. Unaware, Tripp chuckles to himself, feeling an unexpected warmth. It was his first time openly flirting with such a handsome man—and he liked it.

Tripp shakes his head, convincing himself that Geoffrey was just being polite.

"Thanks for coming to Record Changer!" Geoffrey calls out as they exit.

Back at the Mustang, Tripp helps Scott into the passenger seat before circling around to his side. As he settles in, he notices the silence — unusually long and heavy. Glancing over, he sees Scott looking pensive, almost distant, as if a switch has been flipped.

"Ah... everything okay, Scott?" Tripp asks gently, his deep concern lacing his voice.

Scott's expression hardens. "Just thinking about my dad," he replies flatly. "I *hate* him..."

Tripp reaches out, placing a steadying hand on Scott's shoulder. He doesn't know what triggered Scott's response, but the look in his cousin's eyes tells him it's serious — not anger, but fear. He begins to rub Scott's shoulder reassuringly.

"Scott, I'm here if you need to talk. Don't let your dad do this to you anymore. I know it's not easy, but remember, I'm here for you — always. I won't ever leave your side," Tripp promises, voice steady and full of sincerity.

Scott nods, his gaze dropping as he fights to hold back tears. "I know, Michael," he whispers, managing a small, grateful smile. "I'm sorry. I didn't mean to mess up the day."

"Mess up the day?" Tripp's voice rises with warm conviction. "Scott, forget the day and to hell with these records. You're what matters to me," he says, a fierce honesty in his tone. "You come first. *Always.*"

Scott's face softens as he tears up, then reaches over to hug Tripp tightly. Tripp hugs him back, giving Scott a supportive squeeze before pulling away to mess up his hair playfully.

"I love you, Tripp," Scott whispers, his voice full of emotion.

Tripp smiles, pleasantly surprised. "Love you too, Scott. But I thought you didn't like my new name."

Scott starts laughing, breaking the tension. "I don't, Michael... but today I'll make an exception."

The Whole World

October twentieth has been a slow day. The afternoon drags, heavy and slow. It feels like it should be nine o'clock, but it's only four. Mark finishes vacuuming the living room just as Tripp wanders through the front door, looking like a lost puppy unsure where to go.

"Hey, twerp," Mark calls.

Lost in thought, Tripp only shrugs. "Hi, Mark. Sorry I didn't help clean today. Just had a lot on my mind."

Mark sets the vacuum aside and walks over, giving his brother a quick hug. "I've got it covered. Besides, you're the one who does the most around here — and Momma knows it." His smile is infectious.

Tripp's voice cracks. "We're doing this together, Mark. I need you. It's not just about me anymore. Everything we do touches the people we love."

Mark rests a hand on his brother's shoulder. His voice is steady, certain. "Brother, my world is all about you. Go lie down while I finish in here. You look wiped out."

"Thanks, Mark."

Tripp heads down the hallway, a lone figure carrying the weight of two lifetimes. The house is silent except for the creak of floorboards beneath his feet. When he closes his bedroom door, the vacuum roars back to life down the hall.

I'll make it up to Mark, Tripp promises himself, sinking onto his bed. His eyes fall to the photo album tucked on the shelf. He reaches for it, leaning against the headboard, knees pulled up, the book balanced across them.

With a shaky breath, he flips the cover open, desperate for some tether to the past.

The first few pages blur past until a familiar image tugs at him — a picture of him, Mark, and their dad at Lake Norman. He can't be more than eight years old here, just after the divorce. The sadness in his young eyes is impossible to miss. Tripp exhales slowly, fingers trailing across the glossy surface, before turning the page.

Snapshots of family gatherings, birthdays, and Christmas mornings flick past until he reaches the photos from the beach trip — 1976.

He hesitates.

These memories don't haunt me anymore. They won't...

He forces himself to turn the page.

Jeff Tyler's face smiles back at him, frozen in time.

A Quiet Sort of Magic

The world, for a brief, beautiful afternoon, is just the two of them. It is a Saturday in late July, 1976, and the air is thick with the scent of salt and summer, the kind of day that feels endless.

The sounds of the seagulls fill the air as they swoop down over the beach. Mike Carson, twelve years old, is dressed in his brother's old, faded red swimming trunks, they are still a little big on him. His brown hair is almost blonde from the sun and seawater, his skin golden-brown. He lies in the sand, laughing as he makes a sand angel. Jeff Tyler stands over him, laughing and cheering Mike on. This is their world, a perfect day spent outside every hour they can.

When Mike stops, Jeff takes the space beside him, stretching out on his back, their hands touching in the sand, a simple, easy contact. Mike mischievously flicks sand onto Jeff's brand-new teal blue swimsuit. The color is so bright it seems to glow against Jeff's tan skin. Jeff grunts in mock protest. He likes the water, but not the sand.

"That is awesome, Mike," Jeff grins, squinting under the hot sun. "It's better than any snow angel I've ever seen."

"I made it for you."

Mike lifts himself up, resting on his elbows, and Jeff mirrors his movement. Mike takes a deep breath, savoring the ocean breeze. "I'm so glad Momma let you come with me."

"Me, too!" Jeff yells out.

Mike's smile fades slightly. "I think I would've hated being alone."

"Your brother is here, Mike," Jeff says as he brushes sand off Mike's chest.

Mike glances over his shoulder. Mark sits beside a nearby dune, deliberately avoiding them and instead focusing on a group of bikini-clad girls. "I doubt Mark even notices me."

Jeff sits up, brushing the sand from Mike's back. "He's talking to those girls, but his eyes have stayed on you."

"You always find the good in people," Mike says with a smile, shaking his head, which sends sand everywhere.

"Mike!" Jeff yells, playfully.

Mike jumps up, yelling "Tag!" as he taps Jeff's short blonde hair. He begins racing around in circles, Jeff inches behind him, both screaming and laughing in the sun.

Jeff lurches forward, wrapping his arms around Mike's waist. They land with a soft thud, giggling out of control. Mike rolls Jeff over, pinning him on his back, but Jeff counters quickly. A stunned Mike looks up at the sky, wondering how that happened.

Jeff holds Mike by the wrists. Mike surrenders. "You win, Jeff!"

He moves off Mike, and they sit, both catching their breath. Jeff's blue eyes sparkle in the sun. "Winner's choice. What's next?"

Jeff's teeth barely peek through his smile. "Whatever you want, Mike. I'll follow you anywhere."

"Maybe fishing? There's no crowd on the pier," Mike suggests, his breathing back to normal.

"I'm sure we'll catch a shark or something!" Jeff laughs, standing up and offering a hand to Mike.

They run through the water, the surf splashing their bodies as they head to the old pier at the end of town. The wooden planks are warm beneath their bare feet, and the gulls call to one another overhead. Mike insists on going fishing, armed with two hand-me-down rods and a container of bait that smells of earth and ocean. Jeff, who usually prefers a good book to a fishing line, agrees without a second thought, content just to be there.

Jeff sits on the edge of the pier, his legs dangling over the side, watching the waves hit the pilings below. He can feel the vibrations, a steady, rhythmic thrum. Next to him, Mike is all concentration, his brow furrowed as he wrestles with a stubborn knot in his line.

Jeff knows it is a familiar frustration for Mike, a small, easy one compared to the new, sharp anxieties he carries since the divorce. It has been years, but to Mike, it feels like his dad moved out a few months ago. The air around him sometimes feels heavy with it, a sadness Mike tries to hide with a forced smile or a loud joke. But here, with just the two of them and the sea, the sadness seems to melt away.

Jeff smiles, a quiet, private sort of smile that Mike will never see. He isn't watching the fishing line. He is watching Mike. The way his sandy-blond hair, still damp from their earlier swim, falls across his forehead. The determined set of his jaw. The faint freckles dusted across the bridge of his nose that only seem to appear in the summer. It is these tiny, perfect details that Jeff keeps tucked away in his mind, like a collection of precious things.

"Hold on, hold on," Mike mutters, a playful curse on his lips. "This thing is a monster."

Jeff finally speaks, his voice soft. "Need a hand?"

Mike looks up and shakes his head, a genuine smile replacing the frown. "Nah. Got it." He casts the line with a practiced flick of his wrist, and it soars out over the water, a whisper of a sound before it breaks the surface.

They fall into a comfortable silence, the kind that only exists between people who know each other completely. Jeff notices Mark and his harem have followed them to the pier. *See, I knew Mark is watching close,* Jeff thinks. The sun begins its slow descent, painting the sky in shades of orange and pink. The light is golden on Mike's skin, making him look like he belongs in a dream.

Suddenly, Mike's line jerks taut. "I got one!" he yells, jumping to his feet.

Jeff scrambles up to help, his heart thumping in his chest for a reason that has nothing to do with the excitement of the catch. Mike struggles, the rod bending with the weight of the fish.

"You're fighting it too hard, Mike!" Jeff laughs. "Give it some slack!"

Mike laughs too, a sound that is pure and joyful, echoing off the water. "I know, I know! Just got excited."

Finally, with a final heave, Mike reels in their prize: a small, silvery fish. It is nothing spectacular, maybe six inches long, but Mike holds it up like it's a trophy. He is grinning so wide his eyes squint shut. Now, just a few feet away, Mark is trying to impress a new group of girls with a show of strength. They are all giggling, but he glances over at his little brother and is surprised to see Mike's genuine, unrestrained happiness. He looks over at the girls, who have not noticed his momentary distraction, and rolls his eyes before pulling a small instant camera out of his back pocket.

Mark ambles over to them, the girls following and still giggling. "Smile, shrimp," he says, not unkindly. He holds up the camera.

Jeff, in that moment, has an arm slung around Mike's neck, casual and easy. He isn't looking at the fish. He is looking at Mike, at the pride and happiness that has replaced the sadness, even if just for a little while. The camera is just an afterthought, the photo a frozen testament to the feelings that are as vast and deep as the ocean behind them.

Mark snaps the picture, a flash of white light, and then hands the square paper to Mike. The image begins to develop slowly.

Mike, utterly oblivious, just beams at the camera, a boy proud of his small catch. And Jeff, next to him, is just happy to be there, in that quiet, golden light, with him. He never notices that his eyes give him away. He never realizes that he is already lost.

Lost In Memories

The picture doesn't lie. Tripp clutches a small fish in one hand, grinning so wide his eyes squint nearly shut. Jeff has an arm around Tripp's neck—but Jeff isn't looking at the prize catch. He's looking at Mike. And Mike had never even noticed.

Tripp feels the weight of the years pressing in—forty-six years and counting. He presses the photo flat with trembling fingers.

I really messed up with Jeff...

Twelve-year-old Mike hadn't been ready for the confusion that bloomed under the surface that summer — but that didn't excuse the way he lashed out. He owes Jeff Tyler more than an apology. He owes him understanding. He owes him kindness he never gave.

Tripp closes his eyes, the sting behind them growing unbearable, and flips past the beach photos.

He doesn't want to drown in that summer anymore.

The next pages show Steve and Larry, arms slung over his shoulders, their smiles wide and easy. Tripp notices something else, too — his younger self is heavier now, the carefree spark already dimming. He looks happy enough. But the cracks are there. The slow drift toward self-destruction has already begun.

Another turn of the page — and then it hits him.

A Polaroid from 1977, from a school basketball game. Robbie and Mike, captured in a single, perfect moment.

Robbie grins at the camera, all bright energy and sunshine. And Mike?

Mike is looking at Robbie.

It was a day he will never foget..

He flips the pages going through all the pictures with his friend, over and over again At birthday parties. At school dances. Sitting side-by-side on the front steps of the church. Tripp smiles.

Mike looking at Robbie.

Always Robbie.

The truth stares back at him, undeniable and blinding, yet Tripp doesn't fully understand.

Tripp shut the album, but the walls of his room felt too close, too heavy. He needed air, space, something bigger than memory. With a sharp breath, he grabbed his jacket and slipped out into the evening.

Dr. Elmhurst - August 13th, 2021

Doctor Elmhurst is a small, unassuming man with a quiet energy that fills the room. Bald on top with a fringe of fine hair at the sides, he wears round-rimmed glasses that give him an almost scholarly air. At five-foot-five with a lean, athletic frame, he seems younger than his years—full of life and purpose.

His mountain bike is always parked in the office lobby, a silent testament to his passion for cycling. He once tried to get Michael into it, believing that a healthier lifestyle might improve his emotional outlook. To be clear, when Elmhurst said "healthier," he meant physically—not overweight. But Michael wasn't there to see a dietitian. He was there for something deeper—psychological treatment.

Elmhurst is an exceptional therapist. Within just a few sessions, most of his patients begin to trust him, often more than they expect. Michael, despite his passive-aggressive tendencies, was no exception. He surprised even himself by opening up so quickly. Though he wouldn't say it aloud, he's quietly grateful.

Doctor Elmhurst sits in a high-backed chair upholstered in rich fabric. His office, with its Victorian-inspired décor and warm sunlight filtering through the drapes, feels more like a study than a clinic. The space is roomy, comfortable. Michael is stretched out on the couch—his choice. Most of the doctor's other patients prefer to sit, but this feels right to him.

"Michael, is there anything you want to focus on? This is our eighth session and I would like to delve deeper into childhood." the kind doctor begins.

"Hmm-K" Michael shrugs, feeling apprehensive.

"Last week, you spent about fifteen minutes talking about a coworker you like. In previous sessions, you only mention them in passing. I felt good about our discussion. " Elmhurst probes, testing Michael's mood. "Did you try to engage them in conversation?"

Michael looks up at the doctor, fear building within him keeps him from replying. He shakes his head no in shame. Elmhurst makes a few notes in the silence.

"Michael, seem you uncharacteristically quiet today." Dr. Elmhurst adjusts his glasses, watching his patient carefully.

"It's my hour to waste, is it not?"

"No, *it is not.*" Elmhurst raises an eye brow. "Granted, if you don't want the time to work through your issues, that is your choice. However, someone else could use this hour. You need to remember to think of others– a chance for a breakthrough..."

"OK, OK...I get it." Michael admits with a heavy sigh. "I'm...ashamed." Averting his eyes from the doctor.

"Are you ashamed that you like Jamie?" Elmhurst stops writing. "It's the twenty-first century, don't let something like an age difference stand in the way of happiness. From what you have told me, you and Jamie are a good fit."

"I'm ashamed of my attraction in the first place." Michael hangs his head. "What would Jamie see in me anyways?"

"Very well. May I share some observations?"

"If I said no, would that stop you, doctor?" Michael closes his eyes, a juvenile attempt to hide.

"Of course not." Doctor Elmhurst smiles encouragingly. "You said we made progress at the end of that two hour session."

Michael nods, "It was a grand awakening, I felt like my eyes were suddenly open, finally seeing the man in the mirror. It was a man that I *hated.*"

"You also said that you want to be a better man?"

"We keep finding more flaws, my mistakes, so many failures..."

"Yes. With each passing revelation, the list of wrongs would create another regret." Elmhurst leans forward. "Yet you come back. You refuse to accept that paradigm and want to change. I've urged you to embrace *this* new life and make amends to those you could. Michael, you can never change the *past*, but focus on a good life now and matter to those around you."

"I have tried! I'm so worried I'll relapse."

Doctor Elmhurst narrows his gaze, reclining in his chair. "You are afraid of the past?"

"Yes, doctor." Michael sighs.

"I believe there is a memory that is holding you back. You have alluded to it many times," Doctor Elmhurst explains as he flips back through the notes. "What happened at the beach?"

The memories Michael lives with have created so many years of unnecessary pain. As a child, Michael had an encounter with one of his friends. One that a twelve-year-old boy would not ask for.

Michael hesitates, he wants to keep the shame and pain buried deep, yet a part of him needs to be free from this pain. "I was twelve."

"Forty-six years ago, Michael." Elmhurst notes.

Hesitantly, "It shouldn't be hurting me this long."

"Time has no power over pain. Your attachment to the event has crippled you emotionally." Elmhurst leans back in his chair. "If you are ready, I can guide you through this."

Taking a deep breath. "We had gone on a family vacation, to the beach. My momma let me bring my best friend at the time." Michael's eyes avoid connecting with the doctor. "We went to the pier and fished. Made sand castles. Swam in the ocean every day. It was the third day of the trip. My friend and I had been in the water all day."

Taking notes, Elmurst asks. "It sounds like it starts as a good memory."

"It was. We didn't want the day to end. But I was so tired." Michael's voice strains as he fights his fear. "It was a very hot night, even after a cold shower to get the sea water out of our hair."

"I can hear you struggling, Michael. Do you need to stop?"

"No...'" Michael turns his head away. "The rental house did not have AC and there was only one fan. Jeff and I made a fort out of pillows in the living room, we were laughing and having a good time. And. I'm not sure if I should say. He suggested we sleep in our underwear."

Elmhurst nods, taking notes. "It was a hot night, sounds innocent enough?"

"I guess...We'd done that before." Michael clears his throat after a deep breathe. "I fell asleep very quickly. The pillow fort was small, we were in a tight space."

"I am not pushing Michael, this is *your* hour."

"I know, but I don't want to stop now," Michael whispered. "I woke up later...not sure why. It was dark in the room. The only sound was the whirring of the old fan. I could..."

"I'm here with you. You are safe."

Michael swallows hard and nods, "I could feel his hands moving over the soft cotton fabric."

Doctor Elmhurst waits, giving Michael the space he may need. Without the talking, the silence seems overwhelming. Michael turns to look at the doctor. The sadness, the pain is reflected in his eyes, but Doctor Elmhurst did not judge.

"My body reacted to his touch..." Michael hides his face with a throw pillow.

"Were you afraid to say something to your friend?"

"No...I was. Well, doctor, I'm embarrassed to admit, but I enjoyed it. I said nothing."

"You were young, experimenting with a new sensation?"

Michael shrugs. "The next morning, I had time to think it over. I was confused–unable to understand the flood of emotions."

Elmhurst nods, writing more notes. "How did you feel? I'm curious of your reaction."

"I knew I was supposed to like girls. Homosexuals were terrible people; my father hammered that belief into Mark and me for years." Michael's eyes fill with tears. "For a boy to like another boy was just unacceptable. *Unacceptable.*"

"That must've been hard for a twelve year old to reconcile."

"Damn near impossible." Michael snaps. "I hated who I was."

"Did you talk about it with your friend?"

"No." Michael replies flatly. "I didn't end our friendship in a nice way. I never spoke to Jeff after that."

"Maybe you can make amends with him now?"

Sadness washes acrois Michael's face. "It's not possible, I heard he died a long time ago."

Elmhurst laid the notepad down as he slides forward. "I can see how this could scar your emotional growth. A traumatic event can lock your mind in a prison."

The tears flow out of Michael's eyes. "I became too wrapped up in hating who I was. It wasn't until I was in my twenties that I learned that being bisexual was real. But by this time, Caroline and I were married; and had a small child, Gabby."

"Now that we know this, I believe we can get through this."

"For years, even though I knew what I was, I still hated the bisexual nature within myself. I believed there was something wrong with it. I liked women, not men."

"Michael. Do you trust me?"

"I do, doctor." Michael wipes the tears away.

"It will take time, but we can work together and help you to heal."

It was Doctor Elmhurst who helped Michael accept his bisexual nature.

Beneath the Stars

The streetlight overhead hums as the electricity brings it to life. In the darkness, the only sound to be heard comes from Doug's truck, which idles roughly. The combination of the sounds echo in Doug's mind. He considers how the afternoon started out as a day of laughter that has morphed into a somber moment. He gently taps his fingers on the steering wheel while waiting for the traffic light to change.

He and Robbie lost track of time as they had worked on the old pickup. What started as an oil change had morphed into tracking down a vacuum line leak. He glances over to the passenger side. Rob Davis is staring out the window. His friend has been slightly off all day, and Doug is tired of waiting for him to open up about what is bothering him.

"I think you'll need to adjust the carburetor again," Doug said with a laugh, breaking the silence. "Gertie is wheezing..."

"I can do that in the driveway when you drop me off," Robbie replies, not sounding like his usual cheerful self.

Doug notices Robbie's silence and tries to bring him back with a grin. "You know, we've got flames shooting out the back, and a clown car's been tailing us for miles. Should I be worried?"

"Huh? For miles... wait, what?" Robbie blinks and looks over, clearly caught off guard. "Flames? Clown car?"

Doug chuckles, glancing at him. "See? You're a million miles away, man. Seriously though, everything alright?"

Robbie shifts uncomfortably, looking out the window. "It's not that I don't like the new Mike. He's... different. Better, even. But he's just... not how I remember."

Doug glances at him, eyebrows raised. "Different like... how?"

Robbie sighs, struggling to put his thoughts into words. "I mean, the old Mike would sulk if I wasn't hanging out with him.

He'd get all sarcastic and stuff, like I wasn't a good friend for wanting to do my own thing. But now... now he's practically pushing me to spend time with other people. It's like... he's okay with it." Robbie chuckles nervously. "I know it sounds dumb, but it just... feels strange."

Doug tilts his head, nodding as if seeing it from Robbie's point of view. "So you're used to him acting possessive, and now he's giving you freedom. I'd be weirded out, too. But hey, maybe he just wants what's best for you."

"Yeah... maybe," Robbie says, his tone soft. "It just makes me wonder if he still needs me, you know?"

"Needs?"

"Ugh, yeah. He doesn't have that many friends, I'm just..." Robbie replies with a grunt of frustration.

"Robbie Davis," Doug exclaims. "I'm not trying to push you; I just don't like seeing you hurting, that's all."

Robbie smiles sheepishly and answers, "I know, Doug. It sounds stupid. I can't believe I'm letting this bother me."

"Just remember, *you* aren't alone," Doug said, messing up Robbie's hair.

"You're a good friend. So is Mike," Robbie sighs, embarrassed by his feelings. Robbie relents and offers his explanation.

Doug paused, "He's just trying to be your friend."

"Doug, he's my best friend," Robbie answers, looking away.

"You're his best friend, that's for sure," Doug replies as he turns onto a side street. "Is that really what's bothering you?"

"Yeah, stupid, I know," Robbie agrees, staring out the window.

"No, Rob." Doug taps Robbie on the shoulder, getting him to look back. "He's growing. It wasn't until Mike got this second chance at life that I noticed how you see him begin to change. I know that Mike's determination to turn his life around and this vulnerability during his transformation resonate with you. I'm impressed."

"Thanks, Doug," Robbie says, leaning towards Doug. "Mike's honesty and willingness to confront his past mistakes made me see him in a new light."

"And you think he doesn't want to be around you?" Doug asks sincerely.

"No, it isn't that. He does want to be around me," Robbie shakes his head. "But he isn't the sharing type... wasn't..."

"Well, why don't we stop and ask him," Doug said, pointing out into the darkness. "Isn't that his Mustang?"

Doug pulls his truck to the side of the road. The engine struggles, idling like an out of tune trumpet playing. To the left is an entrance to the city park. Robbie scoots forward to see better. Only one light is working, casting shadows across the few cars he can see in the parking lot. Robbie spots his friend, Mike Carson, sitting on the hood of his car, gazing at the sky. Doug turns off his engine, nodding for Robbie to get out.

"Mike and his cousin were together the other day; I think something happened. It really bothered him, but he wouldn't talk about it. He was taking it rough," Robbie admits. "Are you OK with me checking on him?"

"Go, sheepdog," Doug orders with a smile.

Robbie climbs out of Doug's truck and makes his way across the parking lot, his steps quiet in the still night. He sees Mike sitting on the hood of his Mustang, eyes fixed on the star-filled sky. As he gets closer, Robbie feels the weight of his friend's mood and decides to break the silence gently.

"Hey, Mike," Robbie says softly, leaning against the fender. "Rough day?"

Tripp nods, a subtle look of weariness in his eyes. "Yeah, just... trying to make sense of things."

"Making sense of what?" Robbie asks, glancing up at the sky as if it might hold some answer. "Something new happen?"

Tripp leans back on the hood, stretching his arms behind him for support. "No... more like something old," he murmurs, gesturing to the vast sky. "Trillions of stars out there. Makes us feel pretty small in comparison, don't you think?"

Robbie raises an eyebrow, smiling slightly. "Since when did you get so philosophical? Look, if it matters, you're anything but insignificant to me." He gives Tripp a gentle nudge on the arm.

Tripp glances at him, a faint smile tugging at the corners of his mouth. "You're the reason I'm here, Robbie. You're the one who matters."

Robbie chuckles, trying to lighten the moment. "Here as in... the park? Or here on Earth?"

"Maybe both," Tripp replies, a laugh escaping as he looks back at the stars. "There are billions of people on this planet, Robbie—billions, and that's just the ones who are alive now. Imagine how many have come and gone before us."

"I don't care about them," Robbie responds, his gaze fixed on Tripp, trying to understand what's weighing on his friend's heart.

"Out of billions..." Tripp shakes his head, exhaling deeply. "Why me? Why did I get a second chance?"

"Mike, nobody gave it to you—you're *making* your chance," Robbie says, scratching his chin, still watching his friend closely. "We're only sixteen; we've got our whole lives to get this right."

Tripp's expression darkens, and he shakes his head. "I used up all my chances the first time around. My ticket was up—literally. I don't deserve this." He looks away, the memories of his empty, past life clearly haunting him. "I feel like my fate should have stayed in that void..." Robbie, missing the full meaning behind Tripp's words, frowns with concern.

"Mike," Robbie starts, struggling to find the right words. "I know you're carrying a lot, but even if this wasn't 'meant to be,' you're making it real, Mike. I've got your back, always. You won't be going through this alone."

"But I let you down, Rob," Tripp whispers, the shame evident in his voice. He pulls his knees close, resting his head on his arms. "In so many ways…"

"I've never felt that way," Robbie says gently, climbing up to sit beside him on the fender. "I've loved who you've always been. I told you that before." He hesitates; this isn't the first time he's seen Mike so burdened, but something feels different.

"I know, and it's why I can't let myself fail this time," Tripp says, turning to Robbie. "I can't die alone—can't go back to being that guy with nobody left to care."

"Then that won't happen. I won't let it." Robbie's tone is firm but full of warmth. "You're doing everything right, Mike, and I'm proud of you."

A soft smile breaks on Tripp's face, his friend's words a lifeline he hadn't realized he needed. "Thanks, Rob. That means… everything."

As he speaks, Robbie feels a wave of warmth he hadn't fully recognized before—a mix of pride, loyalty, and a bond deeper than he could have imagined. He realizes he loves Mike, not just as a friend, but as something more meaningful. They are, in every way, each other's home.

A Friend's Confession

The bell rings, its sharp sound a welcome end to another day. Blair Nelson pulls her last textbook from her locker, a sigh of relief escaping her lips. "Finally," she mumbles to herself.

"Hey, Blair got a minute?"

Blair turns to see Holly standing there, her expression uncharacteristically hesitant. "Yeah, sure, what's up?"

"I... I just wanted to talk about Mike." Holly's voice is a low murmur, and Lauren, passing by their lockers, slows her pace, her ears perking up.

"That guy you dated a while back?" Blair asks. "Thought you didn't like his reputation?"

"I didn't..." Holly looks to her feet. "I may have been too quick to judge."

"Yeah, you did," Blair replies bluntly.

"Blair." Holly snaps. "This isn't easy. People are talking about him..."

"Oh," Blair says, her smile faltering. "Because he's... different. I'm not sure what's going on with him, but he seems happier. More... himself, I guess."

"I know," Holly says, her voice barely a whisper. "That's what I wanted to talk about. I was so awful to him. I made some terrible jokes, and I've been a total jerk to him since the start of the year."

Blair's expression softens. "Yeah, you were pretty bad, Hol."

Holly smirks. "You didn't have to agree so fast."

"Hol, I love ya, girl, but the boy missed a week of school after your last date."

"I know!" she says, a tear welling in her eye.

"What have you done about that?" Blair asks, pulling sonme chewing gum from her purse.

Holly hesitates, gazing at the ceiling and takin a deep breath. "I've tried to apologize, but he's not talking to me. He just gives me that blank stare. I feel so awful about it. I want to make it right. What do I do?"

Lauren stops completely now, feigning interest in a poster on the wall as she strains to hear their conversation.

"When was the last time you tried?" Blair asks, closing her locker.

"Last month." Holly answers sadly, leaning on the locker doors.

"Maybe he's forgotten all about it?" Blair teases.

"Be serious!"

"Are you still interested?"

"Yes...Please help me." Holly sighs, taking Blair's hand.

Blair thinks for a moment. "You could try writing him a letter. Sometimes it's easier to say things in writing than face-to-face. Tell him how you feel, how sorry you are, and that you want to be friends again. That Mike that everyone's talking about... he'll read it. He might not forgive you right away, but it's a start."

Holly's eyes light up. "A letter... yeah, I can do that. That's a great idea, Blair. Thanks."

"No problem," Blair says, giving her a small smile. "He's a good guy, Holly. He'll come around." Hugging her friend as they head to class.

As Lauren walks away, a new plan begins to form in her mind. Maybe she can use this information to help Tripp, too.

A Slice of Celebration

The following two weeks have gone by fast for Tripp and Robbie. It seems like they closed their eyes, and it is fourteen days later. With Tripp's help, Robbie has finished all the engine and mechanical upgrades. Scott has been with Tripp and Robbie on several afternoon rides. Robbie is getting used to the new Mike Carson but hasn't transitioned to calling him Tripp. He likes the idea that Mike is including his cousin. It is clear that his friend cares.

Tripp found the time to get his haircut. His older brother, Mark, helped him get a job at the local produce store, Maddox Grocery. It is close to home, and the store will make Tripp's work schedule around school. On the way to Robbie's house from school, they stop to pick up his first paycheck. There is a particular plan for hard-earned money. It's a surprise for his mother. They have time today; Lauren is doing something with a friend after school. The friend plans to drop her off at Robbie's house later. It is easier for them, plus Tripp offered to take her home.

Robbie insists on helping Tripp with the reading list and reports in the first hour after school. They haven't made as much progress as they did with the car, but Mrs. Austin is impressed. Tripp has completed the other classwork. If it hadn't been for Robbie, Tripp would not have made it this far or as fast. They plan to celebrate by making a homemade pizza. Robbie's mother has a unique recipe that Tripp loves.

The boys have been doing the homework at the dining room table. Robbie is an excellent tutor, and today has been easy. Tripp stands up, putting the assignments in his backpack. He smiles at Robbie as he straightens up the table. Tripp carries both bookbags over to the front door. They still have time to start working on the car as the pizza cooks. Mama Davis insisted that she help.

"Hey, Mom!" Robbie yells. "We're done with the table. How long will your pizza take?"

"I'm looking forward to this!" Tripp adds, rubbing his hands together. "It feels like a century since I last ate your pizza, Mama Davis!"

"It will take about 45 minutes, Robbie. I am making two for tonight." She calls out from the laundry room.

Robbie laughs, adding, "Good, I'm starving, Mom!"

"Uh, no, Robert!" She snaps back; her voice echoes in the hall.

Tripp gets a laugh out of this exchange. He has spent more time with Robbie since the day he returned to 1980. The fear that he would wake up and be an old man again is less daunting. Tripp feels he has made a significant impact. He is finally content. Michael Carson fixed things with Robbie and strengthened his relationships with his cousin, brother, close friends, and most importantly, his mother. He would accept whatever fate decides to do with him now. He would not let up as long as he was here. It is the only way he can make a difference.

Robbie disappears down the hallway. Tripp walks over to the kitchen bar. He is thankful for the day. Surprised, he turns when he hears movement on the back porch. It is Robbie's older sister, Stephanie. She lives about an hour away with her husband but recently seems to be regularly visiting her family. She is tall like Robbie and has beautiful dark brown hair. It hangs just over her shoulders. She is wearing a casual pantsuit for work. She may be only 24, but her skills landed her a job with Carolina Corporate Bank in their mortgage department. Stephanie opens the door, walking in with a broad smile. Her blue eyes seem to sparkle as she sees Mike Carson. Her brother's best friend has been a part of her family for three years. Plus, she enjoys the flirting they engage in every time they meet. She has been very interested in the transformation of Mike Carson.

"Good evening, Tripp," Stephanie greets him as she closes the door. "Where is everyone hiding?"

"Hello, gorgeous!" Tripp flirtatiously replies.

"Oh, stop it, silly!" She teases, hugging him. "Bud will be here soon anyway,"

"Good! So, you're all mine for a few minutes?" Tripp smiles.

Robbie appears in the hallway, "Well, that explains the second pizza."

"Pizza!" Stephanie exclaims. "Lucky me, I picked the right night."

"It is kinda a celebration. Robbie's car is running great now, and he has helped with my schoolwork," Tripp announces.

Robbie runs in. Wrapping his arms around his sister, he hugs her. Tripp watches and smiles. He always wanted a sister. Mark is great, without question, and Tripp hopes to build a close relationship with his brother, but he has seen how much Robbie and his sister love each other. Mama Davis walks in and heads into the kitchen.

"Hey, Mom, we are going to start sanding the car," Robbie said.

"I will signal with the floodlights. It should be about 45 minutes," his mother replies. "Maybe sooner, with Steph's help."

"Come on, Mike," Robbie heads to the side door. "Oh, Mom, one of our friends may be here soon. Is it ok if she wants some pizza?"

"I will see if we can make three. Bud is coming too." His mother replies, quickly surveying the supplies.

Stephanie watches as her brother and Tripp head out the side door. Robbie is quietly talking to Tripp as they walk. Both boys bust out laughing as they head downstairs. These two have always been close.

Steph has been concerned about Mike. Everyone in the Davis home thinks highly of Mike Carson. She has had multiple conversations with her mother, discussing their concerns; they want to help Robbie's friend, and up until a few weeks ago, Mike seemed distant. They were distraught. That changed one day. It was like overnight, and he had become a different person. More importantly, Steph has been seeing other changes.

Steph cocks her hips to one side while folding her arms, "Mom, does Tripp seem different to you?"

Mrs. Davis shakes her head, "Well, you know that he has decided to change his whole life, basically,"

"I know that." Steph laughs softly and puts her hand on her mother's shoulder. "What I meant was different for today?"

"No..." Mama Davis said as she gathered ingredients. "From what he and Robbie have been saying, Mike has apologized to friends and family even if he didn't need to. Robbie said that Mike's cousin is tagging along some on their excursions to the parts house. Robbie likes this and calls it Mike's best improvement. I have seen a difference, but it is a good thing. Robbie was so worried that Mike was battling with depression."

"There is something else, and I can't put my finger on it. Mike has stepped up his flirtations with me; they are harmless flirtations. But still, Mike is happy. He seems at peace," Stephanie replies as she contemplates.

"At peace? That is a good way to describe it..." Mama Davis nods with an approving smile.

"Have you noticed that Mike behaves differently if people other than us are around?" Stephanie can't let go of her feelings. "I mean, towards Rob?"

"How so, Steph?" Mama Davis asks as she grabs the ingredients for the pizza dough.

"I can't put my finger on it. Mike has a different demeanor; it is a softer side of his personality around just us," Stephanie gazes off and smiles. "He lets his guard down. Maybe that's who he truly is, and he feels safe around us."

"Three years is a long time to get to know someone. I agree that he has changed, but not sure how much," Mama Davis answers, mixing the pizza dough. "Does it matter, hon? Robbie is happy about Mike. I've seen that he's dressing better."

"He's lost some weight too. I'm glad. I wonder if all this is to impress that girl he likes? What is her name, Holly?" Stephanie tries to remember.

"Ahhh..." Mama Davis sighs, "Young love is so fun to watch!"

"And heartwarming. If it is for her, I'm thankful. I like the new Mike," Stephanie laughs. "Tell me what you need me to do, Mom."

Robbie comes out of the garage, arms loaded with sanding equipment. Tripp stands by the car, looking over their progress with admiration. Though they're only focusing on the hood and right fender today, he's impressed by how far they've come. Their task for the day is to sand these areas smooth—a tough job even with the electric sanders.

"Alright, Mike, ready to get dusty?" Robbie jokes as he begins organizing the equipment.

"You swore no grease this time!" Tripp grins back, playfully exaggerating his relief.

Robbie chuckles, holding up one of the face masks. "No grease, but plenty of dust. Just a different kind of messy."

Tripp laughs, giving a nervous nod. "Alright, just tell me what to do, Rob."

Robbie explains the basics and assigns him the hood while he takes on the fender. He hands Tripp some safety glasses and a face mask to keep the dust out.

Starting on the driver's side of the hood, Tripp quickly realizes it's more tiring than he'd expected. His arms begin to ache, while Robbie, now shirtless, sands the fender with practiced ease. Tripp knew cars were Robbie's thing; Robbie's ease only reminds him of his friend's years of experience. But for Tripp, just helping out means more than the car itself. In frustration, Tripp sets his sander on the hood as he he pulls shirt off.

"How do you make this look so easy?" Tripp shouts over the noise, balling up his shirt and setting it at the base of the windshield.

Robbie, already covered in dust, puts down his sander and walks over to help. He adjusts Tripp's settings, then demonstrates the technique, his hands guiding Tripp's.

"Hold it like this," Robbie says, placing Tripp's hands on the sander. "Let the left hand steady it, and pull the trigger with your right. Got it?"

Tripp follows his instructions, his focus intense. "Like this?"

Robbie leans closer, placing his hands over Tripp's for a quick demonstration. Tripp shifts so they're working in sync, and Robbie nods. The sander roars to life, and Tripp lets out a thrilled shout, which makes Robbie laugh.

"Let the sander move in its direction—don't fight it," Robbie yells over the noise. "Just guide it along the lines of the hood."

"Wow, way better!" Tripp shouts, his eyes wide as he sees the difference. They work through the lines on the hood together, dust flying everywhere.

Once Tripp has the hang of it, Robbie pulls down his mask. "Not bad at all. With a few more passes, you'll have that side looking good."

Tripp stops the sander to catch his breath, wiping his forehead with his arm. "Thanks, Rob. Helps to know the technique." He looks over to the fender. "Wait... are you already done?"

Robbie crosses his arms, amused. "The fender's smaller, and I've done this a few times," he teases.

Tripp pulls off his mask and lets it hang. "Let me grab some water, then I'll get back to it."

As Tripp heads into the garage, Robbie inspects the hood, smiling at the progress. "Guess he's not just a Tool Monkey anymore," he mutters approvingly, then shouts out, "Looks great, Tripp!"

"That's all you, Robbie!" Tripp calls back with a laugh.

Robbie stands back, hands in his pockets, and smiles as he envisions the finished paint job on his car. He hopes it'll turn out well; the last thing he wants is a patchy job that stands out. Just then, Tripp walks out of the garage, sipping water from a large glass. He steps beside Robbie, resting his free hand on Robbie's shoulder.

"It's going to look incredible, Robbie," Tripp says confidently, leaning in with a supportive grin.

"Thanks. I hope so," Robbie replies, a hint of excitement in his voice. "It wouldn't be this far along if you hadn't helped."

Tripp chuckles softly. "You're my best friend; I'd do anything for you."

"Even with all the grease, oil, and dust?" Robbie nudges him playfully.

"Absolutely," Tripp nods with a smile. "Robert Davis is worth the mess."

They stand shoulder-to-shoulder, backs to the street, lost in their moment of accomplishment. Behind them, Lauren arrives, dropped off by a friend, and heads down the driveway. She spots the two of them standing close, admiring the car, their faces lit with satisfaction. A smile creeps onto her face as she watches.

"Ah, boys and their toys," she laughs quietly to herself.

Seeing them gearing up with their masks and glasses to get back to work, Lauren makes her way over and sits on the brick retaining wall, observing them curiously. Tripp grabs his sander, preparing to finish the right side of the hood, with Robbie beside him, guiding his friend's hands as the sander buzzes to life. Lauren raises an eyebrow, noting how focused they look. Even though they're sweaty and dusty, they look undeniably dedicated.

"They actually kind of look hot working up a sweat," she thinks to herself, amused. Robbie has always been muscular, and she notices that Tripp's been losing weight, starting to show a bit. She smiles, ready to tease them when they're done.

After about five minutes, they finally finish. Tripp playfully leans his shoulder into Robbie, both of them laughing in celebration. Turning toward the other side of the car, they spot Lauren sitting nearby. Tripp steps back, suddenly aware of his shirtless state.

"Oh, hey! When did you get here?" he asks, a little embarrassed.

"About five minutes ago," Lauren replies, her grin widening. "So... this is the 'lamb' you've been working on?"

Robbie raises an eyebrow, realizing she might be teasing—or maybe she doesn't know. "It's a *goat*, Lauren. GTOs are called 'goats,'" he explains, chuckling.

"Got it. Well, it's impressive!" she adds, hopping off the wall. "Looks like you two have put a lot of work into it."

Tripp nods, wiping his forehead. "Yep, just trying to get this part done before dinner."

"You two make a great team," Lauren compliments, folding her arms. "I didn't realize that you haven't ate yet..."

"Speaking of which, the pizza should be ready in about ten minutes," Tripp adds.

"My mom's making homemade pizza," Robbie says with a smile. "There's plenty—you're welcome to join us."

"I wouldn't want to be a burden," Lauren says, holding up a hand as if to decline politely.

"You're not a burden! They're making extra for everyone," Robbie says, smiling. "We're celebrating Mike's progress in school, and my stepdad offered to help get part of the car painted, so it's a double celebration."

"Well, thanks for inviting me to the...uh, party?" Lauren laughs, looking between the two of them with a grin.

As they chat, the flood lights start flickering on, signaling dinnertime. Both Tripp and Robbie see it and start cleaning up, putting aside the rest of the sanding for now. Robbie begins putting the tools away, and Tripp wrestles the car cover over the newly sanded surfaces. Lauren steps up to help, grabbing the opposite end. Tripp flashes her a big smile.

"Thanks, we just need to cover the front side of the hood," Tripp says.

"Consider it payment for the show," Lauren jokes, playfully looking him over. "Not to inflate your ego, but you look pretty good half-naked."

Tripp chuckles, glancing down. "Does 'half-naked' mean I need to lose the jeans, too?"

"There's my silly dork," she replies, rolling her eyes. "But honestly, you're looking good."

"Thanks, Lauren." Tripp humbly replies.

"Hey, Tripp," she says more softly, "could you drop me at Greg's place instead of home? We had a fight."

Tripp pauses, concerned. "A fight? When did that happen?"

"During fourth period. I snuck off campus to meet him by the convenience store." Lauren shrugs.

Tripp raises an eyebrow. "You know you could get in serious trouble for that, right?"

"Relax, **Mom**. They haven't caught me yet," she teases, sticking her tongue out. "So...do you mind?"

"Nah, I don't mind at all. But can we go after the pizza? I'm starving," Tripp says, patting his stomach.

"Sounds good! Mrs. Davis must be a fantastic cook," Lauren replies with a nod.

"If I could eat her pizza every day and not gain weight, I would," Tripp says, feigning a serious tone.

Just then, Robbie returns from the garage, dusting his hands off. "Mike, you might want to wash up in the downstairs sink. I didn't realize how messy sanding would be."

"Good call," Tripp nods. "I'll be up in a second."

"Come on, Lauren. Let me introduce you to my mom and sister. You better hurry, Mike. We may eat all the pizza!"

Mike throws a shop rag at Robbie and laughs. Robbie easily dodges the slow-moving projectile.

"Try harder!" Robbie taunts, guiding their friend away.

Lauren laughs. Robbie grabs his shirt and puts it on. She smiles, following Robbie up to the kitchen. Tripp quickly cleans up in case they do not wait for him. He has to shake the dust off his shirt. He did not leave it far enough away from the car. He runs up the steps as Robbie finishes the introductions.

Robbie's stepdad is not going to join them for dinner. This is good; it means that there should be enough pizza. Robbie and Tripp sit on the right side of the rectangular dinner table. Lauren sits across from Mike. Steph takes the seat at the head of the table. Mama Davis sits down at the other end after getting the plates for everyone.

"Dig in; we aren't too formal when it's pizza night!" Stephanie announces as if she is calling for a race to begin.

"OK, thank you..." Lauren tries to get out before the boys attack the pizza.

Robbie and Tripp are already grabbing a slice each. Lauren watches Tripp. She is intrigued by the way he enjoys the pizza–like he's never eaten it before. She knows he is trying to eat better, dismissing it as him getting his pizza fix. Tripp leans towards Robbie. He poorly pretends to steal Robbie's pizza. Lauren laughs. Steph is smiling big, carefully watching Lauren. She wonders *is Tripp is interested in her. They seemed to be comfortable around each other.*

Everyone is getting their second slice when the back door opens. Stephanie's husband of two years has arrived. Bud Jansen may appear to be a simple-sounding country boy, but he is brilliant—a talented engineer in his own right. He introduces himself pleasantly, grabbing three slices of pizza. Bud sits beside Lauren, though he is focused on his wife.

"Bud, how was work?" Mama Davis asks her son-in-law.

"A real headache," Bud said in between bites of pizza. "I'm doing an automation project in the secondary assembly room, and the equipment is all..."

Mama Davis gives him a warning look. Tripp and Robbie laugh. Steph lets out a sigh and smiles at her husband. Lauren could tell that this group had spent time together. This family time is a side of her two friends that she is unaware of. She likes what she is seeing.

"Uh, the equipment is all fouled up. They don't take care of the machines..." Bud restates his comment.

"What kind of automation, Bud?" Chewing up his pizza, Tripp asks.

"It is actually a simple upgrade, Tripp," Bud explains. "The machine should unload a conveyor and flip the primary component upside down. The next machine is a welder that will add another piece. The arm is not grabbing the part."

"I would love to see that," Robbie said.

"You will figure it out; nothing has beat you yet," Tripp nods with a smile.

"Thanks for the vote of confidence. It is probably something very simple, and I just haven't seen it..."

"Then it should be easy for you to find since you are very simple," Stephanie teases her husband.

Robbie burst out laughing. Tripp tries to stifle his laughter; he has respect for Bud. In the end, he is not able to remain quiet. Everyone laughs hard. Lauren smiles quietly. She wouldn't presume to be allowed to join in. Stephanie leans over to give Bud a quick kiss. Bud answers with his tiger growl sound. Steph shakes her head no, laughing again. Lauren is unsure when it happened, but Tripp has moved away from Robbie. They sat very close when the meal started, but now they are not.

"So, I hear the goat is almost road-ready?" Bud asks.

"Yes, it is," Robbie said confidently. "Mike has been a big help; we were sanding the hood today. Carlos said he would pay for a partial paint job!"

"All one color? That is fantastic," Bud exclaims. "You two make a great team."

"We are best friends, right Mike?" Robbie smiles.

Tripp has a mouth full of pizza. He stops for a subtle smile and nods in agreement. Mama Davis begins talking about their upcoming family trip to Maine. She is originally from that area. In three weeks, they will see an older aunt and uncle.

Lauren carefully nudges Tripp's leg under the table. It is getting late, and she has to go. Lauren hates that she put this inconvenience on Tripp. It's evident that this is his second home. *The two dorks and their family*. She smiles. It is great that Mike has Robbie as a friend. In many ways, Robbie is a better role model for Mike than Greg. Tripp smiles, focusing on Robbie.

"Mama Davis, thank you so much for making this fantastic pizza; I could die a happy man right now," Mike Carson jokes.

"You are so welcome, Mike," she replies. "You have worked hard—both of my strong men!"

"Exactly, Tripp. We are proud of your efforts at school. I'm sure that Robbie likes having you as a tool monkey," Stephanie said softly. "That car is almost as important to him as you are!"

"At least until the new paint job," Robbie jabs cheerfully.

Tripp pretends to be insulted, "Oh, to be cast aside so easily, what will I ever do?"

"Get a new paint job yourself?" Bud cracks to everyone's amusement.

"As much as I am enjoying this abuse, I need to take Lauren home," Tripp said dryly, wiping his face.

"Thank you again, Mrs. Davis. It was kind of you to invite me in," Lauren politely said as she stood.

"It was a pleasure meeting a good friend of the boys," Mama Davis answers.

"Hopefully, we will see you again, Lauren," Steph adds.

Bud smiles, his muscles raise his eyebrows, "I might even behave on your next visit."

Matchmaker

L auren makes her way to Tripp's Mustang. She pauses, noticing Tripp and Robbie talking on the front porch, illuminated by the soft glow of the lights. Tripp's smile catches her eye as he listens to Robbie, who's animatedly describing his plans for his GTO. One of the porch lights casts a gentle halo around Robbie, which seems fitting to Tripp—his best friend truly is a beacon of goodness in his life.

"Mike, the GTO's going to be so awesome. It's incredible that we've been building it together," Robbie says, tapping Tripp's arm. "Did you get enough pizza? I know you're about to head out."

"Yeah, thanks to Mama D. Be sure to tell her I really appreciate it," Tripp replies warmly, grateful for Robbie's excitement and the chance to be part of his dream.

"You did good today... Tripp," Robbie says, managing a smile. "That name still feels weird."

Tripp chuckles. "It's okay, Rob. I'm just glad to be part of this."

Robbie folds his arms, his voice turning serious. "I owe you for all this, Mike. You've had your own stuff going on, and you're turning everything around... because of a nightmare?"

Tripp's expression softens. "It was more than a nightmare, Rob. That was my future. And I did this for you. You've been my constant, my friend... once I remembered that, everything made sense. Now the hard part is not letting you down."

Robbie, touched, replies, "Even before your change, you were my best friend. You couldn't let me down."

"Make sure to thank Mama D for me, okay?" Tripp's voice wavers slightly, emotions catching up with him.

"Don't get mushy on me now, goober. Besides, the princess is waiting for her ride," Robbie jokes, nodding toward Lauren at the car. "And you know, when I call her 'princess' now, it's because I can see why she means so much to you."

Tripp laughs. "She kinda grows on you, doesn't she? Good night, Rob."

"See you in the morning?" Robbie asks, returning the smile.

Tripp nods, then runs to his car. Lauren watches, both moved and amused by the interaction. As she slides into the car, she murmurs to herself, "Well, it's not eavesdropping if they're your friends."

Seeing Tripp and Robbie together like this reveals a side of them that school doesn't show. Outside of the usual setting, their genuine bond is unmistakable, and she feels lucky to be part of their circle—even if they're still dorks, her dorks as she affectionately thinks. Meeting Robbie's family tonight has left a warm impression.

As she settles in the seat, a name suddenly crosses her mind. "Jeff Tyler..." she whispers, a curious thought flickering in her mind.

She waves goodbye to Robbie as Tripp glances back, watching his friend head inside. After a moment, he gets in, starts the car, and lets the engine idle briefly before turning to her.

"Sorry it's so late, Lauren," he says quietly.

"It's okay; Greg's been mad before," Lauren says with a small sigh. "Besides, I think you needed that celebration. It's clear Robbie means a lot to you."

Tripp nods, pulling out of the driveway. "He really does. He's my best friend."

She reaches over, touching his shoulder gently. "So... are you going to ask Holly out again?"

Tripp glances at her, slightly caught off guard. He hasn't even thought about dating anyone since he began this journey to change. For him, every day has been about rebuilding, making things right. Dating, right now, feels like a distant possibility—like he can't afford any detours. He finally shrugs, smiling at her curiosity. "Hadn't really thought about it. She's nice, I guess."

"Honestly, I don't get the attraction. She doesn't really seem like your type," Lauren says with a playful grin, studying his reaction.

"My type?" Tripp laughs, raising an eyebrow. "Well, I went out with her, so that would make her my type, wouldn't it?"

"Oh, you know what I mean!" Lauren teases, nudging his arm. "Holly's pretty, sure, but... I think your taste leans elsewhere."

Tripp rolls his eyes, leaning into her teasing. "So now you know all about my taste, huh? I'm an open book?"

"It's science, Tripp! Girls are complicated; boys are simple," Lauren quips, folding her arms as if presenting a proven theory.

"Simple?" Tripp's expression grows serious, a small frown forming. "Does everything I'm doing to turn things around seem... simple to you?"

"Not at all." She softens, meeting his gaze. "I think what you're doing is complicated. But your reason for doing it is pretty clear—you just want to make things right."

Tripp's face relaxes, and he nods slowly. "You're right. I guess... I know I have to do this. It's more than wanting. And I'm sticking to it, one day at a time."

"You're brave for that, Tripp. I'm proud of you." Lauren's voice is gentle, genuine. Then she smiles, lightening the mood again. "But... back to Holly."

"Fine, fine." Tripp sighs, looking ahead. "She's very pretty, but she's... focused on the wrong things. All about looks, reputation, like what people think of her, and, you know, what *message* it sends for her to be with me." He does air quotes on "message."

Lauren's eyebrows lift. "She actually said that?"

"More or less. I'm not mad. Her reputation is important to her..."

"But not to you," Lauren says, her tone a little sharper.

Tripp glances at her, her intent piercing through. He sees the way she looks at him, her arms crossed but a softness in her expression, almost as if she's waiting for him to understand something she's holding back. He's not sure what it is but knows he values her honesty more than anyone's. That alone sends a warmth through him, though he quickly pushes it aside.

He sighs, chuckling. "You're right. It's not. What matters to me... that's still a work in progress."

Lauren smiles at his response. With a gentle turning of her head, she pulls more information out of Tripp.

"Well, I get not wanting people to talk badly about you, but with her, it's all about status, isn't it?" Tripp shrugs, his shoulders dropping as he sighs.

Lauren leans closer, her voice a playful whisper. "I know. See, Tripp, I can read you. You're more into the girl-next-door type. Blondes might be fun, but brunettes... they're full of surprises."

"Lauren, you're a blonde," Tripp replies with a smile, his tone light. "And you seem full of surprises, too."

She laughs, nudging him. "Stop it, Mike Carson. This isn't about me. It's about you being happy." She softens, watching him. "So, tell me—what's the most important thing you're looking for?"

Tripp stares ahead as the light changes, gathering his thoughts. "Respect. Honor. I need someone I can look up to. Someone kind, considerate... and someone I can really talk to."

Lauren nods, her eyes thoughtful. "Yeah, I'd say your perfect match would share some of your interests but have others of their own. Gives you both room to grow."

Tripp grins, as if an idea just clicked. "That's kind of what I like about Kelly Albright."

"One of the twins? Hate to burst your bubble, but Kelly's parents are strict. I'm pretty sure they're not letting her date until she's eighteen," Lauren shakes her head, smiling.

He laughs, defending himself. "She's not the only one out there."

Lauren chuckles, seeing the opportunity. "You know, Tripp, if you ever want to talk about Jeff Tyler... I'm here."

"Jeff?" Tripp looks slightly startled but nods as he recalls their last run-in. "Not much to say. We were friends. *Just friends.*"

"Tripp," Lauren says gently, catching his hint. "I'm not here to push you. I just think you might need someone to talk to. Greg thinks the world of you, but sometimes it helps to have someone... you know, trustworthy. And I'm realizing there's a lot more to you than I thought."

As they approach a stop sign, Tripp glances at her, his expression soft. "I trust you, Lauren." He pauses, taking a deep breath. "The only thing I want with Jeff is to apologize. I... I wasn't very nice when we stopped being friends." He looks down, rubbing his forehead.

Lauren's curiosity is piqued by the admission. "Is that around the time you became friends with Robbie?"

Tripp checks both ways before accelerating. "No, Steve and Larry have been my closest friends since third grade. Jeff and I were friends when I was twelve. We had a falling out after... an argument. Robbie and I ended up in the same class the next year. We shared a desk, started talking, and just... clicked."

Lauren leans a little closer, her voice warm. "I'm glad you found him, Tripp."

Tripp takes a second to reflect, smiling. "Me too. Friends like him don't come around twice in one lifetime."

She glances over at him. "So... Robbie's someone you really look up to?"

"Absolutely." Tripp's voice brightens. "He's the most honorable, incredible guy I know. Part of why I'm changing is to be worthy of his friendship."

"Tripp, you know Robbie cares about you. I don't think you need to worry about him."

But Tripp's smile fades, his gaze drifting off into the distance. In his heart, he feels the weight of that worry. He knows all too well the future he's trying to prevent and the hurt that he's hoping to spare Robbie from. Lauren can sense he's deep in thought, and though she wants to keep talking, she decides to give him the space he seems to need.

"Sorry, Tripp. I'm pushing too hard," Lauren apologizes. "It is only minutes to Greg's house now, anyway."

A Friend's Strength

Tripp nods, focusing on the road. The more Lauren considers it, the more she is unsure if coming here is a good idea. Greg had a temper, having flown off the handle over jealousy before. Lauren was never interested in anyone else, but some guy kept asking her out. Lauren loves Greg and him only. She isn't sure why Greg could not see that.

Tripp turns onto Park Lane. They both could see Greg outside. Realizing that Greg is mad, Lauren watches her boyfriend pacing back and forth in the front yard like a panther preparing for an attack. Tripp worries; he has never seen Greg like this before. Mad, a brewing fury in his eyes.

Tripp nervously asks Lauren, "You sure you don't want me to stay around?"

"Oh, it will be..." Lauren starts with a sigh. "Uh, yeah, Tripp, you probably should. That, ok?"

"I would cross the empty void of timelessness for my friends, and you are a good friend," he replies.

"Lauren! What the hell?" Greg yells, tossing an empty beer can toward the porch. "I told you I would come get you, but Ralph has my spare helmet!"

Mike Carson slowly exits the car after Lauren. Tripp tries to defuse the situation with a smile and a wave, but Greg is furious. Mike hopes that he does not make the problem worse by bringing Lauren.

"I thought we needed to talk," Lauren says softly, hoping Greg will reciprocate. "Tripp was willing to help out."

Tripp cannot hide his nervousness. His friend, Greg, has a temper, and beer would not help it. "Yeah, Greg. I would do anything for you and Lauren. I'm sorry it was late. We...uh, that is

Robbie and me. We celebrated my progress in school and his work on the car."

"Mike, I'm not mad at you!" Greg growls, grabbing another drink from the cooler on the steps.

"Oh? Just mad at me, is that it?" Lauren snaps; she hates his drinking.

"Lauren, no! I'm mad because of what happened!" Greg shot back.

"The guy was a dirtbag. I didn't care. He wasn't worth my time. I don't know why you think I could be interested in that loser." Lauren is irritated by the pettiness of the argument.

"He shouldn't be messing with my girl. He should've known better." He grumbles, pacing again.

"So, I am property?" Lauren folds her arms disapprovingly. "I thought we're a couple. Am I just an accessory to make you look good to others?"

Tripp knows he has little time to act, "Hey, wait, both of you. Can I say something?"

"Mike..." Lauren waves her hand, politely telling him to stay out of the argument.

"What?" Greg huffs, "Mike, what could *you* possibly say?"

"Maybe a dose of the truth?" Tripp barks sternly.

"Uh...ok..." Surprised, Greg doesn't know what to say.

"I think you have our attention, Tripp," Lauren said wide-eyed, trying not to get mad.

Greg exhales deeply, "OK, Tripp, I'm listening."

"Greg, you are a great friend. I respect you and look up to you. You've never cared who I was. You accepted me with no questions, but I'm changing. I want to be a better man. I always had faith in you. But, and I say this with all sincerity, you need to let go of this anger!" He scolds.

"Tripp..." Lauren tries to interject. Impressed that Tripp is standing up like this,

"Let me finish," Tripp Carson holds up his hand and speaks even louder. "Greg, this woman right here would follow you to the ends of the world. I don't think it; I know it. Damn it, Greg, *I know it!* I have never lied to you."

"No. You haven't," Greg answers quietly, unprepared for Tripp's assertiveness, gazing at Lauren for help.

"I've changed to be a better person, but you need to change to avoid prison," Tripp said, Slamming the Mustang door. Stepping closer to Greg, Tripp continues, "I do not want that for you. I wish I had someone to love me the way Lauren loves you. Don't throw it away over pride."

"Greg, he is right." Lauren tears up, "I do love you..."

"I know Lauren," Greg sounds defeated, accepting his mistake. "But I am nothing. You could have anybody you wanted..."

"I do have who I want," she whispers warmly.

"I'm sorry, Lauren," Greg admits as he sits on the steps. "I'm sorry to you as well, Tripp. I envy that you can follow through on the changes."

"My strength is my friends—Robbie, you, and Lauren. You said you were going to back me, remember? I will be here for you," Tripp said, calming down.

Lauren walks over, taking Greg's hand. She sits beside him and leans close. Greg shakes his head. Right now, he feels ashamed of who he is and why he is mad, which is a childish way for him to have reacted.

Greg wraps his arms around her. "I didn't think that you would ever treat me that way or even cheat. Lauren, you're too classy." Mike can hear a motorcycle approaching. Greg looks up. He knows the sound of his roommate's bike.

"Greg Dawson, I love you, my classy guy," Lauren whispers, gently showering him with kisses.

"I think that is Ralph," Greg responds, clearing his throat. "Finally. Lauren, I can take you home if you are not mad at me anymore."

"I would like that very much, Greg," Lauren hugs him close. "And thank you."

"Thank you?" Greg asks, still ashamed of his behavior.

"For listening to Tripp," Lauren explains, giving Tripp a wink. "I'm learning a lot about our friend, Mike Carson. Tripp would never send you or me in the wrong direction. It takes courage to listen, baby."

"I love you, Lauren," Greg answers, burying his face on her shoulder.

"I can wait if you need me to," Proud of making his point, Tripp pierces the silence with a softer voice.

The obnoxiously loud motorcycle rounds the corner, heading down Park Lane. Greg stands while holding onto Lauren's hand, straining to look. It is his friend's bike. He could take Lauren home safely. Greg smiles and waves. Lauren gazes at Tripp, grateful he stood up for them. Tripp gets into his Mustang as Ralph rides up into the yard. The roommate has a case of beer strapped on the back of his bike. Tripp is glad to be leaving. He didn't want to see another beer as long as he lived.

A Brother's Burden

Anne Carson sits on the sofa, a new murder mystery in hand. She's distracted, no longer worrying about the electric bill, but keeping her boys toigether. The kitchen cabinets have more than enough. Her sons are becoming men. They're taking care of her, but she knows this is a fragile time, Michael still struggles with school. Mark is taking on too much to become a nurse.

"What am I to do?" she asks the empty room.

Anne sets the book down, hearing Mark emerge from his room. She can hear him cursing softly. Mark enters the living room, startled to find his mother.

"Have you seen Tripp?" Anne asks.

"Left for work, he used all the hot water." Mark growls, buttoning his work shirt.

"Is that why you were cursing?"

"Yes, sorry." Mark sighs as he sits. "I'm not really mad. There is a lot on me, exams are coming."

"I realize you didn't sign up for taking care of us. Am I asking too much?" Anne quietly asks.

"I just don't know, Momma," Mark said, running a hand through his hair, his voice heavy with the weight of it all. "This whole situation... it's just a lot."

Anne Carson sits beside him on the sofa, her hand gently resting on his arm. "I know it's overwhelming, Mark. But Tripp needs you. He looks up to you so much. You're the one person he can really talk to, the one person he can be himself around without fear of judgment."

"I know, but..." Mark sighs, the words trailing off.

"It isn't fair." Anne leans back.

"Fair?" Mark smiles, warmly joking. "When has anything been fair for the Carsons?"

"Mark, you're the strong one," she says softly, her voice an anchor in the storm of his thoughts. "You've always been the strong one for him. He's going through something no one can truly understand. He needs you to be in his corner."

Mark nods, his gaze distant. "I talked to Willis the other day."

"Oh, your father?" Anne's brow furrows. "I don't talk to Willis much, but, let me hear it..."

"He thinks Mike needs a strong man to keep him straight. He's not talking about me."

"Willis wants your brother to come live with him."

"No." Mark recoils. "He thinks Mike needs a more masculine figure in his life to guide him. Willis thinks he needs to be tougher."

Anne's voice grows firm, a protective edge to her tone. "That's nonsense, Mark. Mike is fine. He's a good boy. He's just different—he always has been. He's sweet and kind and sensitive. He doesn't need to be 'tough.' He just needs people who love him for who he is."

"I know," Mark replies, a glimmer of relief in his eyes. "I defended him. I told Willis that he's always been this way and that it's okay. That Mike is his own person and that we love him just the way he is. I told him Mike is better than he ever was."

Anne smiles, a tear pricking her eye. "Thank you, Mark. Thank you for being there for him. He needs you more than you know."

"We all need each other, Mom." Mark squeezes her hand. "You can depend on me."

Flirting With Fate

The sixty-seven Mustang speeds down the road, new music flowing from the speakers. A recent creation, it's a new cassette mix tape for Tripp to listen to as he drives. Tripp left home a little bit early for his shift at Maddox. Wearing his new employee uniform, a pressed white button-down shirt with his name tag above the left shirt pocket. Tripp pushes his glasses back up his nose. He forgot how much he hates wearing them. Though he admits to himself, *the look has grown on me.* He knows that the correct type of Lasik surgery is decades away. Mike Carson shifts in the car seat.

Tripp comments, "Dammit, these pants are a size too small."

Gerry, the manager, has ordered another pair of black dress pants, but they'll arrive no sooner than a week. Tripp changes gears, seamlessly switching lanes. He passes the car ahead and merges back into the right lane. He loves this car.

"Michael, this isn't a good idea..." He reminds himself while shaking his head.

"It is harmless fun..." Tripp nods as he rationalizes his actions. "But it is still not a good idea..."

He glances at the small stack of albums in the passenger seat—three older records that he has not listened to before or after his return to 1980. He's heading to the Record Changer to sell these records and, hopefully, buy another album. He enjoys the album Mark helped him get, and Tripp wants to hear more from that group.

"No, Mike. Stop lying," Tripp growls. "Just admit it; you want to see Geoffrey again."

The next song starts, and Tripp increases the volume of the hard rock song, "This is so petty...you could anger fate, Tripp!"

He is not convincing himself.

He makes a wide left turn into the strip mall parking lot. Pulling into the space out front, Tripp can see through the windows that the store is crowded. Overcome with nervousness, he only wants to flirt with the handsome salesman again, but the other customers may not appreciate it. Public displays of same-sex attraction was not popular in the eighties.

"Too late now," Tripp sighs, checking his hair in the rear-view mirror.

Gathering the items he intends to sell, Tripp sprints to the store. He stands in line, waiting for the customer in front of him to be done. He searches the store, saddened that he cannot see Geoffrey anywhere.

He could be in the back, Tripp mumbles under his breath. *It wasn't like I dressed up and styled my hair,* Mike Carson laughs. In truth, he spent an extra twenty minutes getting ready. Deep down, impressing Geoffrey is important to him.

The young woman behind the counter pleasantly helps the customer. Tripp can't help but stare at her. She has long, wavy, and voluminous blonde hair styled with soft curls. Adorned in a bohemian-inspired wardrobe, the beautiful woman wears a flowing, layered dress. Then it finally hits him; Tripp recognizes her. He recalled that a woman worked here, and she reminded him of one of the ladies from Fleetwood Mac. A free-spirited flower child with a sweet voice. If he wasn't interested in Geoffrey, he might put the effort into talking to her. The customer finally finishes his purchase and leaves. Mike Carson steps up to the counter and places his records there.

"Hey, uh, it's Rosemary, right?" He asks with a clever smile, happy that he remembers after all these decades.

Surprised, she smiles, "Yeah, it has been a while since I have seen you around..."

Rosemary leans in to read his name tag, "So *Tripp*, what brings you to my parlor?"

"Huh?" Tripp is looking down at his shirt. "Oh, my name tag. Sorry. I guess I'm a little dense tonight."

"It's fine..." She winks. "Do you want to sell these or trade them up?"

"Trade up? What is that?" Curious, Tripp runs his hand through his hair as he smiles.

"Something new that Mr. Tynan is trying out. You can get a higher value through an in-store credit than selling them outright for cash," Rosemary explains as she playfully moves her hair behind her ear, leaning closer with a coy smile.

"That is a neat idea; I'm sure there is something in this store I could find interesting," Tripp teases. "I did want to get another album. I bought 'And then there were three' the other day."

"Cool, I love the drummer!" Rosemary picks up the trade-in records and moves them under the counter. "Grab what you want, Tripp."

"OK, thanks, Rosemary!" Tripp Carson timidly smiles, pausing. "I, uh...it has been a long time since I have flirted with a pretty woman. Uh, did I do it right?"

"That depends on why you tried, Tripp..." Rosemary leans on her elbows. "Was it just a simple flirt, or is it more?"

"Can...well...um..." Tripp's face turns red, "Maybe it was both, Rosemary?"

"Mysterious. Hmm, now I'm intrigued," Rosemary whispers. Tripp is distracted by a whiff of her perfume. "That makes it more fun, Tripp. And you can call me Rose."

Embarrassed, he smiles, lowering his head, "Thanks, Rose."

Tripp Carson walks over to the new album section. He wants to see Geoffrey, but it is nice talking to Rose. He doesn't intend to follow through and ask for a date, whether it is Rose or Geoff.

This is simply an ego trip—a moment to enjoy being young and attractive.

Telling himself quietly while looking over his shoulder, "Yes, it was vanity, but I wanted it just the same." Rosemary sees that Tripp is looking and smiles. Tripp can feel his heart begin to race.

Tripp knows he has to keep his focus on fixing the future. He just wants to enjoy the second chance of being a sixteen-year-old. Tripp can see Rose watching him from the register. He wonders what Dr. Elmhurst would say about this excursion. It wasn't difficult to imagine. Tripp knew he would say, *just be truthful; they have feelings just like you, Michael.*

"OK, doc. I will..." Tripp murmurs as he grabs an earlier album from the band.

Tripp feels uneasy as he reads the back cover. Unmistakable, that he is still being watched. He glances around. Rose is engrossed in a magazine. He looks around the room. Several of his classmates are here, but no one he knows closely; plus, he figures his notoriety should have worn off by now, Tripp Carson is just another student. He dismisses it, heading to the register. Rose smiles big as he approaches. Placing the new album on the counter, Tripp attempts to grab his wallet from the rear pocket. This is awkward because the pocket is tight. Rose studies him intently as he struggles; a warm smile grows on her face. Tripp smiles triumphantly when he succeeds in retrieving the wallet.

"Oh, Tripp. This is a good choice. You'll love the drum solos!" Rose nods, adding a wink.

"Drum solos? Great," Tripp is unsure how to respond, "My cousin is teaching me to play the drums. He is an awesome musician."

"Cool, does he play for a band?" Rose asks, leaning closer.

"No, it's a solo career," Tripp Carson laughs. "He's my younger cousin. He's still a great drummer, though."

"I bet you are his hero," she admits, almost whispering. Rose mischievously plays with her hair.

Tripp moves closer, "Why do you say that?"

"Cause you're mine," Rose smiles, sliding the receipt across the counter, revealing she has written her name and phone number on the back.

"562-6969?" Tripp asks as his heart races. This playful exchange is just what he wants. A big smile grows on his face.

Rose replies softly with a seductive smile, "I would like to know more about you."

"Uh, Rose. That is really great," A red-faced Tripp smiles. "But I need to be honest. I uh... I'm only sixteen, just a few months past my birthday."

"You certainly do not act it, Tripp. Listen. If it doesn't matter to you, it doesn't to me. I'm nineteen," Rose whispers, taking his free hand. "I don't really care about what society calls normal. I do what I want. Right now, that is knowing more about Tripp. I get this weird vibe from you. Not a bad one, babe. You have this fantastic aura, like you have an old spirit yet have such youthful energy for life."

"Rose, you are very beautiful. And thanks; you do not know how right you are," Tripp Carson answers, putting the receipt in his shirt pocket. "Can we just start by talking? I want to enjoy every day of life. There is no need to rush." He gently pats the pocket as he smiles.

"Call anytime, Tripp," She replies with a flirtatious smile and a sparkle in her eyes. "Just make sure you do call!"

Tripp nods, nervously walking out. Rose watches as he leaves. She approves the view of his tight pants, hoping he will call. *Sixteen or not, he's cute.* In the back corner of the store, a lone voice speaks. It is too far away for anyone to overhear.

"I don't see him; can we go now?" Emery asks in an annoyed tone.

"Yeah," A sad response follows.

Flirting With Fire

Tripp Carson walks to his car. A new spring to his step as the conversation replays in his mind. He hears someone call out to him. Tripp looks around and spots Geoffrey.

"Geoffrey, hm...I get two flirts in one night," Tripp encourages himself as he straightens his shirt.

The attractive man stands by the corner of the building. The parking lot lights cast odd shadows by the side of the building, as if Geoff is hiding the fact that he is waiting there. Tripp walks over. He has a big smile–fixing his hair as he approaches.

"Hey, Tripp," Geoffrey greets him smoothly, a charming smile on his lips.

"Geoffrey, I was hoping to see you," Tripp answers breathlessly.

"Look at you being all businesslike," Geoffrey says, touching Tripp's shoulder. "I like the look—sophisticated and innocent simultaneously."

"I work in a grocery store, so I'm not sure that qualifies as sophisticated," Tripp sarcastically smiles.

Geoffrey laughs with a pleasant smile, dressed in a silky black shirt under a matching Members Only Jacket. The tight gray dress pants are snug in all the right places. Tripp can't help but look. He finds Geoffrey very attractive. Geoffrey cocks his hip to one side, the goatee highlighting the devilish grin. Tripp stands with his eyes wide, waiting for Geoffrey's next move.

Geoff steps closer, "Would it bother you if I said you were beautiful, Tripp?"

"Me? I'm just a plain old guy..." Tripp coyly answers; all these flirts are becoming addictive to him.

"Don't put yourself down, dude. I think you are hot. Plus, you have a fun personality. Hell, that kid cousin of yours worships you," Geoffrey moves very close.

Tripp Carson knows that Geoffrey is running at full speed. He only wants to flirt, but this man is straight-up hitting on him. Once again, Tripp's face is visibly blushing. *The flirting is nice, kind of intoxicating,* Tripp thinks. *But the mission has to come first.*

"What if I came here tonight to get Rose's phone number?" Tripp asks, testing the response. His breathing increases, becomes heavier; the anticipation consumes Tripp Carson.

"I would still say you are hot. Hell, Rose would be lucky to be the object of your attraction," Geoffrey smiles, caressing Mike's cheek. "She is a free spirit and one hell of a ..."

Tripp chuckles. He is amazed at Geoff's energy. "I give you this, Geoff. You are definitely confident."

"I know who I am. I know what *I like*," Geoffrey says, placing his hand on Tripp's shoulder. "It doesn't matter to me if you aren't gay. I respect you. And you are very attractive..."

Geoffrey slowly removes Tripp's glasses, carefully putting them in the shirt pocket. Geoffrey pulls him closer, Tripp's teenage heart beating faster. The sixteen year old Carson is overcome with multiple feelings, a bold mix of being nervous and excited but cautious. *If I didn't know better,* he thinks, gazing at the man's eyes, *Geoffrey will kiss me next. And why is that bad?* Tripp wonders. The expectation overwhelms him. In a startling move, Geoffrey's strong hand grabs Tripp's butt. But he does not object.

Tripp smiles gently as he stares to the ground. Geoff lifts Tripp's head by the chin with his free hand and smiles. Tripp felt a firm squeeze. Then, Geoffrey slowly caresses the tight pants, his touch gentle and sensational. *Oh my god...* Tripp dares not to pull away. The air between them is filled with Geoffrey's cologne. Tripp inhales a deep breath, looking into Geoffrey's blue eyes. Tripp Carson smiles obediently, not moving. His heart is racing uncontrollably. *Remember the mission!* Tripp scolds himself. *But just a few more minutes won't hurt.*

"Are you going to kiss me?" Tripp's voice creaks, half asking and half hoping.

Geoffrey moves close to Tripp's face. "I want to, very badly and so much more..." Geoffrey answers, yet takes a step back.

"I got that, Geoff," Tripp said, placing a hand on Geoffrey's shoulder. "But I really need to get to work..."

"Then a kiss will have to wait, Tripp," Geoffrey leans in to whisper in his ear. "Plus, I can see you are not ready. Tripp, you are a gentleman, and I respect that. You have my number. Call me. I think we belong together, and I want to do this the *right* way. Call Rose. She is a wildflower and will treat you like a king."

"That's a strange pick-up line," Trip jests, not knowing what to make of what had just happened.

"It's the truth. I want you to be happy. Your smile first attracted me," Geoff answers, running his fingers through Tripp's hair. Tripp closes his eyes, briefly licking his lips. Geoff finishes, "I want that kind of happiness. Tripp, I hope you will call."

Tripp Carson looks toward his feet, briefly glancing up at Geoffrey, "I will call. OK?"

Trembling after the intense encounter, Tripp sprints back to the Mustang. He knows that Geoff is not the reason Fate brought him back to 1980. Mike Carson figures that since his body is physically sixteen, the flood of teenage hormones leads him to these bad decisions.

Bad decisions, and nothing good can come from bad choices.

He takes one last look back at Geoff, flashing a playful wave. Tripp doesn't want to admit it, but he likes the attention. He gives a slight wave in response. Tripp revels in the overwhelming feeling of joy.

Tyrone arrives, stepping out of the shadows to stand beside Geoffrey as the Mustang pulls away into the darkness. Geoffrey has an evil smile on his face. The smug look of satisfaction with his actions. His plan is coming together.

"The Texas weed is top-drawer shit. Nothing less than five hundred, no kiddin' around, G."

"I don't have that kind of cash right now." Geoffrey protests.

"I'm not sure about your offer," Tyrone said and spits on the ground. "It's too much to ask."

"Oh, you did not complain the last time," Geoffrey answers with a wicked laugh.

"Geoffrey, you are one fucked up faggot," Tyrone laughs with a shake of his head. "Guess that is why we get along so well..."

Twists Of Time

Lauren walks slowly this afternoon. Her last class was boring, and she had completed all her work quickly. She worries about Steve's sister, who will be coming to town next weekend. They are going to try to spend time together at the mall. Lauren is excited about it, but Steve mentioned that she has been hanging with the wrong crowd—a group of punk rock types who are nothing but thugs or something worse. Lauren hopes that is not bad news for her former friend.

Lauren slides past the gang of nerds by the door. She does not want to waste any more time. She is sure that Tripp and Robbie will be waiting for her. She never intended to be this late. She slowly walks up the hill. She can see that Robbie and Tripp are leaning up on the Mustang's side panel.

Tripp has his arms folded while moving close to Robbie when he talks. Lauren smiles, seeing they are laughing and having a good time. Mike Carson has been in such a better mood the last few weeks. Tripp notices Lauren walking up the hill, calmly stepping away from Robbie. Tripp waves but sees that she appears to be upset.

She waves, "Sorry, Tripp, it has been a bad day..."

"Did something happen, Lauren?" Tripp asks, his facial expression changes from his concern.

Lauren sighs, "Just the usual bull shit in school, I'm all good now!" Without thinking, she gives Tripp a quick hug, it helps putting the day behind her.

Lauren climbs into the passenger seat, while Robbie settles in the back. Tripp Carson checks the trunk to ensure it's locked. As he heads to get in the car, he spots Jeff Tyler and his black friend walking down the front pathway. He can't help but stop and watch them carefully.

He can see that Jeff appears happy, *still looking the same as he did years ago, only taller.* Closing his eyes, Tripp Carson tries to avoid remembering that last trip to the beach. Old Mike had invited his friend to come; it was supposed to be a vacation. A happy vacation. *It did not end well...for either of us,* Tripp regrets, pushing that out of his mind.

Tripp guesses the black friend is homosexual by his mannerisms and movements; not being judgemental, the gay friend isn't hiding it. *Couldn't loose him in a crowd,* Tripp thinks. Jeff's friend is wearing a peach-colored button-down shirt and pants with bold stripes. The new Mike Carson doesn't care. Overcoming the hatred that had consumed his heart for forty-six years. Tripp smiles, realizing that talking to Jeff might not be as complicated as expected. He briefly thinks about Geoffrey from the other night. Tripp lets out a sigh, finally getting in the Mustang.

"Tripp?" Lauren asks as he starts the car, looking around to see who he is watching. "Is everything okay? I meant what I said when I said you could talk to me."

"Talk to you about what?" Robbie leans forward and asks, looking very concerned.

Tripp figures she's asking about Jeff again, which makes him nervous. He can't speak. Sensing the hesitation, Lauren quickly responds, "Holly. I'm trying to convince Tripp that they make a cute couple."

"Yeah, um...I'm not sure," Tripp replies honestly, glad she gave a quick answer. "I am still trying to apologize to everyone that needs it..."

"Meh, she can be superficial sometimes. Holly's in my biology class," Robbie scoffs. "She is always fixin' her makeup or arranging her hair. Tripp...um, no, sorry, I still can't use that name. Mike, you deserve someone who cares about you. A person of honor..."

"See, Tripp," Lauren smiles with pride. "Even Robbie knows your type!'

Lauren and Robbie start to laugh. Tripp Carson grimaces, quickly racing off from the parking spot. He wants to get Lauren home as fast as he can. There are plans for tonight. He and Robbie need to get to Robbie's house. They plan to work on the last group of assignments from Mrs. Austin. Later tonight, they will watch TV—no working on cars or running around. Tripp just wants some quiet time.

Tripp's thoughts drift back to Jeff Tyler. Robbie and Lauren are carrying on an in-depth conversation about carburetors. Robbie is adjusting the GTO's to run better. He explains what he is going to do and why. Lauren having heard Greg talk about working on engines before, engages Robbie in a thorough discussion. The conversation dominates the ride to Lauren's house.

Tripp begins running through possible outcomes of talking to Jeff. He knows that he has no choice. *Jeff deserves an apology just as much as the others.* Tripp Carson isn't going to back away from that. He worries that it will not come out the way he plans. *I could make things worse; I wish I knew what to do.* Tripp is discouraged by indecision, pulling into the driveway at Lauren's house.

"Tripp..." Lauren said.

"Uh, Tripp..." Lauren repeats, raising her voice.

"Hey, Mike!" Robbie calls loudly.

Tripp snaps out of his trance, "Huh? Oh, sorry. I must have zoned out."

"Zoned out?" Robbie repeats in confusion.

Lauren said, gently caressing his arm. "Tripp, I'm worried. Maybe you need to take a break from your mission; if that's what you call it. This can't be easy on you..."

"Lauren is right, Mike. I will keep you on track, but take some time to focus on yourself," Robbie leans forward between the seats.

"Think about how far you have come. Man, I'm **proud** of you. But I don't want to see you obsessed with reaching out to everyone."

"You're afraid I'm burning the candle on both ends?" Tripp asks quietly.

Robbie nods as Lauren tilts in close, "Listen to Robbie."

"I hate to say it, but I like the new Mike Carson, better known as Tripp," Robbie laughs, resting his hand on Mike's shoulder. "You're my best friend. I just want you to be happy..."

"Better listen to your doctors, young man," Lauren teases, wagging her finger at Tripp. "I'll see you guys tomorrow."

"OK, OK. Y'all win!" Tripp cries in defeat. "See ya tomorrow, Lauren."

Both Robbie and Tripp wave as Lauren walks into her house. Tripp grins at his friend. The red Mustang backs out of the driveway. Revving the motor, Tripp speeds off to Pleasant View Drive. Mike cranks up the radio to listen to the drums playing. Robbie reaches over, lowering the volume of the music.

"Mike, I meant what I said," Robbie said, sounding serious, yet comforting his friend. "Please take some time for yourself. What will one day hurt?"

With a reluctant sigh, Tripp nods. "Agreed. It's time for us. That new Preston Harris TV movie is on tonight," Tripp replies. "No homework, no cars, just best friends being together!"

"I like the sound of that, Mike," Robbie smiles.

"Just one question first," Tripp replies.

Robbie nods yes, as Tripp continues in a worried tone, "Is it okay if Scott comes along with us tomorrow? I know we are just shopping for car parts, but I want to keep spending time with him."

"Of course, Mike. But do you even need to ask?"

"Yes, Robbie. I want to do what's right, I shouldn't assume you'd be ok with it."

Robbie answers, his pride in Tripp shines. "Scott worships the ground you walk on, you know that, right?"

"I know. I just want to do right for everybody. You're my best friend, and *you* will always come first. But I need to be there for Scott; he needs me," Tripp Carson steals the moment to look into Robbie's eyes... "Shit, that sounds so self-serving..."

"Michael Carson, stop right there!" Robbie interrupts angrily. "I like the new Mike, but I can't take it when you put yourself down like this. Everything you've done and said since...well, since October seventh, it's been for everyone else and their feelings. It's always you at the last."

"Sorry, Rob," Tripp is ashamed, avoiding eye contact. "But I haven't put myself last. On the contrary, the truth is that this is my second chance. Perhaps it is my *only chance*. I can erase the bad from my life this time. Everything I'm doing is going to make my life *right*. The way, and I mean the only way to do that, is to put the people I love first. I won't let you down. Just let me know if you need a break from Scott."

"Sure thing. But, if he keeps being a good tool monkey, he can have your old job," Robbie teases.

Tripp joins the laughter and smiles, "Good point, Rob. I prefer being the assistant mechanic anyway!"

"Now that is ambitious, Tripp," Robbie jokes. "But, I believe in you."

Tripp smiles, speechless at his friend's compliment. Robbie raises the volume, but the music can't drown out their laughter. The boys sing along to the rock song as the car races along. The trip takes two extra songs to make it to Robbie's house. An accident on the main road forced Mike to take the long way around.

He parks the Mustang at the bottom of the driveway. They see that Stephanie's car is here. Robbie jumps out of the car to run inside. Mike quickly grabs his friend's book bag from the trunk, they sprint to the house, and head in.

"There is my handsome man! Do you miss me yet, Tripp?" Steph teases, finishing her hug with Robbie.

"I was out collecting treasure for my queen," Tripp smiles triumphantly, holding up Robbie's bag.

"Ugh! She can have that!" Robbie grunts.

"So, what are you guys doing tonight?" Stephanie asks. "Mom and I are going shopping. I have an interview tomorrow, and I need a new outfit."

"Tomorrow, as in Wednesday?" Tripp is concerned and asks. "You aren't moving further away, are you?"

"Actually closer, Tripp. Bud has an offer for a job in Greensboro," Stephanie explains, playfully punching Tripp. "You'll see so much of me that you will be tired of having me around."

"Steph, he'll never tire of you," Robbie teases his friend. "Mike Carson really does love you!"

"Robbie Davis!" Tripp blasts back, looking embarrassed, then reluctantly admits. "I uh...well. You know..."

"I love you too, Tripp," Stephanie replies, ending with an innocent kiss on his cheek.

Tripp blushes. It's true; he's always had a thing for Stephanie Davis Jansen. That's not news. Robbie's sister reminds him of Lauren Becall, only prettier—a classy lady who can do anything.

Robbie playfully snatches the book bag out of his hand while grasping Tripp's arm with the other. He pulls his best friend toward the kitchen. Stephanie sits on the sofa and watches her brother and his friend. They are busy making sandwiches for dinner as she observes Tripp's behavior. It warms her heart that Mike Carson is trying to be a better person.

Robbie removes the sub rolls from the cabinet as Tripp gathers the deli ham, turkey, and roast beef from the refrigerator. Robbie then walks behind Tripp and grabs the Swiss cheese slices. He laughs because this pins Mike to the appliance's door.

"Rob!" Tripp whines, feigning being trapped.

Laughing, Robbie walks back. He begins placing the slices on the rolls. He whistles as he makes the sandwich. Tripp has his hands full. He steps back and carefully closes the fridge door with his left foot. He brings the selection of meat over to the counter, and they make their sandwiches. Robbie walks back to the fridge.

"Want a Coke, Mike?" Robbie asks as he bends down to search the shelves.

"I will stick with water, Rob. But, can you bring the mustard?" Tripp requests with a smile. "I forgot it."

"Water?" Robbie responds with a skeptical laugh. "Are you becoming a vegetarian hippie, Mike?"

"No," he said proudly, displaying the double portion of meat on his sandwich. "I'm just taking a break from soda."

"Yeah, you're a hippie..." Robbie remarks and shakes his head. "I bet Lauren converted you or something."

"That wouldn't be all that bad, would it," Tripp Carson laughs, taking a bite of the massive sandwich.

Stephanie quietly giggles at the bantering between her brother and his friend. *They are so close,* she reminds herself. The two boys gather their supplies and head to the den to eat. Mama Davis comes down the stairs and enters the room. She smiles at Stephanie and greets her eldest child with a big hug. Stephanie grabs her pocketbook as they head out the door.

The den is in the front corner of the house, to the left of the entryway. It has two doors leading into it, one from the living room and the other from the hallway that separates the den from the kitchen. Robbie situates his plate beside the recliner. He lets out a grunt as he bends down to remove his shoes. Immediately,

Tripp notices Robbie's discomfort. Placing his food on the end table beside the couch, Tripp taps Robbie on the shoulder.

"What's the matter?" Tripp asks, sincere concern in his voice.

"Meh, I think I pulled something at school," Robbie replies, rubbing the base of his back. "Doug asked me to help carry out his shop project to his pickup truck. It wasn't heavy, just big and awkward."

Tripp smiles and guides Robbie toward the floor. "If it's sore, I can give you a back rub."

"Really?" Surprised by the offer, Robbie questions, looking at Mike.

"Yeah," Tripp acknowledges, "Mark works hard, and sometimes when he's had a tough day I give him a back rub."

"Oh, well, OK," Robbie smiles and yawns as he stretches his back. "Don't have to ask me twice!"

Tripp places his hands on his hips and motions for Robbie to stretch out on the floor. He looks around the room—knowing that Mama Davis usually keeps skin lotion lying about, finally spotting a bottle. Robbie gets on his knees, pulls his shirt off, and tosses it to the side. Finally, he lies flat on his stomach. Robbie folds his arms and rests his head. Tripp straddles Robbie's upper legs and sits. He squirts out some of the lotion on Robbie's back.

"Hey!" Robbie protests loudly with a shiver. "That was cold. A little warning next time..."

"Cold? You big baby," Tripp teases as he massages Robbie's lower back muscles.

"Am not..." Rob protests but quickly gets quiet as Tripp begins.

"You do have a tight muscle here," Tripp asks, leaning forward. "Is this where it hurts?"

"Yeah, that's it," Robbie grunts. "And I'm not a baby."

"Yeah, you keep telling yourself that, Rob," Tripp teasingly said as he massages.

Stephanie enters through the front door. In a rush, she frantically searches the living room for her mother's wallet. Walking over to the kitchen, she searches the counters. "Where is it?" She walks to the hallway and enters the den from the second door. She spots her brother on the floor.

Surprised, she said, "So, you're a masseuse now, Tripp?"

Smiling, he glances up at her. Tripp laughs, "Yeah, Rob pulled a muscle helping Doug this morning."

"Oh..." Steph is taken aback by surprise. "You know Doug?"

Robbie quickly raises his head, "Yeah, Steph. Uh...We all go to school together..."

"Robbie was helping him with a project for shop class," Tripp explains, leaning into his effort to massage the muscles.

"Oh? OK," Stephanie said, suspiciously eyeing Robbie. "Yeah, I hope you feel better, Robbie."

"I'm in good hands," Robbie replies, resting his head.

"It feels like a pulled muscle. My brother gets them all the time from his job," Tripp explains as he works the deep tissue. "He shouldn't need surgery or anything..."

"Mike! Shut up, goob!" Robbie said without opening his eyes.

Stephanie smiles sarcastically, "OK, we will be a couple of hours. Mom wants to try that Italian place on Main Street afterward..."

Stephanie grabs her mother's wallet off the end table beside Tripp's sandwich and leaves.

"I take it this helps?" Tripp asks as he shifts forward.

"Hm-mmm," Robbie grunts happily in response.

Tripp diligently massages Robbie's back for about ten minutes. Only Robbie's occasional grunts disturb the silence in the room. Tripp's efforts are successful, as Robbie has relaxed to the point of almost falling asleep. Tripp feels the tense muscle relax.

"I think that did it, Rob," Tripp states.

"Thanks..." Robbie's pain has disappeared.

Tripp steadies himself with his right hand on the small of Robbie's back and climbs off. He sits on his knees beside his best friend. Robbie slowly gets up and sits in the recliner to eat his meal.

"I'm gonna wash my hands, Rob."

Tripp steps over to the laundry room. He washes the excess lotion off his hands. It takes only a minute before he walks back into the room and notices that Robbie has not put his shirt on. He doesn't think anything else about it.

Robbie returns their empty plates to the kitchen. As he turns to leave, Tripp notices the white band of his underwear peeking out above his waist, a detail Tripp can't help but see since Robbie has always been thin and his pants hang loosely on his frame. Moments later, Robbie reappears with two buckets of popcorn, and Tripp changes the channel so they can watch the movie, a premier on ABC.

The movie stars Preston Harris, one of Tripp's favorite actors. It is a made-for-TV movie, a film that Mike Carson didn't remember seeing before. That actor appears on many old Twilight Zone and Outer Limits shows.

Oddly, the storyline seems all too familiar to Michael Willis Carson. The story's hero had found this magic lantern that would show the owner the past. A story reminiscent of the Charles Dicken's lecture, changing who you are. The main character was busy trying to fix the problems of his youth using the time-traveling lamp. A second change.

"Mike," Robbie said during a commercial. "I'm proud of you."

"For what?" While focusing on the television, Tripp asks while crunching on some popcorn.

"You let everything go for the night," Robbie explains. "I respect what you are doing. But you don't need to go to *everyone*;

you're a great guy. I know you're set on making apologies to so many people, but you were able just to be you for a while."

"I didn't want to let you down, Rob," Tripp stops eating the popcorn. "Fixing the past is important to me, but being your friend is the most *important* thing. I like just spending time with you, old friend..."

Robbie's eyes sparkle as he laughs, "Old friend, Mike, you're so stupid..."

"Guilty," Tripp answers, raising his hand.

"How are you liking this movie? I think it is one of his best." Robbie comments while eating a handful of the popcorn.

"It is a compelling story," Tripp answers, holding a thumbs up. "But it isn't his best."

"It's okay if you're wrong, goob! So, what would you do if you found a magic lantern like that?" Robbie asks, sitting up.

"Me?" Tripp teases with a smile.

"I don't see any other dorks in here," Robbie jokes, tossing a pillow at his friend.

Tripp watches the pillow miss the sofa, "I would find my best friend and tell him how important he is. Then, I would change who I was and be a better person. Then maybe I would ask everyone to forgive me..."

"Wait!" Eyes growing wide, Robbie laughs hard, "Is this where you got your idea?"

"This is a premier." Tripp smirks with a shrug, "Never seen this movie before, Rob."

"Likely story!" Robbie taunts.

Tripp turns to his friend, "So what? Even if I did, and this is where I got my idea from, it is the right thing to do. But that isn't what happened. My nightmare made me realize what I was doing with my life would end in misery and loneliness. But I am changing because of you."

"You've said that before." Robbie smiles with a nod of approval. "What you're doing takes courage."

"Maybe, but one bad lifetime is enough." Tripp shrugs. "Besides, there is no similarity. My future self was an asshole, unlike the character played by Preston Harris."

"Mike Carson is not an asshole!" Robbie protests, tossing a pillow and not missing.

Tripp smiles, gathering up the loose popcorn kernels. Determined, Robbie tosses another pillow at Tripp, and they both laugh. Tripp throws one back but Robbie is too fast.

They watch the show. The movie concludes with the character just dreaming about what had happened. Tripp Carson dismisses that is a possibility for him. *Fate is not cruel,* but he knows he lives on borrowed time.

It is getting late, and Tripp has to go home. He and Robbie put away the popcorn buckets. Robbie follows Tripp downstairs and out to his car. Tripp digs his keys out of his pocket. The night air is cool, and Robbie realizes he is not wearing a shirt. He tightly folds his arms to keep warm.

"Good night, Mike," Robbie said softly, glancing at the star-filled night sky.

"Hmm..." Tripp makes a sound and teases his friend. "You smell good..."

Robbie laughs, punching Tripp in the arm, "That's my mom's flowery skin lotion, goob!"

"Yeah," Tripp nods. "It does smell nice though..."

"Talk about being a hippie," Robbie rolls his eyes. "That's the only thing it could be! Hippie, now you love flowers?"

"I was just teasin' you, Rob," Tripp defends himself.

"I know, hippie. So, what time will you and Scott be here tomorrow?" Robbie asks as he shivers. "I need to ride home with Doug. He wants to ask me something."

"OK, fine. You just leave me to cater to the princess alone," Tripp scoffs playfully. "That will cost you big time."

"Funny, but she was your princess first!" Robbie points out. "But, if it helps,I will ask Mom to make pizza again."

Tripp Carson smiles big, "Deal! I will grab Scott after school and be here by four?"

"Four-thirty, just to be safe."

Tripp smiles. "Good night, Rob."

Robbie nods and heads back inside. Tripp watches his friend leave. Taking a deep breath, he thinks about the movie they watched tonight. It bothers him; he is trying to remember if he has ever seen it before. Tripp thought he knew all of the films that Preston Harris was in. He shakes his head in frustration. It is getting late, and he needs to get home. As he gets into his Mustang, Steph and Mama Davis are returning. He smiles with a big wave. Tripp is looking forward to Stephanie being around more.

True Intentions Revealed

The final bell rings. The school day for October twenty-ninth is finally over. Tripp shoulders his bag and heads for the parking lot, weaving through the crowded halls. A happy bounce to his step as he thinks of his friend.

Across the school, Robbie climbs the stairs toward the bus lanes, feeling lighter than he has in days. His mind stayed focused on Tripp. Robbie feels a strong pride in their close friendship. *Mistakes happen, we fix them and move on.*

They're good again.

They talked things out. Robbie is glad last night was just him and Tripp — the movie, the way Tripp gave him the whole night, focused only on them. It was special.

His mind drifts to the backrub, the gentle fragrance clinging to Tripp's shirt — earthy, floral. Robbie chuckles to himself. *Hippie.*

He glances over his shoulder, instinctively checking for Tripp.

Robbie smiles as he spots him — a flash of red shirt cutting across the crowd, headed for the grassy hill. But something else catches Robbie's eye. His shoulders tense.

Holly.

Floating through the crowd like she owns it, curls bouncing, books hugged to her chest. Robbie stops in his tracks.

Is she looking for Mike? Robbie wonders, stomach tightening. He shakes his head. "No, no, no, no..." He whispers.

Feeling empty, helpless and stepping onto the bottom step of the bus. One last look at his best friend and Robbie disappears through the doors.

At the top of the hill, Tripp breathes easier. This morning's conversation with Robbie helped — a lot. But the storm inside him hasn't passed.

Not by a long shot.

A voice cuts through his concentration.

"Mike? Hey, Mike Carson?"

He turns —and there's Holly, smiling shyly, shifting her books against her chest. SHe lights up as she approaches Tripp.

"Holly? Hey," Tripp says, surprised. "I don't think I've ever seen you after school before."

Holly shrugs, curls bouncing.

"My mom's picking me up. I'm trying to get a job at Wilson's Family Restaurant," she says. "Gotta save up for a prom dress."

She laughs nervously, giving him a look he recognizes — the hopeful kind. Not the same girl he remembered from the date at the movies.

Tripp smiles politely.

"Well, I'm sure you'll get it. They'll be lucky to have you."

Holly's eyes brighten at the compliment.

"So... I hear you aren't Mike anymore?" she asks, stepping closer.

"Well... yes and no," Tripp says, chuckling. "I felt like I needed to change — be a better person. Asked people to call me Tripp. You know, like 'triple' — third generation."

Holly nods slowly. "But you'll always be Mike to me," she says, brushing imaginary lint off his shoulder.

Tripp laughs lightly. "Sure thing, Holly."

She moves closer, her voice dropping. "I've noticed your changes... not just the weight loss. You're different in class too. I'm proud of you."

"Thanks, Holly," Tripp says, a little distracted by the wildflower scent of her lip balm.

Holly hesitates, fiddling with the edge of her book.

"Mike... are you still mad at me? About what I said after the movie?"

Tripp shakes his head. "No. I kinda was back then, but... I get it now. I was a jerk. You were right to be concerned."

Relief floods Holly's face. *So glad I talked to Mike instead of using a letter like like Blair suggested.* Holly gently touches him on the arm.

"You weren't a jerk, Mike," she says quickly. Her hand lingers.

"I was selfish, but I'm glad you're not mad."

She smiles, big and hopeful. "So... you're not dating anyone?"

Tripp shrugs. "No. There's someone I like, but... it's complicated."

"Oh," Holly says, visibly deflating. "You gonna ask her out?"

Enjoying the flirts, Tripp flashes a grin. "Lauren's been pushing me to ask you out again."

Holly's cheeks flush pink. Her hearts races.

"I'd like that," she says shyly. "I always thought there was more to you... I was just scared to find out."

"There's not much to know," Tripp says honestly. "I'm just trying to do better. Be better."

Holly nods as she steps even closer. The wind a mix of the wildflower scent and her shampoo, clouding Tripp's mind.

"Can I call you sometime? I miss talking to you. You're the only guy I dated who really listened."

Tripp fights to keep his mind from wandering again — distracted by the smell of her lip balm, the closeness.

"Sure, Holly," he says warmly.

"Anytime. But I gotta run."

She leans in, hugging him lightly.

"Thanks, Mike," she says, her voice a soft hum against his shoulder.

Across the parking lot, Robbie watches from the window of Bus 319. He doesn't know why Mike would talk to her. Robbie remembers how she broke his heart. An anger builds in his chest.

His gut twists as he sees Holly leaning in, smiling up at Tripp. *What's going on? Why didn't he tell me he was meeting her?*

Robbie turns away, biting the inside of his cheek hard enough to hurt. Doug leans over the seat.

"Hey, isn't that Holly whats-her-name from biology?"

Robbie nods stiffly. "Yeah. She and Mike used to go out. Lauren is pushing him to ask her out...Maybe they're dating again. I dunno."

He stares at his hands, frustration bubbling up.

"Oh?" Doug asks softly, a growing concern for his friend rises to the surface.

Robbie mumbles. "She has a spell on him..."

Doug chuckles. "Who? Lauren or Holly?"

"Both," Robbie shrugs, crossing his arms tightly.

Doug studies him carefully. "You don't like her very much, do you?"

"I just don't want Mike to get hurt again," Robbie says, turning to the window again. "Holly can be... shallow."

He breathes a little easier when he sees Tripp and Holly part ways, heading off in opposite directions.

Doug grins, clapping Robbie on the knee.

"I'm sure ol' sheepdog Robbie will keep him safe."

"Not the sheepdog again," Robbie groans, laughing despite himself. "I'm not *that* bad."

"No. You're worse," Doug teases, leaning back with a grin.

Robbie rolls his eyes but grins back.

"Alright, funny man," he says.

.The bus rumbles to life, coughing clouds of diesel smoke into the afternoon air. Inside, Robbie leans back against the cracked vinyl seat, arms crossed, watching Tripp retreat toward the parking lot.

Doug nudges him with an elbow.

"Seriously, Rob," Doug says, tone teasing but soft, "You're worse than a sheepdog."

Robbie cracks a grin, tension easing slightly. "Fine. Maybe I'm a little protective."

Doug laughs. "Little?"

"Yeah," Robbie smiles. "Just like you, Doug."

They bump shoulders like little kids, laughing at the absurdity of it all. But beneath Robbie's easy smile, a knot still twists in his chest.

He hates feeling like this — uncertain, jealous, powerless. He just wants Mike — *Tripp* — to be happy. That's all he's ever wanted.

Doug leans closer, more serious now. "You wanna talk about it?"

Robbie shrugs. "I just..."

He pauses, trying to find the right words. "I guess I'm scared. Mike's changing so fast. I don't wanna lose him."

Doug listens carefully, nodding.

"You won't," he says simply. "You two are solid. Even blind people can see that."

Robbie chuckles weakly.

They sit there for a minute, letting the noise of the other students fade into the background.

Then Robbie shifts in his seat, facing Doug fully.

"Anyway... what did you want to talk about?"

Doug's grin softens.

"You," he says.

"Me?" Robbie raises an eyebrow.

"Yeah," Doug says simply. "I wanna make sure you're okay. Because you always worry about everyone else first."

Robbie blinks, caught off guard by the sincerity.

"I'm okay," he says automatically.

Doug shakes his head. "Don't lie to your sheepdog."

Robbie snorts, covering his laugh with a hand.

"Alright, alright. Maybe I'm not totally okay."

Doug claps him on the shoulder.

"Good. Honesty's step one."

They both smile, the tension easing, the friendship anchoring them both.

Outside, the bus jolts into motion, carrying them toward another night of thinking too much, feeling too much, and trying — somehow — to make it all right.

What Lies Beneath

Today is Thursday. After school, Robbie rode the bus with his friend for the second time this week. Later this evening, Robbie and his mother will be doing something for Carlos.

Greg picked up Lauren sometime during the day. Tripp hopes she won't get in trouble for leaving the school grounds. Tripp wanders into the living room. It is just him in the house this afternoon.

Tripp worries about his cousins. Scott and his sister are with their father for the week again. Tripp's happy to help his cousin—doing things together with Scott and more importantly helping the young boy deal with his emotions. Scott channels his anger better, but something remains just under the surface, and Tripp can sense it. He reaches for the phone and dials the number for Henry Graves. As the line rings, Tripp gets comfortable on the sofa.

"Hello?" A girl's voice snaps quickly. It's his older cousin.

"Oh, hi, Regina. This is Michael. Can I speak with Scott?" Tripp asks politely.

"Fine...whatever..." She responds by dropping the receiver on the table and walking away. After 20 seconds of silence, Tripp can hear running footsteps in the background.

"Michael!" Scott yells into the phone, holding back his giggles. "Man, you really ticked off Regina. She's all huffy now, waiting for some dude to ring her up!"

"Hey, Scott, well, that isn't why I called, but glad it makes you happy," Tripp jokes. "I just wanted to check on you. How's my bestest bud holding up?"

"I'm the bestest now!" Scott exclaims. "Hey, it's super cool to hear from you. My dad's been on my case big time, but let's not go there."

Tripp smiles. His heart swells with pride in hearing Scott avoid letting Henry Graves dictate his mood. Tripp laughs. A warm sound.

Scott stops, hearing Tripp's laugh and sensing the pride through the phone. "So, did you find any cool new tunes to jam on? I'm ready to teach you some new stuff, grasshopper."

"Grasshopper?" Tripp laughs, "Yeah, been thinking about it, something easy. It's a Fleetwood Mac song."

"I bet I can guess which one, Michael," Scott can't contain his excitement. "But dude, it's not as simple as it seems. You gotta come over every day to practice. Hear me, every day? Oh, and bring Robbie along!"

"Ok..." Tripp regrets the suggestion but laughs warmly. "Once you teach me, then we can bring in an audience."

"Robbie's special...he isn't an audience," Scott questions.

"You are right about that. I just want it to be perfect when I play for him," Tripp responds with a smile as he thinks about Robbie.

"I think I understand." Scott replies.

"I promise we will do it together. I just called to make sure you are okay. Your last visit was rough..."

Scott gets quiet and speaks softly, "Yeah, it was pretty rough. I was by myself; Regina just stayed at home with her big butt. But that was before you and I became tight, Tripp. Now, it's like you're right here with me."

"That's good, Scott. Don't forget that, bestest!"

"Thanks, Tripp. Because of you, I'm not alone, anymore. Hold on..." Scott says, covering the phone as someone talks in the background.

Scott finishes. "Dang it, Regina says it's time to eat. *He's* making asparagus." Scott makes a gagging sound.

"You'll survive, bestest! I'm going to do some chores." Tripp smiles, realizing that Scott called him Tripp. He feels like he's doing a good thing for his cousin. "Listen, call me if you need to talk."

"Chores? Yuck! You sound like an old man, Michael," Scott laughs.

"Well, I am almost sixty..." Tripp jokes. "Seriously, Scott. I made you a promise. *Call me*; I'm here for you."

"I know you are, Michael. I know..." Scott replies with seriousness, then begins to laugh. "Tell Robbie I says ppppfffttt!" Making a long and loud raspberry sound.

"Goodbye, Scott," Tripp tells him, shaking his head. He carefully hangs up the telephone, and a big smile appears. "Now, what do I need to do?"

It's been a while since Tripp has stayed home alone. He doesn't like the idea of solitude; his older self endured more loneliness than he could take. Scratching his head, he decides to call the store.

"Maddox Grocery," A pleasant woman answers the call. "How may I help you?"

"Evening, Ms. Livengood, this is Tripp Carson. Is Gerry around?"

"Why hello, young man. Yeah, give me a second," She replies.

After a brief silence, the receiver comes alive, "Hello Tripp. What's up?"

Tripp smiles, clearing his throat, "I was calling to see if you needed extra help tonight?"

"You do too good of a job, Tripp! Nothing left to do, ya' stocked the last truckload all by yourself, it's dead here." Gerry explains.

"OK, thank you sir..." Tripp politely responds.

"Tell ya' what, kid. I'll call you at home if I need you," Gerry adds. "Promise."

"Thanks. Good night, sir," A discouraged Tripp answers as he returns the receiver to the cradle.

Tripp Carson starts with the laundry and then the dishes. Cleaning doesn't take long since he and Mark keep up with the cleaning the house. Mike feels boredom setting in.

A thought pops into his head, considering he is all alone. Tripp decides to try his latest purchases.

"Maybe I should try on a new outfit. This is the perfect opportunity!" Tripp proclaims to the empty house.

Tripp felt a little awkward when he made the purchases, but he has always wanted this. After all, he's sixteen, getting fit, plus no one is there with him. Now is the perfect opportunity–going into his room and pulls the outfit from the bag.

"Can't believe I finally get to do this!" Tripp excitedly tells himself with anticipation.

The color purple has grown to his liking, almost a new favorite. Tripp strips down to his briefs. He grabs the white tights first. He looks in the mirror and nods, putting them on. He struggles at first, but Tripp overcomes the challenge. Rummaging in the bag, he retrieves the leotard next—a brilliant color of purple with short sleeves. Tripp guessed the size, *hopefully it fits, fortunately it strectches.* The leotard is easier to put on.

Now fully dressed, Tripp admires himself in the mirror for a moment. The tight material stretches across his young body. *This leotard is a little tight, but I like it,* Tripp thinks, noting the smile on his face. His recent weight loss is highlighted when he turns to the side and runs his hand down his abdomen. Spinning to the other side, he runs his hand down his back, stopping on his hips. Finally, looking back over his shoulder - an enormous smile grows on his face.

Tripp's very pleased with how he looks. He starts whistling one of Boston's songs.

I should take some time just for me, Tripp thinks.

Sitting on his bed, he puts on his tennis shoes. He starts a new album on the record player and gets lost in the music as he works. Tripp spends the next half hour finishing the house cleaning.

He believes he has done an excellent job so far. Tripp heads to the kitchen to get some water–taking a couple of minutes. He leans against the counter in their tiny kitchen and enjoys his beverage, getting interrupted when he hears Mark coming in the front door.

The outfit is so comfortable that he has forgotten what he is wearing.

"I hope Mark likes my surprise for him," Tripp smiles, proud of his laundry efforts. "Ironing those work shirts was no easy task."

"Hey, Tripp?" Mark yells out. "Where are you at?"

"Kitchen!" Tripp calls back.

Tripp hears Mark moving in the dining room. He smiles, guessing that Mark found the folded laundry on the table. Silence.

"Hey, did you iron my work shirts?" Mark asks loudly in a delightful way.

"Yeah, couldn't have my brother going around town all wrinkled up..." Tripp yells back, happily, amid laughter.

"I'm glad you are looking out for me," Mark responds as he leaves the dining room.

Tripp whispers. "You've always looked out for me, brother."

"That was very nice of you. If you need me, I'm going to listen to an album before I head to work."

Tripp can hear his brother going down the hallway. He looks down at the purple spandex. He likes the way it highlights his weight loss.

"It's just an outfit," Tripp reassures himself. He thinks about Mark and how important his brother is. "If I am going to be honest with Mark, I have to start somewhere..." Tripp heads to his room.

Tripp knows he can't overwhelm his brother, especially if he wants Mark's support. He slides on some sweatpants and hoodie over the colorful outfit. Tripp's heart begins to race with anxiety.

'I need you, Mark. Please don't let this be a mistake."

Tripp takes a deep breath, bracing himself. He'd thought about this moment for long time, but now that he's standing outside Mark's room, the words feel thick in his throat. It isn't just about the leotard—it is about wanting Mark to understand him, even if Tripp isn't sure he understood himself. Acceptance.

He knocks softly and waits, his pulse drumming in his ears. Mark's voice, muffled but unmistakable, calls from inside, "Come in."

Tripp steps in, fidgeting with his hands. Mark sits at his desk, headphones on with the cord snaking back to the stereo, a textbook open in front of him. He glances up, eyebrows knitting together as he takes in Tripp's expression.

"Michael, is everything ok?" Mark asks with deep concern.

"Hey," Tripp began, his voice wavering. "I, um...I wanted to show you something. But if it's weird, you can just tell me."

"Weird?" Mark slowly removes his headphones, turning in his chair. "What's going on, Tripp?" His tone is neutral, guarded.

Without another word, Tripp lifts the corner of his hoodie, revealing the sleek purple leotard underneath. He glances down, swallowing hard. "I...I like wearing this. It feels right, somehow. I thought...maybe you'd get it? That you'd get me..."

For a moment, silence fills the room. Mark's expression shifts—something flickering across his face, too quick to name.

"You'd best take that thing off," Mark says, an edge of discomfort in his voice.

"I want this." Tripp pleads.

"If Dad saw you in that, he'd—well, beat some sense into you..." Mark let the thought trail off, but Tripp can tell he's serious.

"This is important." Tripp takes a steady breath. *Here we go,* he thinks, bracing himself. "Dad's not here, Mark."

"Damn it, Michael."

Tripp folds his arms. "But you are, and you've always been here for me. I really like wearing it. It isn't some statement or whatever, it just...feels good." Pulling the hoodie off when he finishes.

Defewated, Mark clears his throat, looking away, and then forces a casual shrug. "Okay. Uh...if it makes you feel good, then...sure. Whatever, man."

"Are you mad at me?" Tripp pleads, sliding out of the sweat pants.

Shaking his head, Mark's expression hardens, his voice rising a notch. "You like dressing up like a girl? That's sissy stuff; I might have to beat your ass!" He huffs, but Tripp senses the half-heartedness in his tone.

"It is just clothes, Mark," Tripp explains, getting defensive. "You gotta see past that...see past the hate Dad taught us." He folds his arms in defense, *I wish he'd get that this isn't about looking 'girly'.*

Mark's jaw tightens, wrestling with his own thoughts, like he wants to defend their dad but can't quite bring himself to do it. "Boys aren't supposed to dress...well, like this," he mutters, gesturing toward Tripp's leotard and tights. "Or even those colors!"

Tripp grunts, rolling his eyes.

"Actually, leotards are unisex. To be perfectly honest, this was designed by a man ," Tripp replies, lifting his chin slightly. "And purple is traditionally the color of royalty; did you know that?"

"Michael Carson, have you lost your mind?" Mark shakes his head in disbelief, slamming the textbook closed. Mark grumbles, but his eyes soften a little, his expression less guarded.

"It was Jules Léotard, a Frenchman in the 1800s—a trapeze artist, I think..." Tripp recalls, scratching his chin. "He wore them to show off his manliness..."

"Bull shit," Mark laughs, not believing the conversation is even happening. His eyes trying to avoid looking at his brother's outfit.

"I'll never lie to you, Mark." Tripp whispers in shame.

With a heavy sigh, Mark releazes that this was important. "What brought this on, Tripp?"

Tripp smiles. "Your opinion matters to me."

"I guess you're old enough to know the risks. I support you, Tripp." He loves his little brother. "I don't want you to feel like you can't talk to me. You, me and Mom against the world."

Mark stares blankly at the text book. His gaze returns to Tripp. *How long has he been doing this?* Mark wonders. Confidence slowly returns to Tripp's demeanor, Mark can see it in his brother's eyes.

Tripp tries to read Mark's reaction, searching for some sign of understanding. "You really think it's okay?"

Mark hesitates, running a hand over his jaw. "I mean, I don't get it, Tripp. But I guess it's your thing, not mine."

A beat of silence hangs between them, heavier than Tripp expected. He forces a smile, though he could feel his shoulders tense. "Yeah, I guess. Thanks for...not making it a big deal."

Mark nods, shifting in his chair. "Just...maybe keep it low-key around other people, alright?"

Tripp's heart sinks a little, but he nods. "Yeah. Low-key." He tries to keep his voice light, but the words feel thin. The confidence retreats, a dark cloud hangs over him now.

As he turned to leave, he senses Mark's eyes on him, not unkind but distant, like he's studying something he didn't quite know how to handle. Tripp walks out, his chest tight, feeling the weight of that unspoken distance between them.

Tripp drops on the hoodie as he walks to the living room. The pangs of regret fill his mind. "I should have waited."

Tripp sighs as he tosses the sweatpants by the doorway, his leotard and tights on full display. He flops on the end of the couch, eyeing the telephone. He contemplates calling Lauren, believing she would be more understanding. Tripp's thoughts are interrupted by Mark clearing his throat. The older brother stands in the hall doorway with his arms folded.

"I know that took courage, Tripp," Mark says calmly. "Tell me one thing. You aren't going to school like that?

"No, Mark. I don't plan on wearing this outside of the house." Tripp answers, standing up. "I'm not an idiot,"

"OK, brother..." Mark relents.

Tripp sees and opening, the confidence races back. He knew his brother couldn't stay mad at him. With a playful grin and patting his bottom, Tripp teases his brother. "I think it makes my butt look good."

Tripp twists his body around to show off his rear end. Tripp giggles at Mark's reaction. Accepting the ridiculousness of the situation, Mark sighs, reluctantly laughing.

"No one cares what a guy's butt looks like..." Mark responds while leaning on the door frame.

"Meh, maybe. Holly liked to grab it when we kissed. I mean when we were kissing while standing up," Tripp blushes.

"At least you are talking about a girl," Mark jokes. "Wait, she *is* a she?"

They both laugh.

"Yes, dufus. You've met Holly," Tripp counters. "I'm also talking to Rose, the hippie girl at the Record Changer."

"Her?"

"She thinks I'm adorable."

"She's hot! Damn Mike, she's my age..." Mark suddenly acts proud. Mark laughs, pointing at his younger brother. "Look at you in all your *manliness!*"

"Mark..." Tripp becomes serious for a moment. "Does it upset you this much? I mean, I like wearing it, really, I do. But I do not want you to think badly of me."

"Your choice, baby brother. I think you've earned the right to make your own decisions," Mark nods to his brother. "Tripp, if you like it and know the risks of being seen in it, I don't see the harm."

"Thanks, mark."

"You kinda look cute..."

"Really?" Tripp hopefully smiles.

"No, dumbass," Mark snaps back, looking frustrated. "I was being sarcastic..."

They laugh. Tripp runs over to his brother, wrapping him up in a big hug. It means a lot to Tripp that his brother accepts him. It will take a long time for Mark to understand Tripp's bisexuality. But he has hope that his brother will always love him—*one day at a time.*

"Uh, OK...Mike..." Mark nervously squirms from the embrace. "Baby brother...let go! Mike...this is weird..."

"What about my butt?" Tripp laughs, ramping up his teasing. "On a scale of one to ten?"

"I'm late for work," Mark yells, ignoring his brother andraises his hands in defeat. Then he dashes out of the room. "I love you, Tripp!"

Tripp switches on the TV and finds reruns of an old cop show. He stretches out on the floor, moving to lie on his stomach. His lower legs point up in the air, and he slowly rocks them back and forth. Tripp folds his arms and rests his chin on his hands. It feels good just to watch TV.

The half-hour show is minutes from ending when Mark comes down the hallway, dressed for work. Tripp leans onto his left side, his right arm resting on his side as he looks at Mark. His brother smiles, and Tripp stretches out on his stomach to finish his show.

"You look very professional in those ironed shirts," Tripp remarks, smiling proudly at the results of his work.

"I do, thanks, Tripp," Mark answers softly.

Tripp softens his tone, "Anything for you, Mark; see you tonight?"

"Probably not. Working late," Mark waves, heading out the door.

"Good night, Mark," Mike replies as his brother leaves.

Conversations With Destiny

Tripp turns his attention to the TV; a sitcom about an astronaut, a rerun he'd loved as a kid. He lays on his back, staring up at the ceiling, lost in thought. *What was it about that almost-kiss?* His mind wanders back to that moment, wondering if Geoff might be home today.

"Bad idea, Mike. Stay focused," he mutters, trying to shake himself out of it. But he finds himself glancing down at the purple leotard hugging his body, wondering what Geoff would think.

He isn't ashamed to feel attractive—maybe it's vanity, but it feels nice to know someone finds him appealing.

"What could it hurt?" he asks himself, sitting up and reaching for the phone. "It's just a phone call...nothing can happen."

Inhaling a deep breath, Tripp dials the number Geoff gave him that first night. Rolling onto his back, he pulls his knees up, one hand resting on his stomach as the other holds the receiver to his ear. His heart races as the line rings.

"Hello," a deep, unfamiliar voice answers, with a hint of an accent.

"Uh, oh—sorry, I hope I didn't call the wrong number," Tripp stammers. "Is Geoffrey there?"

"Yeah, hold on." The man's voice is casual, and he calls out, "Hey, Geoff. Phone!"

Tripp's breath caught, unsure if it was from a flicker of excitement or a twinge of nerves. He had to admit, the attention felt good—especially coming from someone like Geoff with his rugged good looks.

Geoffrey's deep voice comes through. "Hello?"

"Uh...Hi, Geoff...it's, uh..." Tripp hesitates, feeling his face warm.

"I'd recognize that cute voice anywhere! I'm so glad you called, Tripp." Geoff's tone softens, his smooth charm coming through.

"Yeah. I was just...thinking about you—is that okay?" Tripp asks, feeling both nervous and thrilled.

"Okay? Hell yeah, it's OK, Tripp. I think about your beautiful smile all the time."

"Stop it!" Tripp giggles, pulling on the phone cord, his voice barely hiding his excitement. "Were you really? That makes me feel good. Actually...don't stop."

"Then I won't stop," Geoff replies, his voice warm. "I take it you're warming up to me? That's okay, you know. It doesn't make you...weird."

Tripp's face flushes, glancing down at his outfit. "Maybe I'd just like to hear you flirt."

"Now, you wouldn't be teasing me, would you?" Geoff's voice grows serious, though there is a flirtatiousness in his tone.

Tripp freezes. "I...I'm not sure what I want, Geoff. I mean, you don't know me—"

"I realize that, which is why we're talking." Geoff's tone is soft but certain.

"What if...you don't like what you discover?" Tripp whispers, his voice barely audible.

"Tripp, don't worry about that," Geoff said reassuringly. "I like you. I keep thinking about the other night. I wanted to kiss you so bad."

Tripp's heart pounds deep in his chest. "I know. Honestly, I've thought about that, too...about you kissing me. It would've been okay if you had."

"Just a kiss?" Geoff's voice holds a hint of something more.

"Well...you did have your hands on my butt," Tripp said with a shy smile, his heart racing.

"For a straight guy, you sure know how to tempt me," Geoff laughs softly. "I think you're beautiful, Tripp. I think you're incredible...and sexy. Does it bother you that I'm older?"

Tripp hesitates, then gave a small smile. "Not really...my ex-wife was older."

Geoff laughs hard. "Tripp, that sense of humor of yours—it's wicked! You know, even if you're teasing me, I still want to be with you."

Tripp imagines Geoff's arms around him, the brush of a kiss. "Uh, Geoff...just curious, how old are you?" he asks, twisting the phone cord, trying to sound casual but feeling every bit of the butterflies in his stomach.

"I'm 24, Tripp. And you are, what, 17...18?" Geoffrey answers. "You know, age is just numbers that don't really matter if two people like each other..."

Seventeen or eighteen? I must look older than sixteen. Maybe it is because of how I act? He might freak out if he knows I'm barely sixteen, though technically, I am fifty-eight... Tripp decides to avoid the answer altogether. He pushes the image of the kiss from his mind.

"Can we just...get to know each other?" Tripp asks, his voice a little uncertain. "I'm kinda new to all this."

"Sure," Geoffrey replies, his tone softening. Then, in a whisper, "What are you wearing?"

Tripp feels his cheeks flush, suddenly a bit self-conscious. "Well..."

Geoff laughs, teasing gently. "Come on, that should be an easy one. Wait...are you wearing anything at all?"

"Of course I have clothes on, Geoff!" Tripp balks, feeling both embarrassed and amused. "It's just...well..." His mind wanders, almost imagining himself completely vulnerable in front of Geoff.

Geoffrey chuckles, clearly enjoying the playful tone. "Don't be shy, Tripp. Just a minute ago, you said you wished we'd kissed."

"I did say that," Tripp admits with adamant certainty, his heart picking up speed. "And I...guess I wouldn't mind, you know, someday. Just don't laugh..."

"Laugh?" Geoff's voice is smooth and encouraging. "I'd never laugh at you, Tripp. I like you a lot, you know. Best tell me. You better hurry up before my imagination runs away with me."

Tripp smiles, feeling encouraged by Geoffrey's advances. "You like me, or just my, uh...soft lips and firm butt?"

Geoff laughs, his voice warm. "Can't it be both? That's how it is for adults—we're drawn to who a person is *and* what they look like. And with you, I can see both. I mean, your cousin practically worships you! I knew then you were someone special, someone I could really like. That's why I wanted to kiss you."

"I believe you, Geoff," Tripp said softly, biting his lip. "Well...purple."

"Purple?" Geoff echoes, sounding intrigued. "The color of royalty, huh? Okay, purple *what*?"

Tripp closes his eyes, his face heating up. "Purple leotard. With...uh, white tights. I like just wearing it around the house."

"A leotard?" Geoff's voice perks up, clearly intrigued. "I wouldn't have guessed that, but I bet it's a great look on you."

"It's a little, leaves nothing to your imagination." Tripp whispers playfully.

"I'd love to see it." Geoff enthusiastically answers. "I bet that ass of yours is hot as hell in that get-up."

Tripp stifles a laugh, a mix of nerves and playfulness. "Actually, it's not hot at all—spandex breathes pretty well."

Geoffrey laughs heartily. "You with that wicked sense of humor! Next time you pull that on me, I'm going to kiss you so hard—and yes, with tongue!"

Tripp feigns surprise, eyes widening. "Wait, your tongue? Why on earth would you do that?"

"I ...uh..." Geoffrey stutters, caught off guard. "Uh, Tripp. It's just a style of passionate kissing, nothing sinister."

Tripp laughs heartily. Geoffrey scoffs, realizing that he was tricked.

Geoff asks over the laughter. "How much experience have you had? if I can ask."

"I know how to French kiss!" Amid a few remaining giggles. "But not many experiences; I used to date a girl, we made out a lot," Tripp decides to toy with Geoff. "I did get my hand in her shirt. And I...I..."

"You, what?"

"I stimulated a certain region of hers with my fingers," Tripp smiles big.

"Nice, that's all?"

"It was at the moment."

"So, are you a virgin?" Geoffrey asks, his voice ringing with satisfaction.

"I guess," Tripp is having fun toying with him. "Does that make it different?"

"So, no one has ever touched you?" Geoffrey speaking delicately. "You know..."

"Know what?"

Tripp's heart runs wild, he thinks, *This is getting out of hand, Mike. Stop!*

"Uh, how can I ask this delicately?" Geoff ponders aloud.

"You asking if she ever played with my penis?" Tripp knows he needs to stop, but he feels the rush of excitement by the conversation. He wants to see where Geoff will go with the conversation.

Smiling, Geoffrey answers firmly, "Yes, I am, Tripp."

"She never did..." Tripp answers quietly. He smiles bashfully, not realizing his body's reactions.

"I'm not judging you. You are a gentleman." Geoff compliments.

"Thanks, Geoffrey." Tripp admits warmly. "It's good to know I have your respect."

"I can tell you know what you want. I need to ask one more thing," Geoffrey is probing for answers.

"According to my friend, I'm an open book," Tripp playfully answers. "What do you want to know, Geoff?"

"I haven't made it a secret. I want to...uh..." Geoffrey avoids making it about sex. "...make love to you, that includes touching your penis,"

There is a moment of silence. Tripp is deciding what to say, but the images in his mind cloud his judgment.

Geoffrey deserves an honest answer. Ideas are racing in Tripp's mind. Geoff needs an answer—well, as much as Tripp wants to share.

He looks down, seeing the results of this conversation upon him. *This is wrong, Mike!*

"I've had someone touch me there. It was a few years back," Tripp cautiously said. "He thought I was asleep, but I enjoyed it. He was a friend."

"Was? I'm sorry for that, Michael. I would never do that," Geoffrey voice sounds compassionate. "Maybe it's better that your first time will be with me. I'm older and have experience. I can help you do it the right way."

"And not rush you," Geoff adds after a brief pause.

"That means a lot, Geoff. I'm not saying that is what I want, but can we just keep talking for now?" Tripp is short of breath; he knows he must stop.

Gritting his teeth, Tripp closes his eyes tight. He rests his free hand on the floor beside him.

Geoffrey whispers intimately, "Tripp, I would treat you right. This isn't about a single hook-up. Yes, I want to be with you. But only if you're willing. I want to show you pleasure like you could never imagine. I'm not boasting. You will not regret *submitting* to me."

Tripp notes the word 'submitting' and guesses that it means Geoff wants complete control.

Tripp Carson is sure that Geoff has an ulterior motive. *But what?* He asks himself. *It could be as simple as popping someone's cherry or a long-term thing.* Regardless, Geoff is trying very hard to get into his pants. Tripp doesn't want to be a notch on this guy's belt.

Tripp knows that this conversation has gone on too long. He does like the attention, though.

"I...uh..." Tripp hesitates.

"I'm sorry, Michael. Did I come on too strong?"

"Just a little bit, Geoff. I do like you..." Tripp can hear the neighbor's car pull up outside.

"Hey, Geoff, I hate to cut this short, but I think my momma is home. I need to run. OK?"

It is a white lie, but Tripp has to stop.

"Yeah, no problem, Tripp," Geoff is irritated that the call is over. "Just promise I get to see you in that purple leotard."

"Maybe one time for show-and-tell only?" Tripp asks. "Can you live with that?"

"I respect your desires. You remember my address, right?" Geoffrey is careful to choose the right words. "My door is always open. Even, if you just want to talk..."

"One forty Madison Grove Place," Tripp answers. "I know your number by heart as well.

"That is a good sign, Michael. Good night, handsome."

Between Friends and Obligations

T he Mustang is almost empty. Tripp stops at the Exxon station. A friend of Greg's is a mechanic there.

Robbie and Lauren stand by the Mustang, waiting for Tripp. The morning air is cool, and Lauren wraps herself in her sweater and jacket, glancing over at Robbie, who stands unfazed in just a T-shirt. He's been unusually quiet, and Lauren's curiosity is piqued.

She clears her throat, debating whether to ask, but ultimately decides that good friends don't shy away from these moments.

"Hey, Robbie, you've been pretty quiet," she says gently. "Not to pry, but is everything alright?"

Robbie hesitates, a nervous edge in his voice. "Uh, yes and no. One of my other friends really needs my help. His church youth group has a project to clean up an area of the park."

Lauren raises her eyebrows, impressed. "Wow, that sounds like a great cause. So, what's the problem?"

"Sadly, most of the other volunteers backed out at the last minute," Robbie admits, sounding defeated.

"I'm not sure I follow you, Robbie," Lauren adds.

"Doug asked if I could help tomorrow," Robbie quietly continues, looking down. "But Mike and I had plans to go driving up the mountain, and I feel torn. Doug's in a bind, but I know Mike was really looking forward to our day."

"And you don't want to let either of them down," Lauren observes, nodding. "But let me ask you this: What would old Mike have done?"

Robbie sighs, rubbing the back of his neck. "The old Mike would've probably been annoyed and guilted me a little. But yeah, we'd have rescheduled eventually."

Lauren gives him a knowing look. "And don't you think that Tripp will do the same?"

"No..." Robbie gives a faint smile, pointing a finger as if he's making a point. "Not only will Tripp be okay with it, he'll probably end up coming along to help Doug, too. I just... I don't want to feel like I'm taking advantage of Mike's kindness. He doesn't even know Doug all that well."

"Robbie," Lauren says earnestly, "Tripp would do anything for you. Helping you, even if it means scrapping your plans, is exactly the kind of thing he wants. He doesn't see it as 'helping Doug.' He'll be there for you."

Robbie lets out a deep breath, trying to smile. "Yeah, I know. I just still feel a little bad about it."

"Robbie Davis," Lauren says firmly, giving him a reassuring pat on the arm, "you're more important to him than any plans."

"Maybe so," Robbie murmurs, still uncertain. "But don't mention it to him yet, okay? I don't want him to feel like I'm throwing a wrench into things. He's really excited about that mountain trip."

"No promises, Robbie," Lauren says with a grin as she spots Tripp approaching.

"Hey, sorry, guys," Tripp calls out as he begins pumping the gas.

"No problem, Mike," Robbie says, attempting a casual tone. "Will we still have time to change into our costumes at school?"

Tripp nods. Robbie's distracted mood this morning has not gone unnoticed. Robbie's mind is clearly elsewhere in class, and while Tripp had wanted to ask about it, something made him wait. He plans to try tonight before dinner.

Robbie reaches for the seatback latch but stops when he sees Lauren has already settled in the back seat. She glances up with a grin and nods to the front passenger seat, giving him a playful nod. Robbie grins widely and jogs around to the other side of the car, clearly touched. Tripp raises an eyebrow, glancing at Lauren in the back window with a mock look of disbelief.

"Uh, Lauren..." Tripp begins, a bit puzzled. "That's the back seat."

"I know, Tripp," Lauren teases, tossing her hair over her shoulder. "I'll just think of it as a royal gesture—you treating me like royalty."

"Well then, Your Majesty," Tripp laughs, offering an exaggerated bow before sliding into the driver's seat.

"Oh, stop it, you dorky peasant!" Lauren responds in a faux regal accent, adding, "To the parkway, driver!"

Tripp chuckles as he starts the engine, and Robbie settles comfortably into the front seat. He appreciates Lauren's gesture more than she realizes, knowing it was her way of giving him some time with Tripp without making a big deal of it.

As they head down the back street toward the parkway, the breeze begins to tousle everyone's hair. Robbie glances back, ready to offer to close the window, but he catches Lauren tying her hair back into a ponytail.

"Well, Princess, I was going to offer to roll up the windows, but I see you're already prepared," Robbie jokes, grinning.

"It's a nice day, Robbie," Lauren says with a big smile. "Let's enjoy the ride." She smirks at Tripp and raises an eyebrow. "Say, dork—this is all your car's got?"

"Madam, you doubt the Mustang?" Tripp retorts with a mock insulted look. He shifts down a gear.

"Hell yeah, Mike!" Robbie whoops, leaning partly out the window as Tripp steps on the gas.

The Mustang roars down the road, and for a moment, Tripp feels a rare sense of freedom. Something as simple as this—sharing a joyride with his friends—fills him with a gratitude he's learning to savor.

The growl of the engine mixes with the laughter and wind, creating a perfect moment. Lauren, sitting back and watching the boys enjoy themselves, feels a sense of happiness seeing them like this.

Though, she knows that Robbie still hasn't addressed what's weighing on him, and she glances over with a subtle sigh. It looks like she'll need to give him a nudge.

At the next light, she seizes the pause. "Hey, Robbie," Lauren says slyly, leaning forward, "didn't you have something you wanted to talk to Tripp about?"

"Well, I... uh," Robbie stammers, glancing nervously at Tripp.

"What's up?" Tripp asks, turning toward Robbie. "You've been too quiet. I wanted to ask."

Robbie swallows, hesitating. "I know you were looking forward to heading up to the mountains tomorrow..." he trails off, almost a whisper.

Tripp tilts his head, noticing the uncertainty in Robbie's voice. "Yeah, I am! Yet it sounds like there's a 'but' in there. Did something come up?"

Robbie struggles to find the words, his gaze dropping to his hands. Seeing her friend floundering, Lauren can't resist stepping in. She wants to respect Robbie's privacy, but she knows he could use a little help getting it out.

"It's about Doug," Lauren offers, glancing away as if not to put Robbie on the spot.

"Doug?" Tripp asks, immediately concerned. "Is he okay?"

Robbie nods slowly, still looking down. "Yeah, it's just... well, you know he's doing that project with his church group?"

"Yeah, you mentioned it," Tripp replies, smiling. "It's great they're pitching in to help out. Pretty cool, right? Cool is still a word, yeah?"

Lauren lets out a laugh. Tripp always has a way of misusing slang that amuses her.

Robbie, however, only manages a small smile, clearly uneasy. He's worried about how Tripp might react. If what he told Lauren is true, the *"new Mike"* is bound to insist on helping, and Robbie can't shake the guilt.

"Well, most of the volunteers backed out," Robbie finally admits. "Doug asked me to help. Sorry, Mike." He looks down, ashamed.

"Don't be, Robbie," Tripp replies, patting him on the back. "Doug's your friend, and I'd be happy to help both of you."

"You're not mad?" Robbie asks, his voice tentative.

Tripp shakes his head. "Best friends don't do that, Rob. The mountains will always be there."

"Ugh, seriously?" Lauren sighs dramatically. "Is it always this hard for you two to communicate?"

Tripp glances up at the rearview mirror and catches her playful smile.

Lauren huffs. "If I were either of you, I'd go nuts."

He and Robbie burst into laughter. Lauren's glad she isn't part of the Boys' Club.

Tripp Carson revs up the motor. Robbie smiles, nodding back at her to say thank you. Lauren leans back, relieved that the tension has eased, but she's not quite finished.

"Tripp, Robbie was worried he'd been taking advantage of you," Lauren says, nudging Robbie. "He was really upset."

"She's right, Mike," Robbie confesses, his voice heavy with remorse. "I felt guilty... still do, honestly."

"Rob," Tripp says softly, taking a moment to gather his thoughts. "Your friend needs your help. You're my friend, and you need my help. It's that simple. I'm sorry if I ever made you think I wouldn't understand."

"I knew you would understand, Mike. Even the *old Mike* would understand," Robbie tries to make his point. "It feels like I was taking advantage of your new kindness. I was just trying to be worthy of being your friend.'

"Best friend, Robert Davis ..." Tripp smiles with pride. "We are best friends. I will always be here for you..."

Lauren feels proud of herself. She wants to hug them both. She begins to laugh. She imagines that this must be what having brothers is like. Daisy is always talking about her younger brothers. It is tiring but has its rewards. She sits back in the seat. Riding in the back is better than she was expecting. Robbie turns up the radio volume as they finish the ride to Lauren's house. For the moment, everything is right in the world.

The Mustang pulls into the unofficial Tripp parking space, Robbie opens his door, and gets out. He pulls the seat back toward the dash. Lauren hurries out of the back seat.

"Thanks, Lauren. You were right, and I don't think I could have told him without your help.," Robbie admits.

"Robbie, I love Tripp like a brother. I want to think that we have become good friends lately. Y'all may be dorks, but you are my dorks!" Lauren said, giving Robbie a friendly hug.

"We are, princess," Robbie jokes.

"Don't let that go to your head, Lauren!" Tripp yells.

Halloween 1980

E ven older teenagers get into the holiday. Pinewood High was transformed into a circus: cowboys, vampires, racecar drivers, and more. Education had taken a backseat to fun, laughter, and candy. Oliver Hammond dressed as the jolly Green Giant. Mrs. Austin came as Glinda, the Good Witch of the North. But, most of the students agreed the best teacher costume was worn by Brock Summers.

Brock made sure to give credit where credit is due. It was Tripp's idea. Mr. Summers wore his tuxedo and spoke with an uncanny imitation of Sean Connery. An international Spy, and it was a role that Brock embraced fully.

The end of the school day has arrived. The students slowly shuffle around outside. The magic of the day is still flowing strong. Holly darts around some girls dressed as football players. One of Tripp's friends, Peter, faithfully portraying Sherlock Holmes, guides her through the crowd as she looks for Tripp.

"Mike!" she calls out.

Tripp and Lauren are standing by the east wing exits. Holly, in her Ragedy Ann costume, runs over, the fake red pigtails bouncing with each step.

Lauren received a prize for the best student costume. An elegant silk dress adorned with a purple sash and a glittering tiara embodied her correctly. Holly stops, his smile grows. Tripp is wearing black plastic glasses. His white button-down shirt was pinned to remain open to expose the blue shirt beneath that had the bold S on his chest.

"Superman! Not what I expected you would wear, but it totally makes sense." Holly smiles.

"Of course, Miss Masters would appear as royalty, but her Grace should be a queen." Peter laughs.

"Nope, I'm Tripp's princess." Lauren smiles.

Everyone laughs as they admire the costumes. Robbie exits the building behind them and joins the crowd. Holly tilts her head to the side, her brow tense in deep thought.

"Is he Dick Van Dyke from Mary Poppins?" Holly asks. "A chimney sweep."

Robbie is wearing a fine Victorian-looking suit and carries a brass-framed lantern, a large clock centered inside.

Tripp is about to explain, but Peter beats him to it. "No, Holly, Robbie is the character from the new Preston Harris movie."

Tripp finishes the explanation. "The character found the lantern, and it allowed him to time-travel."

"Oh, wow! My dad watched that movie." Holly laughs.

Robbie shrugs. "Only the older teachers knew who I was, and Tripp, of course." Smiling at his friend.

"Of course, I can see everything," Tripp answers, standing in a heroic pose. "Well, except for lead."

Holly playfully says goodbye to Tripp. The trio of friends head to the waiting car, and they start the trip to Robbie's house. Robbie cannot help but smile at Tripp. Guys have a way of communicating with each other without using words. He can tell that Mike Carson knows what he means. Tripp doesn't say much, but Robbie can feel their unspoken understanding. It's been a good day. The mountains will wait, and they both know helping Doug is the right thing to do.

"Hey, Rob. If we aren't going to the mountains, am I still going to spend the night?" Tripp cautiously asks.

"Of course," Robbie replies, winking playfully. "Luaren is welcome to stay with us...uh, not spend the night. Maybe you'll get to hang out with Stephanie, too. Mom and Carlos have dinner planned anyway."

"Greg is picking up from Robbie's, but thanks." Lauren smiles. "I want my dorks to have family time."

"Good," Tripp replies. He loves the Davis family.

Tripp parks up by the street when they get to Robbie's house. Carlos has parked his VW Microbus down by the GTO. They will need to leave room for Mama Davis to park her car. Tripp grabs his overnight bag and retrieves Robbie's book bag from the trunk. He brought a change of clothes because he planned to shower in the morning, though he did not bring work clothes. *Maybe, we could run back to my house later or in the morning*, Tripp thinks.

Thinking of the contents of his bag, Tripp admits, "Hey, Robbie. I didn't pack any old clothes to do that kind of work."

"Yeah, I figured you wouldn't," Robbie replies, thinking for a moment. "I can find you something if you don't mind drowning in tall sizes."

"It's just to do the church group stuff. I can look like a hobo around Doug," Tripp laughs.

Robbie walks ahead toward the house, but stops when they hear another vehicle pulling into the driveway. Both turn to see Stephanie's car pulling in behind Tripp's Mustang. Robbie immediately considers the logistics—if his sister stays the night, it might complicate things. The den, where Mike typically crashes during sleepovers, would likely become her room. He knows Tripp won't care, but still, it's something to think about.

Stephanie has full-sized luggage in her hand. Tripp offers to help, but she waves him off. It isn't heavy. She sees that Tripp is carrying a small duffel bag. She hopes she hasn't upset their plans. When they get inside, she puts the suitcase in the den.

"Well, look at this sight!" Stephanie nods in approval.

"Nobody knew who I was," Robbie answers, forcing a smile.

"Tripp did." Lauren quickly points out, holding Tripp's arm.

"Hey, he's my Superman." Stephanie laughs.

"The way y'all are inflating his ego, there will be enough to share." Robbie rolls his eyes.

"I hope I'm not stealing your room for the night?" She apologizes.

"I wouldn't worry, Steph. He can sleep in my room with me," Robbie said as he put his bookbag near the steps.

"I will make the sacrifice for you, Steph," Tripp teases, placing the back of his hand on his forehead for dramatic effect.

Stephanie smirks. "I'm sure you are. But, Robbie, y'all are sixteen now. Are you seriously squeezing into that tiny bed together?"

"We have done it before. At least Mike doesn't snore like Bud," Robbie laughs, punching his friend in the arm.

"You have a point. Maybe I will join you then," Stephanie answers, and they all laugh.

The four share a laugh. Carlos walks over, sporting a large smile, and he hugs Stephanie.

Carlos looks at Robbie, then Tripp and Lauren. He laughs, grinning widely. "Well, look at this. Superman, a princess, and..." He squinted at Robbie. "A Victorian chimney sweep?"

Robbie puffs out his chest, adjusting the lantern he carries. "Not a sweep. I'm carrying the light. Somebody's got to keep Superman out of trouble."

Tripp shoots him a look — half embarrassment, half something warmer. Robbie just winks.

Lauren smooths the satin skirt of her princess dress and rolls her eyes. "Don't lump me in with these two. At least everyone knows what I am."

Carlos chuckles and waves them toward the kitchen. "Fair enough. I'll give you all points for effort. Though I figured you'd be out trick-or-treating instead of humoring us with dinner."

Tripp shakes his head. "Not this year. My cousin, Scott, wanted Uncle Pat to take him out — it's his first time doing the real rounds, and I didn't want to spoil that for him." He smiles faintly, glancing at Robbie. "So we figured we'd focus on dinner. Just friends and family."

Robbie adds with a grin, "Besides, if Carlos is cooking, who needs candy?"

Carlos laughs, ushering them toward the table. "Flattery will get you extra dessert."

"I wish I could stay, but my boyfriend is coming by to pick me up." Lauren apologizes.

Mama D walks up beside Carlos with a smile. "Lauren, you're always welcome to join us."

"Thank you, Mrs. Davis." Lauren curtseys. "Is there a room I can change in?"

"Let me show you," Mama D takes her by the hand.

"We'd better change as well. It's gonna be a normal night." Tripp laughs.

Greg arrives fifteen minutes later. Robbie and Tripp walk with her to the driveway.

"See ya, later." Robbie smiles.

Tripp waves at Greg, who keeps his distance. "Good night, princess. Thank you for every thing you do."

Lauren hugs Robbie, then Tripp and gives him a kiss on the cheek. "Anything for my dorks."

As Robbie and Tripp head toward the bar in the kitchen, Stephanie watches them, smiling at their easy dynamic. Despite her teasing, she feels a twinge of guilt. She knows her brother and his best friend don't mind the arrangement, but she remembers being sixteen—privacy starts to matter more to teenagers. Then again, Robbie and Tripp seem entirely unfazed, and she realizes that might just be the difference between teenage boys and girls.

Robbie's face lights up. "Let me call Doug and let him know you're coming to help."

"Sure," Tripp replies with a nod, leaning against the counter.

Robbie grabs the receiver and starts dialing. Tripp stands close beside him, casually pulling out a ChapStick. He applies it to his lips, a habit Stephanie has noticed countless times, especially in cooler weather. She watches as Tripp keeps his focus on Robbie, his smile warm and genuine. It's clear how much being here, part of this moment, means to him.

"Mike, Doug says thank you and offers to wash and wax your Mustang," Robbie relays as Doug keeps talking in his ear.

"Tell Doug we're both happy to help a friend. I don't want him to feel obligated, but I'd gladly take him up on his offer—as long as he doesn't do it alone. I have to help," Tripp says with a grin.

"Mike, he's a car guy. It's not an obligation; it's just his way of saying thanks," Robbie explains, his tone reassuring.

"I get it, Rob. He's in a bind, and we're helping because that's what friends do," Tripp replies, patting Robbie on the shoulder.

Robbie feels a swell of pride in his best friend. "Thanks, Tripp...and Doug says he insists!" he adds with a smile, reflecting Doug's determination.

"It's a deal then!" Tripp agrees enthusiastically.

Robbie nods as he speaks into the phone, "Doug, we can do it together whenever you're free..."

Tripp steps back, holding up a finger. "Hey, Robbie, I'll be right back. Bathroom."

"Got it," Robbie replies, watching Tripp head down the hallway. "Sure thing, Doug... OK, talk soon."

Since they arrived, Stephanie has been quietly observing them from the living room. Robbie notices her watchful gaze and feels a twinge of unease. As he hangs up the phone, he walks over to where she's sitting, folding his arms in anticipation of her commentary.

"Robbie," Stephanie asks softly, her tone curious yet cautious. "Does Tripp know about your history with Doug?"

Robbie sighs heavily, glancing toward the hallway to ensure Tripp is out of earshot. "No," he says finally, turning his gaze back to his sister. "Doug's my friend now, and Mike's my best friend. That's all that matters."

Stephanie tilts her head, studying him carefully. "You sure that's the right thing to do, Robbie?" she asks, her expression a mix of concern and suspicion.

Robbie doesn't answer. Instead, he offers a half-smile and a shrug. Stephanie nods thoughtfully, taking a deep breath before picking up a copy of National Geographic from the coffee table. Robbie walks toward the stairs, grabs his book bag, and heads to his room. He pauses midway, glancing back at his sister with a brief, unreadable expression before disappearing upstairs.

Tripp emerges from the hallway a few minutes later, his expression curious as he glances around the room. Stephanie lowers her magazine, looking up at him with a bright smile. As always, Tripp returns her smile, his shyness peeking through. She sees him almost like another sibling, but a part of her enjoys how flirtatious he seems to be in her presence.

"Uh, where did Robbie disappear to?" Tripp asks, puzzled.

"He went upstairs with his stuff," Stephanie replies, leaning back on the couch. "Say, Tripp, what are you guys up to tomorrow?"

Tripp grins. "Doug's church youth group is supposed to clean up a section of the park, but a lot of volunteers backed out. Doug asked Robbie to help, so we're both going to pitch in."

"Church youth group, huh?" Stephanie muses. "Didn't y'all have plans to hit the mountains, or is that next weekend?"

Tripp shrugs lightly, still smiling. "We were supposed to go tomorrow, yeah. That's why I'm staying over. But helping Doug is more important right now."

"You don't sound upset," Stephanie observes, her voice tinged with curiosity.

"I'm not," Tripp replies earnestly. "We can always go to the mountains later. What matters is *Robbie*—and being there for him."

Stephanie tilts her head slightly, studying him. "Robbie's lucky to have you as a friend."

"No, Steph. I'm the lucky one," Tripp says with a warm smile and a wink. "Robbie is the most honorable and incredible guy I know. He's my best friend."

Stephanie can see the sincerity in his expression, and she smiles back. "I'm glad you both feel that way."

"I'm gonna check on him," Tripp adds, stepping toward the stairs. "He's probably lost in some random project by now."

"Fine, just abandon me," Stephanie fakes being insulted. "Tell me, have I lost my true love?"

"Never," Tripp winks, heading up the stairs. "I will be back though."

Tripp makes it to the top of the stairs, turning left down the hall. Robbie's door is closed. Tripp taps a couple of times, then enters. Looking surprised, Robbie finishes buckling his belt in a hurry. He turns around when Tripp enters. Robbie has a big smile and motions to come in.

"Just wanted to tuck in my shirt," Robbie offers as an explanation. "What do you think, Tripp?"

Tripp looks confused, "I don't think I have ever seen you tuck in your shirt. I guess it looks ok?"

"Not a ringing endorsement, oh well," Robbie sighs and yanks the shirt out. "Tripp, is it OK that you can't sleep in the den?"

Robbie sits down on his bed. It is a full-size mattress that is parallel to the wall. Along the opposite wall is his dresser. There is a single lamp and a clock radio with bright green LED numbers. Robbie has a small desk in the corner. A full-length mirror is on the wall between the door and the head of the bed. There are several different posters decorating the walls. All from various bands. One of them is in a frame. It was the Boston concert in Atlanta. It was special because he and Mike attended the concert together.

Robbie's room is in the center of the house and has no outside windows. Tripp grabs the chair from the desk to sit down as well.

"Well, Steph did have a point about privacy. I mean, we are both sixteen," Tripp answers. "We aren't exactly 13-year-old boys anymore. That makes it different."

"I don't think it matters, Tripp," Robbie disagrees. "We've been friends for years."

"True," Tripp agrees cautiously, though a few well-guarded secrets flash in his mind. "And I don't have any secrets from you. Well...mostly."

Robbie grins and narrows his eyes suspiciously. "Mostly? That's not reassuring, Tripp."

Tripp tries to hold his serious expression but cracks a smile. "Maybe one or two. But they involve national security," he says in a terrible mock accent.

Robbie snorts and tosses a pillow at him. "You know, I might already know your secrets, Mike Carson. You talk in your sleep."

"Oh, so that's your interrogation technique?" Tripp counters, catching the pillow and tossing it back. "But to answer your question, yeah, I'm fine sleeping in here. Although..." He glances at the bed and chuckles. "I think it shrank as we grew."

Robbie laughs. "Or we just got taller."

"Maybe. Anyway, I can sleep on the floor if you'd rather. One night won't kill me."

Robbie shakes his head with a smile. "Don't be ridiculous. We'll manage. Besides, I'd never make you sleep on the floor."

"It will be like old times," Tripp laughs, using the accent again. "We can make a fort or something!"

"You are a goober!" Robbie jokes. "Say, Tripp. You getting hungry?"

"In a minute," Tripp clasps his hands together several times. "Can we talk about the car ride home?"

Robbie wonders why Tripp is bringing this back up. "Yeah, I guess. Didn't we resolve everything?"

"Yes...and no. The short-term issue of helping Doug was resolved," Tripp explains. "Long term, I need you to know that I am your friend. I do not want you to feel like we can't talk."

"Best friends, Tripp..." Robbie pauses and raises his finger. " See, I'm getting the hang of your new name, not so weird this time. I'm sorry I did not have the courage to tell you."

Tripp laughs, "You made a face, so a little weird..."

Robbie chuckles and nods, "I will get there; I know it is important to you."

"It is, but whether you call me Mike, Michael, Tripp, or Mr. Carson...all those are just names," Tripp answers. "You always treat me with respect and honor. That's what is important. I want to live up to your standards, Rob."

"You do, Tripp. I was afraid I would make you upset. I'm proud of you. In a short amount of time," Robbie explains, he is impressed by his friend's efforts. "You've turned your life around. Mom and Steph have talked about you a lot lately. They care about you..."

Tripp glances away for a moment. "It was a valid point to care about my feelings, thank you. But *we* need to promise that *we* can talk about anything."

"Anything?" With a heavy sigh, Robbie asks, sliding forward. "Oh...OK. There is something..."

"Robbie! Mike!" Mama Davis yells from the bottom of the stairs. "Do you want dinner with us?"

"Woohoo!" Robbie screams out, "Yes, Mom. Feed us, please!"

Tripp starts laughing as he pushes the chair back under the desk. Robbie heads out the door, flipping the light switch off on his way. The boys charge down the stairs, the thundering sound of their steps echoing through the house like a stampede of wild buffalo.

In the kitchen, the aroma of grilled steak wafts through the air. Robbie's stepdad, Carlos Montepeña, is outside tending to the grill, working on excellent cuts of steak for dinner. Meanwhile, Mama Davis is busy preparing baked potatoes and a fresh salad.

Robbie and Tripp enter the kitchen, immediately quieting down when they see Stephanie on the phone.

"Mike, what do you want on your baked potato?" Mama Davis asks warmly, looking up from her preparations.

"Just butter, please. Do you have any Italian salad dressing?" Tripp replies politely.

"Hippie!" Robbie teases, grabbing the place settings for the table with a mischievous grin.

"I think we do," Mama Davis nods. "I didn't even think to ask if you wanted a salad. I'm sorry about that, honey."

"It's OK if you don't have enough," Tripp assures her with a smile. "Please don't go to any trouble."

"No trouble at all, sweetheart," Mama Davis insists with a warm smile. "There's plenty. It'll just take a moment to put one together for you."

"Thanks, Mama Davis," Tripp says, stepping forward and hugging her without a second thought.

"Aww, thank you!" She giggles, clearly touched by the gesture. "What will the new Mike Carson spring on us next, I wonder?"

Tripp shrugs with a bashful grin, while Robbie pours two glasses of water and slides one over to his friend. Tripp grabs the napkins and silverware, carefully placing them around the table.

Outside, Carlos flips the last of the steaks on the grill. Inside, Stephanie hangs up the phone with a frustrated sigh, muttering something under her breath.

"What's the matter, honey?" Mama Davis asks, concern crossing her face as she pauses her work.

Stephanie sighs, "That was Bud. His shift is running long, so he won't make it tonight."

"Oh, I'm sorry to hear that," Mama Davis says, pulling her daughter into a comforting hug. "Will he be here tomorrow?"

"Yeah, around nine," Stephanie replies, her frustration evident. "We still have to meet with the realtor, though. It's just... annoying."

"Hey, Mike," she says, turning to Tripp with a small smile. "I guess you can have the den tonight. I'll figure something else out."

Robbie looks over at his sister with genuine sympathy. "Sorry Bud won't be here, Steph."

""Hey, Steph," Tripp begins with a warm smile. "You were right about needing privacy, but not for me and Robbie. I think it should be you. Robbie and I have it all worked out."

"You sure, Tripp?" Stephanie asks, her tone laced with concern. "It wouldn't be the first time I've slept in the recliner."

"Yikes! That sounds like a backache waiting to happen," Tripp laughs. "It's already decided, right, Robbie?"

"You might as well accept it, Steph," Robbie chimes in, grinning as he suddenly grabs Tripp in a playful headlock. "Tripp's a stubborn old goat when it comes to these things!"

Laughing loudly as they wrestle, Tripp teases back, "It's called being persistent."

"Thanks, Tripp. I owe you one," Stephanie says with genuine appreciation, blowing a playful kiss in his direction.

"Hey, Robbie, I think Carlos is almost done. Can you and Mike go out and help carry everything back in?" Mama Davis calls out as she finishes preparing Tripp's salad.

Releasing Tripp from his grip, Robbie heads to the door with a grin, "Yes, Mom."

"Yes, ma'am," Tripp echoes politely, flashing his signature smile.

The boys step out onto the deck. Tripp carefully closes the porch door behind them. Stephanie strolls over to the bay window, her curiosity piqued. Carlos waves at the boys but signals that the food isn't quite ready to bring in.

Robbie leans casually against the railing, gazing thoughtfully out into the backyard. Tripp stands beside him while facing the house, catching sight of Stephanie through the window. He grins at her, the look on his face saying, *This feels like home.*

Turning back, Tripp leans his back against the rail and twists slightly, bringing himself closer to Robbie. The two exchange a quiet moment of connection. Inside, Mama Davis steps up to the window to join her daughter.

"I wonder what they're talking about," Stephanie muses softly.

"Robbie seemed distracted when they came downstairs. Actually, he's been out of sorts for a couple of days," Mama Davis observes, folding her arms. "He could be upset about canceling the plans with Mike."

"He cares a lot about Tripp," Stephanie replies, glancing out the window. "And Tripp thinks the world of Robbie."

"That's so true, Stephanie. The whole world can see they belong together," Mama Davis says with a warm smile.

"I know..." Stephanie answers, her voice trailing off as she continues to watch them through the window.

Outside, Robbie fiddles with a loose section of the railing, his gaze distant. Tripp stands beside him, sensing the tension. He knows his friend is troubled and is giving him the space to open up. Robbie glances briefly at Tripp, who responds with his signature big smile.

"I'm glad you're here..." Robbie finally confides, his voice low.

Tripp turns fully to face him, placing a steady hand between Robbie's shoulder blades as he leans in slightly. The aroma of the steaks on the grill fills the air, but Tripp's focus remains on Robbie. He waits, giving his friend the time he needs.

"I'm guessing that *anything* you started to mention earlier is still weighing on you?" Tripp asks gently.

"Yes, Tripp. It's important, but...I don't know how to tell you," Robbie admits, his eyes fixed on the yard.

Robbie looks at Tripp briefly before turning his gaze back to the yard. Tripp moves his hand to Robbie's shoulder, offering a comforting squeeze. His smile is patient, understanding, and unwavering.

"Well," Tripp says with a calm resolve, "we'll stay right here until you're ready to open up."

"That grill smells awfully good," Robbie jokes, trying to lighten the mood. "You can't resist steaks!"

"Not even Mama D's pizza will pull me away. I can wait all night," Tripp proclaims with a grin. "It's you first, then food."

"Tripp, you're a dork," Robbie laughs, the tension breaking momentarily.

"That's why we get along so well," Tripp teases, sliding his hand down Robbie's arm with a smile. Then, his tone shifts to sincerity. "All kidding aside, I'm not going to push. Whatever it is, I want to help. When you're ready, I'll be here."

Robbie sighs deeply, glancing at the ground. "Tripp...it's about Doug."

"Doug was your best friend..." Tripp says softly. "Or maybe he still is?"

"It's different, Tripp."

Tripp nods encouragingly, "Rob, it's okay to have other friends."

"How can I make you understand?" Robbie asks.

"I understand." Tripp stands straight. "I know where I stand, even if you still consider him your best friend. But I need you to know this. You're my first new best friend since the fourth grade. When Daniel moved away, I thought I'd never find another friend like that. Then I met you. It took time, sure, but I'm thankful we built this connection. You complete me in ways I didn't expect."

Robbie turns to face him, his eyes softening. "I've always felt like we're meant to be friends. Tripp, you're important to me. I just didn't want you to be upset."

"I can share..." Tripp says with a playful grin.

Robbie raises an eyebrow skeptically. "No, you can't."

Tripp laughs, holding up his hands. "Okay, sometimes."

Robbie smirks, shaking his head. "No. No, you really can't!"

Inside, Stephanie continues watching them from the bay window. Her protective instincts stir as she observes her brother. Robbie has been so quiet these past few days, and she knows he's not ready to talk to her yet. And she can see how much Tripp's friendship means to him.

As Tripp walks over to help Carlos bring in the steaks, Robbie leans back against the railing, his thoughts clearly weighing on him. Looking back at the window, he meets Stephanie's gaze. She smiles, her expression encouraging, and nods toward Tripp. Robbie shakes his head slightly, his face tinged with uncertainty. Stephanie watches him, her heart heavy but hopeful.

Where Shadows Touch

After the fantastic meal, everyone is in high spirits. Carlos has outdone himself tonight — the meat is tender and perfectly seasoned, the baked potatoes rich and fluffy, the crisp salad rounding everything out. Stephanie finally calls off her secret surveillance of Robbie and Tripp. Whatever doubts she had, tonight's atmosphere washes them away.

After dinner, everyone drifts toward the living room. Mama Davis suggests a game of charades, and soon the room fills with laughter. Stephanie can't help but be impressed — Tripp and Robbie win every round.

Tonight, the seams between them have vanished; they are no longer two people in sync, but two parts of the same inseparable whole.

Carlos calls it a night first, needing to catch an early morning flight out of state. Robbie's mom heads upstairs soon after. Around ten o'clock, Robbie and Mike follow, trudging up the staircase, full and tired. Stephanie disappears into the den, her own day tomorrow weighing heavily on her mind.

Tripp trails behind Robbie, yawning loudly as they reach the bedroom. Robbie closes the door behind them, and Tripp stretches his arms overhead, feeling the fatigue from the day settle deep into his bones.

Robbie moves to the dresser, setting the alarm clock for 7:15 a.m. Tripp kicks off his shoes and sinks into the chair, rubbing his face with both hands.

Robbie peels off his shirt without a second thought, tossing it aside. Tripp follows, unbuttoning his own and folding it carefully into his bag.

"I was expecting the den tonight," Tripp says, glancing over his shoulder. "I didn't bring anything to sleep in. Just my underwear."

Robbie shrugs easily. "Doesn't bother me. But you'll have to sleep against the wall. I'm used to being on the outside."

"No problem," Tripp says with a grin, pulling off his socks and setting them aside.

Robbie finishes stripping down, ending in navy-blue boxer briefs that fit snugly. Tripp catches the sight and chuckles to himself — *guess nobody sticks with plain white underwear anymore.*

He removes his glasses and places them next to the alarm clock, then stands to undo his jeans. As he slides them down, he hesitates for just a second, self-conscious in his favorite pair of deep purple briefs. They're comfortable — soft, silk-like — but loud enough that Robbie might say something.

Sure enough, as Tripp folds his jeans and places them neatly on the dresser, Robbie's eyes catch the color.

"I like the new paint job," Robbie teases with a laugh. "But aren't those, uh, girl's underwear?"

"No," Tripp shoots back quickly, cheeks warming. "They're men's. Just a polyester blend — they feel like silk. They're really comfortable, like you're not wearing anything—"

Robbie bursts out laughing. "That's supposed to make it sound better?" he howls.

Tripp sputters, mortified. "No! I mean— you know what I meant! They're from the men's department, I swear!"

"You keep telling yourself that," Robbie chuckles, settling back against the pillow.

Tripp shakes his head, smirking despite himself. He steps over to the mirror, turning slightly to the side, admiring the fit.

"I've been told I have nice legs," he says, tossing the comment over his shoulder.

"Those white toothpicks?" Robbie jabs.

Tripp laughs, flexing playfully. Facing the mirror, he watches his reflection — the briefs hugging his newly toned frame. *Maybe a little vain,* he thinks wryly.

"One thing I've never been called is a toothpick," he quips.

Robbie grins, giving a lazy golf clap. "Okay, Tripp Carson, I'll admit it — you do look good. Those sit-ups are paying off."

"Thanks, dork," Tripp says, flipping off the light. "Did you set the alarm?"

"Yeah. 7:15," Robbie confirms.

"Plenty of time," Tripp says, navigating carefully through the dark.

The only illumination now is the faint, eerie green glow from the clock radio, casting long shadows across the room. Tripp gropes for the bed and accidentally brushes Robbie's upper thigh — a little too high for comfort.

He yanks his hand back instantly.

"Sorry!" he blurts out.

Robbie laughs. "Was expecting you to stub your toe, not... that. Just climb over."

Chuckling awkwardly, Tripp carefully crawls across the bed. He stretches out on the far side, back against the wall, breathing a sigh of relief.

The mattress is comfortable — way better than his own worn-out single at home. He watches Robbie out of the corner of his eye, lying on his back, one arm bent beneath his head.

The room is silent except for the slow, rhythmic breathing between them.

Tripp exhales, feeling the exhaustion drag at him.

His mind goes blissfully blank for once.

He listens to the sound of Robbie's breathing, steady and familiar, and lets himself drift.

Tripp is almost asleep when Robbie's voice breaks the quiet.

"Hey, Tripp?" Robbie whispers.

Tripp clears his throat. "Yeah, Rob?"

Robbie shifts slightly, his voice soft. "Can I ask you a favor?"

Tripp lifts his head a little, blinking through the dim green haze. "Of course. What do you need?"

"I'm a little cold," Robbie says sheepishly.

"The blanket's in the corner, I think," Tripp offers, squinting toward the shadows. "Want me to grab it?"

"That's so far away," Robbie laughs quietly. "I don't wanna trouble you."

Tripp frowns, confused. "So... what should I do?"

Robbie hesitates, then asks, almost shyly, "Could I... borrow some of your body heat? Just for a few minutes?"

Tripp grins, amused by how serious Robbie sounds. "Sure, Rob. I thought you were about to ask something complicated."

They chuckle softly together, the sound easy and familiar. Tripp scoots closer, careful and deliberate, lying on his right side facing Robbie. He rests his head lightly against Robbie's chest, feeling the solid warmth there, and drapes his left leg gently over Robbie's thigh.

"If this doesn't help, I'll grab the blanket," Tripp murmurs.

"I think this'll work," Robbie whispers, his voice already thick with sleep.

The steady thump of Robbie's heartbeat fills Tripp's ears. He closes his eyes, letting the warmth and rhythm soothe him.

Minutes stretch out.

Robbie doesn't pull away.

Instead, his right arm moves, resting lightly across Tripp's back, his hand warm on Tripp's shoulder.

"Hey, Rob?" Tripp says, voice barely above a whisper.

"Yeah?" Robbie murmurs.

"I'm really comfortable... I'm just gonna stay here, okay?"

"That's fine, Tripp," Robbie exhales, sounding almost relieved.

Tripp smiles against Robbie's chest and lets the quiet of the room wrap around him like a blanket. The darkness, the steady breathing, the comfort of being this close to someone he trusts completely — it lulls him deeper toward sleep.

He drifts off easily, peacefully, without dreams.

A while later, Tripp jolts awake.

Not from a nightmare.

Not from noise.

Just... awake.

His heart races for reasons he can't name.

The room is still dark, bathed only in the faint green blur of the clock. Shapes barely emerge from the shadows.

Tripp's breathing quickens — and then he realizes, with dawning horror, that he's aroused.

Badly.

Oh no.

Fortunately, his right arm — still resting against Robbie — acts as a barrier.

But if Robbie moves... if he notices...

Tripp squeezes his eyes shut, willing the reaction to pass. It has to be a random thing. Teenage hormones. A leftover dream he can't remember.

Except... Robbie's breathing has changed too.

Faster.

Shallower.

Tripp opens his eyes carefully, blinking into the dim light.

Through the green haze, he thinks he sees the outline of Robbie — and if he's not imagining things, Robbie's body seems... equally stirred. Unmistakable.

Maybe it's nothing. Maybe it's just shadows. Or my mind playing tricks.

Still, panic gnaws at Tripp's gut.

He knows he should move away.

He should do the safe thing, the logical thing.

But he doesn't.

He stays frozen, breathing quietly, terrified of making things worse.

Then Robbie whispers.

"Hey, Mike?"

Tripp's heart jumps into his throat.

"Yeah?" he answers, voice rough.

"Did I wake you?"

"I'm not sure," Tripp says honestly. "I haven't been awake long. You okay?"

There's a pause.

"I just... wanted to say thanks," Robbie says, voice slow and sleepy. "For tomorrow. For being there for Doug. And... for me."

Tripp relaxes fractionally, resting his left hand lightly on Robbie's shoulder. "Anything for you, Rob. You're my best friend."

There's a quiet chuckle from Robbie.

"You're more than that," he says after a beat. "You've been like a brother to me."

Tripp's chest tightens painfully. He doesn't know what to say — not when every part of him feels something more than brotherhood, something deeper and heavier and terrifying.

"Same here, Rob," he finally manages, his voice thick with emotion. "I couldn't ask for a better friend."

Robbie shifts slightly, his arm brushing lower across Tripp's back, a casual, sleepy motion — but it sets Tripp's heart racing again.

Tripp fights to focus on anything else — anything but the warmth, the closeness, the confusion knotting inside him.

Minutes pass. Silence, heavy and fragile.

Then Robbie whispers into the darkness:

"I understand."

Tripp lifts his head, searching for Robbie's face through the green-lit shadows.

"What do you understand, Rob?"

Robbie turns toward him, voice soft but certain.

"I understand what you were saying. In the car that day. About what we have. It's not normal. It's not just friendship. It's... something special."

Tripp swallows hard.

"Very special, Rob," he whispers back.

He rests his head again on Robbie's chest, trying to calm the hurricane inside him. Trying hard not to think about how right this feels.

Robbie's hand brushes Tripp's shoulder gently, a simple, grounding touch.

"You're the kind of best friend you don't find twice in one lifetime," Tripp says quietly, voice thick with unspoken meaning. "I mean that."

In the darkness, Robbie smiles.

"Good night, Tripp," he murmurs, voice soft and sure.

"Good night, Rob," Tripp replies, gratitude and longing and something he dares not name filling his chest.

The room falls silent again, but this time, it's not empty.

It's full — of warmth, of closeness, of something growing quietly between them that neither fully understands yet.

Awkward Awakenings

The blaring alarm slices through the heavy quiet, shrill and relentless. Tripp stirs, blinking against the dimness, the green glow of the clock numbers casting soft light across the walls.

For a moment, confusion fogs his brain — the sound reminds him weirdly of sirens in old French police dramas.

His senses kick in, and with relief, he realizes he and Robbie are still lying the same way they fell asleep.

No weird tension. No panicked separation.

Carefully, he shifts his head.

"Good morning, Tripp," Robbie's voice cuts through the noise, dry and amused.

"Uh, yeah. Morning, Rob." Tripp yawns so wide his jaw pops. "What time is it?"

Robbie lifts his head, squinting at the clock. "Think it's 7:25. Can't see much without my glasses, though."

"Same here," Tripp says, stretching and rolling onto his back.

"Maybe we should call the nurse. Vision problems this early? Two old men already."

Robbie laughs, sitting up. "Exactly. But you're worse. The alarm's been going off for like ten minutes and you didn't even twitch."

Robbie laughs and slides off the bed.

"What?!" Tripp bolts upright, swinging his legs over the side of the bed. "You let it go off for that long? That thing was *screaming* at us!"

"You looked like you needed the sleep." Robbie smirks, reaching over to silence the clock with a tap. "Besides, you were talking in your sleep again."

Tripp scrubs his face with both hands. "Talking? Again?"

"Yeah," Robbie grins. "Couldn't make out what you were saying, but it was pretty entertaining."

Tripp groans. "Next time, record it. I'll roast myself."

Robbie's brow tenses, amused by Tripp's strange reference. Without hesitation, Robbie flips on the light switch. The sudden brightness floods the room like a spotlight, and Tripp throws an arm over his eyes with a dramatic whine.

"Great. I think you just burned my retinas."

"You big baby," Robbie teases, rummaging through his dresser drawers.

Tripp grins from under his arm. "Can't do much without my sight, Rob. I'd be wandering around helpless."

"Wandering around helpless?" Robbie says, smirking over his shoulder. "You found your way across this room just fine in total darkness last night. You'd make an excellent blind man."

Tripp chuckles, swinging his legs idly. He watches Robbie — the casual way he moves, the ease between them — and he feels a twinge of nervousness bubbling under the surface.

The memory of last night stirs at the edges of his mind — the closeness, the confusing emotions — and for a second, he debates saying something.

Something real.

But the words catch in his throat. *No, Mike. Bad plan.*

He swallows the impulse and focuses instead on the present moment.

Robbie turns, holding up a pair of khaki shorts and gauging their size. "Try these on," he says, flashing a wide grin.

Tripp smiles back, feeling the tension in his chest ease.

"Thanks," he says, accepting the shorts. "As tall as you are, these might just cover my feet."

Robbie laughs. "You're not that short, Tripp!"

Tripp holds up the shorts for inspection, pretending to squint critically. Robbie digs through the dresser again, pulling out a pair of work pants then grabs his glasses.

Tripp slips into the shorts, finding they extend just below his knees — not quite ridiculous, but definitely not tailor-fit. The waistband feels looser than he expects, and he notes the change with quiet satisfaction.

Maybe all this effort is paying off after all.

"Yeah, these'll work," Tripp announces, checking his reflection in the mirror.

Before he can turn fully, something soft smacks him in the back of the head. He yanks it off, laughing, and finds himself holding a black T-shirt emblazoned with a bold Pontiac logo.

"Pontiac?" Tripp raises an eyebrow. "Hope my Mustang doesn't hold a grudge."

"It's strong." Robbie laughs. "Your Mustang'll survive."

Tripp places the shirt on the bed. "Hey, Rob? I'm thinking about grabbing a quick shower before we head out."

As Tripp steps out of the shorts again, Robbie watches him briefly — casual, comfortable — and Tripp catches the glance in the mirror.

He smiles.

"No problem," Robbie says, leaning against the dresser. "I'll wait till after we get dirty. Clearing all that brush is gonna be sweaty work."

Tripp turns, dropping the shorts beside the bed. "You have a point, I need to rethink this..."

"Change your mind about the work, huh?"

"Not a chance," Tripp asserts, he's going to see this through.

"Ok, let's try this again." Robbie teases, walking over.

Tripp feels the ease between them again — the playful edge that's always been there, but somehow feels sharper now, more real.

Robbie bends down to pick up the shorts Tripp dropped, steadying himself with a hand on Tripp's stomach as he rises.

The touch is brief, casual. But it makes Tripp pause, feeling oddly self-conscious for just a second. His mind flashes the image from last night.

Robbie hands back the shorts with an easy smile.

"You might wanna put these back on," he jokes. "I hear the park has a strict no-purple-underwear rule."

Tripp bursts out laughing, slipping the shorts back on. "Good to know. Wouldn't wanna scandalize the locals."

"Alright, Tripp," Robbie says, clapping him on the shoulder. "We're dressed and ready to tackle the slave pits."

Tripp grins, slipping the shirt over his head. "You gonna feed me before you put me to work?"

"Mom's already cooking," Robbie cheers. "I can smell bacon."

"What are you, part bloodhound?"

Robbie just grins as Tripp sniffs the air — and sure enough, the unmistakable scent of sizzling bacon drifts up from downstairs.

"Okay, fair," Tripp admits, laughing. "Lead the way, Lassie."

Laughing and teasing, they head downstairs, the early sunlight streaming through the front windows, bathing the house in a soft, golden glow.

They reach the bottom of the stairs, sunlight spilling through the front windows, making everything feel warm and alive.

Just as they step into the hallway, Stephanie stumbles out of the den, looking half-asleep. Tripp instinctively reaches out, steadying her with a hand on her arm.

"I've got you," he says with a quick grin as she blinks blearily at them.

"Sorry, Steph," Robbie adds, glancing at her with concern.

Stephanie mutters something incoherent, brushing her messy hair out of her face. She's wearing an oversized white T-shirt that sways around her knees. Tripp catches a glimpse of purple underneath — just a flash — and can't resist.

He lets out a playful, soft wolf whistle.

Stephanie shoots him a glare, though it's softened by how obviously tired she is. "Too early for flirts, Tripp," she mumbles. "Let me drink a pot of coffee first."

Robbie snorts, and Tripp laughs, following her into the kitchen like mischievous schoolboys. Stephanie slumps into a chair at the dining table with a sigh. Robbie slides onto a stool at the breakfast bar.

Mama Davis bustles around the kitchen, moving plates to the counter. She glances at Tripp — and hides a knowing smile behind her hand.

Tripp freezes midstep, realizing it instantly. The way the khaki shorts hang ridiculously below his knees, the way the black Pontiac shirt almost swallows his frame — it's obvious.

I'm wearing Robbie's clothes. He thinks, feeling self conscious.

Instead of teasing, Mama Davis just shakes her head affectionately and chuckles softly under her breath.

Tripp, recovering quickly, heads for the fridge. He pours two glasses of orange juice first, hands one to Robbie, then goes back to the counter. Grabbing the coffee pot. Stephanie watches as he stirs creamer into a steaming cup of coffee. The metal spoon clinks softly against the ceramic. Stephanie watches all of this with bleary curiosity, her head resting against her hand.

Since when does Mike Carson drink coffee? she wonders.

Tripp carries the mug over to her carefully, setting it down in front of her like an offering.

"Here you go," he says with a warm smile. "Perfect way to start the morning."

Stephanie smiles back, touched despite her exhaustion. She takes a cautious sip, savoring the warmth.

"Thanks, Tripp," she says. "You're such a gentleman. Your coffee's better than Bud's — he couldn't even get the creamer right the first time."

Laughter ripples around the table.

Tripp shrugs dramatically. "Guess Bud needs to step up his game. Although, to be fair..." — he pauses, shooting a sly look at Stephanie — "he probably didn't have the view I do."

Stephanie groans, shaking her head. "You're incorrigible."

"Completely hopeless," Robbie agrees, nudging Tripp lightly with his elbow.

Tripp smirks, settling into the seat beside him. For a few minutes, the kitchen fills with the comfortable clatter of plates and forks and the smell of bacon and eggs.

Mama Davis watches them from the stove, her heart full. She sees what's happening — sees the easy bond Tripp has slipped into with her children — and she says a silent prayer of thanks for it.

Saturday In The Park

Tripp sits, unusually quiet during the ride to the park, his head leaning against the passenger window. Robbie notices him sneaking glances his way now and then but doesn't think much of it.

We were up late, Robbie reasons. *And he was talking in his sleep again.*

He recalls how hard it was to wake Tripp up this morning — harder than usual. If it had been up to Robbie, he would've let the alarm keep ringing, giving Tripp as much rest as he needed. Robbie remembers past sleepovers when Tripp would toss and turn all night.

But last night had been different — Tripp had seemed at peace until about five a.m. (as best as Robbie could guess) when he started murmuring again.

Robbie frowns slightly, recalling the name he heard: *Leigh. Who's Leigh?* he wonders for a moment, then shakes the thought away.

Focusing back on the road, Robbie smiles. He loves driving Tripp's Mustang — smooth, powerful, well-maintained. Keeping it running like new is almost a personal mission at this point.

"You should've made yourself a cup of that coffee this morning," Robbie finally says, breaking the heavy silence. "You're too quiet."

"Sorry, Rob," Tripp answers, voice distant as he stifles a yawn.

"I was just thinking about what you said last night."

Robbie glances over, concerned. "What part?"

Tripp shifts in his seat, hesitating for a beat before speaking.

"I'm just... really glad we can be honest with each other," he says, his tone soft.

Robbie nods in agreement. "That's what best friends do."

"I can't stop thinking about how lucky I am to have you as a best friend."

"We're both lucky, Tripp." Robbie smiles, tapping Tripp's arm lightly. "I meant what I said, too. Thanks again for helping with Doug's project today. It really means a lot. Doug's—well, he's been a good friend for a long time. But not many people would do this just because I asked."

Tripp notices the way Robbie says it — no pressure, no guilt. Just... gratitude.

He smiles. It would've been okay if Robbie had kept calling him Mike. But the fact that Robbie fully embraces calling him Tripp now, warms something deep inside him.

"I'm not selfless," Tripp chuckles, staring down at his feet."I just love being around you, that's all. Makes me feel good when you're happy."

He looks up, catching Robbie's eye briefly before glancing away again.

"Really?"

"I can still picture the look on your face when we fixed those rocker arms," Tripp adds with a smile. "That made everything worth it. We're best friends, Rob. Best friends for life."

"For life," Robbie echoes, his smile deepening as he tightens his grip on the steering wheel.

They pull into the park entrance, gravel crunching under the tires. The parking lot is empty on this early morning.

Doug Barrett waits near his truck, waving as they approach. He's almost as tall as Robbie, wiry and athletic, with wavy red hair and a face that still clings to boyishness. Doug's reputation at school is golden — easygoing, strong, someone everyone likes.

A tall girl stands beside him, thick glasses perched on her nose, long black hair cascading down her back. She looks familiar, but Tripp can't place her.

Doug looks relieved when he spots Robbie and Tripp climb out of the Mustang, stretching.

Doug grins and waves them over.

"Hey, Rob! You remember Al?" Doug calls.

Doug gestures toward the girl.

"Hey, Alice, this is my best friend. Mike Carson — he goes by Tripp now," Robbie says, voice ringing with pride.

Tripp smiles, remembering. *She's Jeff's friend.*

"Hey, Alice," Tripp says, offering a handshake.

"Hello, Mike," Alice replies pleasantly, shaking his hand with a firm, awkward smile.

They move toward the shelter where the real work waits. The area's a mess — weeds choking the supports, trash scattered everywhere.

Alice grabs a trash bag and gets to work gathering debris. Robbie and Doug handle cutting the brush, while Tripp hauls the branches toward the tree line, sweating steadily under the midmorning sun. Tripp pauses to wipe his forehead, he realizes how much material they're going to have to move. Placing his hands on his hips, surveying the mess, he gets an idea.

"Hey Doug," he calls out, scratching his head, "Wouldn't it make more sense to bring your truck over now? Save us a lotta hauling."

Doug wipes his brow and laughs. "Good idea, Mike! I'll go grab it."

Doug and Robbie head off together. As they walk, Robbie looks back — and catches Tripp smiling faintly before turning back to work. Doug leans toward Robbie, voice low but amused.

"He really has changed," Doug says, shaking his head with a grin. "Though I gotta ask... who dressed him this morning?"

Robbie smirks. "Yeah, he didn't bring work clothes. I loaned him some stuff."

Doug raises an eyebrow. "What were the other options?"

Gently laughing, Robbie rolls his eyes. "Stop it."

"He looks like a toddler playing dress up." Doug hides a smile.

Robbie shakes his head. He remembers when Doug didn't aprove of the friendship he had with Mike Carson.

"He's growing, changing for the better." Robbie looks at Doug. "I've never doubted Tripp was a good man."

But Doug's teasing smile fades quickly, replaced with something more sincere.

"I believe you, Rob. I'm proud of him too. What he's doing... takes guts."

Robbie nods, glancing back toward where Tripp drags another pile of branches. "I'm glad you're giving him a chance to prove it."

"No doubt he's changed," Doug says. "He talks to me now in math class, you know? Never used to before that day he *jump started*."

"What?" Robbie chuckles. "Jump-started, huh?"

"That's one way to put it," Doug laughs.

"You're talking about October seventh."

"I figured he was just helping today because you asked," Doug adds, voice softer, "but he's working hard. Really hard. He's a good friend."

"Best friend," Robbie says firmly, meeting Doug's eyes.

Doug grins.

"No offense taken, Robbie Davis. Makes me happy to see you two together."

They reach the truck, and Doug hops inside to start it up.

Robbie lingers for a second, looking back at Tripp — still working, still hauling, still trying so damn hard.

"Tripp Carson means a lot to me," Robbie says under his breath.

While Robbie and Doug fetch the truck, Tripp hauls another load of branches toward the tree line, lost deep in thought. He tries not to stare after them — after Robbie — but it's harder than it should be. The easy laughter between Doug and Robbie stings somewhere deep inside him, even though he knows it shouldn't.

You're just tired, Tripp tells himself. *Late night. Weird dreams. Hormones. That's all.*

He tries to focus on work, tossing branches into a neat pile, but his mind keeps drifting. Tripp's mind centers on Robbie, bringing a smile to his face. Closing his eyes, he can feel the warmth of being beside Robbie.

Tripp exhales sharply. His thoughts tangle worse the more he tries to straighten them out.

Why am I even thinking about Robbie like this?

Why does it feel different now?

Why can't I just stop?

Earlier, even seeing Steph — pretty, bright, familiar Stephanie — barely registered. The old Mike would've fixated on that moment: Stephanie in the oversized T-shirt, long legs catching the morning sun. Her hidden purple attire.

But this morning? The memory of Robbie lying beside him—warm, breathing, safe—overshadowed everything else.

Tripp shakes his head, frustrated. "I love him like a brother."

"Dammit," he mutters under his breath, dragging another fallen branch toward the trees.

Maybe Geoffrey stirred something up, he thinks. The phone call. The casual flirting. Tripp remembers the way Geoffrey flipped the script on him, and how strangely thrilling it had felt to be out of control for once.

He clenches his jaw.

It doesn't mean anything.

It's just leftover confusion. That's all.

And yet, when he glances up and sees Robbie and Doug approaching with the truck, laughter still echoing between them —

his heart squeezes, tight and aching.

Doug parks the truck along the tree line. Tripp steps forward, waving him into position. Doug cuts the engine and leans out the window, grinning.

"You really have changed, Mike," Doug calls as he hops out. "You're actually working."

Robbie laughs, circling around the truck bed.

"I gave Robbie my word I'd help." Tripp stops. "His friends are my friends." Tripp is amazed how statisfying that feels.

Doug smirks and nudges Robbie as they walk. "You sure he's the same guy? I mean, October 7th wasn't that long ago."

Robbie grins to himself. *Yeah. October 7th. The day everything changed.*

Tripp frowns slightly. *Doug mentioned the day I woke up. What could they have been talking about?*

They get to work tossing branches into the bed of the truck. Tripp focuses on the motions — bend, lift, toss — trying to drown out his thoughts with sweat and muscle memory.

It almost works.

Almost.

Until he glances up and sees Robbie helping Alice with a stubborn vine. Robbie's laughing again — that easy, open laugh that Tripp knows too well — and it hits him like a punch to the gut.

Tripp forces himself to look away.

You're overthinking everything, he scolds himself.

It's just friendship. It's always been friendship.

But somewhere deep down, he knows he's lying to himself.

He finishes heaving another large branch over the truck rail and steps back, wiping his forehead. He sees Robbie across the field, sunlight catching in his hair, a smile lighting up his whole face — and Tripp feels the ground tilt under him.

Best friends, he whispers inside his head.

Best friends. That's all.

He scoffs quietly.

If that were true, why does it hurt so much?

Later, as he works alone gathering stray debris, his mind spins out again. He thinks about Jeff Tyler — the friend he pushed away long ago. About Geoffrey — the casual way he'd turned Tripp's world upside down with a few whispered words.

He thinks about Doctor Elmhurst, sitting patiently in that office, telling him:

> *"Michael, sometimes the thing we love is right before us, and we cannot see it..."*

Tripp drags another branch, chest aching. A tear forms in the corner of his eyes. The realization blooms in him slowly, painfully:

He's not just confused.

He's not just lonely.

He's in love.

Robbie and Doug move on to trimming a small tree near the shelter. Tripp watches them for a moment, heart aching — but smiling too.

If Robbie's happy, that's enough, he tells himself. *That has to be enough.*

Robbie waves, catching him staring. Tripp smiles back, forcing the ache deeper into his chest.

"See?" Tripp whispers under his breath. *"I told you I can share."*

He keeps working, throwing himself into the labor, trying to sweat out the feelings he can't admit — not yet.

Maybe not ever.

Asking For Help

A nne Carson sits on the edge of her bed, exhausted. It's been a rough day at the office. November first was the day they reconcile the receipts, and the weight of it clings to her like damp clothes. When she arrived home earlier, she found the house spotless — Mark and Tripp have cleaned most of it again without being asked.

She nearly cried.

Sometimes, she thinks, *it's the small things that leave the biggest impact.*

Tonight, Anne can relax. This is her ner normal. Only one basket of laundry waits by the door. A tear stings the corner of her eye again. She is so proud of her boys. So proud — and still so bewildered.

Anne leans over and picks up the telephone from the nightstand. It's been weeks since she last spoke to her baby brother, John.

They've both been so busy, and she misses him terribly.

She starts dialing the D.C. telephone number she knows so well.

"Be nice to share some good news for once," she says aloud as the line rings.

"Good evening," John Dalton Jr. answers, his voice immediately familiar.

"Hello, John! How are you and Jake?" Anne asks warmly, her tone lifting with genuine happiness.

"Doing great. The new client signed a two-year contract and doubled the scope of their project with us." John replies.

"Oh, John, that's wonderful news."

"Jake's thrilled about it too, We have to hire another designer." John says, his voice carrying the easy joy that always makes Anne smile.

"You'll have to tell me all about it," she says. "I just thought I'd call and update you on the oh-so-dreary life of your older sister."

"Anne, my dear," John laughs warmly, "your life is anything but dreary. I admire you for keeping everything together. I'm proud of you, sis."

"Thank you, John. I've missed you."

Just then, she hears the front door open and close.

Footsteps.

Quiet ones.

Anne covers the receiver. "I'm back here in my room," she calls out.

John can hear her voice and instantly knows something is wrong. Before she can reply, a soft, strained voice cuts through the air.

"Momma?"

Anne's heart leaps. The voice is fragile — like something precious about to break.

She covers the receiver again. "I'm in here, Tripp," she calls out.

Michael appears at her doorway, wearing oversized clothes she doesn't recognize. There's dirt on his shirt and sadness in his eyes. Anne's chest tightens instinctively. Something is wrong.

"Sorry, Momma," he says, voice low and defeated. "I didn't realize you were on the phone. I'll come back."

Panic rises in Anne's chest. "I'll be done in just a minute, honey. I'll find you when I'm finished talking to your uncle—"

"Is it Uncle John?" Tripp perks up slightly.

"Yes," Anne says gently. "He's telling me about his new clients."

Tripp hesitates, then shuffles closer. "Can... can I speak to him?"

Anne blinks, startled. Michael — *asking* to speak to family? Voluntarily?

"John," she says cautiously into the phone, "Michael wants to talk to you."

"Voluntarily?" John echoes in surprise. "I'd like to hear this firsthand."

Anne offers the phone to her son with a smile of encouragement.

Tripp sits gingerly at the edge of the bed, gripping the receiver like it might slip from his hands. He clears his throat once, twice — steeling himself.

"When one door closes, another opens," he remembers faintly.

"Uncle John?" he whispers into the receiver.

"Hello, Michael," John replies warmly. "I hear you've made a lot of changes."

"Yes, sir," Tripp says quietly, barely above a whisper.

"Sir?" John chuckles softly. "Your mother's so proud of you, and I am too."

"Thank you, sir," Tripp says, taking a shaky breath. He closes his eyes.

"It's been a long time since you wanted to talk on the phone."

"Uncle John," Tripp replies, voice cracking, "I love you. I don't think I ever told you that."

Silence falls across the line.

John Dalton Jr. swallows hard, caught off guard.

And Anne, sitting there beside her son, feels her heart crack wide open. This is not what she expected...John takes a moment before answering. His voice, when it comes through the line, is gentle.

"I love you too, Michael. Or is it Tripp now? Your mother has bragged about everything you've been doing."

Tripp smiles weakly, a flicker of pride and sorrow mixed. "I'm asking people to call me Tripp... as a symbol of the change." He clears his throat.

"You sound different," John says after a pause. "In a good way."

Anne watches closely, her heart catching at the vulnerability in her son's face.

"I'm trying," Tripp whispers. "Uncle John, I'm sorry. If I ever said anything to hurt you... I didn't mean it."

"You've never hurt me, Tripp," John says, voice steady. "Never."

Tripp exhales, the tightness in his chest loosening just a little. "I just... I needed you to know."

He grips the receiver tighter, words tumbling out before fear can steal them away.

"I... I'm not the same person anymore. I'm trying to be someone better. A man... someday."

Anne presses her hand against her mouth to keep from crying. She can see it now — the rawness, the longing for approval, the deep fear of slipping backward.

"I can hear it in your voice," John says warmly. "Your mother told me how hard you've been working."

Tripp hesitates, weighing how much to say. "If I didn't change, I was going to lose everything."

"Everything?" John prompts gently.

Tripp fidgets, biting his lip.

"Uncle John..." he says instead, voice small, "Uh, when are you coming down again? Or maybe visiting Papa Dalton at the lake?"

Anne stays quiet, sensing how much this moment matters.

"Not until the holidays," John answers slowly. Jake murmurs something in the background. "Why, Michael?"

"I just need to talk to you," Tripp whispers. "I need ... your viewpoint."

The air between them thickens.

"I have time now," John offers. "If it's something you want to talk about—"

Tripp squeezes his eyes shut. "It's not... it's not something for the phone."

He looks at his mother, sitting there, love radiating from her — and yet something inside him recoils from hurting her with the truth he carries.

"I can wait," Tripp says quietly, voice cracking. "It'll keep."

"Is it something you can't talk to your mom about?" John asks carefully.

Tripp swallows hard. "No, sir. It's just... it's not ready yet. It needs time."

Anne fights the urge to reach out, to demand answers. She knows — knows — that pushing him now would only drive him deeper into himself.

John's voice is steady on the line. "Will it wait until I can get there?"

"It has to," Tripp says, so softly Anne barely hears him. "I don't... I don't have anyone."

"You mean no one to trust?" John asks, alarmed. "Your mother's right there. You can trust her."

"I know," Tripp says miserably. "But not until it's right."

There's a pause — Jake whispering again on the other end.

John clears his throat.

"Michael, let me speak to your mother for a moment, okay?"

"Yes, sir," Tripp whispers, handing the phone back.

Anne takes it, heart hammering. Tripp's hand lingers for just a second longer than necessary, like he's afraid of letting go.

"John?" she says into the receiver.

"I guess you figured out he wants to talk," John says dryly.

"Yes," Anne says, brushing Tripp's hair back with trembling fingers. Her son looks so fragile sitting there — so young and scared.

"I have a hunch, based on what you've told me about his changes. Maybe I'm wrong. It could be drugs..."

"You're never wrong, John."

John laughs under his breath. "Jake's insisting I fly down. He's booking the ticket now."

Anne closes her eyes, overwhelmed with gratitude. *What could Tripp have said to him?* She wonders, fearing that she knows.

"I love you, John."

"I love you too, sis. Don't panic. We'll figure this out."

Anne cradles the receiver against her shoulder, tears brimming. She watches her son, who is holding himself together by sheer will.

John's voice returns. "Let me talk to him one more time before we hang up."

Anne hands the phone back.

Tripp's eyes are red and shining. His lip trembles, but he clenches his jaw, trying to be strong. He takes the phone carefully.

"Yes, Uncle John?"

"Michael," John says, voice rich with feeling, "I spoke to my business partner. He'll cover my meetings. I can fly down tomorrow if that's what you want."

Tripp's hands tremble around the receiver. "Would you..." His voice breaks. "Would you really do that for me?"

"Yes, Michael," John says gently. "Family is important."

The words cut straight through Tripp's defenses. Tears spill down his cheeks — and for the first time in what feels like forever, he lets himself be small, lets himself be loved.

"I'm sorry," he chokes. "I didn't want to be a problem..."

"You're not a problem," John says firmly. "You're family. You're loved. *Never* forget that."

"Good night, Uncle John." Tripp hands his mother the phone.

Anne sets the receiver gently back in its cradle. She wraps her arms around her son and kisses the top of his head, rocking him like she did when he was small.

"Baby," she murmurs, "Uncle John will be here tomorrow night. Can you wait until then?"

"Thank you, Momma," Tripp sobs. "My life was supposed to be better this time."

Anne's heart twists painfully. "This time?" she repeats gently.

"I thought I was here to make things right. I was making it right. But I'm failing all over again," Tripp whispers.

He slams his fist weakly against the bedspread, the fight draining out of him. He sees his mother's loving gaze.

"Why?" She whispers.

"It's complicated," he says, voice breaking. "I'm still that damn old man deep inside. No matter how hard I try."

And somewhere in the haze, Robbie's face flickered across his mind — another truth he couldn't face yet.

Tripp's mind races however.

Last night. Robbie's bedroom. The blurred, confusing boundaries of friendship and something more. Doubt consumes his mind. Had they shifted without realizing it? Had Robbie noticed what Tripp tried so hard to hide?

Questions swirl like smoke, impossible to grasp.

The truth, Tripp thinks bitterly, *is never what we expect.*

He closes his eyes, forcing the memories away.

There's still so much he needs to fix. So many people depending on him — even if they don't know it.

He clears his throat, voice scratchy.

"Momma," he says, sitting up carefully. "I'm going to my room, okay?"

"Of course, honey," Anne says gently. "Call out if you need me."

"Thank you, Momma," Tripp whispers.

Tripp returns to his room. Stretching out on his bed, the photo album beckons from the night stand. He tries to resist. *Jeff is in there. Robbie...how could I be that blind?* Tripp remembers the photos, the similarity between him and Jeff. *Our eyes always find the the heart's desire.* Tripp hears Doctor Elmhurst's advice echoing from a future he desparately wants to change.

From the doorway, his mother's voice floats in, gentle but firm.

"Michael." She clears her throat and amends, "Tripp."

Startled, he almost drops the album. "Oh — yes, Momma?"

"Robbie's on the phone. He wants to talk to you."

Tripp closes the album with a soft thump, cradling it against his chest for a moment longer than necessary.

"I'll use the living room phone so I don't disturb you, okay?"

Anne Carson smiles, the kind of mother's smile that expects nothing but offers everything. "That's very thoughtful, honey."

Tripp sniffs, blinking rapidly, and slides off the bed. In a few steps, he's at the living room door. Shadows stretch long across the carpet, the only light is a single lamp near the couch.

He picks up the receiver, forcing cheer into his voice as he calls out, "OK, Momma!" before pressing it to his ear.

The line crackles softly before Robbie's voice comes through, tentative. "Hey, Tripp?"

"Hey, Robbie..." Tripp whispers, heart thudding painfully.

"You left so fast this afternoon..." Robbie sounds unsure, fragile. "Doug didn't really pick up on it, but I thought... I thought maybe you were mad."

"Mad?" Tripp swallows hard. "No, no... I just had to swing by Maddox for my Momma. And I figured maybe you wanted to hang out with Doug for a while... without having to lug dead weight around."

Robbie chuckles, but it's thin, nervous. "Just as long as you're not mad."

"I'm not, Rob," Tripp says, closing his eyes but the tears escape. "I promise."

"You sure? You sound... different."

"Long day, I'm tired." Tripp leans back against the couch, the old frame groaning under his weight. "I found out some family's making a surprise visit tomorrow. Uncle John's flying down."

"Your Uncle John? Isn't he the one in D.C.?" Robbie asks, confused. "That's a long trip for a surprise visit."

"He gets better rates. For his work, or something," Tripp says quietly, wishing he had a better lie.

There's a pause, then Robbie asks, softer now, "Do I need to take the bus Monday?"

"No, no," Tripp says quickly. "I'll drive y'all to school. I just... I won't be able to drive you home. Sorry."

"No problem," Robbie says, the brightness forced and brittle. "So... I'll see you tomorrow, right?"

"Yeah, tomorrow." Tripp breathes. "My old friend."

A beat of silence.

"Okay. Goodnight," Robbie says, voice breaking just a little. "Old friend."

The line clicks dead.

Tripp hangs up the phone and lowers the receiver slowly, like it weighs more than he can bear. He tosses his glasses aside, but the motion feels hollow, automatic.

He just sits there, the silence of the living room pressing down on him.

Frozen.

Ashamed.

He knows he heard it — the shift in Robbie's voice, the sadness Tripp put there. Another friend slipping through his fingers, another heart he didn't know how to hold.

Why do I always do this?

He presses the heels of his hands into his eyes, trying to hold back the tears.

But the shame clings to him, thick and heavy.

"Dammit," he growls under his breath, voice raw and shaking. "Way to go, Michael. Just like the selfish old fat man."

Monday Morning Misunderstandings

M onday morning feels heavier than usual. Robbie slumps in his seat, staring out the window. Tripp grips the steering wheel tighter than necessary, his mind racing with everything he wants to say — and everything he's afraid will make it worse.

He still feels like a scrambled mess of nerves and second-guessing. And now Uncle John is part of the equation. *Please don't let this blow up in my face,* Tripp thinks grimly.

"Uncle John's my only choice," he mutters. "It's 1980 — Doctor Elmhurst is probably just starting med school."

The thought makes him chuckle under his breath. Tripp is glad they didn't hear the comment, he doesn't want to lie to Robbie or Lauren. Not now, it would make things worse.

Tripp cautiously glances at Robbie. His friend focuses on the passing landscape. No music, only the hum of the V8 engine disturbs the silence. Neither of them talked during the short ride to Lauren's house.

When Tripp pulls up to the curb, Lauren climbs in, immediately sensing something is wrong. She glances between them. Robbie's slouched posture screams sadness. Tripp looks like his brain is a million miles away. This isn't the condition she'd expected this morning.

Lauren considers staying quiet — just letting it ride —but that's not who she is. Her dorks need her.

"Hey, Robbie," she asks gently, testing the waters. "How did Saturday go? Did y'all save Doug?"

Robbie lets out a sigh so heavy it fogs the window.

"Yeah," he says, voice hollow. "Mike made a big difference. Doug said we finished..."

"Finished?" Lauren asks, leaning forward, hopeful.

Robbie nods blankly. "Yeah. Finished faster than Doug thought we would. Beat the afternoon rain."

Tripp stares straight ahead. Moving like an automoton at an amusement park. Lifeless and empty.

"I had to head home after we wrapped up," Tripp says, his voice flat.

"Oh... well, okay." Lauren hesitates, then presses, trying to spark some life into the conversation. "What did you do for the rest of the day?"

Robbie answers before Tripp can.

"Doug and I dropped Alice off, then went to his house to work on his truck," Robbie mumbles, his voice barely audible.

Tripp tries to force a smile, fails. His chest feels the weight of his failure. This is his doing, his fault that a wedge has grown between them.

"My uncle's coming to town. Had to do something for my mom," he says. "So... I can't give y'all a ride home this afternoon."

"I'm taking the bus," Robbie says quietly, still staring out the window.

"Well, I can get Greg to take me," Lauren adds quickly, trying to ease the tension. She studies them both, her gut knotting.

"Did something happen Saturday?" she finally blurts. "I feel like I'm at a funeral or something."

Tripp lifts his head, catching Robbie's reflection in the rearview mirror.

"Nah," he says lightly. "Robbie's just worried he upset me. He didn't. He did a great job balancing his time between me and Doug on Saturday. It was hard work though. I guess I'm just sore. Old fat man and all."

Lauren giggles despite herself. Even Robbie manages a small, reluctant laugh.

Tripp clings to the humor — the old Michael Carson method of survival. He parks the car, pulling into their usual spot.

Before the ignition's even off, Robbie grabs his bag and bolts for the school, his head down, his shoulders tight. Tripp watches him go, his heart sinking.

Lauren grabs his arm before he can follow. She yanks him back hard enough to startle him.

"So, Michael," she snaps, arms crossed. "You expect me to believe all that bullshit?"

Tripp sighs heavily."Yeah, I guess not," he mutters.

Lauren narrows her eyes.

"What about you?" she demands. "You're acting just as bad."

Tripp rubs the back of his neck.

"It's like October seventh never happened and the old Michael Carson showed his ass this weekend," he mutters bitterly, hanging his head low. "I owe Robbie an apology."

"Yes you do." Lauren barks, folding her arms. "Want to start from the top, Tripp?"

"Something changed." Tripp hangs his head low. "We helped Doug. I could see that they are best friends."

Lauren's anger softens. "Was it hard?" she asks quietly. "Seeing your best friend with someone else?"

Tripp's laugh is dry, almost painful.

"Truthfully?" he says. "No. It;s good seeing him happy. It was weird. I didn't feel like a third wheel or anything. I just... I dunno. I guess I was wrapped up in my own head."

Lauren nods, reaching out to squeeze his arm.

"I meant what I said before. You can talk to me, you know. You can trust me."

"I know," Tripp says, voice cracking slightly. "I just... I don't even know what to say yet."

He slings his bag over his shoulder, trudging toward the school.

"I'm going to talk with my uncle tonight," he calls back. "Maybe figure out what the hell I'm supposed to do."

Lauren jogs to catch up, falling into step beside him.

"I'm not mad at you, Tripp," she says gently. "I care about you — both you and Robbie. But seriously — I can't have sad dorks following me around. I have a reputation to protect!"

That earns a real laugh from Tripp.

He slows as they approach the main doors. *She's only trying to help,* he thinks.

"I left Saturday without saying anything," he says quietly.

"And I was a coward on Sunday, I was supposed to go to his house but kept overthinking what could go wrong. So, to make sure nothing happened, I stayed home. Robbie probably thinks I'm mad... or jealous... or just a shitty friend."

His answer stings, Lauren pulls him into a quick, fierce hug. "Tripp, I don't think that of you, neither will Robbie."

Tripp smiles, taking the hug. "Thanks..." He whispers.

"Then tell him," she says firmly. "Don't let a stupid misunderstanding screw everything up. You've worked too damn hard to throw your friendship away now."

She pats his shoulder and walks off, giving him space. Lauren struggles to keep the tears inside, the pain of not being able to help is a tidal wave crashing down on her.

Tripp watches her go, heart hammering in his chest.

I need to fix this, he tells himself.

No more waiting.

He glances at his watch and bolts for the building, weaving through clusters of students.

He's not sure what he's going to say yet — only that he has to say something before it's too late. Tripp bursts into the hallway, dodging through the morning chaos. He barrels toward the main wing, heart hammering.

Gotta fix this. Gotta fix this.

He slides into the classroom, barely managing to stop himself from crashing into a desk.

Robbie sits near the windows, his bag slumped at his feet. Their spot in the class. He stares blankly outside, his face guarded, distant. Tripp beelines for the desk beside him and drops into the seat, tossing his bookbag onto the floor. Robbie turns, forcing a small smile — but it fades before it even reaches his eyes.

Tripp leans in.

"Robbie, I..." He shakes his head, frustration boiling over. "I'm a fucking idiot."

Robbie blinks, startled. "Huh? What are you talking about, Mike?"

Tripp rubs his face, struggling for the right words.

"I've been... worried about some stuff. With my cousin. It's nothing major, but..." He trails off, searching Robbie's face. "Thruth is, I'm failing. I'm losing my life, my future, my cousin, everything, it's closing in all at once."

"You coulda said something, Mike..."

"I couldn't risk telling you. I'm afraid. Saturday just... triggered some stupid thoughts."

"Triggered?" Robbie repeats, eyebrows knitting together.

Tripp hurries to explain.

"You weren't doing anything wrong. I'm sorry, Rob. I shouldn't have left like that. I *wanted* to help Doug — and it was great seeing you happy with him. I just got stuck in my own head. After our call Saturday night, I realized how much **I** screwed up. I was afraid to call yesterday. Your friendship means everything to me. I'm afraid to lose you..."

He clenches his fists.

Tripp shakes his head and continues. "Dammit. It's all my fault. The old Mike Carson — the one who overthinks everything —

it's a monster still lurking inside me. I didn't think about how my silence would make you feel. Forgive me?"

For a second, Robbie just stares at him. Then, slowly, he smiles — a real one this time.

"You never have to be afraid, Tripp," he says softly. "I'm always beside you. Your friendship is a big part of who I am."

"I didn't want to lose you." Tripp hangs his head, his voice cracking. "I crawled into a shell. I should've trusted you."

"You're the one who told me we should always talk it out. I was just... worried. I thought you changed your mind about us hanging out. And you *did* work hard. Doug and I both saw it."

Tripp swallows hard.

"I owe you, Rob."

"You don't," Robbie says, shaking his head. "I'm just glad we're okay."

Tripp pats Robbie's arm gratefully. In a blink of an eye, he almost lost everything...

They exchange a quiet smile — the bond between them pulling tight again, stronger than before.

Before Tripp can say more, Suzanne approaches quietly, a folded jacket in her hand. She coughs softly to get their attention.

"Hey, Mike," she says shyly.

"Oh — hi, Suzanne."

Robbie scoots back, giving them room. Suzanne clears her throat, holding out the jacket.

"Thanks again," she mumbles. "My mom washed it... I mean, I didn't... uh, it's clean now."

Tripp chuckles gently, his kindness disarming her embarrassment, taking the jacket and folding it onto his bag. The veil of nervousness disappears from her face.

"Don't worry about it," he says. "Anytime you need help, just ask."

"Thank you, Mike," Suzanne whispers. "See ya, Robbie."

Suzanne beams at him, then flashes a playful glance toward Robbie before scampering off to her seat.

Robbie raises an eyebrow.

"I loaned her my jacket," Tripp says, shrugging.

"I gathered that," Robbie replies, amused but curious.

Tripp leans in closer.

"Remember last week? Those tan pants she wore?"

Robbie grins, nodding. "Looked like they were painted on."

Tripp lowers his voice. "Well... she, uh... had an accident. Early."

Robbie's eyes widen in sudden understanding. "Oh."

Tripp answers, "Yeah." Nodding.

Robbie slides a little closer. "That's rough."

Tripp nods grimly. "At the beginning of class, it was just a small spot. Could hardly see it. By the end? Huge. I gave her my jacket to cover it."

Robbie nods in approval. "Smooth, Carson. Very smooth."

Tripp smiles faintly, but a shadow passes over his face.

"It was just being nice. It happened to Gabby once; boy, was she embarrassed," Tripp chuckles, leaning back in his chair; remembering a happy moment with his daughter.

"Gabby?" Robbie asks curiously.

"Huh?" Tripp realizes he shared his memory aloud.

"You used to never talk about family," Robbie adds. "So, what happened?"

"Yeah," Tripp says quickly, covering his slip. "A cousin. From Gable. South Carolina."

Robbie frowns slightly but lets it slide.

"What happened?"

Tripp smiles at the memory, though it's tinged with sadness.

"We were at an amusement park. Gabby was wearing white pants... it caught her by surprise. I had a T-shirt under my button-down, so I gave her the shirt."

Robbie watches him closely. Tripp feels the pain of her absence.

"You were her hero," he says simply.

Tripp laughs softly, but it's hollow.

"For a while," he murmurs, smile fading. "I guess the old Mike Carson isn't quite the mean bastard I make him out to be."

He leans back in his seat, blinking hard against the sudden burn behind his eyes.

Gabby... Leigh... I promised I'd be better. I can't never make this up to you. Another lifetime's promise I'll never get to keep.

Robbie sees Tripp's withdrawal into deep thought and nudges him gently with his shoulder.

"You know, Tripp," he says, "I keep telling you — you weren't all bad. You had a good heart then, too. I wouldn't be your best friend if I didn't believe that."

Tripp exhales slowly, fighting back the wave of emotion.

"Thanks, Rob," he says quietly.

They sit in comfortable silence for a moment — two boys, two lifetimes of weight pressing on Tripp's shoulders, leaning into the only thing that really matters: trust.

Affections of the Heart

Tripp makes it home quickly. Traffic is light and he makes good time.. Still fighting nervousness, he isn't sure how to start the conversation with his uncle. He bursts into the house, tosses his bookbag onto the couch, and heads to the kitchen. He needs a moment to breathe.

Grabbing a glass of water, he leans against the counter, staring out the window.

"I need a plan," Tripp mutters. *"Break it into three parts. Keep it simple. Keep it calm."*

He knows better, though. Fifty-eight years of hard living taught him that no plan goes the way it's intended, regardless of considering all the alternatives. Today will be no different. He'll just have to adapt.

A car pulls up outside. Tripp peers through the window and spots a gleaming yellow Cadillac — a rental, no doubt. His heart leaps.

He sprints to the door and it swings open just as John Dalton, Jr. steps onto the porch. Tripp can't stop himself — he rushes forward and hugs his uncle tightly. John laughs warmly, wrapping his arms around him without hesitation. Time stands still.

His uncle is Anne's youngest brother. Always stylish, always composed. Gray slacks, tan sports coat, neat hair brushed to the side — the same height as Michael, but far leaner and more athletic.

Tripp pulls back, blinking rapidly, trying not to cry.

"Thanks for coming, Uncle John," he says, voice thick.

"I know this wasn't easy — or cheap. It means a lot."

John smiles, steady and reassuring.

"I could hear in your voice that it was urgent," he says.

"How about we take a drive? Neutral ground. Sometimes talking's easier that way."

Tripp nods quickly. "Yes, sir. Great idea. Let me leave Momma a note first."

John smiles approvingly as Tripp dashes to the fridge, scribbling a quick message for Anne. John takes this thoughtfulness as a good sign.

Minutes later, they slide into the Cadillac — a plush luxury compared to Tripp's tiny Mustang — and head out onto the quiet roads of Glade Avenue.

Tripp stares out the window, fidgeting, feeling the weight of the moment pressing down on him. John drives in comfortable silence for a few minutes before speaking.

"Okay, Michael. Just you and me now. Do you want to jump right in, or ease into it?"

Tripp shifts in his seat, heart hammering.

"I have a plan... sort of," he says. "It might take me a few minutes to, uh, land the plane."

John chuckles. "Your granddad would love the airplane reference."

"Yeah." Tripp nervously adds.

They drive past rolling hills and clusters of trees, the sun dipping low in the sky. Tripp thinks this is a perfect day. It has to be.

"I'm here for you," John says. "I'm staying with Uncle Pat all week. No rush."

Tripp swallows hard. "All week?" Tears prick his eyes again. He wasn't expecting that.

"I didn't mean to be a burden," he mutters. "I respect that you came all this way."

"Michael," John says firmly, "I wouldn't be here if you weren't important."

The words break something loose inside of Tripp Carson.

"I didn't think it would be this hard," Tripp whispers, scrubbing a hand over his face. He draws in a shaky breath.

"I love you, Uncle John. I really do."

He hesitates, voice cracking under the weight of everything he's carrying.

"And I'm sorry," he chokes out. "Not just for anything I ever said...

but for everything I might've said if I hadn't been trying so damn hard to be better."

John's voice is soft but steady.

"It takes courage to admit when you're struggling," he says.

"And even more to ask for help. This stays between us. Always."

Tripp nods, fighting back fresh tears.

"It's not easy... being Willis Carson's son," he says bitterly. "He instilled some... pretty ugly ideas. Ideas I hate that I carried for too long."

John doesn't interrupt.

He just listens.

"You've always been your mother's son, too," he says finally.

"And she gave you a good heart."

Tripp breathes out slowly. His heart races from the fear of getting this wrong.

"I guess... it just took me forty-six years to realize it."

John chuckles. "Quite a long meditation."

Tripp manages a small smile.

"I used to worry about you, Uncle John. Spending holidays alone... being one of seven kids, but living so far from everyone else. It hurt me to think you didn't have anyone."

John smiles sadly. "I like my life, Michael. I have friends. A business. A home in DC. It's not empty."

Tripp nods, though a sadness lingers.

His eyes drift to John's left hand on the steering wheel — to the gold band shining there. An enigma to the younger Mike, before he learned the truth.

He blurts before he can stop himself.

"I always wondered about your ring. At first, I thought it was for the church... but even pastors can have wives."

John stiffens slightly, glancing down at the ring.

Tripp plows ahead, heart hammering.

"I'm not asking, Uncle John. Whoever it is... I'm just glad you have someone to love. Someone who loves you back. I hope someday I get to meet them."

For a long beat, the car is silent except for the hum of tires on asphalt. John considers the motivators pushing this conversation.

Then John says softly, "Let's take care of you first."

Tripp exhales shakily. "Yes, sir. That's fair."

John glances at him sideways, reading the tension still coiled in his nephew's shoulders.

"You're scared," he says gently.

Tripp nods. "I think... there's something wrong with me."

John's voice tightens with concern. "Have you told your mom?"

"No. I needed to talk to you first." Tripp shakes his head quickly. "I needed someone who... might understand."

John stays silent, letting him find the words.

"I think I am broken. I like girls..." Tripp lets out a heavy sigh.

"You're sixteen, Michael. It is natural for you to like girls," John smiles with a pleasant chuckle.

Tripp hangs his head down. The sudden realization that before coming to 1980, only Doctor Elmhurst knew this secret about him. Tripp did not have many people left in 2022 that he could tell, but he never tried. John Dalton notices that Tripp is very nervous and holding back. He knows he has to break through that wall between them. John gently pats Tripp on the knee.

Tripp smiles briefly at John and then looks away. His uncle will be the first person in his family to know the truth. Granted, John Dalton will be, or so Mike Carson hopes, that his uncle should be the most sympathetic to what he's going through, but it will still be hard. Michael Willis Carson must have blind trust. The moment of truth has come. He takes a deep breath. *Please....do not let this be a mistake...*

"I also like boys..." Tripp admits softly. He closes his eyes, worrying that this is the wrong action. John understands that Michael is struggling.

The silence forces Tripp to squeeze his eyes shut, bracing for rejection.

Instead, John's voice is calm, steady. "I'm listening, Tripp. No judgment here."

Tears slide down Tripp's cheeks as he nods.

"I'm bisexual, Uncle John. Guess I always was. There was this incident... at the beach. With a friend."

He struggles through the memory.

"I didn't say no. I didn't want to." Tripp struggles to breathe. "But after...the next morning, all I could hear was my dad's voice."

Tripp buries his face in his hands. "Telling me it was wrong. That *I* was wrong."

John tightens his grip on the steering wheel but stays quiet, listening.

"I spent a lifetime hating myself for something I couldn't change," Tripp whispers. "It poisoned everything I cared about. Friends ... Family." His last thought, *my children.*

John finally speaks.

"Sometimes... boys are just curious, Michael. One experience doesn't define everything."

"It's more than that," Tripp says. " When I like a girl, the physical attraction comes first, then the emotional connection.

Easy, natural. When I like a boy, the emotional connection is first, then I am physically attracted. It feels right. It's based on my heart. Maybe in a sense, I would have a better relationship with a guy..."

He wipes at his face again. The tears aren't stopping. He sees his uncle watching him.

Tripp adds with hesitation. "It's not a phase. This is **who I am**."

"Some men go their entire life battling the same thing." Uncle John explains, focusing on the road. "It takes courage to look inward and accept yourself.

"I thought I could improve my life this time, but it has recently become complicated." Mike explains with an eye roll. "Very...**complicated**..."

John stops at a light. He touches Trip on the arm, hoping to comfort his nephew. "Tell me, Michael. What is this complication?" John asks.

"I'm in love with someone," Tripp answers sadly as the smile fades from his face.

"It doesn't sound like you are happy about it," John moves the car when the light turns green. "Do you want to keep talking?"

Tripp nods, appreciating his uncle's patience. "I wanted to focus on fixing myself. Finding love was something to pursue after graduating high school. I knew what I had to do. I had a mission. Fate has a funny way of disrupting the best of plans. I did not know that I loved him the way I do. It took me by surprise."

"Does he know how you feel?" John asks, proceeding with caution. "I can say from personal experience that the hardest part is trusting the right one."

"He knows I think very highly of him..." Tripp struggles to smile, "But my true feelings? I don't know, Uncle John. He is my best friend..."

"Oh," A smile grows on his face. John guesses. "Robbie?"

Tripp quietly answers, "Yes, sir."

"Best friends have a strong bond." John nods and answers softly, "And one day, you realized there was more to your feelings?"

"I didn't see it, but it was there. Always there," Tripp nods yes, remembering the events. "Robbie doesn't know. You are the only one I have told about my bisexuality since it came out in therapy..."

"Therapy?" John questions quickly.

Tripp gasps and quickly replies, hoping to correct his slipup, "Uh, the school psychologist. I can trust him. I don't know what to do."

John takes a breath.

"Truthfully, Michael... I didn't expect you to say this."

Tripp's heart sinks — until John adds:

"I'm homosexual. I'm married. His name is Jake. And this," he lifts his left hand briefly from the wheel, "is **his** ring."

Tripp stares at him, blinking in disbelief — and overwhelming relief.

"I'm glad, Uncle John," he says thickly. "I'm so glad. Thank you for trusting me."

"You trusted me. Together, we'll work this out."

They drive on in silence for a few minutes, the weight of the confession lifting, replaced by something gentler. Stronger.

A Mother's Love

"So, Tripp, ready to go home?"

With his uncle's help, he will be able to tell his momma.

"Yes, sir."

The Cadillac pulls quietly into the driveway on Glade Avenue. Anne paces anxiously inside, wearing a trail into the living room carpet.

She sees the car pull up — bright yellow, impossible to miss. Through the window, she catches a glimpse of John and Tripp stepping out, both smiling.

Relief floods her chest, but nerves still twist in her stomach.

Tripp leads the way to the door, glancing once at John, silently asking for strength. John nods back, steady and reassuring.

Inside, Anne wrings her hands. When they step through the door, she moves to meet them immediately.

John gently rests his hands on Tripp's shoulders, steering him to stand directly in front of his mother.

Anne's heart races. She can see the fear in her son's eyes, the way he trembles slightly under John's touch.

John smiles at Anne, calm and confident.

"I think Tripp has something he needs to tell you," he says softly.

Anne moves to stand so she's eye-to-eye with her son.

"Michael Willis Carson," she says, her voice shaking but full of love, "you can always tell me anything. Anything important to you."

Tripp swallows hard.

"I know, Momma," he whispers. "But I'm scared."

Tears brim in his eyes, and Anne instinctively reaches for both of his hands, holding them tightly.

"Tripp," she says, voice breaking, "you know I could never think less of you. Never. Please trust me, baby."

Tripp glances helplessly at Uncle John, who nods encouragingly.

"You can do this," John says quietly. "We're right here. We believe in you."

Tripp inhales sharply, struggling against the tide of emotions. He's terrified, but somewhere deep inside, he knows — he *knows* — he has to do this.

Anne watches him closely, her heart breaking at how scared he is. Not because of what he's about to say, but because he feels like he can't trust his own heart.

"Momma..." Tripp begins, voice trembling.

His eyes search out for hers. "I've known for a long time that I was... different."

Anne doesn't move, doesn't blink — just holds his hands and listens.

"I've accepted who I am," Tripp says. "And it doesn't change me for the worse. It's given me peace. And I wouldn't have found that without you... and Uncle John."

Anne's lips quiver, tears spilling freely now.

Tripp squeezes his eyes shut and blurts it out before he loses his nerve.

"I like both boys and girls." he says, the words rushing out in a breath. "I'm bisexual, there's... there's a boy I love. But I can't tell him. Not yet."

For a moment, there's only silence — the heavy, breathless kind that fills a room right before it shatters.

Then Anne lets out a trembling laugh through her tears.

"Both boys and girls?" she repeats, smiling even as she cries.

"Tripp, honey... you never did anything the easy way."

He lets out a shaky laugh, sobbing openly now as he collapses against her.

Anne pulls him close, cradling her son like she did when he was little. They cry together — not out of sorrow, but relief.

Love pours between them, raw and unconditional.

John steps forward, wrapping his arms around both of them, completing the circle.

This is what family is supposed to feel like, Tripp thinks through the tears. Not fear. Not shame.

Just love.

Later, after emotions settle, Anne teases lightly, wiping at her face.

"Well... we thought this was going to take all week," she says, nudging John. "Guess you weren't completely right, huh?"

John chuckles.

"Anne, my dear, Tripp and I broke through most of it tonight.

But he still needs us. I'm staying the rest of the week.

He's not alone anymore."

Tripp sniffs, laughing, voice thick with gratitude.

"I love you both," he says fiercely. "So very much."

Anne ruffles his hair and pulls him in again.

John smiles warmly, thinking about Jake — about the family they'll finally be able to share.

"Well then," John says with a grin, "I think this calls for a celebration. Italian, anyone?"

Anne laughs and grabs her pocketbook. Tripp practically races to the door, excitement bubbling up now that the worst is behind him.

Just before they leave, John gently tucks a white envelope into Anne's purse, despite her playful protests.

She knows better than to argue. John Dalton, Jr. never does anything halfway.

Outside, the night air feels lighter, the world brighter.

Tripp grins as he climbs into the back seat of the Cadillac.

"I'll take a small lasagna," he announces proudly,
"and a salad!"
John laughs from the driver's seat.
Anne chuckles as she buckles in beside him.
The road ahead is still uncertain, but one thing is clear —
They'll face it together.

Ties That Bind

When they get home, it's already close to nine o'clock. John needs to return to Uncle Pat's house for the night.

Tripp slouches onto the couch, exhaustion sinking into his bones. He feels better — lighter — after everything that happened today.

But a deeper realization gnaws at the edges of his mind:

I have very little control over how my life will unfold.

Still, he believes he can succeed — because of the people who love him, and whom he loves in return. Whether that gratitude belongs to God, fate, the universe, or some unseen guardian angel, Tripp doesn't know. He only knows this second chance is a gift — and he won't waste it.

Uncle John wants to meet Scott first tomorrow — then meet Robbie afterward. He and Tripp devise a simple plan:

John will handle Aunt Linda and Scott directly. Meanwhile, Tripp will call his friends and tell them to ride the bus home after school.

John will pick him up out front when the final bell rings and they will get Scott together.

Tripp grabs the phone, heart racing with a nervous kind of excitement, and dials Robbie first.

The plan is set quickly. Robbie sounds thrilled to meet Uncle John — so thrilled, in fact, that it lifts Tripp's spirits more than he expects. Hearing Robbie's excitement feels like a promise: No matter what happens, their bond will endure.

After hanging up, Tripp immediately dials Lauren's number.

"Good evening," a deep voice answers after a single ring.

It's Lauren's dad.

"Yes, sir. Good evening," Tripp says politely. "This is Mike Carson. May I speak with Lauren?"

"Of course, Tripp," the man replies warmly. "Hold on a moment."

Tripp hears him call out: "Lauren! Telephone. It's Tripp."

"Thank you, sir," Tripp says again, smiling.

He leans against the wall, thinking about it — *Lauren's dad called me Tripp without hesitation. She must talk about me at her home.* That realization leaves a warm glow in his chest.

"Hey, Tripp!" Lauren's voice bursts through the line, full of energy.

"How are things going with your uncle?"

Tripp feels the tension ease out of his shoulders.

"It went really well," he says, smiling into the receiver. "We... had a good talk."

"Awww, Tripp," Lauren says, voice soft with pride. "I'm so glad. I figured you just needed someone you could trust."

Tripp's voice falters slightly.

"Lauren... I *needed* to talk to my uncle first. There wasn't another choice — the mission, you know..."

He trails off, heart heavy. He doesn't want her to think she wasn't enough.

"I know you offered to listen," Tripp continues, voice shaking lightly. "and that meant the world to me. God, it really did. I want you to know... I do *trust* you."

"Tripp," Lauren cuts in, gently but firmly. "We're good. You don't have to explain. I get it."

Relief floods Tripp's chest.

"Absolutely," he says quickly. "And... thank you."

"You're welcome," Lauren says, her voice warm.

"Hey, uh... can Greg pick you up after school tomorrow?" Tripp asks. "My uncle wants to visit Scott first. After that, we'll meet up with Robbie."

"I'm sure he can," Lauren says brightly. "Can I at least meet your uncle too? It'd be nice to see more of your family."

Tripp's eyebrows shoot up.

"You'd really want to?"

"Of course!" Lauren laughs. "We're friends. Unless it's supposed to be a *'boys only'* thing?"

"No — no way!" Tripp says quickly, feeling a rush of happiness. "I'd love for you to come. Honestly... it'll probably help having you there."

"I'm always here for you, Tripp." Lauren replies.

Barely able to contain his excitement, Tripp asks. "I was thinking maybe we could meet at the café?

Lauren giggles. "Then it's a date. I mean — not a *date* date — Ugh, you know what I mean."

Tripp grins. "I know exactly what you mean."

Lauren's voice softens. "Now *this* sounds like the Tripp I know. Have the demons been cast out between you and Robbie?"

Tripp sighs, running a hand through his hair. "Well... we're not mad at each other."

Lauren picks up on it immediately. "Hmm. That *sounds* like there's a but in there, Mister Carson."

"There is..." Tripp hesitates. "But I'm not ready to talk about it. I'm sorry, Lauren."

"Ssshhh," she soothes him immediately. "Michael Carson, you'll tell me when you're ready. I trust you. And just so you know — I'm always on your side."

Tripp's eyes burn with emotion. "I do trust you, Lauren. You're amazing. I never realized how incredible a friend you are. I don't deserve all these good people in my life..."

Lauren cuts him off gently. "Don't say that. You *do* deserve it. And Robbie would be furious if he heard you doubting yourself."

Tripp chuckles weakly. "You've been so helpful. I just... I need a little more time."

"And you'll have it," Lauren promises.

There's a soft pause — one of those rare, comfortable silences that only true friends can share.

"Sleep on it tonight, Tripp," Lauren says at last. "Don't worry. Robbie and I aren't going anywhere. We've got your back."

Tripp's voice cracks as he whispers, "Thank you. I don't even know what to say."

"You don't have to say anything," Lauren murmurs. "Good night, Tripp. Everything's going to be okay."

"Good night, Princess," Tripp whispers.

He hangs up the phone and leans against the wall, heart full.

A Subtle Influence

The first period ends with a shrill ring of the bell. Tripp weaves through the crowd, heading down the north wing of the school.

He needs to return a workbook to Steve — his friend needs it for an afternoon class. As he strolls along, Tripp frowns slightly.

Have I ever even been down this hall before?

The walls feel unfamiliar, almost alien. It leaves him feeling a little lost, but he shakes it off. The uneasy sensation bubbles gently under the surface, reminding him that he has changed his future.

Not important. He picks up the pace. *The next bell will ring soon. Steve's class is all the way at the end.*

As he hurries down the hall, a voice calls out behind him.

"Hey, Mike!"

He turns, heart lifting slightly.

Kelli Albright jogs up, her face bright with excitement, her short hair bouncing as she moves. The old Mike had barely spoken to her — maybe a few words during assemblies. Nothing personal.

But Tripp remembers clearly: He was infatuated with her once, long before February 17th changed everything.

"Hey, Kelli!" Tripp calls back, flashing a playful grin.

Her dark brown eyes sparkle as she approaches, holding her binder close to her chest.

"Or should I call you Tripp?" she teases, smiling warmly. "I heard you're making changes."

"I'm just trying to be a better person," he says, smoothing his hair unconsciously. "I prefer Tripp — but either one's fine. I'm still Mike Carson underneath."

"I like Tripp," Kelli says, tucking a curl behind her ear. "Sounds mysterious."

She leans in slightly, voice dropping slightly. Kelli carefully pushes some hair from his face. "I like your haircut too."

Tripp grins, feeling his face flush slightly.

"Yeah? Thanks. I got it because my brother helped me get a job at—"

"Maddox Grocery! I know!" Kelli interrupts, laughing. "I've seen you there a couple times."

"Really?" Tripp asks, surprised. "When?"

"A few weeks ago, I think. You must've just started. Your uniform still had that 'just ironed' look," she teases, her eyes twinkling.

Tripp chuckles, remembering how ridiculous he felt crammed into those tight, stiff pants.

"If I'm not too busy, you should stop and chat sometime," he offers, feeling unexpectedly bold. "I'd like that."

"I will," Kelli says brightly, then glances at the clock. "Hey — almost time for the bell. Gotta bounce! But you should go meet the new guy in Mrs. Jankowski's room!"

Tripp blinks. "The new guy? Last I heard, they couldn't find a replacement."

Kelli shakes her head, curls flying.

"Someone accepted! You should go say hi!" She gives a playful wave as she dashes off toward her class.

"See ya, Tripp!" Her voice echoes in the hallway.

"Bye, Kelli!" he calls after her.

Tripp watches her disappear into the crowd, smiling to himself. *Was that flirting?*

Or just friendliness?

He can't tell — and maybe it doesn't matter.

Either way, it feels good — normal.

He heads toward classroom 301 — Mrs. Jankowski's room. He had her last year, but always thought highly of the teacher, she was kind—even to the old Mike Carson. The door stands slightly ajar. No students inside. He knocks lightly.

"It's open, come on in," a voice calls.

Familiar. Friendly. Tripp steps inside.

"Good morning," he says — and then stops short, blinking.

"Good morning." The man greets.

"Mr. Summers?"

The young teacher glances up from a stack of papers.

"Yes? Hey, you're one of Mrs. Austin's students," Brock Summers says, snapping his fingers as he tries to place him. "Uh... you wrote the poem about the void, right?"

Tripp smiles proudly. "Yes. I named it 'And We Did Nothing.' It was about a nightmare I had."

Mr. Summers nods thoughtfully, studying him.

"Michael Carson?"

"That's me," Tripp says with a laugh. "My friends call me Tripp."

"Tripp?" Brock repeats, raising an eyebrow.

"Yeah. I'm the third generation. It's a nickname. After... well, after that nightmare, I wanted a fresh start. New name, new outlook."

He spreads his arms wide in a mock showman's pose. Mr. Summers chuckles.

"I like that," he says warmly. "And that poem — Erika, I mean Mrs. Austin — talked about it for days."

He sets the papers aside. "Mind if I call you Tripp?"

"I'd like that," Tripp says, stepping forward to offer a handshake. "Tripp Carson."

"Brock Summers," the young teacher replies, gripping Tripp's hand firmly. "Good handshake. Grandfather teach you that?"

"Yes, sir. Papa Dalton's old school."

Mr. Summers grins. "Impressive. So what brings you here?"

"I heard you took over for Mrs. Jankowski," Tripp says sincerely.

"I just wanted to say congratulations."

Mr. Summers leans back in his chair, looking more relaxed than Tripp remembers. Then it hits Tripp, there's a noticeable difference about Mr. Summers — his face looks thinner, lighter somehow. Tripp wonders if this is how things unfolded originally... or if the timeline is shifting in subtle ways.

"Thanks, Tripp," Brock says. "Despite life's little setbacks, I've always loved teaching, but lately... I feel reinvigorated."

"Really? What changed?" Tripp asks, genuinely curious.

Brock sighs heavily.

"You probably can't imagine this," he says. "But most kids either shy away from me or fixate on my weight. It's exhausting."

"I might understand more than you think," Tripp offers gently.

Brock smiles faintly. "I believe it. Anyway, something shifted. One day, the kids started asking about *me* — my hobbies, my background. They saw me as a person, not just a teacher or a... label."

He laughs, almost shyly. "Made me remember why I love this job."

Tripp feels a warm glow in his chest. Even if he didn't directly cause this shift, maybe his changes nudged the world slightly — for the better.

"That day Jerry Riggins got sick?" Tripp asks.

Brock's eyes widen in recognition.

"Yeah," he says slowly. "I think it started then. Something was different after that."

He leans forward, smiling genuinely. "And it hasn't stopped. I have hope now."

"Really?" Tripp asks.

"Oh, that must sound ridiculous?" Brock chuckles, shaking his head. "Listen to me — getting all sentimental."

"That's not ridiculous," Tripp says firmly. "It's passion. It's about living your life."

Brock's smile softens. "Thanks, Tripp. That means more than you know."

He sits back, looking almost boyishly happy.

"If you ever need anything — advice, help, whatever — you know where to find me."

"Yes, sir," Tripp says, grinning as he heads for the door. "Have a good day, professor."

They both laugh.

As Tripp walks back toward Steve's class, he briefly considers asking Mr. Summers about Caroline — another ripple he might be able to change.

One thing at a time, he tells himself.

Michael Carson strides down the hallway, heart lighter, steps sure. He didn't mean to — but today, he helped shift another life for the better.

And somehow, that feels like the greatest victory of all.

Crossroads And Second Chances

Doug Barrett walks across the courtyard, shoving his hands deep into the pockets of his jeans. Alice strides beside him, backpack slung lazily over one shoulder, her head bobbing slightly to the rhythm of her own thoughts.

"You know, Doug, for a guy who claims he's not worried about anything, you sure do look like you're about to puke," Alice says, smirking.

Doug laughs under his breath. "Thanks, Alice. Real supportive."

She nudges him playfully with her elbow. "You're welcome. By the way, you're buying the fries if you chicken out."

Doug rolls his eyes but doesn't argue. His mind isn't on Alice's sass anyway.

It's on Kai.

And Robbie.

And Mike — *no, Tripp* — sitting somewhere at the front of the school, waiting for his uncle.

Doug wonders if it's weird that part of him misses how simple things were — before everything started shifting. Robbie making new friends. Doug finding someone new to talk to, to laugh with, to maybe... something more.

He doesn't know what to call it yet.

He just knows he wants things to stay good — for all of them.

They reach the front walk where students wait for rides. Alice gives a lazy wave and peels off toward her brother's car.

Doug spots Tripp sitting alone on a bench at the far end.

For a moment, Doug hesitates.

Mike Carson... Mike used to be cocky, sharp-tongued, and sometimes flat-out mean.

But Tripp Carson — this new version — looks different even from a distance. Calmer. More open.

280

Doug adjusts his backpack strap, steels his nerves, and heads over.

"Hey, Mike!" he calls.

Tripp looks up immediately, his face lighting up.

"Doug!" Tripp says warmly, glancing around like he half-expected to be alone.

Doug laughs as he plops down beside him on the bench.

"What happened? Mustang break down?" Doug teases.

Tripp laughs with him, shaking his head. "No, Robbie's my mechanic, remember? My uncle's in town. He's picking me up today. We're gonna visit Scott."

Doug nods approvingly. "Tell Scott I said hey. He talks about you all the time, you know."

Tripp blinks. "You know my cousin?"

Doug shrugs like it's no big deal. "Yeah. He's in the youth group I help lead at New Bethlehem. Was supposed to help us at the park last weekend, but his dad pulled him last minute."

Tripp frowns, absorbing this new piece of information.

"I didn't know that..." he says quietly.

Doug studies Tripp's face — how genuinely surprised and concerned he looks — and feels a sudden surge of loyalty.

There's real kindness under there now. Maybe there always was, but now it's not buried so deep.

"Say, Mike," Doug says, lowering his voice, "You got a minute?"

"Sure," Tripp says, scooting closer.

Doug leans in. "Just... don't tell Robbie we talked, okay?"

"Is it serious?" Tripp raises an eyebrow. "And why not Robbie? He's my best friend."

"You'll understand," Doug says quickly. "It's not bad. It's just... Robbie was kinda upset after you left Saturday. He hid it pretty well, but I could tell."

Doug watches Tripp's shoulders sag slightly.

"I wasn't mad at him," Tripp says softly. "I was worried about,.uh, it doesn't matter. There's something weighing heavy on me. I thought maybe Robbie wanted to spend time alone with you. You two go way back."

Doug smiles faintly. "Yeah, five years. He ever tell you about us?"

Tripp chuckles. "He didn't need to. It's obvious. And I'm glad he still hangs out with you. New best friends don't erase old one best friends."

Doug feels a knot untangle inside his chest.

Maybe Mike — *Tripp* — really gets it after all.

"Thanks," Doug says quietly. "I was worried."

"That's what good friends do," Tripp says, patting Doug's arm. He hesitates, then adds: "I apologized to Robbie Monday morning. For leaving without explaining. For everything."

Doug nods, feeling a weird mixture of relief and admiration.

"You really have changed," he says, smiling. "It's almost like... you're a different person."

Tripp freezes for half a second.

Doug catches it, but before he can backpedal, Tripp smiles again — a little sadder this time.

"So, was I a jerk to you?" Tripp asks lightly.

Doug stiffens. "No — I mean — well, not really. Just... different. Angrier, maybe."

Tripp claps Doug on the shoulder.

"I'm sorry, Doug. For whatever I did. The old Mike wasn't someone I'm proud of."

Doug shrugs.

"We teach the kids at youth group — the past's gone. Be the best person you can today. That's all that matters."

He offers a handshake.

"Welcome to the future, Tripp Carson."

Tripp grips his hand firmly.

"Thanks," he says.

And this time, Doug believes him.

A sleek yellow Cadillac glides around the corner. Doug watches Tripp's face light up.

"That's him," Tripp says, grabbing his bag.

As the car pulls up, Doug rises too. Tripp motions him over.

"Uncle John, this is Doug Barrett — one of Robbie's best friends."

Doug sticks out his hand. "Sir."

"Nice to meet you, Doug," John Dalton, Jr. says warmly, shaking firmly.

"Come on, Michael," John adds, smiling. "We've got a stop to make."

Doug steps back, waving goodbye as Tripp clambers into the car.

The Cadillac pulls away.

Doug watches until they're out of sight, feeling a weird mixture of pride and hope.

People can change, he thinks.

Maybe not all at once.

But they can.

Threads of Family

The Cadillac glides away from the school, and Tripp leans back in the seat, still smiling from the bench conversation with Doug. He's glad they talked. Glad Doug is staying in Robbie's life. And glad he's slowly repairing the bridges the old Mike burned.

Uncle John taps the steering wheel lightly to the beat of the strange music playing through the speakers.

Tripp tilts his head.

"What are we listening to?" he asks, curious.

"Synthesizer music," Uncle John replies, smiling. "Jean-Michel Jarre. French artist. You like it?"

Tripp grins wide. "I do! I've never heard anything like it before. Feels like the future."

John chuckles. "Maybe after we pick up Scott, we can stop at the Record Changer. See if weu can find a copy of the album."

Tripp's heart lifts at the idea. "Really? You know the Record Changer?"

"Yes, Mark and I have been there, though it was last year," John smiles.

"I don't know what to say. That'd be awesome! Thanks, Uncle John!"

He leans his head back, letting the layers of sound wash over him. Maybe it's the music, maybe the warm spring sun — but for the first time in a long time, Tripp feels like things are going to be okay.

Simple joys, he thinks. He's finally learning to appreciate them.

They pull up outside the elementary school. Before Tripp can even climb out, he sees Scott tear across the lawn, backpack forgotten in the grass.

"Michael! Uncle John!" Scott yells, arms flailing wildly.

Tripp barely braces himself before Scott crashes into him, hugging tight. Laughing, Tripp ruffles Scott's messy hair.

Then Scott throws himself at Uncle John, squeezing just as fiercely.

"Whoa!" John laughs. "Easy, tiger!"

Scott beams up at them, talking a mile a minute.

"Hey, Uncle John! Did Michael tell you about my drums? Oh, and Regina's got a new boyfriend — he's stupid! Is this your car?! It's awesome!"

Tripp tries not to laugh.

"Slow down, buddy," he says, slinging an arm around Scott's shoulders.

John smiles warmly, watching the easy affection between the two boys. The last time he saw Scott, the kid was sullen, withdrawn. Now he's practically buzzing with life.

Maybe Michael really is making a difference.

This second chance is working.

As they load Scott's backpack into the car, Tripp offers the front seat, but Scott waves him off.

"Nah, I'm good in the back. We needs to take care of you!" Scott says with a mischievous grin.

They pull away from the curb.

John glances at Scott in the rearview mirror.

"You know, Scott... I heard you've been worried about Ashland Academy."

Scott crosses his arms, his whole body stiffening.

"My dad wants me to be a toy soldier," he mutters, staring out the window. "I'm not a toy."

John keeps his voice calm.

"Being a soldier isn't bad, Scott. Your grandfather served in World War II. But I think your dad's hoping you'll learn discipline, not just follow orders."

Scott grumbles something under his breath.

Tripp shifts in his seat, turning slightly to face him.

"From what Scott's told me," Tripp says carefully, "his dad doesn't like the drums. Doesn't like that Scott's... different, a free spirit. But I think Scott's soul is meant for bigger things."

Scott glances up, meeting Tripp's gaze — and beams. The validation means everything.

John smiles quietly to himself, noting how important Michael's influence has become.

"See, Scott? You've got people who believe in you," John says gently. "I love you, kiddo."

"Love you too, J!" Scott yells, bouncing in the seat.

He hesitates, then blurts: "Can I come live with you in D.C.?"

John chuckles, though there's a hint of sadness.

"I live pretty far away from your mom, Scott. It wouldn't be easy."

Scott pouts. "I don't care. She just listens to my dad anyway."

Tripp reaches back and touches Scott's hand.

"Scott... remember what we talked about?"

Scott exhales loudly, cheeks puffed.

"Yeah, yeah. They'll always be my parents. Doesn't mean I gotta like it."

John clears his throat, steering the conversation gently.

"Your dad agreed to a compromise, Scott. If you behave — show him you can be responsible — he won't send you to Ashland."

Scott stares out the window, silent.

John had hoped for a bigger reaction — relief, maybe excitement.

But Scott just looks tired.

Worn out by battles too big for a kid his age.

After a long minute, Scott pipes up, voice lighter:

"Hey, Michael! We seeing Robbie next?"

Tripp smiles. "Yeah, buddy. We'll meet him at the café."

Scott grins wide. "I like your friend, Michael. He's cool."

"He's my best friend," Tripp says softly. "He's really important to me."

Eyes lighting up as Scott laughs."Everybody knows that."

Tripp chuckles, but his heart twists a little. Scott's right.

It's obvious — maybe even more obvious than Tripp intends.

He pushes the thought aside.

"You're important too, Scott," Tripp says, ruffling his cousin's hair again. "Never forget that."

Scott half-smiles, nodding.

It's not the enthusiastic reaction Tripp hopes for, but it's real.

Sometimes that's enough.

The rest of the drive is quiet. Until they pull into the mall parking lot. Suddenly, Scott's energy returns full force.

He bounces from store to store, inspecting everything, bargaining over clothes, complaining loudly about tight collars and itchy suits.

Tripp and John laugh through it all, letting him be a kid for a while — no battles, no broken promises.

They manage to find four new school outfits and a sharp navy suit for church. Scott proudly demands a "big boy" real tie — no clip-ons — and insists that Tripp promises to teach him how to tie it.

Tripp grins, sealing the promise with a pinky swear. John Dalton, Jr. is amazed by his nephews...more like strangers to hom since the last visit to North Carolina. *Families can be repaired,* John assures himself.

By the time they load everything into the trunk, even John looks exhausted. Scott collapses into the backseat, clutching his new bag of sneakers like treasure.

As they head toward the café, Tripp leans his head against the window, watching the sunset bleed gold across the sky.

It feels like today matters.

Maybe not in big, history-book ways. But in the ways that count.

Second chances.

New threads of family being stitched together.

And somewhere, not too far away, his best friend waits — part of that tapestry too.

Approval and Acceptance

Robbie drives his mother's car, arriving first at the café. He grabs a table near the window, tapping his fingers nervously against the surface. This feels more like an interview than a casual meeting. Tripp never talks about his uncle much, but when he does, Robbie can tell — this matters.

Robbie glances down at himself. New blue jeans, the right length this time, and a borrowed blue button-down from Carlos. It's not tucked in — a little rebellion he can't quite shake — but he looks good. He hopes it's enough.

Through the window, he spies Greg's motorcycle sliding into the parking lot. Lauren leans over, gives Greg a kiss goodbye, and hurries inside.

Robbie straightens up.

"Hey, Lauren!" he calls, waving.

She smiles brightly and heads over.

"Hi, Robbie," she says, sliding into the seat across from him.

"I might've come a little too early," Robbie jokes, scratching the back of his neck. "But hey — good table, right?"

"It's perfect," Lauren laughs. "I see you clean up nice. That shirt looks good on you."

Robbie ducks his head, grinning. "Thanks, princess."

"I've always wanted to ask." Lauren raises an eyebrow, amused. "Princess? Where did that come from?"

Robbie chuckles. "At first? Sarcasm. Tripp always talked about you like you were royalty. But after the jump-start, when he began to change... I guess I started seeing it too. You're important to him — and now, to me."

Lauren blushes lightly, pleased. She settles into her seat, smoothing her pink Oxford shirt.

"Jump-start?" she asks, tilting her head.

Robbie laughs softly. "Doug's term. The day Tripp had that dream in Mrs. Austin's class — when everything shifted. Whatever it was, I'm glad it happened."

"I am too," Lauren agrees, resting her chin in her hand.

Robbie smiles warmly. "He said... he turned everything around for me. That's what he told me. And you know what? I believe him."

They share a laugh, the tension easing.

Lauren leans in slightly. "I'm glad we're better friends now, Robbie. I always thought maybe you didn't like me much."

Robbie grimaces. "I think... it was more about not liking Greg than you. You're a good person, Lauren. I respect you."

She beams at him, genuinely touched.

"You seem nervous," she teases gently.

Robbie laughs, covering his face briefly. "I am! I want to make a good impression for Tripp's sake."

Lauren watches him carefully, her smile softening.

"Since we have a few minutes," she says carefully, "can I ask you something? Just between us?"

Robbie nods. "Of course."

Lauren lowers her voice. Her mind settles on Jeff Tyler. She knows she needs to be careful. Lauren knows she could be wrong about this.

"I think... Tripp has feelings he doesn't fully understand yet. For someone important to him."

Robbie immediately thinks of Holly and fights back a grimace.

"You mean Holly," he says flatly. "He's had a thing for her for ages. But honestly? She's not right for him. He needs someone who sees who he really is, not someone chasing popularity."

Lauren hesitates.

"I'm not sure it's Holly," she says carefully. "I think Tripp... feels deeper than he realizes. He's scared to let his guard down."

Robbie frowns, confused but thoughtful.

"I just want him to be happy," Robbie says quietly. "I don't want him hurt."

"You care about him a lot," Lauren observes softly.

Robbie exhales, cheeks reddening.

"I do," he admits. "He's my best friend. I love him."

Lauren's expression doesn't change — only grows warmer.

"Like a brother," Robbie adds hastily. "You can't ever tell him I said that. Please, Lauren."

"I promise," she says, squeezing his hand. "I would never betray that."

Robbie ducks his head again, hiding a shy smile. It feels good to say it aloud, even if only to her.

"Tripp's hinted about liking someone." Robbie grimaces. "He hasn't told me who it is, I think he's scared."

Lauren thinks for a moment. "Tripp will let us know when he's ready. It's important we stand beside him. Offer support."

"Always, Lauren." Robbie smiles. "He's my best friend."

Before they can say more, Lauren spots movement outside. She points. "They're here."

Robbie's heart leaps into his throat.

Through the window, he sees Tripp walking across the parking lot with Scott bouncing beside him and a tall, sharply dressed man he assumes is Uncle John.

Tripp's face is pure sunlight — radiant with excitement.

Robbie stands quickly, brushing imaginary lint off his jeans.

Lauren rises too, smoothing her shirt.

They brace themselves as the trio approaches.

"Uncle John, this is Robbie — Robert Davis," Tripp says proudly.

"My best friend."

Robbie steps forward and offers a firm handshake. "It's an honor to meet you, sir."

John smiles warmly. "Pleasure's mine."

"Uncle John, this is Lauren... uh..." Tripp freezes for a half-second, realization dawning with a jolt of embarrassment. After all the rides to school, all the conversations, the years of friendship — he had never known her last name.

Before the moment grows too awkward, Lauren smiles warmly and steps in without missing a beat.

"Lauren Masters," she says, offering her hand to John with a graceful nod.

Tripp exhales quietly, grateful — and silently promises himself to do better from now on.

Lauren steps up, smiling brightly. "A pleasure to meet you, Mr. Dalton."

"Please — John," he says kindly.

Scott chimes in, beaming up at Lauren. "She's pretty, Michael!"

Lauren laughs, ruffling Scott's hair. "You're a charmer, Scott Graves."

John chuckles and gestures toward the table. "Shall we sit? I'd love to hear more about Michael's friends."

Tripp and Robbie head off to grab drinks, Scott tagging along eagerly.

Lauren sits with John, smoothing the front of her shirt nervously.

John smiles kindly across the table at Lauren, sensing her nervousness.

"Relax," he says gently. "We're all here for Michael. But... I suspect that's not the only thing on your mind."

Lauren hesitates, fiddling with the corner of her napkin.

"I guess I just worry about him," she admits. "He's fighting so hard to change, but sometimes I wonder if he even knows how much he's already grown."

John leans back thoughtfully. "Finding yourself isn't easy," he says. "Especially when you're trying to rebuild what you never knew you lost."

"He's becoming a man I respect dearly." Lauren says.

"As well as I have become." John gently laughs, disarming the tension. "Tripp trusted me with his heart."

Lauren nods, chewing her lip.

"There's someone he cares about," she says cautiously. "I think... I think he has feelings for Jeff Tyler he doesn't fully understand yet."

She stops herself just short of saying too much, not realizing she said a name. Inside, her mind races. *Did I say Jeff Tyler? They used to be close... maybe closer than they realized?*

Or maybe someone new?

The thought tugs at her heart, but she says nothing more aloud.

John watches her carefully, his expression kind but knowing. He knew the name, from years ago. *Tripp never said anything about him.*

"For someone at school?" he asks, his tone casual.

Lauren catches herself, quickly schooling her expression. She almost says something — fearing she could say the wrong thing.

John smiles a little more and steers the moment away with a gentle nudge.

"Jess? Who is she? That a friend of his?" he teases lightly, misnaming him on purpose.

Lauren blinks, startled, then laughs softly, grateful for the graceful rescue. "No... I mean... maybe. Honestly, it's hard to tell with Tripp. He's got a big heart... sometimes I think even he's still figuring out where to put it."

John chuckles warmly. "The heart rarely shouts," he says. "It whispers when we least expect it."

Lauren relaxes slightly, her worries easing.

"You're good for him," John says simply. "I can see that."

Lauren swallows hard, blinking fast.

"I'm lucky to know him," she whispers. "I don't know why... but somewhere along the way, he stopped being just a ride to school and became someone I can't imagine losing."

John's smile widens. "You two have a friendship that goes deep, I gather?"

"I don't know what to call it, to be honest." Lauren looks timidly at John, a feeling of trust washes over her. "I love Tripp Carson. Not romantically, but still very deep. He matters to me."

"You remind me of someone," he says. "My sister — Tripp's mother. You have the same kind heart."

Lauren blushes, grateful but embarrassed.

"I just want him happy," she adds.

"I see that, Lauren."

Moments later, Tripp, Robbie, and Scott return with drinks.

Scott plops into the seat beside Lauren, grinning.

"I'm the lucky one!" he declares, clutching his cup proudly as he sticks out his tongue at Tripp.

Everyone laughs.

They settle around the table, passing out drinks and laughing quietly as Scott proudly claims the seat next to Lauren.

John steers the conversation casually. Robbie talks at length about how he and Tripp became friends. The pride Robbie has in Tripp shines like a beacon, a clear sign to John.

Tripp explains about Robbie's GTO project. Lauren's dream of becoming a chemist. Tripp's new ambition to teach. The conversations seem simple, but expanded the depth of the friendship between Robbie,, Lauren, and Tripp.

Each answer weaves another thread between them — a patchwork quilt of trust, hope, and connection.

And then Tripp says it.

"I just want a simple life... with someone who completes me."

For a heartbeat, everything freezes in Lauren's mind.

She catches Robbie's startled glance at Tripp — quick, almost hidden — but there. And something clicks deep inside her.

Not a full picture.

Not a certainty.

Just a spark.

A whisper in her heart.

Maybe it's not Jeff, she realizes. *Maybe it's someone standing right in front of Tripp.*

But she says nothing. Just smiles and takes a slow sip of her drink, letting the moment settle like falling snow.

Eventually, John checks his watch and sighs.

"I hate to end this, but we need to get Scott home."

Everyone stands reluctantly.

Robbie shakes John's hand again, feeling proud. Robbie believes he made the right impression.

Lauren hugs Scott tightly, laughing.

John smiles at the group warmly.

"You're remarkable young people," he says. "I won't worry about Tripp. He's exactly where he's meant to be."

They wave goodbye as John, Tripp, and Scott head to the car.

Lauren stands for a long moment, watching them go, heart full and aching all at once. She looks at Robbie. All the history they have. Tripp's feelings had always been there, open, obvious, yet hidden and protected.

"Lauren?" Robbie asks gently. "Is Greg picking you up?"

Lauren wipes at her eyes and smiles. "No... I'll call my dad."

Robbie hesitates, then offers his arm.

"Or I could drive you home?"

Lauren loops her arm through his.

"Thanks, Robbie. I'd like that."

They walk to the car together, the fading sunlight casting long shadows behind them.

U ncle John helps Scott climb into the car. Tripp settles into the passenger seat, excitement buzzing under his skin. Scott is in a good mood, bouncing with energy — but even so, Tripp senses there's something more simmering beneath the surface.

The car hums to life, and they pull away from the café.

"That was fun, J!" Scott calls from the back seat, drumming his heels lightly against the seat.

John chuckles and glances over at Michael. "Well, Michael, I like your friends. They'll have your back."

Tripp smiles, gazing out toward the distant horizon. "I'm lucky. To have good people twice in one lifetime is a blessing."

Scott bounces along with the music, peering out the window. John checks the rearview mirror, then nods at Michael, giving him an opening.

Michael bites his lip, heart pounding with hope. Maybe — just maybe — his uncle saw it too.

John speaks carefully. "Lauren will be a good person for you to confide in. I have a good feeling about her."

"I wanted to tell her... about my feelings," Tripp says quietly, fighting the lump in his throat. "But I had to talk to you first.

It means more than I can explain *that you came*, Uncle John.

You came for me, even when it wasn't easy."

John's voice is soft, steady. "I'll have to thank Jake — he insisted I come straight down. I thought about waiting until after my business meetings, but you're more important. Now I see that clearly."

Tripp sniffles, scrubbing a hand across his face.

He reaches out, palm flat against the seat between them.

John grasps his nephew's hand and squeezes firmly — no words needed.

In that moment, John sees only the best parts of Willis Carson in Michael. But the boy's heart — that belongs entirely to Anne.

"So..." John says, steering the conversation gently back, "Robbie is a good guy. I can see why you're friends."

"Friend," Tripp echoes, glancing nervously over his shoulder.

Scott is still occupied with the window.

"Just friend?" His voice wavers, and his eyes plead for something more.

"For the moment," John says kindly. "You can't rush things, Michael. You need time. But if it means anything, I think it would be good — for both of you."

A shy smile tugs at the corner of Tripp's mouth. It isn't the answer he wanted, but it's hope enough.

John switches on the cassette player.

Bright, ethereal synth fills the car as Jean-Michel Jarre's melodies float through the air.

"Oh cool! That's Jean Jarre!" Scott yells from the back seat, pounding an invisible drum against his knees.

"You know him?" Michael asks, surprised.

"Yeah! Uncle John had this tape last time he visited!" Scott says proudly, tapping along to the beat.

Michael grins, turning to glance back. "I've never heard anything like it. It's got a great rhythm."

"It relaxes me," Scott says, nodding to the music. "I listen to it when I can't sleep."

"How's that been going?" Michael asks gently.

Scott bobs his head. "I'm... handle-ling it better. You've helped a lot, Michael."

"I'm glad you two have each other," John adds, smiling at the easy affection between them. "Family is important."

"Me too!" Scott chirps. Then, out of nowhere, he leans forward between the seats. "Say, Michael — what did you and Uncle John talk about?"

Michael freezes for a beat. "Uh... I had a question I needed advice about."

John steps in smoothly. "Michael needed a fresh perspective. Someone outside the situation to help him see things clearly."

"Oh." Scott fakes a smile and slumps back into his seat.

He goes quiet, his gaze slipping back to the window.

Michael watches him in the mirror, heart tightening. There's something Scott isn't saying — something heavy he's carrying.

Trying to lighten the mood, Michael asks, "So... how was school today, Scott?"

Scott slides forward again, energy returning — at least on the surface. "Um... recess was fun! My teacher was sick, and there was this old lady in our class. We colored all day. Boring! My friend and I played tag. I ate peanut butter."

He pauses, then tilts his head. "Is it that pretty girl?"

"What?" Michael blinks.

"Do you love her?" Scott asks bluntly.

"Lauren?" tripp answers, taken aback. "No, buddy. She's beautiful, but she's dating one of my other friends. She's like a sister to me."

"Okay," Scott says, smiling wide. Then he asks, "Where we going?"

"I thought I'd buy Michael the album since he liked the music," John explains, turning left at the light.

"Yeah..." Scott's voice softens instantly, like someone flipped a switch.

"It's like nothing I've ever heard." Tripp smiles.

"We're going to your music store, Michael?" he asks quietly.

"Yeah," Michael replies. "They've got good prices. It's just around the corner. Won't take five minutes."

"Okay," Scott answers again, even quieter.

Scott slouches back, pressing his forehead lightly against the window glass. His small hands fidget with the seatbelt. The bright spark he had a few minutes ago dims noticeably.

Michael feels a heavy unease settle over him.

He glances at his uncle. John catches his eye in the mirror and gives a slight shake of his head.

Let him have his space.

Michael nods silently. Sometimes the hardest part of loving someone is knowing when to give them breathing room.

The car hums along toward the record store, music filling the silence with soft electronic waves.

Tripp leans his head back, letting the melodies swirl around him, and tries not to think too hard. Today is supposed to be about hope. He clings to that.

Even when that hope — like Scott's moods or the future with Robbie — still feel so uncertain.

J ohn knows something is off. *But what?*

Both of his nephews are different — almost unrecognizable — from the last time he visited North Carolina. Since Tripp seems to have broken through to Scott, John decides to let him take the lead. He parks the Cadillac in front of the record store and glances at Tripp.

"Hey Scott, I need to review some work files. Can you help Michael find the album?" John asks lightly.

Scott bounces in his seat, grinning. "Yeah! Just me and Michael again?"

"Like Butch Cassidy—" Tripp grins.

"And the Sunflower Kid!" Scott finishes with a laugh.

John chuckles, shaking his head. "Sunflower Kid... that's a new one."

Tripp and Scott tumble out of the car, the door thudding closed behind them. John watches, pretending to shuffle through his briefcase, but mostly he's just thinking — watching — and hoping.

Inside the store, a cheerful old man waves from behind the counter.

"Hello, Mister Tynan!" Tripp calls, smiling big.

"Welcome back! Let's see... Boston, Journey, Fleetwood Mac, right?" the old man guesses with a twinkle.

Tripp gives him a thumbs-up. "That's me! But today, I'm hunting for something new."

"Let me know if you need a hand, Boston," the man chuckles.

Scott is already bouncing toward the back wall where the specialty records are kept. Tripp follows, heart lighter for the moment.

"So, Scott," he says, keeping his voice soft, "you doing okay now?"

Scott nods, pulling a comic face. "Yes, Michael. I'm sorry. I didn't mean to make you worry..."

"Don't be sorry." Tripp sweeps Scott into a playful headlock, rubbing his knuckles against his cousin's head. "I *like* worrying about you."

Scott giggles. "'Cause you loves me?"

"That I do, Sunflower Kid." Tripp grins, letting him go.

Scott beams, cheeks red from laughter. They flip through the racks together, Tripp stopping every few records to make funny faces. Scott's laughter echoes off the dusty shelves. Tripp finally spots it — Jean-Michel Jarre. He turns with a dramatic gasp, holding it up like treasure.

Scott bursts out laughing. But their joy shatters when a voice cuts across the room.

"Tripp?"

Tripp turns, spotting Geoffrey approaching from the far side of the store. His Wrangler jeans fitting tight, a loose fitting t-shirt with a tie-dye colored peace symbol on the front. Geoff's hair perfect.

He smiles automatically. "Hey, Geoff. Thought I missed you."

"I was in the back. Glad you came in." Geoffrey flashes a grin. "How's the little drummer?"

Scott stiffens, gripping Tripp's hand tightly. His face, moments ago open and playful, slams shut.

Tripp notices — and frowns — but keeps his tone light. "Doing fine."

"You didn't have to get dressed up for me," Geoffrey teases, stepping closer.

Tripp plays along, laughing. "Well, how else am I supposed to get five-star service?"

Geoffrey laughs. "You'll always get five-star treatment from me, Tripp. What're you hunting today?"

Tripp lifts the album. "My uncle turned me onto it. Jarre."

"Good music to get stoned to.," Geoffrey says, winking. "Especially if you're, you know, *relaxing*."

Tripp chuckles dryly. "Trying to stay boring these days. No more partying."

"I don't party, Tripp." Geoffrey leans in, voice dropping. "I still like a joint now and then... just loosens me up."

Tripp shrugs, shielding himself with the album. "No judgment here. AA cured me of being high and mighty.'"

Geoffrey's grin widens. "Hang tight. Got something for you in the back."

Tripp nods stiffly. He watches the man sprinting away, admiring his rugged qualities. As Geoffrey disappears behind the swinging stockroom door, Tripp crouches down beside Scott.

"You okay, buddy?"

Scott's eyes are locked on the storeroom door. He doesn't answer.

Tripp stands, heart tight with unease. "C'mon, let's check out the rock section."

Scott clutches his hand and tugs him toward the end of the aisle — but his breathing is faster now, shallow.

Halfway down the row, Scott tugs harder.

"Michael... can we just go?" he whispers urgently.

Tripp's stomach twists. Scott's fear is palpable. This isn't a small thing, Scott is petrified.

Before Tripp can answer, Geoffrey reappears, carrying a small frame.

"Tripp," he says softly, smiling slyly, "I got something for you."

Tripp straightens warily as Geoffrey approaches.

Inside the frame are two concert tickets — both autographed by members of Boston.

"I can't accept this!" Tripp protests immediately. His fingers brush the frame but doesn't take it. "This is a collector's item."

Geoffrey laughs and pushes it toward him anyway, tapping Tripp's shoulder with his free hand. "Take it. I've got extras. Planned to sell a couple, but... I think you're more valuable."

Scott stiffens, staring hard at Geoffrey. Tripp forces a smile, heart hammering. The whole encounter feels wrong — off-balance, scripted. He doesn't want to insult Geoffrey, but he doesn't want to encourage him either, well not too much.

He glances down at Scott's pleading eyes.

Scott tugs Tripp's hand again. "*Tripp...* Uncle John's waiting."

Tripp smiles warmly at his cousin. "You're right, Sunflower Kid. We need to get moving."

Turning back to Geoffrey, Tripp accepts the frame reluctantly. "You sure about this?"

"I want you to have it," Geoffrey says smoothly, brushing his fingers along Tripp's arm as he hands it over.

From his back pocket, Geoffrey pulls out a crumpled piece of paper and scribbles something quickly.

"Here." He tucks it between the album and the frame. "Just so you don't lose track of me."

Tripp reads the note silently. He wants to belive it. Geoff's nice handwritting was beautiful. It said: *That kiss still haunts me, Tripp.*

Tripp nods, feeling more trapped than flattered. He holds the items carefully against his chest, stepping away.

"We'll talk later?" Geoffrey presses, voice low.

"Maybe," Tripp says noncommittally. "Got family in town right now."

Scott presses even closer against Tripp's side. Geoffrey flashes a lazy wink at Scott.

"Good wingman you got there, Tripp."

Tripp ruffles Scott's hair, steering him toward the counter.

"He keeps me out of trouble."

Scott doesn't laugh. He keeps glancing back over his shoulder at the stockroom door until they're finally outside.

The bell jingles overhead as they step into the fading evening light. Thoughts race through his mind, *Scott tugs closer against my side. I smile and ruffle his hair, but something about the way he won't meet my eyes makes a sliver of unease prickle in the back of my mind.*

Tripp barely has time to breathe before Scott blurts out, "I didn't like him, Michael. He's... he's wrong."

Tripp swallows hard, heart aching for his cousin. He clasps Scott's small shoulder and steers him toward the Cadillac, forcing himself to smile for Uncle John's sake. Tripp pushes his thoughts to the back of his mind as he helps Scott into the car.

"I was about to call in the Canadian Mounties," John jokes from the front seat. "Everything okay?"

Tripp slides into the front seat, setting the frame and album gently on his lap.

"Yes, sir," he says brightly. "Sunflower Kid came to the rescue."

Scott beams at the nickname, but Tripp notices the way he presses tight against the door, shoulders tense.

And for the first time all night, Tripp truly feels the cost of the things still hidden inside both their hearts.

U ncle John pulls the Cadillac away from the store, heading toward Linda's condo. Tripp sits quietly, casting quick glances at Scott, then at his uncle. Something is wrong — badly wrong.

"I don't wanna go there again," Scott says suddenly, his voice trembling. "Michael, you shouldn't either."

Tripp twists in his seat, facing the back. Scott is hunched in the center of the seat, legs pressed tightly together, hands wringing, breathing fast and shallow. He looks devastated. Tripp's stomach knots. *Panic attack,* he realizes. *Geoffrey triggered this.*

"Alright," Tripp says carefully, "we'll only go if Mr. Tynan is working. Deal?"

Scott shakes his head furiously. "I don't like him."

"Mr. Tynan?" Tripp blinks, surprised. "Scott, he's one of the nicest—"

"No." Scott's voice sharpens with rage. "Not him. Jeffery."

"It's Geoffrey," Tripp says gently, confused. "And he's just a friend. Nothing more."

"I hate him," Scott snaps, folding his arms and staring out the window. His voice wobbles. "He reminds me of my father."

The car grows heavy with silence. Tripp exchanges a worried look with John. His uncle keeps his hands steady on the wheel, his jaw tightening. He's letting Tripp lead — for now.

"I don't understand, Scott," Tripp says cautiously. "Geoffrey's... just been friendly."

"I don't like the way he *looks* at you," Scott whispers, his voice breaking.

John's voice is stern. "Looks?"

Tripp feels the weight of those words. He turns fully in his seat now. Scott's eyes are wide with pure terror. A deep, primal fear.

John glances back in the mirror but stays silent, trusting Tripp to keep guiding the conversation.

"I guess," Tripp says softly, trying to diffuse Scott's fear, "Geoff's just been flirting a little. I didn't take it seriously."

Scott rocks gently in his seat, arms locked around himself. "Michael," he mutters, "you and Uncle John are alike."

"Alike?" John asks quietly.

Scott keeps staring out the window, his small body rigid. Tripp feels a cold sweat bead along his hairline. Scott's not talking about hobbies or politics. He means something deeper. Something hidden.

"It's okay that you're like Uncle John," Scott says at last. His voice is tiny. "I won't tell anybody."

Tripp's heart aches. His throat tightens. How could Scott possibly know?

"I don't want Jeffey to hurt you, Michael," Scott whispers, his fingers trembling against his jeans.

"I promise, I won't go back." Tripp says urgently. "Scott, you matter more to me than anything."

Tripp sees it now — the way Scott's pressed into the seat, arms clutched over his lap, head ducked down.

It's not just Geoffrey's flirtation that scared him.

It's something deeper. Older. A memory. A pattern. Things Tripp learns years from now, helping kids at the shelter in Rhode Island. The stories of abuse he learned to recognize.

Tripp closes his eyes.

Oh, God. Please, not that...

He finally understands.

"Scott," he says carefully, opening his eyes again. "Geoffrey reminds you of your dad, doesn't he?"

Scott slowly nods, each movement weighted with grief.

Tripp leans closer. His voice breaks. "Scott... ...has your father ever... hurt you?"

Scott shudders. His face crumples.

"Yes," he whispers, barely audible.

"And it hurts bad."

John jerks the wheel sharply, pulling the Cadillac onto the shoulder with a screech of tires. Cars honk as they pass. Tripp grabs the door handle to steady himself, heart pounding.

John throws the car in park and bolts into the backseat, pulling Scott into a fierce embrace. Tripp scrambles over the seat to join them, wrapping his arms around both.

"You're safe," John says, voice shaking with fury and love. "You're safe now, Scott. No one will ever hurt you again. Not ever."

Scott clings to both of them, his small body racked with silent sobs.

Tripp buries his face against Scott's hair, tears burning in his eyes.

He wishes he could go back and erase every terrible thing that had ever touched this boy's life.

He can't — but he can be here now.

And he will be.

No matter what it takes.

Shaking Off the Past

S cott stands in the doorway, looking at his new home. The oversized shorts and shirt, stolen from Tripp, hang loosely on his frame, a physical representation of how much he has changed. He hears the quiet hum of the refrigerator in the kitchen and the distant sound of a television.

It's so different from the silence of their old condo and the quiet that had descended on them in the weeks before they moved. But here, with his aunt and uncle, it's the kind of quiet that feels like a blanket, a warm, comforting peace that wraps around him.

Scott feels a strong hand on his shoulder. Looking up, he sees Pat Dalton. Scott remembers that he used to be afraid of the man—a mystery with rules and little time to play. Since the day he and his sister were welcomed into this home, Scott has realized how wrong he was.

"In or out, buddy," Pat jokes, his voice laced with love and devotion.

Scott moves into the kitchen. "Sorry, sir."

Pat kneels, bringing them face to face. "How about a PB and J sandwich? I'll remember to cut off the crust this time."

His smile is warm, and Scott can't help giggling. "Thanks. Can you eat with me?"

"I will, but I prefer a ham and cheese." Pat laughs. "Grab some glasses for the tea."

WIth a broad smile, Scott hugs his uncle. "Thanks, should I get Regina?"

"Gina said she isn't hungry. I'll eat a small sandwich so I join her later." Scott's uncle pats him on the rear and motions to the cabinets.

Scott dashes over to the table, sliding a chair to climb onto. He carefully retrieves two of the blue-tinted glasses—the same style that Papa Dalton has. Scott keeps looking at his uncle as the man meticulously crafts lunch.

Scott pushes the chair back to the table and runs to the fridge, grabbing the tea pitcher as his uncle deposits the sliced ham and cheese on the shelf.

Pat Dalton watches his nephew with pride as Scott pours the tea, seeing the boy struggle to keep from making a mess. Pat thinks of his daughter, now a grown woman, and the special moments they shared in this kitchen.

"I'd be lost without your help, Scott." Pat grabs the plates. "Let's feast."

Scott lets out a hoot and jumps into his chair. *This is what home feels like,* Scott thinks as he stuffs the sandwich in his mouth.

"Slow down, buddy." Pat reaches over, ruffling the boy's hair. "Glad your appetite has returned."

"Thamfff que," Scott tries to say with a mouth full of peanut butter.

"So, your teacher called last night." Pat starts. Scott freezes, fearing a lecture is coming.

"Guess she told you..." Scott hangs his head low.

"She told me that you are doing well in school."

Scott blinks, his chewing slows to a stop. He thinks of the test he just failed. His father would have been yelling. But his uncle is smiling.

"She mention the test?" Scott places his sandwich on the plate.

"She did, Scott. It's a big improvement over the last test. Mrs. Tracey is very impressed by your efforts. Remember, if you need help, just ask me."

He wipes his eyes. Scott is silent, waiting, but Pat Dalton is not his father.

"You already do too much." Scott hangs his head down.

Pat reaches across the table, lifting Scott's chin. "You're family, Scott. There isn't anything Aunt Eve and I wouldn't do for you and your sister. Love makes time."

"Tripp says that, too." Scott's eyes well up with tears.

"Your cousin loves you very much. I'm very proud of both of you." Pat answers with a twinkle in his eyes. "Finish your sandwich before I start tickling you."

Scott giggles, feeling safe. "I like living here!"

He runs his hand along the smooth wooden banister, feeling the grain beneath his fingers. He had come here before with his mom, but the house feels different now. It feels like a safe harbor, a place where he and his sister can finally breathe. He is so tired—tired of worrying, of being scared. Tripp changed that. He smiles to himself. He can sleep here, really sleep. He hears footsteps on the floor below and he heads to his room, not wanting to disturb anyone.

Just outside his door, he looks across the hall. Her room was their uncle's office, but now it is hers. Scott sees his sister, seated on a small wooden bench by the window, a book in her hands. Her long shirt covers her colorful dance outfit. He smiles. *Gina loves to dance,* he thinks. She looks at peace. He had not seen her smile since their father left years ago. The small lamp casts a soft glow on her face, illuminating the subtle changes he has noticed over the past few weeks.

"Hey, Sis. What are you reading?" Scott asks, his voice soft.

She looks up, her face lighting up. "Hey. Just some poetry. It's pretty good."

Scott's brow tenses, his nose wrinkles up. "You okay?"

"Yeah, I'm good. Just reading." Gina smiles, her eyes sparkling. "I'm good, really."

He nods. "Good. Just wanted to make sure."

He turns to go into his room when she calls out, "Hey, Scott. Can I ask you something?"

He turns back. "Yeah, sure. What's up?"

"Why does Uncle Pat call me Gina?"

Scott pauses, thinking. "I dunno. Maybe it's just a nickname?"

She shakes her head. "No, it's not that. It feels different. It feels... special. Like he's known me forever."

Scott looks at his sister, really looks at her. He sees the quiet confidence that has replaced the timid, selfish girl he knew. He thinks about Tripp, about how he had changed so much since he apologized. He thinks about the way his sister looks at Tripp, with a sense of awe.

"I think... I think it's because he sees something in you that you don't see in yourself," Scott says, his voice soft but firm. "You've been so strong, with everything that's happened. Taking care of me. You've been so brave. It's like Tripp. You're not just my sister, you're your own person."

She looks at him, her eyes wide with surprise. "I didn't think about it like that."

"Yeah, well, you should," he says, his voice a playful tease. "You're the smartest person I know. You're better than me at school."

"Scott, don't say that. You're awesome at drumming, and I've seen you writing in those notebooks."

Scott giggles. "You actually read books instead of just pretending. You're going to be a doctor or a lawyer or something important."

She blushes, a shy smile on her face. "You're an idiot."

"I'm not the one reading poetry," he says, a grin on his face. "Come on, let's go see what's on TV."

She shakes her head, a soft laugh escaping her lips. "Go away. I'm reading."

He feigns a hurt look. "Fine. I'll just go watch TV by myself. See if I care."

Gina playfully smiles, not looking up from the book. "I love you, Scott."

"Eww..." Scott groans before he runs to her and wraps her up in a hug. "Love you, Gina."

He turns and walks into his room, a smile on his face. He closes the door and leans against it, a feeling of hope in his heart. They're going to be okay. He knows it.

The Brothers' Truth

Mark sits at his desk, the phone call with his grandfather running through his mind. One of his favorite songs by Foghat plays in the background. *1980 is becoming complicated,* he thinks. He glances at the old photo on the corner of the desk. Mark, standing tall to be like his father, Willis Carson, Jr. A faded black and whte picture. Tripp, next to him, wears a tight, forced smile that barely reaches his eyes, even back then the spark of life faded from his brother.

The picture, taken in 1973, is supposed to be a fun picnic on the Blue Ridge Parkway. Mark had a good time, but Tripp did not. Mark knows he should have defended his brother. Their father criticizes everything the young boy does, and Mark remembers being just glad it is Tripp getting the lecture, not him.

"I let you down," Mark mumbles under his breath, flipping the frame face down. "But, not any more, Tripp."

Mark grunts as he closes the anatomy text book and heads down the hallway. He hesitates at Tripp's door. His brother is listening to music he is not familiar with. Mark shakes his head and raps on the door.

Mark enters and is about to speak when he realizes that Tripp is only wearing his underwear. Bright and form fitting, a color that a boy shouldn't be wearing. *Relax, Mark,* he tries to restrain himself. *At least he's stopped wearing those ridiculous leotards.* The restraint was short lived.

"Michael Willis Carson!" Mark hears himself yell. "Girl's underwear, too?"

Tripp turns and smiles. The gentle response hampers the anger swelling in Mark. Tripp does not seem embarrassed; he is relaxed, calm. He waves with a silly giggle.

"Mark. These are not girls' underwear," Tripp explains. "Mom got them for me–from Sears. The men's department."

"They're yellow." Mark growls, shaking his head.

"Meh, they're comfortable." Tripp timidly answers. "It's just a color."

"This is *slightly* better than girls' dancewear," Mark mutters.

Tripp struggles with his identity, the pain of not telling Robbie last night burns in his mind. He understands that Mark has a point. Something Tripp doesn't want to consider.

Avoiding his brother's eyes, Tripp looks to the floor, a flicker of something in his eyes. "I only wear those when you aren't home."

Mark grunts with suspicion, a pang of guilt hitting him. He looks away briefly. "Can you at least put on some shorts? That color is bright enough to blind me."

Tripp walks to his dresser, pulling out the long cargo shorts and slides them on. "Sorry, Mark. I kinda like being a minimalist. Too many years being morbidly obese, it feels refreshing."

"Fifteen pounds isn't obese, Tripp," Mark says, his sarcasm barely concealing his concern.

Tripp sighs. *I would've preferred fifteen pounds.* He notices how closely Mark is watching him.

"What are you listening to?" Mark knits his brow. "Sounds like... some kind of pop music."

"Olivia Newton-John," Tripp smiles. "She's Australian. Love the accent, pretty lady."

"Speaking of ladies, what ever happened between you and that girl, uh, Holly?"

"She didn't want to date me any longer. She worried what people think of her with me..." Tripp sighs and sits on his bed. "Lauren is trying to fix me up with her."

"Doesn't sound like that is what you want, little brother." Mark sits beside Tripp. "Sorry... I didn't mean to open an old wound. I'm just worried about you. I've noticed some *different behaviors* you've started using."

"I am who I am, Mark." Tripp offers quietly. "I thought you believed in me."

"I do, Michael. I'm worried how what the world will believe about you."

Tripp leans in, resting his head on Mark's shoulder. "Thank you for looking out for me, Mark. You'd make a good dad..."

"Not dad material," Mark mumbles, his voice softer than he intends. "But I love you more than you know..."

Tripp reaches around Mark's broad shoulders, hugging him tighter. Tripp tries to hide his tears, burying his face against Mark's shirt. "Is that what you want to ask me?"

Mark hears the stress in Tripp's voice. "No. I spoke to Papa Dalton. Uncle John has been bragging about us both. Papa and Anne Dear want us to come visit, just you and me."

"Can Robbie come?"

"We'll see. I'll call him back." Mark smiles. "Finish getting dressed, I have a friend coming over."

"Thanks, Mark. I love you."

The Price of A Promise

Tripp pulls on his red Boston T-shirt and blue jeans. The clothes fit baggy now, a constant reminder of his weight loss, and he has to pull the belt tight to keep the pants from falling. As he ties his shoes, he spots the framed concert tickets on the shelf. He stops. It doesn't matter how he looks. Today has a purpose. He knows he never should have accepted the gift in the first place. With everything that happened with Scott, he cannot keep it.

He had called Geoff an hour ago, asking if he could come by tonight. He could hear Geoffrey's excitement. The more Tripp thinks about it, the more he wants to get it over with very quickly.

But Geoffrey didn't do anything... Tripp rationalizes. *I mean, Scott just reacted to his fears, not Geoff directly.*

Tripp takes a deep breath and sits on his bed, replaying every interaction he has had with Geoff since that first day at the record store.

He's attractive. He is a gay man in 1980. It isn't the same to what I knew before...

He looks at the ceiling, then focuses on the window. He knows that he is trying to convince himself, but it isn't working.

Geoff is definitely aggressive.

Tripp shakes his head.

Nothing I can't handle.

His mind keeps returning to the encounter outside the Record Changer that night. Tripp struggles with the idea that he is infatuated with the attention given by Geoff rather than honest feelings about someone.

Tripp's mind floats to the moment they almost kissed. He wants to see Geoffrey, but he can't risk missing out with Robbie.

Tripp looks down at the frame. *Is it worth the price?* he wonders. He gets up, grabbing a ballcap from his closet.

"No..." Tripp growls, heading to his car. "It isn't."

Tripp's red Mustang pulls up to the curb in front of 140 Madison Grove Place. He spots the van in the driveway. It is a quiet neighborhood, filled with mothers in the front yards with their kids. It seems out of place to think this is where Geoffrey lives.

"Just give him the gift back...be nice and leave," Tripp plans out loud.

He runs up to the front door, pressing the doorbell. A tall man answers the door. He has short, thick black hair and a dark complexion, and the wear on his face makes Tripp guess he is much older than Geoff. A tight-fitting tank top strains over his torso, and he is wearing snug terry cloth shorts. The man has muscles on top of muscles, and Tripp is instantly intimidated. *He must be a bodybuilder,* Tripp thinks. The man grunts, his accent thick.

"Which one are you?" he barks.

"Huh?" Tripp answers, startled by the man's sharp tone.

"You lookin' for Geoffrey?" he says, his voice a low rumble. His tight tank top strains across his muscular chest and biceps. "You gotta be Tripp. Geoff talks about you all the time."

The man gives Tripp a slow, appraising look. His sneering gaze reminds Tripp of an animal, a predator sizing up its prey. Tripp feels like hundreds of ants are crawling all over his body.

"Yes. My name is Tripp. Is he home?" he asks nervously.

"He'll be back real quick," the man replies, not hiding the fact that he is looking at Tripp intently. "Say, you've gotta be the prettiest boy I've seen down here."

"Uh, thanks, I just need to talk to Geoff."

"So kid, my name's Ernesto. You want to come in and wait?" He gestures toward the house. "I'm sure we can find something to do while you wait."

"I just came to return something," Tripp answers, stepping back.

Without waiting for an answer, Ernesto takes a confident step back and gestures for Tripp to come in. "Don't just stand there, kid. Come on in. It's colder than a witch's tit out here."

"He won't be gone long?" Tripp asks, as he is pulled inside.

"Ten minutes, tops."

Tripp doesn't look at the guy, but he imagines Ernesto is focused on his body. That's when he hears it, a metallic clank. Tripp spins around. Ernesto pulls the key from a double-sided deadbolt. Tripp's eyes widen with fear, his heart races in panic. He stands frozen in the hallway, uncertain of his next move.

Ernesto walks past him, patting Tripp's behind, his grip firm. "I'd offer you a joint, but Geoff said you're a choir boy or something. You can chill on the couch and watch some TV. The living room's right down the hall. Just make yourself at home."

He pauses at the end of the hall, looking back at Tripp. "Don't worry, kid. Neighborhood's a little rough. My doors are always locked for a reason."

"Uh, OK." Tripp hesitates, the fight or flight instinct pushing him to escape.

"Had I known you were this cute, I would have told Geoff to bring you 'round sooner." Ernesto smiles while adjusting himself. "We can talk till Geoff gets back."

Tripp is repulsed, the sensation of ants increases. "I...uh, I need to be at work soon...can only wait a few minutes."

"You ain't sociable." The man snaps. "Nothing wrong with being polite."

Ernesto walks over to the TV. He flips it on, and a cartoon Tripp doesn't recognize appears. Tripp shudders. It's for much younger kids.

"That should keep you entertained. I babysit a couple of the neighbor's boys. They eat this shit up." Ernesto stands by the TV.

Tripp looks around the sparsely decorated room. A large bag is on the couch, papers stacked around it. The sound of the TV is distorted. Tripp hopes the guy was lying about babysitting. The rest of the room is dark, but Tripp can see several mirrors in the far corner. In front of them is a stand with a blanket draped across it. It looks out of place, but familiar.

"Watch the tube, kid. Remember to play nice," Ernesto says, switching on a tabletop lamp.

Tripp steps back, pressing against the wall. *Hurry up, Geoff.* Tripp wants to leave.

The man pulls off his tank top, squatting to pick up a pair of dumbbells. He begins doing arm curls. Tripp is frozen with fear.

"Bet you've never seen muscles like mine, huh?"

Tripp's voice cracks. "No, sir."

"Come here, you can feel my biceps if you want." Ernesto offers, cliking his teeth at the end.

Tripp's eyes go wide. He doesn't want to imagine what the man has in mind. "I think I need to leave."

Ernesto stops the arm curls. His eyes lock onto Tripp. "Suit yourself, kid. Does Geoff know you're such a puss?"

"Please," Tripp whispers.

Ernesto sets the dumbbells on the floor and quickly moves to the wall. He steps close, invading Tripp's personal space. A sickly smile crawls on his face. Ernesto presses in, placing his hands on the wall. His thick arms are on either side of Tripp's neck. The man's body odor from exercising fills Tripp's nose.

"I said play nice." The tone is cold, low. A command.

"Do you...uh, treat all of Geoff's friends like this?" Tripp can feel sweat rolling down his face.

"No. Most wanna be here. They have *manners.*" Ernesto's stare is cold, but he holds up the door key. "I'll tell him you stopped by."

Tripp timidly takes the key from him. "Thanks, Ernesto. Sorry, I need to be heading to work." Tripp ducks down below the man's arms. "Sorry."

"Whatever, kid, just leave the key in the lock." Ernesto returns to working out like nothing has happened.

Tripp's body trembles as he steps backward down the hall, watching Ernesto, hoping the man will stay put. Tripp stumbles and runs into the door. He spins, hands shaking as he turns the key and escapes.

Tripp runs, skipping the steps altogether as he heads for the Mustang. He spots a cab pulling up in the driveway. Geoffrey rolls down the window.

A head pops out as the motor idles roughly. "Tripp?"

"Yeah, sorry to just drop by, Geoff," Tripp's voice cracks as he calls out, out of breath.

"I wasn't expecting you until this evening." Geoff answers, looking concerned.

Geoff climbs out of the yellow car. He digs in his pocket and tosses some money at the driver. Geoffrey stands, eyes locked on Tripp as the cab pulls away.

"I had to do this now. I was called in for a shift tonight."

Geoff walks over, noting that Tripp isn't being his usual self—not casual, not joking. He is tense.

"That's not a problem...you OK?" Geoff asks, placing a hand on Tripp's arm.

Tripp stops, taking several deep breaths. "Uh...your friend..."

"Ernesto?"

Tripp hangs his head. "He, uh..."

"He's my lover, Tripp. We share a home, but we have our own thing."

"It wasn't that, Geoff." Tripp's voice cracks.

"Oh. You stunned him with your beauty, huh?" Geoff says, his expression softening with concern. "He can be a bit...intense. What did he do?"

Tripp looks over his shoulder at the house. "I didn't feel...safe."

Geoff rubs his chin, his brow furrowed. "I'm sorry, Tripp. I forgot Ernesto can be, well, a lot to take in."

"It's not a personality quirk," Tripp snaps. "He's a monster."

Geoff's face hardens. "Oh? We can't all be saints like you. He's been nothing but nice to me. You just met him; that's a bit judgmental, don't you think?"

"I didn't mean to be, Geoff," he says quietly, his voice pleading. "I actually came here for a reason."

"To see me, I hope," Geoff says, his smile returning as he tries to diffuse the tension. "How about we forget about all this nonsense and just hang out for a while? We can talk."

Tripp takes a deep breath, staring down at his feet. "I felt bad about accepting that gift. I don't want to give you the wrong idea. I'm still trying to find my way."

"Tripp, it was a simple gift that I thought you'd like."

"I know, but..." Tripp pulls the frame out from his back pocket.

Geoffrey smiles. He lifts Tripp's chin to look him in the eye. Tripp feels overheated, but he isn't sure if it's the sunlight or Geoff's body.

"Don't fret, beautiful," Geoff says as he cups Tripp's face in both hands. "I can respect that. You're just trying to be honorable."

"You aren't mad?" Tripp asks, wetting his lips.

"No. How about a hug?" Geoff asks. Tripp nods slowly.

As Geoff wraps his strong arms around Tripp, he whispers in Tripp's ear. "If anything, this just makes me want you more. You are always focused on doing the right things, out of concern for me. I dig it, Tripp."

"Why is it you make me feel wrong when I have every right to be mad?" Tripp gumbles.

"I'm not trying to do anything. I'm here for you, Tripp. I want to be that person." Geoff responds, his hand gently slides down to Tripp's bottom. "If you're not up to talking, there's other things. We could kiss for a while and forget about all this nonsense."

Tripp hestiates. He looks into Geoff's eyes. A smile grows on Geoffrey's face as he leans close, kissing Tripp on the cheek.

Tripp lets out a loud huff. He pulls away, his body shaking with a mix of fear and anger. He shoves the gift back at Geoffrey's chest.

"And if I say no?"

"Then you say no, but there will be consequences," Geoff replies, his tone changing. "Damn, you come to my house and insult my friend? You need to grow up."

Tripp lets go of the frame and it drops to the ground. He shakes his head. Tripp wants to say, *I'm over twice your age, jerk,* but he is too mad.

"The grown-up thing to do is move on. Goodbye, Geoff."

Tripp gets into his car and quickly leaves.

Something Old; Something New

The road winds through rolling hills, past fields of cotton and old barns that lean in silent defiance of time. Mark's Olds Cutlass 442 flies down the back roads of rural South Carolina, soaring like an eagle. The shortcut to the farm bypasses Gable by twenty miles, but it has added time to the trip.

The classic rock showers the inside of the car with electric guitars and drums. Robbie sits quietly in the back, his head bobbing to the beat. Tripp glances over his shoulder and smiles at his friend. Tripp chose to sit up front. Mark's talk the other night made Tripp feel that Mark is having doubts about the path Tripp is taking.

Tripp is saddened by Mark's continued disapproval of the leotards. Mark's reaction to seeing Tripp in the bright yellow underwear didn't help. *What behaviors is Mark worrying about?* He asks himself. Glancing to his brother, Tripp sighs and focuses on the road ahead.

Tripp is wearing the shorts Robbie loaned him. *I should return these,* he thinks with a soft chuckle. His light purple button down shirt isn't tucked in. Robbie is wearing his black shorts with a white stripe. The blue and gray t-shirt hangs loosely on his tall frame. Mark wears faded blue jeans and a Foghat t-shirt.

"How much longer, Mark?" Tripp asks.

"How ten minutes, Michael. I guess I didn't read the map correctly." Mark still feels aggravated by the miscalculation.

"At least you have some good music playing!" Robbie yells from the back seat.

The sun hangs low, casting a golden light over the Dalton farm. Papa Dalton's familiar Ford truck sits in the driveway, its worn tires a testament to a life spent working the land. Tripp, Mark, and Robbie step out of Mark's car, their city clothes feeling out of place in the quiet country air. Anne Dear appears on the porch, a loving smile on her face as she hugs Mark, then Tripp.

"Oh, my sweet boys, I see you've brought a friend" she says, her voice thick with emotion. "It's so good to have you."

"Hi, grams." Mark replies warmly, hugging his grandmother.

"Anne Dear, this is my best friend, Robbie Davis." Tripp adds as he joins the hug.

"Pleasure to meet you, Mrs. Dalton."

"No need to be so formal, Robbie. Everyone calls me Anne Dear."

"Yes ma'am. Uh, Anne Dear."

Anne Dalton invites everyone to join her on the front porch. Anne Dear takes her seat, a delicate shaw draped over the back. Mark takes Papa Dalton's chair, leaving Tripp and Robbie sit on the small love seat.

Mark talks about his nursing classes. Tripp smiles seeing his brother light up. Mark proudly proclaims he's made the dean's list. Robbie talks about his car and hopes to become a mechanical engineer. Tripp talks about becoming a teacher, much to the happiness of his grandmother.

"I'm so proud of you, Tripp. I think your other grandmother was a teacher. Good foot steps to be following in." Anne Dear smiles, Tripp is heartwarmed by her approval.

Papa Dalton emerges from the barn, his shoulders stooped but his eyes sharp and full of life. A broad smile emerges as he waves to the group. As he comes up the steps, both Tripp and Robbie stand.

"Mark, looking good, son." their grandfather remarks.

"Thanks, been too long since our last visit."

Tripp extends his hand. "Papa Dalton, this is my best friend, Robbie Davis."

John Dalton, Sr. firmly shakes his grandson's. "Been hearing great things about you."

Robbie offers his hand, his nervousness evident in his voice, "Mr. Dalton, pleasure to meet you, sir."

"Welcome to our home." John Dalton smiles, impressed by the good handshake.

Mark stands, offering his seat. John nods as he sits. Anne Dear takes Mark's hand, pulling into the house to help carry back drinks.

"So, I understand you're Tripp now?"

"Yes, sir. I've begun putting effort into being a better person. My friends Robbie and Lauren have helped." Tripp explains. "I felt going by a new name to symbolize my change. Momma wanted to call me that when i was born."

"Then Tripp it is. My older brother was a third. He spoiled your mother when she was a little girl."

"I didn't know that."

"They were close, very close. We lost him during World War II."

""I'll have ask her about him."

"I'll get Anne Dear to find a picture of him."

Anne Dear and Mark emerge with several glasses of tea. As they pass them out, Robbie notices she didn't bring any water.

"Hey, Tripp. Want me to grab you some water?" Robbie asks as he stands.

Tripp smiles. "Thanks, if it's OK, Anne Dear?"

"Yes ma'am, I'm sure this is great tea, but Tripp has been making better choices about eating and drinking. He's lost a lot of weight." Robbie explains.

"Certainly, the kitchen's this way, Robbie."

Robbie follows Anne Dalton into the kitchen. Papa Dalton watches Tripp with a judicious eye. His grandson appears to hang on Robbie's every move. Robbie returns with a glass of ice water. Sitting close to Tripp, they answer questions from Tripp's grandmother. John Dalton sees all he needs to see. The tall man rises from his chair.

He claps Tripp on the shoulder, his gaze unwavering. "Son, come with me for a minute. Mark, you help your grandmother with the dinner. Robbie, you can come down to the lake when they're done." Papa Dalton's voice holds a tone of authority that Tripp hasn't heard in years.

Tripp follows Papa Dalton toward a small shed. The air is still, the only sound the crunch of their footsteps on the gravel. Papa Dalton leans against the weathered wood, his gaze fixed on Tripp.

"I'm very proud of you, Tripp. You've provided for your mother. That takes a man. I know Mark has helped, but Anne says you are the reason."

Tripp listens, his heart swelling with a warmth he hasn't felt since he was a child. "She gives without any thought for herself. I want her to know that I am so lucky to have her."

Papa Dalton's voice drops, a hint of suspicion entering his tone. "Your Uncle John tells me you've found a good friend. Says he's got a big heart and a good head on his shoulders."

Tripp stiffens. He fears what's coming.

"John doesn't talk about family much," Papa Dalton says, his eyes searching Tripp's. "So when he does, I listen. But I'm just an old man with old ways, son."

"Uncle John stopped everything to come help me...I was in a bad place. I couldn't talk to my dad..."

"Hm. Interesting." Papa Dalton thinks for a moment. "Why is that?"

John Dalton, Sr. was never a fan of Willis Carson, but he does value family, tradition and honor and he knows there is something driving Tripp. He is also a very smart man. Tripp knows his grandfather never asks a question without a good idea of the answer.

"Uh.." Tripp stumbles on his words. "Momma says Uncle John is smart...uh, plus I thought since he doesn't have kids, he could offer advice..."

Papa Carson's expression tells Tripp that his grandfather isn't buying these excuses. The silence is demanding Tripp to answer.

Tripp sighs, glancing to the house and quietly answers truthfully. "I felt he would understand me better than anyone else. He didn't hesitate when I needed him." Tripp hangs his head low.

"John cares deeply for you, as well as Mark and Scott. Just tell me... is this friend a girl or a boy?"

Tripp's heart pounds in his chest. He knows he can't lie. "He's a boy, Papa. And he is my best friend. But I can't tell him my feelings."

Papa Dalton nods slowly, his face unreadable. "Well, that's what I thought. Just be careful, son."

"Do you..." Tripp hesitates. "Papa, do you hate me?"

John Dalton turns to the house. "It's not that simple."

"I'm sorry I let you down." Tears stream down Tripp's face.

His grandfather takes out a red handkerchief and wipes his face. Gentle and caring like a father. "You didn't. I want you to live your life. I've had mine, and it is priceless. I don't begin to understand what your feelings are or how to deal with them. Between your mother, Pat and John, I know they will be able to help."

John Dalton points at the old farmhouse. "That said, my door will always be open for you." He takes Tripp in a hug. "For you and your friend."

"Papa, if that's true." Tripp hesitates. "What about..."

His grandfather gives him a stern look. The elder man's generation can speak volumes without words and Tripp knows it. John Sr. wraps his arm around Tripp's shoulder, pointing him toward the lake. And just like that, the conversation is over.

Tripp steps through the trees and down the path. Smiling, he sees his friend waiting. Robbie stands on the small wooden dock by the lake. The water is a perfect sheet of glass, the setting sun painting the sky in shades of orange and pink. Robbie sits, letting his feet dangle in the cool water.

Tripp walks to the edge and stands beside him, gazing out at the setting sun. The air is cool, the water a perfect sheet of glass.

"You gonna join me, or are you too scared to get your feet wet?" Robbie asks, a half-smile playing on his lips.

Tripp laughs softly and sits down, his legs close to Robbie's. The warmth from Robbie's skin is a sudden comfort. Robbie rests a hand on Tripp's back, his fingers tracing a small, gentle circle.

"Guess that your grandfather asked tough questions about your desire to change?" Robbie asks warmly.

Tripp holds his breath for a moment, the simple touch sending a jolt through him. He looks at Robbie, whose eyes are filled with a sincerity that makes Tripp's heart ache. He wants to lean in, to close the small distance between them, but he is too afraid.

"He was tougher on me than I could've imagined."

"I need to tell you something," Robbie says, his voice a low murmur.

Tripp's throat tightens. "I know." He looks out at the water, his chest tight. "Can't we just pretend for a little while?"

Robbie pulls his hand back slowly. The absence of his touch is a tangible ache. "Pretend what, Tripp?"

"That we can be here forever. That we don't have to worry about anything," Tripp says, his voice a whisper.

"Anything for you, Tripp." Robbie pats him on the back. "Say, are those new shorts?" He teases.

"Nah..." Tripp laughs. "Stole them from a hobo in the park."

"Well, they hide your good looking legs, you should toss them"

Tripp sticks out his tongue playfully. "Can't do that, strict no purple policy at the lake."

"Purple?" Robbie asks incredulously. "It's almost Christmas, you should switch to red or green."

"It's less than a week to Thanksgiving." Tripp ponders aloud. "What colors is that?"

"Uh...well you have cranberries and apples with the dinner. So a red to burgundy?" Robbie rubs his chin in a thoughtful manner.

Tripp laughs hard. Robbie bumps shoulders with him. With a sly smike, he adds, "Then get the shorts tailored to fit you or ask Stephanie for help."

"Nope, these are original designer shorts!" Tripp jokes. "I've been meaning to return them since that day in the park."

Robbie's smile is sad but understanding. He takes a piece of gum from his pocket and unwraps it. "You want some?" he asks, his voice back to its usual easy tone.

Tripp accepts it. Their fingers brush, a tiny, charged moment that feels bigger than it is.

"What did you want to tell me, Rob?" Tripp asks softly.

The lake water pats softly against the dock posts. The moment of silence between them feels reassuring, anchoring. The colorful sky backdrops Robbie's profile. Tripp tries to not stare.

"You're my best friend. I'm glad we fixed our friendship." Robbie looks at Tripp, his smile infectious. "We should make a pact to never go to asleep when we are mad at eachother. I don't want to lose what we have, Tripp. It's priceless."

"Promise." Tripp's voice cracks.

Tripp knows that Robbie understands. As much as Tripp wants it, they are not ready for a relationship, not yet.

Dinner is a loud, lively affair. The table is filled with food, and the conversation is easy. Robbie is polite and respectful, his southern charm on full display. Anne Dear smiles warmly, her eyes twinkling as she looks at Robbie. He's exactly the kind of boy she hoped Tripp would be friends with. Mark and Papa Dalton are in a heated debate about a recent football game. The laughter is genuine, the atmosphere warm and loving.

Then, Anne Dear turns to Tripp, her smile still in place, but her eyes a little colder. "I have to say, son, I'm so glad you're finding your way. And I'm glad you're not hanging around Uncle John so much anymore. He's a bad influence on you." The room goes silent. Robbie looks at Tripp, a silent question in his eyes.

Tripp's voice is calm, but firm. "Grandma, Uncle John is a good man. He's been there for me when no one else was. He helped me get through a really tough time. He taught me about being a good man."

Papa Dalton watches Tripp carefully. Everyone in the family knows not to disagree with Anne Deear when it comes to her son, John. *This is Willis Carson's arrogant mindset showing through.* But John Dalton, Sr. remains quiet.

"But he's just too busy, son," Anne Dear says softly, her voice filled with a quiet denial. "He runs a successful business in DC and lives in a big city."

"Maybe Scott and I can stay with him for a weekend."

Anne Dear carefully spreads butter on her dinner roll. "Poor Scott has been through enough, it would be too traumatic to uproot him from Pat's stable home."

"I've spent time with Scott every week. He's stronger than we give him credit for." Tripp defends.

"Y'all have nothing in common with your uncle, Michael." Anne Dear's voice is firm, decisive.

Tripp hesitates, like a timid animal about to be trapped. "We are his family. He's coming to spend Thansgiving with us this year."

"Coming for dinner isn't the same. He's single. He doesn't have time to be a father figure to you. He has his... *friends*." She looks down at her plate. "He can't just be flitting back and forth from the city to the country every time you need him. He's far too busy for that sort of thing."

Tripp looks at his grandmother, then at Papa Dalton, who is staring at his plate. "Being a family man isn't about having a wife and kids, Grandma. It's about loving the people in your life, about being there for them, and about being honest."

Anne Dear's eyes fill with tears, and her lips press into a thin line. "You're just like him, can't listen to reason. Michael, I've said no.." The words are a quiet indictment.

The silence is thick and heavy. Tripp feels a knot tighten in his stomach. He knows he's said too much, but he can't take it back. Tripp feels Robbie tug on his hand under the table, a quiet message to stop.

He looks at Robbie, then at Mark, who is staring at his brother with a combined look of admiration and fear. He knows that his family is watching him, and he knows that his love for Robbie is something he must continue to hide.

"I'm sorry, Anne Dear." Tripp looks down and finishes the meal in silence.

Invitation Avalanche

Lauren spots Jeff Tyler walking down the steps just ahead of them. She glances at Tripp, who has clearly seen him too. She knows she should stop pushing. This is his mission, not hers. Then again, when had details ever stopped her before?

Where would Tripp be without me pushing him? she thinks with a smirk.

"It looks like Jeff is alone," she remarks casually. "What about it, Tripp?"

Tripp frowns. "I don't want to feel rushed. Talking to Jeff might need more time. The bell's going to ring soon."

"Just an apology?" Lauren raises an eyebrow and crossing her arms, her eyes locked on him. "Sounds like you're stalling, Carson."

Tripp stops walking. "It's complicated. When I do talk to Jeff, I want to give him all the time he needs. It's not procrastination."

"Hmm," Lauren replies, clearly skeptical.

"It isn't..." Tripp sighs. "I'm not proud of how I ended things with him. He might need to tell me just how much of a jerk I was. He deserves that. And I don't want to make it worse."

"I get it," she answers, pulling him into a hug. "I'm always here for you."

As they embrace, Tripp notices Jeff chatting with someone by the steps. *Ken,* he remembers suddenly. An idea hits him like lightning. He pulls back from Lauren, a grin spreading across his face.

"Come on, Lauren. It's showtime."

"Showtime?" she echoes in confusion, trailing after him as he hurries down the steps.

"Ken! Hey Ken, wait up a sec!" Tripp calls out.

"Mike? Damn, it is Mike Carson," Ken replies, waving.

Tripp catches his breath as they reach him. "I'm glad I caught you. You know Lauren?"

"No, I'm Ken Terrill. Are you Mike's girlfriend?" Ken asks with a grin.

"Sadly, no. Tripp's heart belongs to another," Lauren says with a laugh, resting her hand on Tripp's arm. "I'm dating one of his friends. He just drives me to school."

"She's been pushing me to ask out Holly again," Tripp chuckles.

Ken looks puzzled. "She called you Tripp?"

Tripp nods. "Yeah. I gave myself a life do-over. I'm trying to be a better person. The nickname's symbolic of that change. I'm the third—Tripp."

"Cool. So, Tripp it is. How have you been?"

"Better. Thanks. Listen, we're having this get-together by the river in a couple weeks. Just a few friends blowing off steam. Want to come?"

"Uh, yeah," Ken grins.

Lauren adds quickly, "It'll be huge."

"Huge?" Tripp repeats, surprised.

"The river? Sure. Can Betty come? She's my girlfriend."

"Absolutely," Lauren confirms. "Hey, were you just talking to Jeff Tyler?"

"Yeah, he's in my science class. Why?" Ken looks cautiously between them.

"You should invite him," Tripp suggests.

Ken hesitates. "Mike, I thought you knew... he's... gay."

"We don't care," Lauren anssers, wrapping her arms around Tripp's.

"Yes, I want him to come," Tripp adds. "I know I used to be opinionated. That's fair. But Jeff and I were friends. I want to make things right. If he wants to avoid me, he can."

Ken looks amazed. "You've changed? Betty mentioned it, but I wasn't sure."

"Ken, I believe in Tripp Carson," Lauren tells him. "He's been trying to find the right way to talk to Jeff. I wouldn't support this if I didn't believe in him."

"Okay. I'll talk to him. Oh, here comes Betty."

Betty jogs up, bright-eyed. "Morning, babe! Do you know Mike?"

"English Lit," Betty smiles. "You look nice this morning, Mike. Who's your girlfriend?"

"Thanks. Betty Kinsey, right? This is Lauren Masters. She's dating one of my friends."

"Really? Y'all make a cute couple," Betty teases.

"Just close friends," Lauren smiles.

"Can't hide love," Betty winks.

"Mike invited us to a river party," Ken steers the conversation back.

"Sounds like a blast!" Betty beams.

"He suggested we invite Jeff Tyler too."

"That'd be wonderful. Just don't invite Randy. I don't think they're together anymore."

"Uh, Betty," Ken begins, "you know Mike... didn't like gays"

"This Mike?" she asks. "Or the old one? Mike's changed. He used to be a jerk. He's not anymore. Sorry if I offended you, Mike."

"No offense taken," Tripp replies. "Ken needs to hear that I've changed from you too."

"It's true," Lauren adds, hand on his shoulder. "Tripp really has changed."

Ken raises his hands. "Okay. We'll come. I'll talk to Jeff but can't promise anything. I don't want him hurt."

"Neither do I," Tripp promises. "Thanks, Ken."

"We gotta run," Betty urges. "Can I invite others?"

"The more the merrier," Lauren jokes.

"More?" Tripp echoes, eyes wide.

As Ken and Betty walk off, Lauren exhales and looks at Tripp.

"That was quick thinking," she compliments him. "But next time, give me a little warning. I better go plan this out."

"Thanks, Lauren. I mean that... but inviting everybody? Is that wise?"

• • • •

• • • •

TRIPP HEADS TO CLASS. Robbie sits at his desk and waiting. Looking up at the sound of the door opening, he smiles when Tripp enters the room. He walks over, casually tossing his bookbag into the corner, and sits down. Tripp exhales while moving closer to Robbie.

Tripp whispers, "Uh, just so you know, we are doing a thing by the river in a couple of weeks."

"A thing? By the river? What do you mean?" Robbie asks, scooting closer to his friend.

"I needed a way to apologize to someone, so Lauren and I came up with the idea of a few friends having a nice party by the river. Somehow, I lost control of the conversation, and I think it may get way bigger than that..."

"All just to apologize?" Robbie is amazed by his friend's dedication.

"Yeah," Tripp shrugs. "He may not take my apology. Also, I need to be able to give him time to say whatever he needs to say, but also give him a way to avoid being around me if he chooses."

"That is a good idea. Can Doug and Gary come?" Excited by the prospect, Robbie grins.

"I was going to suggest it anyway. But at this point, I think most of the school will be there!" Throwing his hands up in the air, Tripp laughs.

The Night Before

T he following days come flying by in a blur. Tripp finally comes
up with a way to apologize to Jeff and it turns into a circus.
He knows he has waited too long. Mad at himself, Tripp makes a
promise to make it up to Jeff—or at least that's his plan.

What started out as a few friends gathering has exploded into
something far bigger. Lauren loses count after confirming fifty-two
attendees. Tripp doesn't know how he can ever repay his friends.
Robbie and Lauren stand beside him through every challenge since
he that day in Mrs. Austin's class.

The air buzzes with anticipation on the Friday before the big
event at the river. Tripp dresses in such a hurry that morning he
doesn't notice he puts on one blue sneaker and one white one. He
wears khakis and a red polo-style shirt with a small, dark blue logo
on the chest—not a name brand, just something comfortable. The
stress of planning leaves him unable to focus in class.

He sits in the back corner, his blue windbreaker draped over
the chair. His mind wanders between the party and Jeff. What
starts as a plan to give Jeff a safe space turns into an all-school event.
Tripp isn't sure how Jeff will take the apology—or if he'll even
show. Ken has been intentionally vague, but Tripp doesn't press.

The only rule Tripp Carson insists on is simple: no alcohol. So
far, no one complains.

The final bell jolts Tripp from his thoughts. He grabs his
bookbag and heads toward the lobby. Robbie has to stay after class
to discuss a project, so Tripp figures he'll catch up with Steve and
the guys. It's been weeks since he's really talked to them. With
everyone in vacation mode—Monday is a conference day—it
seems like the perfect time to reconnect.

Exiting the building, he spots Jonah leaning against the retaining wall. The rest of his friends are not there. Jonah waves him over.

"I want a minute to talk to you," Jonah says nervously.

Tripp offers a reassuring smile. "Sure, Jonah. I'm all yours until Robbie gets here."

"So, I know you're like this world traveler and wise beyond your young age type guru, but what's the story about the shoes?" Jonah asks, pointing at Tripp's mismatched sneakers.

"I wasn't paying attention," Tripp laughs. "It's the truth."

"Well, I heard after second period that a couple of guys swapped shoes in the bathroom. Now you're not the only one sporting a mismatch!"

"I'll be more careful next time," Tripp says, laughing.

Jonah leans in slightly. "Hey, Tripp, can I ask about something you said the other day?"

"That sounds ominous," Tripp jokes.

"No, it's not like that. You said the worst thing you believed could happen was *being in love with someone who's never gonna love you back*. Is it Lauren?"

"She's dating my friend Greg. We're just friends."

"Yeah, I wouldn't admit liking her either. Greg might kill you!" Jonah teases. "Still, you can't deny there's something between you..."

"He won't, and there isn't. She's my friend," Tripp replies flatly. "Is that what you want to talk about?"

"No," Jonah laughs nervously. "But if you were in love with her, I'd have your back. I just want to say... I think you've really changed. When you apologized that day, I thought it was just that—a one-day thing. But you've really changed, Tripp. Changed for the better."

"Thanks, Jonah. I'm glad. I want to be the kind of friend people cherish."

"Larry and I talk about you a lot. He says it's like a different person is walking around in Mike's body. He thinks the world of you. And so do I."

"Thanks," Tripp says, offering a handshake. "That means more than you know."

Just then, Robbie emerges from the building. Jonah spots him first, nudging Tripp.

"Hi, Tripp," Robbie greets. "It's Jonah, right?"

"Yeah, we had geometry together last year," Jonah replies.

Peter and Steve appear next, followed by a few others. Tripp waves as Steve breaks into a jog.

"Wanted to say goodbye before you left," Steve calls out, slightly winded.

"Just finishing up with Jonah. I'll see y'all tomorrow?"

They all confirm, and Tripp hands Robbie his bookbag before heading across the field to the Mustang. Jonah's comments still swirl in his head. He chuckles at the idea that anyone thinks he's in love with Lauren. She's beautiful, yes—but more importantly, she's a true friend.

Tripp opens the trunk and tosses his bag inside. Robbie follows, carefully placing his own bag next to Tripp's.

"Should I pack pillows around it?" Tripp teases.

"My project, Tripp. Two lantern pieces in there. Carlos is doing detail work with a router at his shop. Should be fine if you don't drive like me."

"Under a hundred, got it."

"And keep all four tires on the ground," Robbie adds with a grin.

"Now that's asking too much!"

They climb in, and Tripp fires up the V8. It doesn't purr like the GTO, but it's enough. Robbie reaches behind the seat.

"No tunes?"

Tripp sakes his head. "Took 'em in last night. Needed different music for working out."

Robbie laughs. "Trying to impress someone?"

"Just myself. It's easier to keep weight off than lose it."

"Makes sense. Doug's bringing his stereo tomorrow. Cassette player. Would've been nice to have some music now."

"Want to swing by my place and grab the tape case?"

"Yeah. Until then, we can listen to 97.4."

They drive in silence, music filling the background. Tripp pays attention to every bump and curve, not wanting Robbie's project to shift. Tripp has gone the entire day without seeing it. Tripp never realizes how similarly they're dressed.

As they turn onto Glade Avenue, Tripp notices Mark isn't home.

Tripp shuts off the moter. "Wanna come in for a minute?"

"Yeah. Got anything to drink?"

"Tea in the fridge okay?"

"Perfect."

Inside, Robbie notices the living room has been rearranged. He suspects Tripp and Mark did it for their mom. He admires that.

In the kitchen, Tripp pours two glasses. Robbie teases, "The hippie takes caffeine?"

"Saving the bad stuff for tomorrow."

"How do you stay so disciplined? I need my soda for everything."

"You've been drinking more water lately, Rob." Tripp picks at him. "Joining the hippes?"

"No hippie vibes. Just following your lead. I feel better for it."

"You've never had to worry about weight. I look at cake and gain ten pounds."

They laugh, rinse their glasses, and head toward Tripp's room.

"That's kinda why I drink whatever you drink," Robbie says, placing a hand on Tripp's shoulder. "I loved the old Mike, but I really enjoy having the new one around. I told you I'd do anything to help."

Tripp smiles. "My success comes from you. I can't really say how much it means..."

"Don't get all mushy again!" Robbie laughs, nudging him.

"I think my mom has some flowery lotion around here, comrade," Tripp shoots back, grinning as they disappear down the hall.

Signals and Silence

TRIPP WALKS DOWN THE hall into his room. He reaches for the light switch, but the bulb doesn't react. Robbie notices. He walks in and flips on the lamp beside the bed. Tripp's bedroom is ten feet square, with a single twin bed pushed against the wall. A small dresser with a stereo sits beside the window. The shelves are far more organized than they used to be. A Boston poster covers the bare wall—from the concert they went to together. Robbie smiles at the memory.

"Thanks, Rob," Tripp says.

Robbie spots Tripp's photo album on the table next to the lamp. It's open to a page with the Polaroid of them at the basketball game. A big smile spreads across his face. Tripp heads to the shelves, gathering cassette tapes and carefully arranging them in the case. Robbie keeps smiling at the photo, but something else catches his eye.

His gaze shifts toward the bed. Tripp turns, curious, then freezes. His heart skips. The red leotard and baby blue tights are sprawled out in full view. He used them for his workout last night, and they definitely look like they have been worn.

"Uh... Tripp... what's that on your bed?" Robbie asks, confused, setting down the photo album.

"It's a leotard, Rob," Tripp replies, trying to sound casual. "I've got the cassettes..."

"Duh." Robbie glances at him, eyebrows drawn. "I know what it is. Why is it on your bed?"

Tripp hesitates. He considers telling the truth but doubts how Robbie would take it. It's 1980, and boys in leotards aren't exactly a thing. He defaults to deflection. "Uh, it belongs to Holly. I like seeing her in... tight, clingy outfits."

"So, are you getting serious with her?" Robbie asks, concern creeping into his voice.

"Not really. Something wrong?" Tripp replies, growing uneasy. "We talk on the phone. Maybe she's trying to cast a spell on me?" He ends with a goofy grin, hoping to derail Robbie's curiosity.

"Meh... I've never been a fan of hers, but I know you like her," Robbie mutters, shrugging. "I just don't want to see you hurt."

"I know. And I appreciate that you have my back," Tripp says, patting Robbie on the arm. "We probably need to get to your house."

Tripp feels uneasy. He hadn't left the leotard out on purpose. *How could I be so careless?* he scolds himself. He didn't expect that reaction from Robbie, though it makes sense. As far as Robbie knows, Tripp is into girls and once had harsh opinions about anyone different. This secret isn't something people understand.

He snaps the latch on the cassette case shut. They head out to the car. Robbie stays quiet, not seeming angry, so Tripp doesn't press the issue. *Mark warned me. Did I jinx things?* He wonders.

Meanwhile, Robbie wrestles with what he saw. *A leotard? On Tripp's bed? It doesn't make sense. Holly? Maybe. But the way Tripp stumbled through that answer... it doesn't sit right. Tripp's been different lately—more open, more thoughtful. Better. But also more complicated.*

He wonders if there's more to his friend than he's ever realized. Maybe something Tripp isn't ready to say. Robbie doesn't want to push, but he can't ignore the knot in his stomach. He told Tripp he didn't want to see him get hurt. But now, he's not sure who he's really worried about.

"Mind if we stop by Maddox? I want to get drinks and things for tomorrow," Tripp asks.

"Yeah, Mike. Maybe some chips or pretzels," Robbie responds flatly.

Tripp notices the name. *Mike, not Tripp. Is that a message?* He doesn't know what he'll do if Robbie's upset.

They head into Maddox Grocery. Tripp pushes the cart while Robbie walks alongside, still replaying the scene in his mind. As they pass by a rack of athletic wear near the pharmacy endcap, Robbie imagines Tripp in the leotard—not in a mocking way, but with a strange mix of curiosity and discomfort. It feels personal, like catching a glimpse of something not meant for anyone else. The image is so vivid it startles him. He quickly glances away, cheeks warming. *Why am I picturing that?* he wonders. He doesn't even know how to process the thought. It's not judgment—just confusion, curiosity, maybe a little fear. *Tripp is still Tripp... right?*

Robbie blinks, shaking the image away, but it lingers.

The store isn't crowded. Gathering supplies is quick. But Robbie still says little. Tripp understands. Robbie never liked Holly. He even gets why. Holly cares too much about appearances, though she's trying to change.

Back in the Mustang, Tripp puts in his Boston mix tape. Robbie begins to loosen up as the rear speakers blast their favorite songs. Boston has always been their thing. Robbie stares out the window. Tripp heads to Rob's house, taking the quickest route he can think of. The silence hangs over them, and he wants to discover why Robbie has changed. A new song begins playing.

"Can I turn that up, Tripp?"

Hoping to keep the momentum, Tripp backs the tape up and restarts the song. "Remember that concert, Rob?"

"Yeah, we had such a great time," Robbie says with a smile. "I didn't want that night to end."

"We should make plans to see them again."

"Yeah. Hey, look! Stephanie's home," Robbie says as they pull up.

"Time to dust off my flirts," Tripp laughs. "Any word on how the interview went?"

"She and Bud are making an announcement after dinner. Safe bet she got the job. They've been meeting with that realtor."

"It'll be nice having her closer," Tripp agrees, grabbing his overnight bag, packed for any contingency.

Robbie thinks about Tripp's responses. *He's always had a thing for Steph.* Robbie lets out a sigh. He replayed the events through his mind. *It has to be Holly's leotard...*

"Honestly, I wish they'd move to this neighborhood. But they're looking on the east side," Robbie says, carefully removing his bookbag.

"I hated when Mark moved away..." Tripp starts.

"When did he do that?" Robbie asks, confused.

"Huh? Oh, I meant he was thinking about getting an apartment. Closer to school," Tripp answers quickly. "Mom talked him into staying."

"Oh, that makes sense," Robbie nods as they walk to the door. "With school and work, he's got zero free time..."

Reading Between The Bites

STEPH RELAXES ON THE sofa with her feet tucked beneath a throw pillow. Bud and Carlos talk quietly in the kitchen while Bud stirs a pot of sauce. It's his specialty—lasagna—the only thing he can cook, but he makes it with pride. As he preps the garlic bread, he glances occasionally out the window. Stephanie notices. He sees something but doesn't comment.

Outside, a car pulls up. Steph turns to see who it is. Robbie carefully holds his bookbag, Tripp trailing several steps behind with a grocery bag and a small duffle.

"Twins," Stephanie whispers to her mother as the boys approach the house.

Robbie climbs the steps and opens the door. "Come on, Tripp."

"Right behind you," Tripp replies with a grin.

When they walk in, Robbie notices Steph and their mom watching. He offers a sheepish wave. Steph lets out a soft giggle.

"Hon, ten more minutes," Bud calls from the kitchen. "Just putting in the garlic bread."

Robbie motions for Tripp to follow him upstairs. Steph's eyes track them like a cat watching birds. Robbie notices. Tripp doesn't. Robbie bolts up the stairs and into his room with Tripp close behind.

Robbie empties his pockets onto his dresser and kicks off his sneakers. Tripp sets his duffle on the corner of the desk.

"Is Bud's lasagna really that good?" Tripp asks. "Steph's always bragging about it."

Robbie leans back against the wall, crossing his legs. "Let me put it this way—this is the only thing he can cook."

"That isn't giving me a good feeling," Tripp replies with mock concern. He slides out the chair to sit.

Robbie laughs. "I can't lie... it's good. Like if Mom's pizza turned into pasta."

"I'll hold you to that," Tripp says with a grin.

"Rob!" Stephanie yells from the bottom of the stairs. "Come eat, guys!"

They race downstairs. Steph returns to the couch, eyes trained on the boys. Mama Davis finishes setting the dinner table as Bud pulls the garlic bread from the oven.

Robbie grabs two glasses, fills them with ice, and pours water.

"Sorry, Tripp. I don't know how to cook a salad," Bud jokes, drying his hands on a dishrag.

"No problem. I've only heard good things about the pasta plate from heaven," Tripp replies with a theatrical bow.

Carlos laughs. "That's the most accurate description I've heard."

They all sit. Tripp waits for Robbie before taking his seat. Again, Stephanie watches their every move. She notes how close they sit—closer than usual. Conversation fades during the meal. The lasagna is indeed a masterpiece. Tripp savors each bite. Robbie finishes quickly. Bud sits quietly, scanning the table. He notices the way Tripp glances at Robbie during the silence. The way Robbie leans slightly toward his friend. He doesn't say anything—not yet—but he sees it.

No one wants dessert after such a filling meal. Steph and Carlos clear the kitchen. Mama Davis settles on the couch with a murder mystery novel. Plans for a card game hover in the air.

Carlos attacks the dirty pans while Steph wipes the table. Her eyes wander toward the fireplace where Robbie and Tripp stand talking with Bud. She isn't paying attention to the conversation. She's watching her brother. Tripp pulls out chapstick, applies it slowly, but keeps eye contact with Robbie. Stephanie notices how he mirrors Robbie's posture.

She thinks back to dinner: same drink, same closeness, shared silences. Her gaze sharpens.

"Hey, Bud," Steph says casually. "Babe, come here a moment?"

"Sure," Bud replies, patting Robbie on the shoulder. He walks over, and Steph leans in.

"Bud, we need to stay the night," she says quietly.

"Steph, we're meeting with the moving van company in the morning..." he starts, but trails off when he follows her gaze.

"No, Bud. We're staying," she says with a grin, eyes fixed on her brother and Tripp.

Bud looks between the boys, then back to his wife. He doesn't say it out loud, but now he understands what he noticed earlier. He nods slowly. "All right," he says. "We're staying."

Lucky at Cards, Unlucky at Love

"I NOTICED ROB AND TRIPP are wearing matching outfits. Did they have a function at school or something?" Bud whispers quietly, pretending to help wipe off the table.

Stephanie shakes her head. "Not that I'm aware of."

Bud shrugs and jokes, "Coincidence, maybe? Remember when we were young and dating? We did silly things like that, Steph."

"Bud, we matched on Tuesday when we went to your boss's house for dinner," she reminds him, placing a hand over his.

Bud looks confused, then chuckles. "That was on purpose. But we did that a lot when we were dating. I never knew how you always knew what to wear."

"Bud, my love, you are an open book to my heart," Steph says, leaning in to whisper and kiss him.

"How long have Mike and Rob been best friends?"

"They've known each other for three years, but I would consider them best friends for the last year abd a half," Stephanie answers, careful not to speak loudly.

"They seem to have gotten closer since Mike began his self-improvement journey," Bud gives Stephanie a comforting tap on the arm. "I can see how much Mike means to Robbie."

Carlos emerges from the kitchen. "Who's ready for cards?"

Everyone gathers around the couch. The night moves quickly as Robbie and Tripp dominate hand after hand. Steph notices that, as the games progress, Tripp inches closer to her brother. Her smile grows. Bud bows out around 9:30 and heads to the kitchen for a drink. After two more rounds and another clean sweep by Tripp and Robbie, the group calls it a night. Robbie heads upstairs with Tripp close behind.

"Just going to brush my teeth and get changed," Tripp says as he grabs the small duffle bag.

"OK, Tripp," Robbie answers as he heads into his room.

Tripp crosses the hallway and enters the bathroom. He quickly brushes his teeth. Tripp thinks about Robbie's reaction earlier, hoping it was something passing. Robbie appears to have loosened up during dinner and the card game afterward. Tripp removes his shirt and khakis. He steals a moment to gaze into the full-length mirror on the door.

Tripp is sporting a new pair of briefs. He gives himself a nod of approval. "This paint job should impress. I sure hope that Robbie likes these," Tripp whispers to himself as he turns sideways and studies the reflection.

"It took two hours and three stores to find the right color..."

Tripp is wearing a dark blue pair of briefs. The color is as close to the paint on Robbie's GTO as he could find. Tripp is trying one of his uncle's suggestions and making a subliminal connection between him and what Robbie likes. He removes the brush and carefully brushes his hair. He wants to look perfect.

"Maybe tonight is the night?" he softly asks himself as he puts on the running shorts. There is no sense in risking being seen by someone in the hallway.

What We Don't Say

AS ROBBIE CLIMBS THE stairs ahead of Tripp, his thoughts drift. He keeps thinking about the leotard. *Tripp said it was Holly's. That made sense—kind of. But something about the way Tripp said it didn't feel right.* Robbie's not sure why it's stuck in his head. Maybe it's because it was just lying there, like it wasn't hidden at all. Like Tripp didn't expect anyone else to be there.

Robbie hears Tripp saying something and robotically answers, not even catching what the words were. His mind is elsewhere, filled with doubt. Robbie hears the bathroom door close as he enters his bedroom.

Robbie drops his bookbag in the corner and starts arranging the blankets. He glances at the door. Tripp's still in the bathroom. Part of him wants to ask again—but what would he say?

"Hey, do you wear your girlfriend's leotard?"

That sounds ridiculous. But the image flashes through his mind anyway—Tripp, not Holly, in that bright red leotard, maybe stretching before a workout. Robbie shakes his head quickly.

Come on, man. Don't be weird. Tripp's your best friend. He's been through a lot. Don't make it worse.

Still, Robbie can't ignore how Tripp has been looking at him lately. Not just in the "I respect you" way—but really looking. Watching. Observing. The matching outfits didn't help either. It was a weird coincidence... or maybe it wasn't. Steph noticed too. And Bud—he definitely clocked something, even if he didn't say much.

When Tripp enters the room, Robbie turns toward the wall, pretending to be settling in. He can't bring himself to look. Not just yet. He doesn't want to make assumptions—or say something he'll regret. As Tripp moves around the room, Robbie rolls to face his friend. He sees Tripp hesitating, like he was about to remove his shorts but had second thoughts. *Maybe the thoughts aren't there?*

"You want me to sleep on the floor, Rob?" Tripp asks, gently.

Robbie shakes his head. "Nah, just figured you should get the outside this time."

He hears Tripp click off the light and slide into bed. The glow of the small lamp near the bed gives the room a warm amber hue. Robbie listens as Tripp begins to talk. At first, it's casual—about the lamp, sleep preferences, harmless small talk. But then Tripp asks for advice.

Robbie smiles despite himself. "Anything, old friend," he says. He's not sure why Tripp's being so careful, but he knows something is coming.

Then Tripp says it—he might want to ask someone out.

Robbie's heart lurches a little, but he hides it well. He gives the same advice he always does: be yourself, don't rush, follow your heart.

Then Tripp says, "Thanks, old friend. It is someone I look up to. I respect them very much. Uh, they're older..."

Robbie lets out a soft chuckle, but there's an edge of something else behind it.

"Older, huh? Sounds like you're chasing wisdom, not just a pretty face."

Tripp grins, trying not to sound nervous. "I respect them, Rob. Maybe more than anyone."

But when Tripp mentions Jeff Tyler, everything inside Robbie jolts.

Jeff? Jeff Tyler?

Robbie's mind races. He knows Jeff's gay. Everyone does. And Tripp—Tripp used to be the kind of guy who made life hard for kids like Jeff. That's part of what changed after Mike Carson became "Tripp." He let go of that hate. Started becoming someone better.

But now, if Jeff's the one Tripp wants to apologize to—or worse, if he's the one Tripp wants to ask out—Robbie's chest tightens.

He stays silent for a long moment.

"We were close when we were eleven," Tripp says, "After an...argument, I said some awful things."

Robbie listens carefully. It doesn't sound like Tripp is trying to flirt with Jeff. It sounds like guilt. A need to make something right.

Still... the way Tripp hesitated. The way he keeps looking at Robbie. Something doesn't add up.

"I'm sure you can work things out with Jeff," Robbie finally says. He doesn't want to press tonight. Not while Tripp's already so tangled up inside. "You're trying. That's what matters."

Tripp promises not to beat himself up anymore. Robbie lets it drop—for now.

But he'll be thinking about it. And watching. Because he's starting to wonder if the person Tripp wants to ask out... isn't Jeff at all.

And if that's true?

Then things might get even more complicated than he thought.

What He Doesn't Know

Tripp is startled by a gentle rap on the door. He opens his eyes. Another gentle rap follows:

"Robbie, it's time for you and Mike to wake up, honey. It is 7:15 like you asked."

Tripp clears his throat. "Thanks, Mama Davis. Just a few more minutes, okay?"

"Alright, Mike. I will be in the kitchen," she replies.

Tripp lays facing away from the wall, his back pressing against Robbie. At some point during the night, Robbie has moved closer. Now, their bodies fit together perfectly, with Robbie's left arm casually draped over Tripp's side. Tripp can feel Robbie's slow, steady breaths on the back of his neck. He wants to stay motionless, savoring the warmth and comfort of Robbie's embrace. It probably means nothing—Robbie often gets cold at night.

Tripp hesitantly tugs on Robbie's arm. "Hey Rob. It's morning..."

Tripp is the first to make it downstairs. Robbie is still moving slowly. They stayed up until 1 a.m., talking about Jeff and the river trip. Tripp isn't tired now—he's too excited. It's finally the day they've been planning. Friends, music, the river. Tripp feels like he's on top of the world. Still, he knows the lack of sleep may hit him later. He wears dark blue running shorts and a gray tank top.

"Morning, Mama Davis," Tripp greets her, crossing the living room to the kitchen bar.

"Good morning, Mike," she sings, gracefully moving about the kitchen.

Thumping feet signal Robbie barreling down the stairs. Stephanie emerges from the den in sweatpants and a Detroit Lions T-shirt. Her hair hangs in her face. She doesn't look fully awake.

"Morning, Tripp," she mutters. "Mom. Please tell me there's coffee."

"Steph," Tripp answers politely, resisting the urge to flirt.

"Mom!" Robbie calls. "Are there any clean towels? Mike and I need to shower before heading out."

"Laundry room, hon," Mama Davis calls back from the fridge.

Tripp heard the name. He watches as Robbie, still in sweatpants and shirtless, jogs through the living room. He hides a smile, quietly admiring Robbie's strong arms and chest. Stephanie sips her coffee while carefully observing Tripp. Mama Davis returns with two plates stacked with eggs and bacon. She hands one to Tripp with a warm smile.

Robbie comes dashing in, tossing a towel at Tripp's head before pulling on a red shirt and plopping down beside him. They both laugh.

"Let me shower first," Robbie says, leaning his shoulder playfully into Tripp.

"Sure," Tripp replies, smiling.

"When I get done, you'll need to shower quickly. I want to clean the Goat and pack up."

"I can help with that," Tripp offers, perking up.

"Eat while it's warm," Mama Davis urges.

"Yes, ma'am," they chime together.

Stephanie steps beside her mother, sharing a quiet nod. The two women watch the boys—how they laugh, how they move around each other. It's obvious to them now.

"Heavens, Robert. Take time to chew your food," Mama Davis scolds.

"Sorry, Mom!" Robbie says with a full mouth. "I've gotta shower!"

As Robbie sprints upstairs, Tripp leans back to stare. He moves to take another bite and catches the women watching him. The smile fades from his face.

"Does he know?" Stephanie asks.

"Does he know?" Tripp echoes, startled. "Know... what?"

"Robbie," Mama Davis says softly.

"Does Robbie know that you love him?" Stephanie folds her arms, smiling.

Tripp checks the stairs. Still quiet. He fidgets with his napkin.

"Robbie's my best friend..." he begins.

Mama Davis arches a brow. "And?"

"Best friends can love each other... like brothers."

"Tripp," Stephanie sighs. "All that flirting with me—you were covering, weren't you?"

"It's okay, Michael," Mama Davis says warmly. "It's perfectly fine that you're gay. You're welcome here."

"You've always made it feel like my second home," Tripp says cautiously.

He glances again toward the stairs. He's not scared, exactly—just not ready.

"Mike, I want you always to feel like this is home," Mama Davis reassures.

"I'm not mad," Stephanie adds, teasing. "But it was nice thinking you worshiped me."

Tripp doesn't want to lie to them; it feels right, and he trusts them. "Well, technically, I'm not gay," Tripp explains nervously. "I like boys. And girls. It's bisexual attraction."

"So you still love me?" Stephanie laughs.

"If only your husband weren't sleeping in the den," Tripp jokes.

"You should talk to Robbie," Mama Davis urges. "You've been friends a long time."

"I never thought anything about it until a few months ago," Stephanie adds. "But then I saw it. You let your guard down around him."

"And in front of us," Mama Davis agrees.

"Last night during cards," Stephanie says. "You sat close. You kept watching him. I noticed how you matched your clothes. Once you see love, it's hard to miss."

Tripp leans back, sighing.

"I couldn't tell him. I can't risk losing him."

"Michael," Mama Davis says gently. "Robbie will understand."

"Maybe," Tripp admits. "Up until two months ago, I hated myself. I hated being broken. I was on a self-destructive path. If I hadn't changed, I would've dropped out."

"I suspected you were depressed," Mama Davis says.

"We all did," Stephanie adds, brushing his hair.

"I didn't like who I was. I was becoming a narcissist. I'd have lost Robbie. I didn't want that dark future. I changed because of Robert Davis."

"Oh, Tripp," Stephanie says, eyes moist.

Tripp leans back and looks to the stairs, then continues, "He saved me. He saved me in a way no one else ever could. It took forty-six years to accept that my attraction to boys *and* girls is a part of who I am. It's taken me time to figure all this out. Robbie has been my friend for a long time. I did not know I had feelings for him. I have strong feelings, but I never understood them until now. I didn't want to, but I admit that I love Robbie. I could not lose him again. I would rather keep my secret than risk losing him. No matter his reaction to a confession of my feelings, he would never look at me the same way."

No one catches Tripp's mention of "forty-six years."

They hear footsteps pounding down the stairs. Robbie bursts into view.

"I'm heading to the garage! Hurry up, Mike!" he shouts.

Tripp watches Robbie leave, still smiling but aware of how much weight this moment carries. He grabs the towel from the floor.

"Please keep this between us," Tripp says quietly. "Only my mom and uncle know. Maybe a few others suspect."

"We won't betray your trust," Mama Davis says. "But you really should tell Robbie."

Tripp nods. He heads upstairs for his shower, mind spinning.

Tripp zones out in the shower, grateful Robbie didn't use all the hot water. The conversation with Mama Davis and Stephanie loops in his head. Their support means the world to him. Still, he isn't ready. How would he even start?

He dries off, slipping into silky red briefs, the Boston concert tee, and khaki shorts borrowed from Robbie. He styles his hair with extra care.

"He isn't going to see..." he mumbles to himself, then sighs and heads out.

Tripp dashes through the house and out of the garage. Robbie slams the trunk shut.

"I thought you went back to bed!" Robbie teases.

"I had to use all the hot water," Tripp grins.

Robbie hops behind the wheel. Tripp jumps into the passenger seat as the GTO rumbles to life.

"Mama Davis doesn't like that!" Tripp laughs.

"She has to catch me first!" Robbie grins as they peel away into the morning.

The River

The muscle car rumbles and leaps forward. Robbie catches second gear and peels onto the street. Tripp leans out the window and hollers like a man on fire. None of the neighbors seem to care. Tripp's never felt so alive.

He doesn't know why fate picked that day in Mrs. Austin's class to send him back—but he counts it a blessing. Robbie cranks the radio, flooding the GTO with classic rock. Tripp drifts off, thinking about this morning. Stephanie and Mama Davis. Their questions. Their warmth. Their insight. Several songs pass before he realizes Robbie has turned the volume down.

"You okay?" Robbie asks, glancing over.

"Huh?" Tripp blinks back to the present.

"You've been zoned out since we left."

"Sorry," Tripp shrugs. "I was thinking about something."

"I said the Albright twins aren't coming today—family's in town."

"That's a shame. I was going to ask out Karrie."

"I thought you had a thing for Kelly?" Robbie chuckles.

"Karrie, Kelly... goob, they're twins. Does it matter?" Tripp playfully grins.

"It does! Kelly's the girl-next-door type. Isn't that more your speed?"

Tripp hesitates, then smiles. "I prefer someone sincere. When you love someone, you should also like them."

"Oh, that's deep," Robbie laughs. "Wasn't it you who convinced the cheerleaders to wear their leotards every day during Spirit Week?"

"I can be deep and superficial. Multitasking."

Robbie laughs, but something flickers behind his eyes. He remembers last night in Tripp's room—Robbie remembers imagining Tripp in a leotard, Robbie had pushed it out of his mind. Seems Tripp has always liked to see girls in spandex, that and he liked girls.

Robbie shakes the thought away. "You didn't hear me complaining."

"Let me see. Cheerleaders in tight, clingy outfits?" Tripp laughs. "We are men after all!"

They both laugh loudly and then Robbie changes the subject, "So what were you so deep in thought about?"

Considering how things went last night, Tripp decides to try a roundabout way gauge Robbie's feelings, "I was thinking about my cousin in Gable, South Carolina. You remember Dusty?"

"He was here last summer?" Robbie nods.

"Yeah, he and Mark did some mountain camping thing. Well, recently, he and I got close. I guess he needed someone to reach out to and listen. I talked to him a few days ago. He told me some things."

"Is everything ok?"

Tripp suddenly gets cold feet.

"It isn't important," Tripp points down the road. "Besides, we are almost to the turnoff."

They slide off the main road, Robbie handling the GTO like a rally car. The tires kick up dust as they veer onto the dirt path that leads to the river. Tripp grips the door, grinning as the car fishtails before sliding perfectly into a spot between two trees.

"You're getting better at reckless driving," Tripp deadpans.

Robbie looks smug, pops the trunk, and they grab the cooler and chairs.

They set up under the trees. Ken and Betty are already wading in the water. Chris tosses a football with his brother. Robbie cracks open a Coke. Tripp remembers when he and Chris were fourteen. They would play football in the open lot near the Perry's house.

"I'm gonna talk to Doug and Gary. Back in a bit."

"Tell Doug I said hi," Tripp says, pulling a fruit punch from the cooler.

A shadow appears beside him.

"Uh, Mike?"

Tripp turns, surprised. "Jeff! Glad you came."

"I almost didn't," Jeff admits. "I thought... I mean, you said you hated me."

"I did," Tripp says softly. "I was wrong. I'm sorry. I didn't know how to handle what happened."

Jeff fidgets, stunned. "If anyone should apologize, it's me..."

"You already did. I wasn't ready to listen back then. But I am now." Tripp hands him a grape soda—Jeff's favorite. The gesture makes him blush.

"Still, Mike. I was being honest when I apologized..."

"You've done that. You apologized years ago. I was freaked out, Jeff. I wasn't going to listen then. I did not know how to deal with those emotions. I didn't have anyone to talk to. It was hard for me to process what happened. We were twelve. I was wrong to overreact. But today, I can listen."

"Thanks, Mike." Jeff replies with a smile and a drink of the soda.

"So, why tell me now?" Jeff asks, taking the open seat.

"Jeff, I did not like who I was or would become. I am asking my friends to forgive me."

Jeff looks down at the drink. "You don't need to ask my forgiveness, Mike."

"Call me Tripp. My friends do."

Jeff smiles. "Because you're the third?"

Tripp nods. "Mom wanted to call me Tripp from the start. Dad didn't."

"Tripp it is," Jeff says. "So... can we be friends again?"

"I'd like that very much."

Jeff glances around. "Do you ever... think about boys that way?"

Need to be careful about what I tell people. Tripp thinks. *I'm just fixing our friendship.*

"I like girls," Tripp answers. "But I'm not freaked out anymore. Can we just be friends?"

Jeff nods. "I'd like that."

Tripp sees Jeff's friend, lurking in the tree line, keeping a protective watch over the conversation. Jeff spots his friend, "I need to catch up with Em, can we talk later?" Tripp nods. As Jeff walks off to join Emery, Tripp watches his smile linger. There's hope in it. Hope Tripp isn't ready to match. Not yet.

Tripp watches Robbie laughing and shirtless, tossing the football. He sighs, catches himself staring, and scolds himself inwardly. *Better not. Too many people around.* Chris and his brother head off.

"Well, I haven't made any progress with the direct approach..." Tripp says softly as he thinks.

Robbie returns and flops into his chair, still glowing with energy.

"You okay?" Robbie asks. "You've looked preoccupied all day."

"I'm worried about my cousin," Tripp lies. "He came out to me—said he's bisexual. He doesn't know what to do about someone he likes."

Robbie blinks. "Bisexual?"

"Yes, Dusty is one of my cousins," Tripp nods yes. "Who he likes doesn't change that."

"I thought you disapproved of... them?" Eyeing his friend with suspicion, Robbie answers in a concerned way.

"Well, as he explained it, a bisexual can be attracted to boys and girls. So, it isn't really homo...not that it makes a difference, I understand that now," Tripp said. "After he told me, I knew that

Dusty is still the same cousin I have known all along. I realize I was wrong for hating homosexuals. I mean, sometimes you cannot help who you fall in love with..."

"Do you mean that, Tripp?"

Tripp nods. "Said he's into guys and girls. He's in love with his best friend but scared to say anything."

"Whoa... That could go really wrong," Robbie says, eyes going wide. "Does the friend know?"

"No. That's the problem."

Robbie shakes his head, "Then he shouldn't tell him. Not unless he's sure."

Tripp swallows hard. "You think it's that risky?"

"I mean, some people's friendships are fragile. Better safe than sorry."

Tripp tries to nod, but the weight in his chest grows. "I trust your advice."

"He must trust you very much, Tripp. It can be terrifying for some gays," Rob explains to his friend.

"Hearing you call me Tripp makes me smile."

Robbie sighs. He thinks for a minute. The images of Tripp in the outfit race in his mind. *I can't tell him that.* Robbie considers alternatives.

"I was mad...I felt hurt that you kept Jeff a secret from me. Sorry, I know you're apologizing to everyone.

"Thanks, Robbie," Tripp answers, hiding his sadness. "It wasn't on purpose."

Before Robbie can say more, Doug and Gary come running up.

"Suzanne's into you!" they shout.

Robbie nearly leaps out of his seat. "No way!"

"Holly's friend?" Tripp asks, stunned.

"Yes, She's coming later!" Robbie beams. "Maybe we can double date!"

Tripp forces a smile. "I've only talked with Holly lately..."

"Not for long," Robbie says, still euphoric. "Let's do this!"

Tripp watches Robbie run off to tell more friends. He exhales slowly, pain tightening in his chest. Thank God he hadn't pushed the conversation further. His love—for now—would remain secret.

Later, the sky turns orange. Jeff brings Emery over to say hello. Emery is all flair and sparkle, dramatically singing along with the music. Jeff takes the chair beside Tripp's. The sit and listen the song.

Tripp leans over and asks. "Y'all dating?"

Jeff rolls his eyes.

"He's not my boyfriend," Jeff explains. "Too theatrical. I like regular guys. Like you—uh, I mean..."

"It's okay, Jeff," Tripp laughs. "Actually... can I ask something?"

"Shoot."

"Do you know any bisexuals?"

Jeff quirks an eyebrow. "Why?"

"My cousin. He came out to me."

"Ah." Jeff leans back. "That's brave. So... is this why you forgave me?"

"Partly," Tripp admits. "I see things differently now."

"Thanks for telling me. Honestly, I always wished I'd just talked to you first... that day. You're so cute, uh, I meant you were cute. I...uh, shit. The twelve-year-old Mike was cute. Damn it, you know what I mean."

"Yes," Tripp laughs

Jeff nods. "You were cute then. But that day—I didn't want to scare you. I just... liked you."

Tripp couldn't help a lighthearted tease. "So, just to be clear. Am I still cute, or was I cute only when I was twelve?"

"Jerk, you know what I meant!" Jeff smiles with a laugh.

"You were the first person I should have apologized to," Tripp says. "I just didn't know how."

"You did it now. That counts."

Tripp offers a handshake. Jeff pulls him into a hug instead.

"You gave me courage, Tripp," Jeff says. "I think I'm finally gonna say yes to the guy who's been asking me out."

"I hope you do," Tripp says sincerely.

They part with a smile.

Jeff runs off, jumping in victory. Tripp sits back down. He thinks he can relax some. Thanks to the new bond with his uncle, Tripp is not alone. His mom unconditionally loves him and Mark is beginning to accept who he is. Scott is doing so well. Robbie is still his best friend.

Maybe this second chance was never about Michael Willis Carson. That could be the only explanation. Fate, the universe, or God, whomever it was must have wanted to help all these people. Tripp was only the tool. *Fixing my life may have been my reward for touching so many lives,* he ponders. Tripp is OK with that.

"I am ready to go..." Tripp gazes at the sky and closes his eyes.

"Go where, dork?" Lauren laughs. This startles Tripp, causing him to jump up out of the seat. Lauren and Greg stand in front of him, their faces sparkling with huge smiles. Tripp runs over and gives them both a big hug.

Tripp suddenly notices something, Lauren and Greg appear to be glowing. Lauren holds up her hand to show the new ring.

"We're engaged!" she beams.

Tripp shouts with joy, hugging them both.

Greg grins. "And I'm going to welding school—figured it was time to grow up."

"You inspired him," Lauren adds. "You changed his life."

"I didn't do much."

Lauren stops him. "You did, Tripp. You make people matter. Don't forget that."

"Lauren is right. That night, you brought Lauren to my house, and you...well, you gave that lecture to us both..." Greg laughs.

"I only said what I thought y'all needed to hear, Greg. I am sorry; I did not mean for you to dwell on it..."

"I did need to hear it, Tripp," Greg responds with a wave. "You always treated me nice, even when others called me a criminal or a thug. You stood up for me. It made me realize that I matter. I wanted to matter. I knew I had to do what was right so I could love Lauren with all my heart..."

Tripp tries to resist the emotions, but tears appear in his eyes. Lauren touches him on the shoulder. Greg laughs warmly. Michael Carson started as a stranger but has treated Greg better than any of his family ever did.

"I just wanted to thank you, Tripp. I mean that." Taking Lauren by the hand, Greg nods. "I am going to tell my class buddies the news next. I think Lauren wanted to talk with you."

"Greg, I am very proud of you," Tripp could feel several tears running down his face.

Greg kisses Lauren and walks off. The sounds of the music and people talking ring in the background.

"He was so afraid he was going to fail, Tripp. He kept going on because of you."

"He has you, Lauren," Tripp answers. "It was good to see something besides a beer in his hand."

They sit, sipping fruit punch. Lauren takes Tripp's hand gently.

"I have counted myself as lucky to be your friend. I don't know all the specifics of that nightmare you had, but you've made such a difference to the people you care about. I have seen that with my own eyes."

"I think I was here for them, the ones I have helped. This is their second chance. It was never about me."

Lauren gazes at Tripp with affection, "Maybe. But it should be, Tripp. It isn't selfish to desire a better life and to have love. It was your mission. How did things go with Jeff? I saw him earlier and assumed you were finally ready..."

"I apologized. We're friends again."

Lauren watches him carefully. "Is that who you're in love with?"

Tripp shakes his head. "No. I like Jeff. But not like that."

Nodding her head, her voice softens. "Then... Robbie?"

Tripp nods, unable to speak.

"I saw how you looked at him, Tripp. It wasn't subtle—not to someone who cares about you."

"Do you think anyone else knows?" tripp asks fearfully.

"I had a feeling," Lauren says, eyes misting. "You hide it well, but not from me."

"I can't ever tell him," Tripp whispers. "He asked out Suzanne. He was so happy."

Lauren squeezes his hand.

"How do you feel?"

"Heartbroken," Tripp confesses. "But I'd rather be heartbroken than lose him."

She whispers reassuringly, "I am so sorry, Tripp. But, you and he?"

"Best friends for life," Tripp smiles and nods. "Thankfully, I was cautious enough not to make my confession of love."

From the parking area, Robbie and Doug wave. Tripp stands, brushing away tears.

"Is it okay?" Lauren asks, quick on her feet.

Tripp nods. "Let's tell them the news."

As Lauren shares the engagement story, Robbie wraps an arm around Tripp's shoulder.

"I already knew," Robbie whispers. "Greg asked for my help. He said he wanted to change because of you."

Tripp laughs, eyes brimming again. "You're a good man, Robert Davis."

Robbie squeezes his shoulder. "So are you."

Lauren grins. "Party next week. Bring everyone."

Tripp watches them, heart aching, but full of love. His secret is safe. His mission, unclear. But for now, this moment is enough.

Crossroads and Echoes

The uneventful Sunday brings a surprising tension. Tripp, Robbie, and Doug are gathered around Doug's new Camaro, tackling an oil change and installing headers on the engine. Rock music hums from a small stereo, but the usual rhythm between the friends feels off.

"I thought you had the car running smooth, Doug. Something happen?" Tripp asks, walking over to the engine bay.

Doug's eyes are dull, maybe due to a lack of sleep. "Not sure what happened, Mike..."

"You two are the geniuses of the auto world, What do you want me to do?" Tripp nods toward the car.

"Can you lay the headers over here?" Doug points to the tool box near the driver's side door.

Tripp smiles and grabs the exhaust parts. His mind wanders. The events at the river seem so distant to Tripp. The emptiness in Tripp's heart crushes the success of finally apologizing to Jeff. *Don't discount what you've done for Jeff,* Tripp scolds himself.

Robbie is unusually talkative—bouncing between stories about Suzanne and joking about how good his GTO looked tearing down the river trail. Doug, on the other hand, is quieter than usual. He wipes his hands on a rag and focuses on the engine.

Tripp tries to break through the wall that surrounds his friends with a light tease, "You've been kinda quiet, Doug. Everything cool?"

Doug shrugs, not looking away from the engine, "Just tired. Long week."

Tripp exchanges a quick glance with Robbie, who doesn't seem to notice the subtle shift. Doug switches the ratchet in his hands, a soft metallic noise echoes in the garage.

Tripp nudges Doug on the arm, "You hear Robbie's big plans? Cherry pie and Wilson's Diner. Real Casanova stuff."

Doug grunts, not looking away from the car.

Robbie chimes in, grinning ear to ear, "I'm telling you, man—Suzanne's going to be impressed. Might even wear my clean jeans."

Tripp puts his hands on his hips in response, "You better. It'd be a shame to ruin dessert with those raggedy ones."

They all laugh, though Doug's lasts only a few seconds. For a moment, the tension eases, but Tripp still feels it—something changing. Tripp is happy for Robbie; *Suzanne is a sweet girl. If Rob wants this, I will wrestle the stars to help him.* Tripp mindlessly helps clean up the garage. By the time the tools are put away, he realizes that though his hands are greasy, it's his heart that feels empty.

Monday carries the weight of too much silence. His mind is numb, his heart fully protected now. The day feels like the calm before a storm. Tripp spots Doug and Robbie in the hallway. He does not think they see him. Tripp presses up to the wall, right at the corner and watches. *This feels wrong, I shouldn't spy on them,* Tripp whispers. *But they both are not acting like themselves.*

Doug is talking to Robbie, his hands are very animated as he moves closer to Robbie. Doug is upset. *Upset about what?* Tripp wonders. Robbie looks sad, like he is doing something he knows he shouldn't. He wishes he could hear what they are talking about, Tripp only wants to help them.

"Mike?" Holly interrupts his thoughts, Tripp jumps.

Moving away from the corner, "Oh, Holly. Hi. I didn't see you."

"You looked like you were focused on your friends. I just wanted to apologize for missing the party."

"It's uh, OK. I think you would have enjoyed it."

"So... you have anything to ask me?" Holly smiles, playing with the curls of her hair.

Tripp's mind clicks, turning momentarily in the direction where Robbie was standing. "Uh, yeah. I need to get with Robbie and find out when he and Suzanne are going to the movies...so we can double date?"

"Yes!" Holly giggles with excitement. "I know it's just a friendly night, Mike. But I am looking forward to another date with you."

Tripp smiles. Holly is a nice girl, and they have learned a lot about each other by talking on the phone. Holly steps close, and Tripp catches the fragrance of the sweet perfume. He grins. *It would be fun to be a simple sixteen year old on a date.*

"I am too, Holly." Tripp bows like a gentleman. "I'll call once I tie off with Robbie, OK?"

"I'd like that, Mike," Holly's eyes sparkle, looking like she wants to say more. She quickly leans in and gently gives him a peck kiss on the cheek and darts off down the hallway. The bell rings, Tripp is going to be late...

Tripp drifts through the rest of the day on autopilot. When the final bell rings, he lingers at his locker longer than usual. The talk with Holly should have lifted his spirit, but it hasn't. *It isn't her fault,* Trip thinks. *I'm in love with someone else.* That's when Steve and Larry pass by.

Steve runs up to Tripp, punching him in the arm. With an ear-to-ear grin, "Yo, Rob's finally going out with Suzanne tonight."

Larry laughs, pointing at Tripp, "Took him long enough. She's been giving him the eye for weeks."

Tripp forces a smile and nods. The words hit harder than they should. He stands and listens to his friends gossip, the words dissolve before they enter his mind. *I should be happy for Rob, I really should...*

As he walks to the parking lot, the ache inside him intensifies. Robbie rode the bus today—to talk more with Doug. That shouldn't sting. But it does.

Tripp struggles walking up the hill. "Maybe I should've never admitted it. Maybe that's when everything changed."

He reaches the Mustang and leans on the door before getting in. The cool metal beneath his hand reminds him of who he used to be. And who he's trying not to become.

Home is quiet. Tripp changes clothes carefully—nothing too fancy, but no old t-shirt either. He settles on a button-down. Brushes his hair. Checks his wallet. Enough for one used record. He steps into the bathroom, gazing at the reflection.

Tripp whispers, muttering to the mirror, "Desperate to feel like you matter. That's all this is."

He laughs, but the sound is hollow.

Tripp hits the light switch, "Let's go pretend this is about music."

The Mustang rumbles to life. He drives slowly, careful not to waste gas. He'll give most of his paycheck to his mom—that's the plan. No slipping back into old habits. He reminds himself to be smart, and the fuel will last him.

When he pulls into the Record Changer parking lot, the sky's fading with twilight. He checks his reflection once more in the side mirror.

Tripp snaps, "Is this wise? You're acting like a child."

But still, he goes inside.

The Record Changer

Tripp grabs his keys and heads into the shop. The store is empty. A handwritten note taped to the door reads, *I'm in back. Come on in.* He chuckles softly—very eighties.

Inside, he's grateful to find the space empty. He browses quietly, letting the silence settle around him. An older album catches his eye—something not in his collection—and he picks it up. Still, something feels off. He came here for a distraction, a chance to flirt, to feel wanted. But as he turns the record in his hands, doubt creeps in.

Why do I still feel so bad? No... I feel stupid.

He sighs and steps back toward the rack, ready to shelve the record and leave.

Then a voice.

"Tripp, you look like a glass of water to a man dying of thirst..."

He turns. It's Geoffrey.

Tripp glances out the window. He didn't see the Dodge van in the lot. Unease tickles the back of his neck. Geoff looks different tonight—tighter shirt, better jeans, boots, and his hair styled with more volume. Tripp's heart skips a beat.

Tripp steps toward the counter, record still in hand. He runs a hand through his hair, suddenly self-conscious.

"Hello, Geoff," he says flatly.

"Ah, still mad at me, I see?"

Tripp gives him a blank stare.

"I'm sorry about the gift...and Ernesto."

"It's not that, Geoffrey."

Geoff leans back against the counter, arms loose. "Can I at least know what I did?"

"Sorry. I've been busy. Something happened with my cousin..."

"The drummer?" Geoff tilts his head, expression shifting. "Is he okay? I know you two are close."

"He's good now. I'd rather not go into details, but we had to get him and his sister out. Their home wasn't safe."

"Damn," Geoff says sincerely. "I'm sorry. Here I was worried you were still mad, and it's not even that. Drummer boy OK?"

"They're okay. Thanks."

Tripp hesitates. He knows Geoff might be a wolf, but even wolves are human. And tonight, Geoff doesn't seem like a predator—just a guy with kind eyes and good hair. He sets the album down. Tripp smiles, catching the hint of Old Spice in the air.

"I must've seemed like a jerk before," Geoff says. "I came on strong, and I thought I scared you off. If there's anything I can do..."

"I appreciate that. I actually came in to talk with Rose."

"She was supposed to work tonight. Her grandma had some emergency—just a broken toe, I think." Geoff nods to the album. "Want me to ring it up?"

"Can we talk instead? Just talk. No games. No weirdness."

Geoff softens. "Of course. Come over here."

He leads Tripp to a lower counter. Tripp hops up, resting the album beside him, shoulders hunched. His legs dangle. Geoff leans against the register a few feet away, arms folded.

"We can talk about anything you want," Geoff says. "Or we can sit here and say nothing. But I can tell you need to let something out."

"Thanks," Tripp exhales. "I need a moment to *not think*."

"Start there. Or start wherever you want."

Tripp stares at the floor. Then, carefully: "Did you always know you were gay?"

Geoff nods. "Yeah. Grew up in Atlanta. Big cities are more forgiving. I thought everyone liked who they liked. Took a while before I realized people, *some people*, saw it as wrong."

Tripp doesn't look up.

"Are you worried you're gay?" Geoff asks gently.

"I'm not gay."

Geoff raises both hands in surrender. "Okay. Just trying to understand. What do you need?"

"I don't know," Tripp murmurs, looking into Goeff's eyes. There is a softness in them tonight. "I knew I liked boys when I was twelve. I hated myself for it."

"That must've been hard. Were you alone?"

Tripp nods.

Geoff nudges him gently. "You should accept who you are. Whether it's Rose or someone else—they deserve honesty. So do you."

"I like girls too."

"Bisexual?"

Tripp nods again.

"So... I'm guessing the person you're in love with doesn't feel the same?"

Clearing his throat, Tripp mutters, "Yeah. I almost told him. But I realized he's not into guys. I thought I could handle just being friends."

"Your Boston friend?"

Tripp nods. "Best friend."

Geoff sighs. "I know that feeling. I wish I could say the pain goes away."

"But it doesn't."

Geoff smiles sadly. "Nope. But life goes on. You'll find someone. Won't be the same. But it'll still be love."

"Do you have someone?"

"You met Ernesto. Kind of a roommate I sleep with. We got tegther in Philly six years ago."

"Do you love him?"

"I do. But I love a lot of people." Geoff chuckles. "It's not always easy. But I know where I stand."

He gently takes Tripp's left hand. Tripp doesn't resist. Geoff's touch is steady.

"I love him," Tripp whispers. "I'm not wired to love more than one."

"Then he's lucky. Even if he doesn't know it."

Geoff watches him closely. "Have you thought about telling him?"

"I thought I could accept just being his friend. But this hurts more than I expected. I came here tonight just to feel desirable."

"By someone like Rose?" Geoff smiles. "So... you're not mad at me?"

"No," Tripp says, voice cracking. "And Geoff... I could fall for you."

Tripp hides his face. "I did fall for you."

Geoff's expression shifts, sincere. "I don't know if I could be loyal—I've been wild too long—but I'd try for someone like you."

They sit in silence. Then Geoff puts an arm around him, warm and steady.

"I still think you're beautiful," Geoff says softly. "And kind. Your cousin thinks you're a hero. You're not a one-night stand kind of guy. I can respect that. Can we be friends?"

"Yes," Tripp says. "But I should get going. Got to clock into the coal mines at five A.M."

Geoff laughs, prompting Tripp to laugh, too. First real laugh of the night. Geoff lifts Tripp off the counter effortlessly, surprising Tripp with his strength.

At the register, Geoff almost lets Tripp have the record for free—but he stops himself. If he's going to win Tripp's trust, it has to be real. He rings up the album. Tripp pulls out a few bills and pays.

"Think you can come by tomorrow?" Geoff asks. "I'll leave a note for Rose too."

"Thanks, Geoff. I'd like that."

Tripp heads to the door, waving with the record in hand. Geoff watches him through the window, tracing every movement.

Innocent. Graceful.

I want him, Geoff thinks. *So badly.*

Best Laid Plans...

It is getting late—almost a quarter to seven. Geoff worries that Tripp is not coming. *At least the other kid was hot for some action. He better be, I shaved for that little shit!* Geoff can't shake being mad about that. Saturday will be a good night. But it is for a purpose.

Goeff successfully convinced Tyrone to commit to one full bag of the Texas weed. He hears the bell on the door ringing and glances out the stockroom door. It is just a customer. Goeff feels sure that he read Tripp correctly. Geoff acted well and said all the right things. Goeff walks out to the register. The young girl wants to trade up an album.

"OK, miss. I'll evaluate the record if you want to shop around," Geoff points to the back of the store.

"Thanks, I won't be a moment!" She answers with enthusiasm.

The bell jingles again and Geoff can see out of the corner of his eye, it's Tripp. He smiles. Not too much, Geoff knows that Tripp is wrapped up in new emotions and can be easily scared off.

"Hey Tripp, I was beginning to think you weren't coming," Geoff smiles when he sees that he is wearing the grocery store outfit.

"I had to earn some money somehow; the mines don't pay that well. I have Christmas presents to get," Tripp jokes. Geoff is pleased that Tripp's in a better mood tonight.

Tripp walks around and sits on the short counter. Geoffrey smiles, realizing he's broken through the wall Tripp hides behind. He brings a soda for Geoff. Geoff nods in gratitude and takes a long sip.

"Tripp, thanks. I was getting thirsty. I did not think about you having to work," Geoff said softly. "I am glad you came. You looked like you had more talking to do last night."

Tripp takes the drink, taking in some for himself, much to Geoff's approval. He just smiles and hands the cup back. Goeff has to service the customer.

"I found it!" The girl screams, holding up an Andy Gibb record. "I must have it!"

"Nice choice, this is his latest, excellent singer. He is lucky to have an adoring fan like you," Geoff plays into it. "The in-store credit is four dollars. It's just three-seventy-five, and Andy is all yours!"

The girl pays quickly and skips out the front door, the excitement of the purchase fueling her joy. Geoff thinks that Tripp is up to something but does not know what. The bell rings gently as the door closes. When the customer leaves, Tripp gets relaxed.

"Tripp, I have to say, you are...well, you appear to be in a better mood tonight," Geoff said smoothly.

"Things are still the same, Geoff. I realized last night that I can't change everything. Honestly, I can't change anything. As much as I have tried these last few months, my life will not be different," Tripp sighed, shrugging his shoulders.

"You don't strike me as a quitter, Tripp," Geoff offers a sincere compliment.

"I was the first time, Geoff. I turned everything around for...uh, my Boston friend," Tripp admits.

Geoff did not want to follow up on that, he focuses on Trip, "After we talked last night, I thought long and hard about the things you told me. I like you a lot, Tripp. But I want to put my feelings on hold and just be your friend. In confusing times, dealing with your feelings can be difficult."

Geoff smiles as he places his hand on Tripp's right knee. Tripp could not help but be mesmerized by his good looks. He takes a deep breath, putting his hand on Geoff's.

"So, we don't have school on Tuesday, Wednesday, and Thursday. I haven't heard from...Boston," Tripp's still leery of giving Geoff too much information. "I only saw him in the hall on Monday..."

"I guess you and he are inseparable?" Geoffrey nods. He has been working on his tone and the way he speaks.

"Pretty much this year and... yeah, last year, too. His mood changed early Friday at my house. I don't know why. However, he lightened up when we made it to his home. Sleeping was...weird," Tripp pauses; giving Geoff a sharp look. "Just **sleep** before you ask. He, uh...well, he asked a girl out Saturday. Maybe he sensed I liked him, and he did not know how to let me down?"

"So why do you think his mood changed? Did you say something or do anything that might have set him off?" Geoff leans against the counter. He makes a loud sipping noise with the drink and folds his arms.

"We stopped at my house..."

Geoff tosses the empty cup into the trash, "Was that your plan?"

"I...uh, well. Please don't laugh, but I left one of my leotards on the bed. I worked out the night before..." Tripp lowers his head. "Maybe it freaked him out? I quickly tried to play it off as something I bought for ... a girl I like. I know he disapproves of her."

"Is she a...uh, someone that stays in trouble?" Geoff is briefly distracted, thinking about Tripp in spandex, but decides to keep his comments to himself.

"No, Holly...um, no, she is on the honor roll," Tripp freezes. Geoff keeps a calm smile and waits. "What other people say about her is important. I'm just a nobody."

"I bet he doesn't think that."

Tripp shakes his head no. Clearing his throat, he said, "He's worried she will hurt me."

Geoff points at Tripp, "That could be possible. Do you know how he feels about homosexuals in general?"

"Not really, no. He's never talked about same-sex attraction. And I used to be very vocal in my hatred of gays. Though, deep down, I was hating myself because of denial," Tripp explains, thinking Geoff isn't bad when he isn't hitting on him. "Talking with a therapist helped me come to terms with it. Forty-six years later..."

"Forty-six..." Geoff laughs briefly, "Maybe he is worried that you still hate gays?"

"I dunno, I just miss my friend. I think I can live with him only being my friend," Tripp wipes his eyes. "...but I need him to talk to me..."

"Tripp, would you like a hug? I will keep my hands up here," Geoff grins, pointing at Tripp's shoulders.

Tripp deeply exhales and nods yes. Geoff wraps his arms around Tripp and gives him a gentle hug. Tripp slowly leans into Geoff. Tripp breathes slower now. Geoff slowly runs his hand over the back of Tripp's head, though he can tell the young boy keeps space between them. He decides to take a different approach, playing on Tripp's kindness and empathy.

"Not that it matters, but I told Ernesto I wanted more. Talking to you last night made me think how empty a life I have been living. He is fun, and we like each other, but he isn't my soulmate..."

"How did he take that, Geoff?" Tripp asks, pulling away and looking at his face.

"Thankfully, what we have is very open. He said to go for it if I can find someone with a good heart." Geoff answers, still gently caressing Tripp on the back of the neck and head.

"You have anyone in particular in mind?" Tripp let that slip out, his heart rate has increased.

"I thought we were talking about you? I can see you are still hurting from the situation with your Boston friend," Geoff replies softly. "What is it about the way he looks that you like?"

"Uh...well. When I like a guy, it starts with an emotional connection. The physical attraction comes later." Tripp explains, Goeff keeping eye contact. "We've known each other for three years. But he is tall, almost as tall as you. Dark black hair and blue eyes. His smile comes straight from his soul. He is the most incredible and honorable man I know."

"Damn, Tripp. That is a deep love; have you tried to tell him that?" Geoff moves his other hand to Tripp's waist.

"Actually, yeah. Well, just the 'most incredible and honorable person' part of it. I think it impressed him. Geoff, can I ask you something?" Tripp whispers softly, holding his head down again.

With a warm tone, Geoff answers, "Tonight is all about you, Tripp."

"What is it you want from me?" Tripp begs, looking Geoff in the eyes. "Truthfully."

"The truth?" Stunned, Geoff asks sincerely.

"I think I deserve it, don't you?" Still making eye contact.

"Yes, that you do," Geoffrey clears his throat and takes a deep breath. "I have loved so many people. I guess you'd call me an instant gratification junkie. I never thought about the next day. Tripp, you are not the kind of guy I like. Everyone I have been with was gay, openly gay. No one besides Ernesto has been with me for any amount of time. I do love Ernesto, but he isn't my true love. From that first time, when I saw you with Scott..."

Tripp smiles, impressed that Geoff remembers his cousin's name, "I remember that day."

"As do I, Tripp. You were so beautiful, but it wasn't about your looks, though you are hot. I saw something special. I didn't know if you were gay or not, but it didn't matter. I could see your honesty.

You care about people. I saw that and wanted that for myself. Listening to you talk about your friend, Boston, only solidified my belief in you. You cannot fake love. I hoped you could feel that way for me. I did not know how to...well, what to do. That is why I went after you so hard..."

Tripp's heart fills with curiosity, "What changed?"

"I...uh, well, Tripp, after talking to Ernesto, I called my sister in Atlanta. We talked about you. She said if I wanted something meaningful, something long-term, I would have to let go of who I was." Geoff gives a brief smile and looks away.

"And I just thought you shaved..." Tripp smiles, joking with a warm chuckle.

"You noticed." Geoff thinks quickly, "It was for you. I like my name, but I felt the change should be visible. I want to be the kind of man you are..."

Tripp looks down for a second, "I always liked your looks. I just never thought you were serious."

"I wasn't. Not until now." Geoff removes Tripp's eyeglasses. He is surprised that Tripp doesn't object.

There's a long pause.

"Geoff, can I ask something?" Tripp says.

"Anything."

Tripp meets his gaze. "That night you almost kissed me... I think about it more than I should."

"I wanted to. I still do. But not until you're ready. I can wait."

"Would you kiss me right now if I asked?" Tripp searches Goeff's eyes.

Geoff holds the side of Tripp's face. He leans in, their lips touching gently. Tripp's heart races. He doesn't know why he doesn't stop Geoffrey. Tripp wraps his arms around Geoff's neck as the gentle embrace continues. Tripp likes the kiss, but in the back of his mind he knows the truth.

Geoff backs away, saying softly and taking Tripp's hand. "You need time."

"You mean that?" Tripp gazes into his eyes, eager for this to be the truth.

"Yes. That kiss was worth the wait"

Tripp smiles, looking at his feet. "Then why stop it?"

"I do want to be with you. Tripp, you're an awesome guy and worth doing it right. I also need that time; I want to be worthy of someone like you. I mean that," Smiling, Geoffrey leans closer to hug him.

Nervously, he asks, "Are you getting overheated, Tripp?"

"Uh, yeah...work clothes," Tripp rolls his eyes. Geoff looks closely at the shirt.

"Tripp," He starts, hoping he is correct. "Are you ok? I can get you some water from the stockroom..." Geoff pulls the white shirt back, exposing the secret beneath.

"Yeah, Geoff...I uh..." Tripp hesitates, realizing that Geoff is aware. "I...I wanted to get your attention, I guess..."

"I don't follow you, Tripp," Geoff takes a step back and folds his arms. "You don't have to try for that; I figured you knew that by now."

"Yes," Tripp bashfully averts his eyes by looking down. Geoff lifts his chin back up so they can look eye to eye. "Geoffrey, I may have worn something for you..."

"Oh, first a delicious kiss and now show and tell?" Geoff smiles approvingly. "Is this a distraction from Boston, or do you really want me to see you in your outfit?"

"I think it is a little of both, Geoffrey," Tripp giggles with the flirt. "Remember, it's just **show** and tell..."

"I would not think of pushing you, not after all that we have said tonight. I like you a lot, Tripp. You know that," Geoff almost whispers. "I can wait..."

Geoff stops talking; Tripp has already started unbuttoning the white uniform shirt. He has a smile on his face. Geoff watches carefully as Tripp jumps off the counter to pull the shirt off. He gives Tripp a nod of approval. The spandex snuggly clings against Tripp's young chest. The short sleeves of the purple material highlight the upper arm muscles. *Tripp did say he was working out.* Geoff gives him a comforting pat on the shoulder.

"Wow..." Geoff said breathlessly. "Is it ok for me to gawk at you for a second?"

Tripp giggles, "Yes, Geoff. Get it all out..."

Geoffrey lets out a loud wolf whistle. Tripp watches as Geoff looks at him. He can see the desire in the older man, and for the moment, Tripp is okay with that. *The kiss was delicious.*

"I can see you've been working out. May I?" Geoff asked, pointing at Tripp's chest. Tripp approves. "I am impressed," Tripp ends with a laugh as Geoff caresses his arms and shoulders.

"Aren't you glad you came back?" Geoff sings out, running his hand over Tripp's chest.

"Yes, I am. Thanks, Geoff," Tripp slowly spins around. "I don't know why I like wearing these. I guess all that time as an old fat man made me appreciate having a nice body..."

"Nice is an understatement, Tripp! But I couldn't imagine you fat..." Geoff laughs, unaware of that comment's source, "However today, you do have a superb body, Tripp. Those pants fit you right. Can I say that's an awesome ass?"

With a coy smile, Tripp stops, looking over his shoulder, "Nobody cares what a guy's butt looks like..."

"Well, not in those pants," Geoff laughs admiringly. "Are you wearing the tights as well?"

Blushing, Tripp smiles, knowing Geoff is being clever. He thinks for a moment, then Tripp puts his foot against the cabinet and pulls the pant leg up past his socks to reveal the white tights

"Say Tripp, maybe we should move to the stock room. If someone comes in the store, I mean, just in case, you are wearing a leotard after all..." Geoff explains with care. "I would not want you to get embarrassed."

Glancing at the back room door, "I...I, uh, I dunno, Geoff." Tripp is hesitant. "It's show and..."

"Tripp, Tripp, I wasn't suggesting anything underhanded. I meant what I said. I want to be with you and understand that you need to move slowly. I respect that. Seriously, I did not want you to get embarrassed. A boy in tights? Depending on who came in, they might stare. Scandalous..." Geoff said, holding his hands up defensively.

"Well..." Tripp sheepishly answers, feeling uncertain of what to do. He thinks *I need to go...*

"Tripp, it's just show and tell. **Show and tell**," Geoff explains, emphasizing and taking Tripp's left hand.

Tripp takes a deep breath. He was enjoying the attention. "I still love Robbie; this is just show and tell..."

Raising his hands in surrender, Geoff smiles. He noticed that Tripp let the boy's name slip out. He chose to ignore that. He steps over and puts his hands on Tripp's shoulders.

"I promise, you are in complete control. I will listen to whatever you say, ok Tripp?" Lifting Tripp's chin to look into his eyes.

"Thanks, Geoff. Guess I am just being silly..." Feeling embarrassed, Tripp tries to look away.

"No, you aren't. I realize you act like you know how the world works, but you are almost eighteen and scared. It would be best if you didn't feel scared. I don't want that for you. Never."

"Thanks, Geoffrey. OK. I trust you," Tripp said, looking at the stockroom door.

Geoff takes his hand, and they go into the back. The stock room is a big square room. Beside the door is a corkboard with employment posters and several handwritten schedules. A small time clock is attached to the wall near the door. There are several shelves with boxes on the back wall. Hanging overhead are fluorescent lights, but half of them are turned off. Tripp is glad; he feels exposed wearing this tight, revealing outfit.

Tripp can see that a workbench is in the center of the room. There is one open box on the left side. He notices a sawhorse off to the left - modified with a flat board nailed to the top of the cross beam. Something familiar. Tripp notes how it does not fit with the rest of the stock room; *that's strange; maybe they have a reason for that.*

Goeff leans back against the sturdy wooden table. He has a pleasant smile. The lion is proud. Outwardly, he acts like a gentleman, inwardly his hungry runs wild.

Tripp thinks that maybe he read Geoffrey wrong. He kicked off his tennis shoes and smiles.

"There you go, my feet!" Tripp laughs, and Geoff joining him. Tripp feels that Geoffrey is trying to be a gentleman. Tripp feels safe.

"You don't know how glad I am to hear you laugh again. I was worried," Geoff said, hoping there will be more. "But your smiles and laughter give me hope."

"I see that now, Geoff. I appreciate that," Tripp trusts Geoff. He smiles and starts to unbuckle his belt.

"I meant everything I said," Geoff replies, tone soft and measured.

Grinning ear to ear, Tripp pulls his pants off, tossing them beside his shoes. He stands with his feet shoulder-width apart and puts both fists on his hips. He has a confident smile on his face..

Without his glasses, the shadows blur the room. It's oddly comforting.

"You look very heroic," Geoff says with a chuckle. "We need to find you a superhero name."

"Well, then you'd need a name too!" Tripp spins around, laughing.

Tripp has strong, muscular legs. There is no hiding anything in that tight outfit. Geoff is pleased. Geoff's eyes linger, hungry but contained. He scratches his chin. "How about the Purple Knight?"

"Oh, yes! I like that...now for you..." Tripp stops, cocking his hips to one side as he contemplates a hero's name for Geoff.

"I am... the Louisville Slugger," Geoff says, lips curling into a grin.

Tripp snorts. "A baseball bat?"

"Well, to be honest... you look really sexy. And I'm only human."

Tripp raises a brow, amused. "A baseball bat, huh?"

"I didn't name it," Geoff says, laughing. "But if that worries you—if this is too much—you can say so. No pressure."

Tripp hesitates, then shrugs with a smile. "I'm okay. Is my outfit really that distracting?"

"You can't hide anything in spandex," Geoff says, still keeping his distance. "But it's not just the outfit. You're beautiful, Tripp."

Tripp blushes. "Thanks. You've changed. I see that."

"I'm trying. For you."

Tripp knows this is wading into uncharted waters. He isn't afraid, yet overcome with his teenage hormones. *I am still in the store; it will be safe here.* Tripp blushes when he realizes that he is staring. Geoff remains a gentleman, though his reaction is obvious. Tripp wonders if Geoffrey has genuinely changed. Geoff can see the teenage boy focusing on him.

"You like staring at me?" Tripp teases.

"Yeah, but I also like to see you in your work uniform. Remember the night we almost kissed?" Geoff leans back on the table. Tripp glances down, unsure. Geoff senses his hesitation and reins himself in.

"I do remember." Tripp answers, his heart races. "Your hand was on my butt."

"I was tempted to ask if you wanted to... you know, touch it. But I know that's a step too far." Geoff backs away slightly. "Maybe you should put your pants back on. I want you to know I respect you."

"I don't want to be a tease." Tripp exhales. "But I kinda... I'm curious. Over your pants. Is that okay?"

Geoff nods solemnly and takes his hand. "Only if you're sure."

"I'm sure."

Tripp is very nervous and not sure what to expect, but he still feels in control. Geoff guides him gently, turning Tripp to face away. The air thickens. Tripp's breath catches. Geoff moves slowly, respectfully. Tripp slowly moves his hand behind him.

"Oh!"

Geoff whispers near Tripp's ear.

"Not what you expected?"

"N-no..." Tripp stammers, "No... but... it's okay."

Tripp's hand moves slowly. Geoff lets the moment stretch, careful not to push. The lion waits. But before he can go further, the bell above the front door jingles. Tripp flinches.

"I'll be right back," Geoff says, stepping away. "If you want to get out of that leotard, you might be more comfortable."

Tripp hesitates. "I'd like that... but, Geoff, will you be able to stop?"

Geoff meets his gaze. "You're still in control."

Geoff walks to the door, looking over his shoulder and smiles. He exits the storeroom, leaving the door partial ajar. Tripp tries to control his breathing. He knows this is going to end badly.

The kid in the store has a couple of albums in his hand. Geoffrey figures if he helps the guy, he can get him out of the store faster. Geoff realizes *the longer Tripp sits idle, the harder it will be to get some tonight.* He walks over to the customer and smiles.

"Need any help?" Geoffrey politely inquires.

"Yeah, I am getting a Christmas present for my best friend. I am not sure which one he would..." Holding up the two albums.

"Well, Kansas is a solid choice—rock band with an excellent violist. The vocals are outstanding. ELO, or Electric Light Orchestra, is a different genre. You would not go wrong with either choice. What music does your friend prefer?"

"He likes a wide variety of bands. I've heard him play Elton John, Journey, Fleetwood Mac, Boston, and Triumph. Plus, he's not easy to get presents for..." the guy laughs nervously.

"I'd go with Kansas then," Geoffrey grins, hoping to get this clown out of the store.

In the stockroom, Tripp freezes. He knows that laugh. Carefully, he peers through the cracked door. His heart stops. Robbie is at the register, holding two albums.

"You sure?" Robbie asks, staring at the Kansas cover. "I want my best friend to know how much he means to me."

"Dammit," Tripp whispers, retreating from the door. His heart pounds.

He turns away, eyes stinging. The moment with Geoff is shattered. All he wants is to disappear.

What Else Could Go Wrong?

"**R**obbie..." Tripp softly gasps after Robbie's last statement. "How could I be this stupid?"

His best friend works hard to get presents, and Tripp is acting foolishly over Geoff. Tripp begins to panic, tears streaming down his face. His shirt, jacket, and glasses are on the counter behind the register. He thinks through everything that has happened tonight.

This is wrong, all wrong. Geoff will ask too many questions if I try to leave when he returns. Tripp thinks, scooping up his pants. He desperately searches the pockets. *Good, here are the keys!* Watching through the cranked door, he kneels to grab the shoes. Tripp hopes the back exit isn't locked. He has to get out of there.

"Sir...Excuse me, sir?" Robbie asks.

"Oh, sorry. I am thinking about what to do tonight after work. Do you need some other titles to look at?" Geoffrey's patience running thin.

"No thanks, I've narrowed it down to these two. I asked, which of these Kansas titles would you suggest?" Robbie is torn between the choices, reading the back of the second album.

"Hmm, you said this was a Christmas present?" Geoff wants to get back to Tripp. "How about I sell you both? Buy one, get one free kind of thing?"

"Can you do that?" Robbie is in awe, with his eyes wide.

"Yeah, Mr. Tynan has a contract with the distributor and gets twenty units monthly at no charge. Been with them for a decade. I can't do it for everybody, but Mr. Tynan is ok giving a few out like this. And it sounds like you need to do something extra special for your friend." Geoffrey admits, rushing to get it done.

"Wow, thank you very much. Two gifts will blow him away!" Robbie smiles, wholly consumed with excitement.

Tripp works the latch on the door, and it opens. He takes one last look at the stock room door. He decides that staying here is not in his best interest. As much as he wants to make it work with Geoff, Robbie is his priority. Leaving this behind is the best thing to do. He carefully steps out, closing the door behind him. Tripp shivers in the cold night air.

"No time to get dressed; I must leave before Geoff discovers..." Tripp wastes no time.

He takes off running to his Mustang. Thankful that he has socks on over the white tights. The pavement is rough, and he can feel it on his feet. Tripp can see the parking lot is empty. He hopes that no one sees him running in this outfit. Tripp finds relief in that he parked his car on the side of the building...

He reaches his car and quickly grabs the door handle, forgetting that he locked the doors. Fumbling with the keys, it took several tries to unlock the door. Taking a deep breath, he can see that Robbie's still in the store. Within seconds, Tripp starts his car and drives out the side entrance. Once on the main road, Tripp floors the accelerator, unleashing the engine and allowing it to roar into action.

Tripp is several blocks away from the store. He keeps driving fast. Tears running down his face. He feels that he has betrayed Robbie, though they are friends. He knows that Robbie isn't his soulmate. Tripp knows that he should not have been thinking of himself like that. Tripp forgot his reason for being here was to fix his future. His actions tonight were selfish and could have ruined everything.

Geoff was trying so hard, Tripp tells himself. Tonight, it has been bad decision after bad decision. Tripp jerks the wheel sharply to the left just barely missing an object in the road.

"What the hell was that?" Tripp asks himself, barely able to see. "I really should not be driving at night without my glasses."

He just wants to get home. He isn't watching his speed. He flies past a stop sign without realizing it. Then, the Mustang starts to kick and sputter. Bucking like a wild horse, struggling for life. Tripp tries to baby the accelerator, but the engine dies without the precious flow of fuel to keep it alive.

Tripp strains to turn the steering wheel and coasts to stop on the shoulder of the road. *I ran out of gas, how stupid am I?* he condemns himself. He is stranded and alone. Tripp slams his hands down hard on the steering wheel and lets out a grunt of frustration.

"Dumb ass!" Tripp screams, slamming a fist in the steering wheel one more time. "You're such a dumbass. What else could go wrong?"

Tripp hangs his head in shame. Still a mile or more to his house and this hunk of metal is practically worthless. He begins to shiver. His jacket and shirt are still at the store. He doesn't have his glasses. He looks down. The leotard he likes so much would not protect him from the cold.

At least I have my pants, he thinks with a laugh. Tripp reaches over to the passenger seat for his work pants. His eyes catch the flickering of light from behind his car. His heart stops. The lights are blue and could only mean one thing! Tripp glances up at the rear-view mirror and sees a city cop car has pulled in behind him. Tripp sighs. He leans across and rolled down the passenger window.

"This is not good..." He gripes as he waited for officer to approach the car.

"Hey, pal, I'm on the clock here. Toss me your license and registration real quick, alright?" The officer barks using his ring to rap hard on the driver's side window. This startles Tripp.

Tripp quickly rolled the window down, "Sorry, sir. I'm having a bad night..."

Tripp grabs his pants and starting looking in the pockets. He spots his wallet, Tripp lets out a heavy sigh. It must have fallen out of the pocket and landed in the floor board.

"Uh, sir. My wallet's on the floor. Is it ok for me to reach down there?" Tripp asks, he can't remember the proper things to do with cops in the eighties.

"It ain't gonna magically appear up here. You ain't pulling some funny business, are ya?" He replies, leaning down closer to the open window.

Tripp has a nervous smile, "No, sir..."

Tripp leans over and stretches to get the wallet. Tripp feels self-conscious knowing that his outfit is on full display. The cop shakes his head as he realizes what Tripp is wearing. Tripp has to move closer to the passenger side and grunts as he strains.

"Almost have it, sir. Sorry," Tripp apologizes.

He finally grabs it and sits up straight. He opens his wallet and pulls out his driver's license. The registration is above the sun visor. He hands them both to the cop. Tripp can see that this cop is not in a good mood.

"Yo, buddy, what's with the getup? You rocking tights and a leotard. Lose a bet or something?"

"Uh...no, sir. I can...uh explain..." Tripp has trouble getting the words out. He hasn't figured out a good reason.

The cop shines his flashlight into the window. It is very bright. Tripp covers his eyes. The light goes down Tripp's body. The cop scans the floor of the car. He stops at Tripp's feet. He shines the flashlight on Tripp's license.

"Hey, Michael Willis Carson, **the third**. How 'bout you come outta the car for a sec?" The cop commands, emphasizing Tripp's name.

Tripp nods, opening the car door. He steps out. The cold air causes him to shiver. Tripp folds his arms tightly to keep his chest warm. He fidgets nervously. The cop shines the flashlight on him one more time. Tripp hopes none of his friends ride by. He can see the cop is stunned by seeing a teenage boy dressed in a purple leotard and white tights. The cold air is not helping. Tripp notices the name tag. Officer J. Nowak and he has two stripes on the sleeves of his uniform.

"Kid, listen up. Your license has a restriction for glasses on it. Cruising without shoes? Totally against the law in North Carolina." Officer Nowak states as he shakes his head. "Got no clue how to deal with your purple leotard, especially when you can't even give me a reason, huh?"

"I can't think of a good lie, Corporal Nowak. And I am afraid to tell you the real reason..." Tripp hangs his head in shame.

"I gotta hand it to you for nailing my name, kid. Not many southerners can spit it out right on the first try." Officer Nowak sighs.

"Yes sir, my Uncle John works in DC. I have met some of his friends before. I am guessing either the Bronx or Jersey. But I could be wrong, sir." Tripp replies as he shivered. It was a white lie; Tripp knew several people from New York when he lived in Rhode Island.

"I'm a Bronx native, born and bred in the heart of it all." He said with a smile.

"Never been to New York, I bet North Carolina was quite a change for you?" Tripp asks, regaining his confidence. At least he is treating the policeman with respect.

He laughs, "Not too shabby. Can't stand the damn cold, you know?"

"Yes, sir." Tripp nods as he shuffles to combat the cold.

Officer Nowak quietly grunts as he closes his citation pad and puts it in his back pocket, "Alright, it's just you and me, kid. Spill the truth about this outfit. I could haul you to the station for driving without glasses and rocking those bare feet, you know?"

Tripp holds his head low and lets out a deep sigh. The cold air made the exhale visible, "I uh...I was trying to impress..."

"Impress?" The cop growls.

"Uh, yes, sir. A guy that I like, well he likes me too. Please don't take me jail wearing this. Please let me get some clothes..." Tripp pleads. It is in that moment that the cop notices that Tripp has been crying.

"A guy? Toss on a jacket and pants, and for sure, don't forget those shoes, kid." Corporal Nowak instructs.

"I uh, I only have my pants and shoes. I sorta left in a hurry." Tripp is cold, embarrassed and tired.

Officer Nowak nods and points at the car. Tripp smiles and leans in to grab his pants and shoes. He puts them on quickly as the cop watches him.

The burly cop puts his hand to his chin, "I got a feeling I've seen you around, kid. You pulling shifts at Maddox Grocery on King Street, huh?"

"Yes, sir, Corporal Nowak. My brother helped me get a job there. I help my momma, well so does he. It's just the three of us.," Tripp answers, thankful for the pants, but he is still cold.

"Stay right there. You mentioned you bounced out real quick. Worried about your safety or something?" He starts as he walkes back to his cruiser and reaches in the front seat.

"Maybe," Tripp admits, avoiding eye contact. "I was really worried at first, but now? More of a bad decision. I suspect he was only wanting to have sex."

"You're sixteen, kid!" Officer Nowak barks. "What's his age?"

"Geoff? Uh, he is older. Uh, maybe 24, Corporal Nowak," Tripp admits.

Officer Nowak looks at Tripp. It was of utter disapproval; Tripp could feel it. The cop clears his throat, "Jakub. Jakub Nowak. I'll let your folks handle the official lecture, but here's my two cents. He ain't worth it; that creep's a pedophile."

"Yes, sir. It's Tripp. My friends call me that because I am the third," Tripp replies as he nods.

Jakub Nowak walks over to him, "Alrighty Tripp. Hey, put on my jacket. You might catch a cold in that flimsy leotard, you know?"

Tripp laughs, "Yeah, but they are comfortable. Thank you, sir, Thank you." Tripp lets out a sigh of joy getting wrapped up in the coat.

"Well, Tripp. You gonna manage driving home without them glasses of yours from here?" He asks.

"Uh, if I drive slow I could...but I kinda," Tripp hates to admit this. "I, uh, ran out of gas, sir. And officer, what about your coat?"

"On my next shift, I'll swing by Maddox Grocery. You can hold onto it until then," Corporal Nowak shakes his head and pulls out a small business card and hands it to Tripp. He looks confused as he takes the card from the policeman.

"It's a business card, kid. That's my number. Give me a shout if you ever need help. I mean it."

"I don't...I don't know what to say, but thank you. Very much, sir," Tripp could not help but tear up.

Officer Nowak waves his hand in dismissal. He isn't the type to dwell on helping people. He knows that most of Tripp's story has to be true. *Can't make that shit up*, he laughs. He grabs the red can from the trunk of his car. Tripp starts taking off the gas cap to his car.

"Uh, Corporal Nowak..." he begins, but the cop gives him a look. Tripp tears up. "Uh, I am grateful, but Jakub, why are you doing this for me?"

"Take it easy, Tripp," The veteran cop said in a rough voice. "It is simple. You remind me of my son, he's called Jakub too. I'd want someone lookin' out for him like I'm doin' for you, that is if he were to be caught with his drawers down. Though he can't stand purple."

Late night, but finally home...

Tripp drives as cautiously as he can. Getting home isn't as far as he thought. Corporal Nowak follows him the entire way, and Tripp counts himself lucky. But he also knows he's used up a lot of mercy for the foolish things he's done in 1980—maybe all of it. He can't afford another mistake.

As he turns onto Glade Avenue, Corporal Nowak gives a couple of quick horn taps and keeps going. Tripp exhales a heavy breath of relief. The kindness of others, he thinks, is a blessing he cannot take for granted.

But his heart freezes when he spots a familiar car parked by the curb.

"Did Robbie see me at the Record Changer?" he whispers as he parks the Mustang.

For a moment, he just sits there, his pulse pounding. Then he sets aside his worry—*Robbie is here. That's what matters.* Tripp climbs out and hurries to the front door. Inside, he finds Robbie sitting on the couch, looking uneasy.

"Uh, hi Robbie," Tripp says, his voice nervous.

Robbie stands, trying to smile. "Hi, Tripp. I hope it's okay—Mark let me in before he left for work."

"Yeah, of course. I just wasn't expecting you." Tripp closes the door and walks toward him.

"Guess you worked late, huh?" Robbie asks, seeming to relax.

"Yeah, but I made a few unplanned stops on the way home. How about you?"

Robbie draws a deep breath, eyes not quite meeting Tripp's. "Long day. But it was worth it. Uh, Tripp—it's my turn."

"Your turn?"

"I'm the idiot this time." Robbie sighs, sitting back down, head bowed.

Tripp joins him. "Why would you think that?"

"I was upset with you. Upset for a dumb reason. I still worry Holly's going to hurt you. She's not your type."

Tripp chuckles gently. "I know you're worried. But that's not a reason to feel like an idiot."

"If she's changing clothes here, that must mean it's serious. I just want you happy, Tripp. I love the new Mike Carson. You've come so far. I hate thinking she might do something to set you back..."

"Rob, I'm humbled that you care. I'm grateful to have you as my best friend. Not many people can say they've got honesty like this between them. I believe we can tell each other anything."

"Yeah, Tripp. Anything. I'm sorry—I didn't know how to bring it up. Then I had to work. I kinda missed you."

"That's not dumb. I miss you when we're apart, too. Uh, Rob..."

Tripp hesitates. He thinks Robbie was upset about the outfit. *Maybe honesty is the best path.* He doesn't know how Robbie will take it—but he has to try.

"You're worried about Holly because of the leotard you saw the other night?"

"Yeah... I know it sounds ridiculous," Robbie says with a laugh, then looks ashamed. "It's just—she must really like you to wear that here."

Tripp clears his throat. "Well, I've got an *'anything'* I need to tell you."

"An *'anything'*? Oh. Yeah. You can trust me." Robbie reaches over, touching Tripp's sleeve. That's when he notices the police jacket.

Tripp sees the glance and removes the jacket. Beneath it, Robbie sees the purple spandex. There's no judgment—just curiosity. Tripp slowly removes his pants and sits beside him.

"I like to wear them," he explains. "It's the fabric or something—I don't know. I was afraid to tell you."

"Purple and red?" Robbie asks, "Because these are girls' clothes?"

"And blue," Tripp admits. "Technically, a guy invented them. But yeah, I get that it probably looked weird. And no, Holly and I have only talked on the phone. We may go bowling if I can save up some money. I know you have my back, and I'm sorry you were upset over the wrong reason."

Robbie's relieved. "So... why are you wearing it now? Weren't you at work?"

Tripp laughs. "I wear them at home sometimes. I like how I look in them. I also wear them to work out—like I did this afternoon. I lost track of time and had to rush, so I threw my uniform on over it."

"Can you show me?" Robbie gestures for Tripp to stand.

Tripp stands and turns. He even flexes a bit, making a muscle. Robbie stands too and playfully inspects the arm.

"Seems to have helped," Robbie jokes. "Hey, if you like to wear them, I support you. Sorry I acted like a jerk."

"You weren't. You're my best friend," Tripp says, putting a hand on his shoulder. "You were looking out for me. I'm glad I could show you. You didn't laugh—that means a lot."

He still doesn't have his glasses. He's leery about returning to the Record Changer after how he left Geoff, but he remembers Corporal Nowak's advice. He'll take things slowly—verify Geoff's sincerity. That's a task for another day. Sunday belongs to Lauren and Greg.

Aisle Twelve

Tripp fights the onslaught of boredom. Usually, it's a quiet night at Maddox Grocery, but tonight is dead. He needs the extra hours—Christmas is not far away, and he still has gifts to buy. He chose between stocking shelves in aisles 12 and 13 or cleaning the restrooms. An easy decision, but now he's tired, bored, and only halfway up the first row. It's going to be a long shift.

Without his glasses, it's hard to match items to shelf labels. He hopes he's not making too many mistakes. Stocking shelves isn't quite the six-figure career he had in Rhode Island, but he's happy. Tripp likes the people here. Happiness outweighs money most of the time.

He opens a box of green beans—only two slots on the shelf. He stretches on his tiptoes to place them. Tripp chuckles thinking about the challenges from working in the grocery store.

"What's so funny, gorgeous?" a soft voice calls behind him.

Tripp turns. "Oh, Rose! Hey! You're the last person I thought I'd see shopping tonight."

"Hippies gotta eat too, you know!" she laughs.

Tripp grins. "How's your grandma?"

Rose smiles warmly. "She's better. Just a broken foot—wearing one of those big boot things. Thanks for asking."

"You're welcome. Say, can I interest you in a case of New England's finest green beans? Buy one at full price, get the second for the same price!"

Rose chuckles, touching his arm. "Quite the salesman. I'll take three. Gift wrap included?"

"Half price, but you'll have to see the butcher. Be quick—he passes gas a lot!"

She laughs harder. "You're nuts! I've missed seeing you at the store. I hoped I hadn't made you mad."

"Mad? At you? Impossible," he replies, trying to lean coolly on the boxes but laughing instead.

"I found your glasses and shirt. Geoff left a note that you were looking for me. I thought maybe... you weren't interested."

"I, uh... can explain."

"It's okay. Geoff's hot. I'm not upset. I just thought you liked me."

"I do. I also like Geoff... though I'm leery."

"Both?" She smiles. "Interesting possibilities."

Tripp blushes. "Afraid to ask what you mean..."

"Just teasing. But I'm glad you like me." She pulls out his glasses. "Found them behind the register. Not asking about the shirt."

"It was after work. I... stopped by to flirt with Geoff," he admits.

She nods, serious now. "Be careful. You're not the only young guy I've seen around him. Most just want weed. You don't strike me as a pothead."

"Not even alcohol. AA cured me."

"I'd hate to see you hurt. Geoff likes young sex, I think."

Tripp nods, surprised by her candor. "I want love. I can wait. I just like the attention. Does that make me bad?"

"No. Just honest," she says gently. "You just want my attention now? Because I'm nineteen?"

"My ex-wife was older," Tripp shrugs. "That's the truth."

"I didn't know you were such a worldly man. So, does that mean I could be the next ex-Mrs. Tripp?"

"When I marry, it's forever." He takes her hand. "Are you asking me out? I'm nervous. Never asked someone out surrounded by vegetables."

They laugh. Rose hugs him gently, then pulls back and looks him in the eye.

"Soda shoppe?" he offers.

"I'd love to. Call me next week, okay?"

"Promise. Thanks for the glasses. I was afraid to go back and face Geoff."

"I figured. He was in a mood. Something about his dealer. Be careful."

"I will."

Rose hugs him again and leaves. Tripp smiles to himself. He feels good. As much as he wants Geoff to be different, fate has sent too many warnings.

"Well, at least I have my glasses. Easier to fix than replace," he mutters. "How much do glasses cost in 1980 anyway?"

He finishes his shift. Gene compliments him but points out one mix-up with the corn. Tripp apologizes, but Gene waves it off. "We've got your back."

Mark picks him up right at seven. Tripp sees Robbie waiting in the driveway.

"Thanks, Mark!" Tripp yells. "See ya tonight?"

"Eleven, probably." Mark punches his arm. "Tell Robert I said hi."

Tripp runs to the door. His friend is waiting. Robbie grins. "Hi Tripp!"

"Hey Rob! What brings you over?"

"My job was boring. Felt stiff. Thought we could work out?"

"Lifting beans all day. I feel like Mr. Universe! Come inside—Mark found a new bench at a yard sale."

Tripp heads inside with Robbie close behind. "Oh, and I have something for you from Steph."

Robbie hands him a small wrapped gift.

"A surprise for me," he says.

Tripp opens it carefully. It's a short-sleeved button-down shirt in deep yellow. "Nice! I'll wear this to Lauren's party."

"Awesome. Guess I should dress up too," Robbie teases.

Tripp beams. "I'm just glad my best friend will be there."

He hangs the shirt, and Robbie asks to change in the bathroom. Tripp nods, grabbing sweatpants. But he reconsiders... *maybe today's a leotard day.*

Robbie changes, looks in the mirror, and exits. "Ready?"

Tripp emerges in a dark blue leotard with baby blue tights and white sneakers.

"Blue. Much more respectable for a Maddox employee," Robbie laughs.

"I like purple too! Want me to change into red? We could match." Tripp laughs.

"Wear what makes you comfortable," Robbie says sincerely. "Funny how this would have freaked me out a few days ago. You look good, Tripp, I mean that."

"Thanks. Let's try that bench!"

In the basement, Tripp lies on the leg curl bench, and Robbie adjusts the weights. They take turns doing sets. Robbie smacks Tripp playfully, then shows him how it's done. They finish their workout smiling.

"You know a lot about this. Secret training?" Tripp teases.

"Nah. Doug and I hit the gym a lot. He's intense—probably has a black belt by now."

"Really? That's awesome!" Tripp grins. The words from Robbie still ringing in his mind, the fact that Robbie said he looks good in the outfit.

Party Before The Storm

The party will be early on a Sunday evening. Lauren and Greg want to celebrate their engagement. She quickly planned a party at her house for a bunch of their friends. Nothing fancy—just friends, music, and pizza. About twenty people are inbited. The party takes place in her basement—a nicely finished space with several rooms and a large family area.

Tripp is looking forward to going. He wears his tan cargo pants and a yellow Oxford button-down shirt—a surprise gift from Stephanie a couple of days ago. Stephanie and Mama Davis were so happy to see him. Tripp's thankful to spend the afternoon with the Davis family. After their recent talk, he feels confident about his friendship with Robbie. The honesty between them has only strengthened their bond.

Since Tripp can't see well enough to drive, Robbie brings them to Lauren's house. Robbie wears a yellow t-shirt with a crisp Boston logo on the front—it looks new—and a pair of khaki pants. He tells Tripp he wants to dress up for Lauren and Greg. Along the way, they pick up Doug and Gary. Everyone is excited for the party.

When they arrive, several people are already there. Robbie and Gary grab the sodas, while Doug heads to the back of the car with Tripp to help carry in the chips and other supplies.

"Say, Mike. Is that a new shirt?" Doug asks politely.

"Yeah, Steph gave it to me a couple of days ago. I think she secretly loves me," Tripp jokes.

"Stephanie? Yeah, she is awesome. Bud's lucky to have a classy lady like her," Doug says with a grin.

"She reminds me of Lauren Bacall. Everyone in Robbie's family is important to me," Tripp says, grabbing the grocery bags.

"Is that your color?" Doug asks, nodding toward the yellow shirt.

"No, I like blue, but I've started liking purple too," Tripp laughs. "I guess it's her favorite."

"I think yellow is Robbie's favorite," Doug says knowingly.

"Really?" Tripp smiles, hopeful. "I think she was just trying to be nice."

"Stephanie is nice to everyone. It looks good on you," Doug says, adjusting the bag in his hands.

"Thanks, Doug," Tripp replies as they approach the back door. "Did you ever figure out what was wrong with your Camaro?"

"Yeah, cracked fuel basin and several bent linkages. Should have it back on the road soon."

Doug and Tripp make it to the side entrance, Daisy, a neighbor and friend of Lauren's, opens it for them.

"Hey, Daisy!" Tripp greets her. She gives him a quick hug.

Daisy smiles, "That color looks perfect on you!"

"Thanks." Tripp answers, heading inside.

"Oh, hey, Mike. I see Al. Mind if I step away?"

"No, Doug, tell Alice I said hello. I'll catch up soon. I want to speak with Greg," Tripp says, taking the second bag from Doug.

The next half hour is filled with loud music and junk food—though Tripp avoids eating most of it. He works his way around the crowd. Steve and Larry are there, Tripp catches up with his nerdy friends. *Tonight is the perfect night,* he tells himself. *I'm so fortunate to have so many good people in my life.*

He spots Betty and Ken over at the pinball machine. Lauren's dad borrowed it from someone who owns an arcade or bar. Doug had come over earlier to deliver it for them. Tripp decides to say hello. Ken twists and dodges as he plays, while Betty encourages him.

"Hi, Ken! Hello, Betty. Enjoying things so far?" Tripp calls out over the music.

"This is a blast! I'm so excited. I've never known anyone who was engaged before!" Betty laughs.

Tripp nods and grins. "I kinda knew Lauren and Greg would end up together. He's really trying hard for her."

Ken keeps his focus on the game. "Yeah, I hear he's getting certified to be a welder. Good money if you do it right."

"Welding, blah! They're in love, Ken!" Betty says, hugging him.

"That they are, Betty," he says, sneaking a quick kiss. "Hey, Mike."

"Yeah, Ken?"

"I just wanted to say thanks," Ken says as he pulls the plunger back. "For what you did for Jeff. He's been a new man since the river. I'm glad you could see past your hate."

"Ken!" Betty scolds. "Mike is a new man. That's not nice!"

"No, he's right, Betty. I'm glad I can see past the hate. Jeff deserved my respect," Tripp says.

"Well, it takes an honorable man to admit a wrong and make up for it. I'm glad Lauren believes in you. She's the reason I trusted you," Ken says. "You did good."

"Thanks, Ken. I mean that," Tripp replies, feeling proud. The old Mike is gone.

Ken plays more aggressively now, and Tripp stays to watch. Doug and Alice stand on the other side of the room. Robbie and Gary are in the far corner, talking to Greg and Lauren. Alice leans closer to Doug and nudges him toward Tripp.

"Oh, Doug, how utterly surprising! If you had forewarned me about the riveting prospect of gracing a soirée hosted by the illustrious Lauren Masters, I would have gladly seasoned my hat with condiments and devoured it on the spot," Alice says with a flourish.

Doug laughs. "Maybe, but you do seem to be enjoying yourself, Al."

"I never said I wasn't, geez. But think about it. There are cheerleaders, athletes—uh, *pretty people*—at this party. Not where I thought we'd end up."

They both laugh. Doug sips his soda and glances at Robbie, who seems to be enjoying himself. Doug smiles. Alice watches Doug. They've been good friends since first grade. If anyone knows Doug, it's her.

A new song starts—"Stay Awhile" by Journey. Out of the corner of her eye, Alice catches something about Tripp. She watches him closely. The couple at the machine talks to Mike, but his gaze is fixed across the room. She follows it to where Lauren and Greg stand talking with Robbie. She smirks.

"Isn't this an engagement party, Doug?" Alice asks, keeping her eyes on Mike.

"Yeah. Lauren and Greg. Greg's one of Mike's friends. I think a dropout, but he's going to tech school," Doug says. "Why?"

With deadpan delivery, Alice says, "Mike's got it so bad for that girl, I'm considering sending a sympathy card to his heart."

Doug chuckles. "What do you mean?"

"What do I mean? Doug, are you blind? I think Mike's in love with Lauren. She's in one of my AP classes. She talks about him *all—the—time*. And he's wearing a brand-new shirt for her."

"Uh, Al. This is a party about Lauren getting engaged to Greg. Engagement means she's marrying him?"

"Yes, but when has that stopped love? She and Mike have gotten close. He's fallen hard. He's not even hiding it. That's one lovesick puppy. Helen Keller could see that."

They both laugh. Doug finally says, "I'll give you that. But you're wrong about the shirt. Robbie's sister gave it to him."

Alice grins. "Ah, dearest Doug, my memory wizardry is astounding. You once said Rob has a thing for colors—and yellow happens to be Michael's favorite now, doesn't it?"

"Al, I meant he didn't wear it *for* her... well, maybe he didn't." Doug points. "Looks like Ken and his girl are heading to the drinks. Let's corner Mike and solve the mystery of the Yellow Shirt!"

As Doug and Alice approach Mike, Robbie and Gary yell, "Hey guys, we're making a run to the pizza place. Back in a few!"

"Bye, Rob!" Tripp calls, waving.

Doug and Alice wave too. Alice surprises Mike with a big hug. He laughs and returns it.

"Thanks, Alice! It's good to see you too," Tripp says.

"I'm glad you invited me. I never knew the cool kids were this much fun," she jokes.

"I think you're pretty cool. You make me laugh. You should do stand-up," Tripp says. "I'm glad you came. So is Lauren."

Alice glances at Doug with a grin. "Good to know. She and I talk about you in AP all the time."

"She's a good friend," Tripp nods. "Say Doug, enjoying the party too?"

"Absolutely. It's a blast. I can't believe they have this huge basement and hardly use it."

"This is actually my first time inside her house. I give her a ride to school. She's been helping me. She planned the river party."

As Doug and Tripp talk, Alice notices something new—Mike isn't watching Lauren anymore. Not like earlier. She wonders if Doug has noticed. She wants to whisper in his ear, but he hates that. Doug starts talking about his truck, which bores Alice. She rolls her eyes, waiting to drop a clever line. Ken and Betty walk up, and Doug stops talking.

"Hey Mike, we need to head out. I've got a family thing in the morning. Just wanted to say thanks again for Jeff," Ken says.

"Good night, Ken. Night, Betty," Tripp replies.

Doug and Alice wave goodbye. Doug watches Tripp, grinning. It makes Tripp self-conscious.

"Did I say something wrong?" Tripp asks.

"No, Mike. You did something good. I thought Robbie was joking, but you really planned the river party just to talk to Jeff?"

"It wasn't a secret, but I didn't tell everyone," Tripp says with a shrug. "I wanted to apologize. Lauren and I thought a party would help."

"That's so sweet," Alice beams. "Jeff's been in a good mood—because of you."

"Uh, Al. But tonight's date night. I think Jeff's good mood is because of *that guy*..." Doug grins. "He's cooking for him. Kinda romantic..."

"Don't get me started again, Doug!" Alice warns.

"The guy who's been asking him out?" Tripp tenses.

"More like harassing," Alice says. "Emery doesn't approve..."

"Alice, you're assuming things," Doug says, trying to wave her off.

"Jeff seemed to like him, or at least that's how it sounded at the river," Tripp says. "Is something wrong with the guy?"

"Alice doesn't like him," Doug says. "She's our mother hen."

"Well, mother hens keep you safe," Tripp says pointedly to Alice.

Alice huffs, "He's too old. It's gross. I think he's in college or something."

"Alice!" Doug sighs.

"Jeff is sweet but naive. Easily distracted," she says. "Like with Randy."

"Jeff likes pretty boys," Doug nods.

"Yeah, well, Randy wasn't up to something," Akuce says.

"Not the present thing again?" Doug groans.

"Yes, **AGAIN**. That collector's item wasn't cheap—"

"What?" Tripp interrupts, putting a hand on her arm. "What do you mean?"

"It's a framed autograph. Doesn't even look real," Doug mutters.

"Whoa, whoa—start from the beginning!" Tripp snaps.

Doug hesitates. Alice pushes forward. "Some guy's been hitting on Jeff for weeks. I love Jeff, but he's an idiot. A college student shouldn't be chasing him."

"You're overthinking it," Doug mutters.

"How old?" Tripp asks firmly.

"He's a creep," Alice says. "Big-big trouble."

"Where did Jeff meet this guy? Does he work around here?" Tripp presses, putting his drink down on the table.

Doug notices Mike's concern. "Some record store off Cherry Street..."

Tripp looks around—Robbie's not back. Greg's nowhere to be seen. He looks at Doug. They don't have time for a crowd.

"We need to go," Tripp says, pointing to the door.

"Huh?" Doug blinks.

"You ain't leaving me behind!" Alice growls, punching Doug's arm.

Tripp grabs Doug's hand and pulls him toward the exit. Several guests look on curiously. Alice smiles politely and says, "We're out of dip... Come on, Dougie."

Outside, it's raining. That doesn't stop Tripp or Alice. Tripp runs to Doug's truck. Alice sprints after him. Doug knows he's lost this battle. Alice jumps in and slides to the middle of the bench seat. Tripp slams his door. Doug climbs in behind the wheel.

"OK, we're in my truck. Is there a plan?" Doug asks, glancing at Alice.

Alice shrugs.

"One forty Madison Grove Place," Tripp says coldly. "We need to go, Doug. **Now.**"

A Word of Caution: The chapters "Under The Rainy Skies" and "The Prayer Meeting" explore intense subject matter and contain vivid imagery. This content is intended for mature readers.

Under the Rainy Skies

T he sun has set under a dark cloud that has loomed over the city all afternoon. One forty Madison Grove Place is a nice ranch style house built in the late 1970's. It is a plain white house with gray shutters. The time is 7:30 and the rain comes down steadily.

Geoff paces the living room floor. Tonight is the night. He has planned it out well. Tyrone is set to arrive at 8:15. Geoff hopes to have everything ready for him by that time. *If I read the young guy correctly, it was not going to take a lot of effort.* Geoff pats his left shirt pocket. The magic joint is in this pocket.

Geoffrey is dressed in the dark gray dress pants. He is wearing a tight black button-down shirt, made of silk. The top four buttons are left open to expose the tone chest underneath. Goeff takes a moment to check his hair in the living room mirror.

The kitchen is on the front of the house. As you enter the modest home, there is a door way to the kitchen on the right. The hallway empties out in the living room. It is 20 feet long and 16 feet wide. In the center of the back wall, is a small sized fireplace. There are a couple of logs already glowing with warmth. To the left of the fireplace is a small television in the corner. To the right of the fireplace are several full-length mirrors attached to walls in the corner. Sitting at a 45° angle to the array of mirrors is a wooden saw horse.

Across the spine is a wide board with a faux leather cushion affixed to it, it is almost two feet long. The legs closest to the corner have two medium sized holes in each leg. The legs on the side facing to the center of the room has one large hole in each leg. A small box is under neath that contains multiple ropes of various lengths.

A small sofa is on the opposite wall. Dark blue fabric decorated by the fleur-de-lis in an exquisite pattern. A cheap black colored coffee table is arranged in front of the sofa. A door to the kitchen/ dining area is just to the left of the sofa. On the right-hand wall is a large recliner with black fabric. A large sized cardboard box rests in the center of the seat.

Only the two table lamps are on, keeping the room in a slight state of darkness. To the left of the living room are the two bedrooms and a single bathroom.

Geoff heads into the kitchen. He has a head of lettuce and several vegetables beside the cutting board on the counter. The L shaped counter and cabinets form the perimeter of the kitchen. Beside the sink is a white refrigerator. There is a small dining room table with two chairs.

Goeff checks the glass he has prepped for his guest. It sits by itself on the counter. Geoff pours himself a glass of wine. *The trap is set, just need my little virgin to show up,* Geoff thinks with an evil grin upon his face.

Geoff perks up when he hears the doorbell ring. He darts through the side door of the kitchen and into the entry hallway. He checks his hair one last time before opening the front door. He smiles big.

"Hello beautiful, I have been dreaming about you all week!" Geoff told the young man at the door.

Jeff Tyler blushes. He is not used to all this attention. He immediately notices that Geoffrey has shaved the beard. He does not like beards, the prickly hair always reminded him of his Uncle Chester. That man gave Jeff the creeps as a child.

Jeff is wearing a nice pair of designer jeans. He has on a white oxford button-down with a white undershirt beneath. He has on a pair of penny loafers that he borrowed from his dad. His blonde hair is styled with a gel. Emery helped him prepare for his date tonight. Everything had to be perfect.

Geoffrey motioned for Jeff to come in. He heads to the kitchen, with Jeff following closely behind. Jeff has a large smile on his face. Geoffrey gets to the counter and takes a sip of his wine.

"Want something to drink, love?" Geoffrey asks sweetly.

"I...uh, can I try some of your wine?" Jeff nervously inquires.

"Ever had wine before?" Geoffrey checks, offering his glass for Jeff to sample.

Jeff takes a small sip and nods to indicate he hasn't. He takes a bigger sip, "I like it, it is the sweet wine you were talking about. May I have a glass of this?"

Geoffrey smiles, "Yes, hon." He motions for Jeff to sit on the counter. Jeff walks over and Geoffrey picks him up easily and helps him to sit to the left of the sink. Geoffrey moves in close, pushing Jeff's legs apart at the knees. Jeff blushes again. Geoffrey leans in closely.

"It will cost you a hug, love," Geoffrey commands as he puts his arms around Jeff's waist–pulling him closer to the edge of the counter. Their bodies are almost touching in this embrace. Jeff wraps his arms around Geoffrey's broad shoulders and hugs him tight. His heart races.

"I see you shaved for me," Jeff whispers.

"I wanted you to know how much I care about you, hon. From the way you described your uncle, I could understand why it turned you off," Geoffrey smiles. "Does this mean I finally get a kiss?"

"May I have some wine to go with it," Jeff laughs.

"Absolutely, love. Anything for you," Geoffrey said as he steals a brief kiss on the lips.

Jeff closes his eyes and enjoys the tender moment. For a man, he is amazed how soft Geoffrey's lips are. Jeff likes the shirt that he is wearing, the bare chest has Jeff's mind racing. Geoffrey grabs the special glass. Jeff could not see from this angle, but there are about

20 cc's of a blue liquid in the bottom of his glass. Geoffrey quickly pours the wine into the glass and hands it to his prey.

"I'd suggest going slow until you get a feel for the alcohol. Wine is subtle, but you can get drunk quickly," Geoffrey explains as he rubs Jeff's upper thigh.

Jeff takes the wine glass and takes a few sips and smiles, "I am not sure what is sweeter, the wine or your kiss."

"I know which I prefer, Jeff," Geoffrey replies, placing his hand behind Jeff's neck and pulling him close to give Jeff a passionate kiss.

After a minute, Geoffrey pulls away. Jeff takes a moment to catch his breath, "Geoffrey. That was...amazing. I have never been kissed that way before."

"Hon, as our love grows, I will show you even more passion than you can imagine. But, like I told you, Jeff you have the control. I will not force you," Geoffrey comforts Jeff as he gives the boy another kiss.

Geoff pulls away. He can see that Jeff is flushed in the face. Jeff's tight jeans betrayed the young boy's arousal. *Wow, this kid's in the fast lane,* Geoff thinks.

He movess over to the far counter and starts chopping up the vegetables. He watches as Jeff takes another small sip of the wine. *He's a slow drinker, better break out the heavy artillery* Geoff smiles as he thinks of the plan. He sets the knife down beside the cutting board.

"I have another surprise, babe. I found some local weed for you," Geoff explains, pulling the joint from his shirt pocket. "Nothing too extreme. Should give you a nice buzz, if you want."

Jeff giggles, "I've smoked pot before. I warn you; I get silly..."

"You have a beautiful laugh, hon. Shall we light up before dinner?" Geoff extends his hand with the joint to Jeff.

Jeff can see that the wrapping paper has a blue tint to it. "That looks cool."

Geoff smiles; he sees that Jeff notices the blue color.

"It's a flavored paper," He explains. "I'm all out of the cherry, though..."

Jeff takes the joint from Geoff with a big smile, "Thanks, you think of everything!"

"I do," Geoff smiles and grabs one of his joints from his pants pocket.

"Can you show me how to French kiss?" Jeff asks.

"I will show you a good time, hon."

Geoffrey pulls a nice silver lighter out of his other pocket and lights his joint. Jeff puts his in his mouth. It dangles on the edge of his lips. Geoff thinks that Jeff really hasn't had pot before. It did not matter; he comes closer and lights up the blue tinted joint.

Jeff takes a long deep puff and smiles. He slowly blows the smoke out. Geoff smiles. Taking a few hits off his joint. He slowly begins to massage Jeff's thighs. Geoff watches the young boy inhale several more times as he his hands move up the legs..

Soon the magic would be working on Jeff. Geoff leans in and gives Jeff a kiss. He pulls away–walking back to the fridge and grabs his wine glass. As he turns around, he sees Jeff take a very big swallow of the wine.

He gets concerned, Jeff has smoked the joint and just consumed a lot of the wine. Both of these items are treated with the blue DMR concoction, Geoff worries that he may have given too much to the virgin.

Dihydrogen Monoxide Ribotoxin is a cleaning solvent that Ernesto used to clean his deli back in Philadelphia. It is touted as an all-natural and non-toxic cleaner.

It also has the unique ability to render a person unconscious for ten minutes. It works without any dangerous side effects. It leaves no traces in the blood. It's the perfect tool for Geoffrey to use. When the black out begins to wear off, the subject will be very suggestable, though the time that lasts varies from person to person. Geoff made the mistake once of not securing one young tart fast enough.

"Hey, babe. Maybe slow down a bit? We have all night..." Geoff warns, but pauses.

Geoff can see the stunned look in Jeff's eyes. The DMR works quickly in a regular dose, but the double dose seems to be putting Jeff out in the kitchen. Geoff takes his hand and pulls Jeff off the counter.

"Come on, babe...let's move this party to the living room," Geoff tells himself.

"Huh? Yeah...Geoff...that would..." Jeff's knees go weak.

Forcing him to grab a hold of Geoff. Jeff puts the joint on his lips and takes a long drag even though he can barely stand. Geoff is trying to get him into the living room quickly. Jeff stumbles, his mind in a complete fog. As they exit the kitchen, Jeff goes limp. Goeff holds on tight.

"Dammit!" Geoffrey curses.

He almost has Jeff to the saw horse. He reaches down and unfastens Jeff's belt. With his agile hands, Geoff is able to unfasten the pants and lower the zipper. The pants slip down to rest all bunched up below Jeff's thigh. Geoffrey unbuttons the white button down and pulls it away. Lifting Jeff up, he moves the boy to the sawhorse.

Geoff leans the boy on the soft leather cushion and pulls off the white undershirt. Pausing a moment to admire the soft pale skin of his prey. He runs a finger down Jeff's bare back. Geoff has a sinister smile on his face. This is the part he enjoys the most before they wake up. He carefully lays Jeff face down on the cushion.

Jeff's arms dangle to the sides. Geoff centers the boy on the cushion and walks around to the front. He reachs into the small box underneath and pulls out two thin ropes. With a practiced motion, he threads one rope through the holes in the leg of the sawhorse and wraps the rope around Jeff's left arm. Geoff quietly whistles a happy tune as he ties Jeff up. He repeats this intricate binding and tied the right arm next. This secured Jeff's hands tightly.

Geoff walks to the opposite end. He tugs hard and pulls off the pants. Leaving Jeff dressed in white briefs and his socks. Geoff kneels down and threads two more ropes though the back legs of the sawhorse. Jeff's legs are immobilized. Geoff pats Jeff's cotton covered bottom.

The DMR has Jeff out cold. *Within ten minutes, he should be awake,* Geoff reminds himself. He likes to watch their shock as they wake up and see themselves in the mirrors and struggle to get free.

Geoff is getting excited just thinking about it. He stands there admiring the bound-up teen bent over the sawhorse. Geoff loves this thing. He has all kinds of sick acts he could perform. There is no escaping this trap.

"Let the party begin!" Geoff laughs. "Tyrone better hurry, I am not sure I can wait."

Geoff glances at his watch. The time is now a quarter to eight.

"Hm, way ahead of schedule," Geoff congratulates himself. "Damn, I am good!"

Within five minutes, Jeff will start to wake up. It's different for each guy Geoffrey's had in this trap, but for at least a minute, the drugged person will do as ordered. It would not be long before the full effect of the DMR would wear off. Then he would stop and hear them plead and scream. That is when Geoff really unleashed his perversions on the unsuspecting partner.

But he will have to wait. Jeff is payment for the high potency weed from Texas. Tyrone wants a virgin. He also liked to abuse white guys. Jeff Tyler fits both of those requirements perfectly. Geoff thinks that was the deciding factors for his dealer.

Tyrone Bascome is physically fit and well endowed, even for a black man. Geoff wants to fully enjoy the show. He glances at his watch again. It is eight o'clock. He stops and looks at the mirrors. Jeff is still out.

"Damn it!" Geoff complained. "The little shit took too much. That joint was too much. I should have waited..."

The front door bell rings twice. Resuming the whistling tune, Geoff walks through the kitchen and grabs his wine. After a quick glance and a fast smoothing of his hair, the bell rings again. He took a long sip as Geoff answers the door.

Tyrone waits on the front porch, an imposing man at six feet tall and weighs a solid 225 pounds. Large biceps are tucked away in the sleeves of a brown jacket. He is wearing black leather pants. Under the jacket is a basketball jersey with the number 69. Tyrone smiles big–holding up his satchel.

"I brought a little extra for us to celebrate after I have my cracker and cheese," Tryone laughs, forcing his way past Geoff and into the house.

"Hot damn, Ty. I have your meal tied up in the living room," Geoffrey announces and reaches for the bag.

"Kink first, fag! I want my payment in full," Tyrone demands as he walked into the room.

"That was the deal, Ty. He should be fun," Geoff said walking in front of Tyrone and pointing at Jeff. "Hell of a kisser, too. Hope you don't mind?"

"Kiss? Pfft, I don't really care about that, it's just another hole to me," Tyrone lets out a sinister laugh.

"And you call me sick..." Geoffrey starts but is interrupted.

"Ooo, my fucked-up fiend, those mirrors are wicked," Ty yells, rubbing his leather pants. "I love this. That white boy's ass is up in the air, just perfect! The horse at the record store is nothing compared to this set up. You can see everything this way..."

"It's an incredible show to watch," Geoff proudly declares. "I even have an instant polaroid camera if you want!"

"You deviant!" Tyrone laughs. "You said he'd be ready at 8:15. Shouldn't he be awake? "

"It was a larger dose. He's still sleeping off the magic cocktail. I am guessing you want him fully awake?" Geoffrey nods and laughs in an evil manner.

"Absolutely. I want to see his fear when I unleash the anaconda up his ass!" Tryone pulls off his jacket and heads to the corner. "He'll be crying for momma in two minutes."

"He's all yours, Ty. I wasn't sure what kind of lube you wanted, so I have an assortment..."

"Lube? Shit, that's for sissies! I want to rip this cracker in two!" An angry Tyrone answers with a sadistic laugh.

"Can you leave him in one piece long enough for me to finish him off?" Geoffrey asks.

"No guarantees. This little bitch is making me hard now," Tryone smacks Jeff's butt.

"You paid for him, well at least you will..." Geoffrey points at the satchel, hoping to get some weed up front.

"One full bag of Texas, all for you, my sick friend!" Tyrone laughs. "You may even get a bonus for this pink little piggy."

Jeff's mind is a complete fog. He heard distant voices, like echoes in an empty cave. At the moment, he does not understand the words. He doesn't know where he is. His body tingles all over. The confusion runs through his mind as Jeff struggles to remember where he is and what he is doing.

The Prayer Meeting

Doug drives fast. He does not understand why Mike has this urgency to find Jeff. *This will just embarrass Jeff when we show up out of the blue. He will hate me,* Doug thinks as he turns onto Maplewood Road. Tripp lets out a grunt of frustration when the traffic light turns red and Doug stops.

"How much further is it, Doug?" Alice asks, looking at Doug.

"I dunno, Al. About ten minutes. A lot of lights going down the parkway..." Doug answers with a shrugging of his shoulders.

Tripp leans forward and looks at them, "Doug, **I can drive**, we don't have time for this!" as the stop light glows intensely red.

"Mike, you don't even have your glasses..." Doug replies, pointing at Mike's face.

"Doug," Frustrated, Tripp growls and reaches for the door handle. "Just fuckin' move over!"

Seeing that his friend is serious, startles Doug. Doug looks both ways and revs up the big block motor– releasing the brakes. The truck screams to life and leaps through the intersection. Doug is glad that there isn't much traffic. Driving like a madman is not unfamiliar to him, but Doug never attempted this at night, and in the rain. He glances at Tripp, *whatever is driving Mike is real.*

Doug floors the accelerator as the oversized four-barrel carburetor whines. Alice wraps her hands around Tripp's arm. She can see Tripp gripping the dash with his free hand.

He is focused. This isn't folly; his fear is real. The reality of the situation overcomes her. She has been complaining many times about Jeff's new interest. Though she knew she was right, she never thought it would have been this bad.

Doug darts around a couple of slow-moving cars. Alice and Tripp sway back and forth from the motion of the truck maneuvering at high speeds. The longer the silence continues in the cab of the truck, Doug becomes more anxious.

"On the left, Doug. Herbwood, it is a short cut!" Tripp yells.

Doug slams on the brakes as the tires screech loudly in protest. Doug turns the wheel–flooring it once again. The truck lurches forward as the motor propels the trio down the road. Doug has no words. He can see that Alice is worried. *How could I have been blind to this?*

Tripp thinks about the words that Rose used. Her warnings about Geoff and the history that she knew. He remembers the intense reaction that Scott had around Geoff. Alice digs her hands into Tripp's arm as the ride becomes more volatile.

"Mike...Jeff's going to be ok, right?" Alice asks with fear.

Tripp looked into her eyes with a slight shrug of his shoulders, he did not want to think of the consequences should they be late, "Turn right, Doug!"

Doug spins the steering wheel to the right and the truck leans from the force of taking a sharp turn at high speeds. The rain unleashes a constant sheet of water on the old truck's windshield. Doug has never been this afraid in his life. His heart feels like it is about to explode.

"Mike..." Alice begins in a weak voice, the tears starting to flow.

"There's Madison Grove, which way Mike?" Doug yells slamming on the brakes.

Tripp slides forward and looks to the right, then he strains to look to the left, "Uh..." He really needs his glasses at the moment.

"Oh, Mike! Please!" Alice cries out.

Tripp spots an old 57 chevy on the side of the road, "Left Doug! Six houses on the right!"

Doug revs the motor and follows Mike's directions.

"Oh my God! That's Jeff's car!" Alice screams, spotting the brown Pinto in the driveway.

Doug pulls his truck over to the curb in front of the small ranch styled house, "OK, Mike...what's the plan..."

He isn't fast enough; Tripp jumps out of the truck and runs towards the front door. He can see Geoff's van and an old Impala he does not recognize. The front porch light is on and Tripp makes a bee-line to the door. Doug scrambles to get out of the truck and dashes to the same location. Alice slides out of the cab of the truck, wiping the tears away as she follows close behind.

"Mike!" Doug calls out. "Mike, wait. What are we going to do?"

Out of breath, Tripp stops on the porch and presses the doorbell button, "Whatever we have to do, Doug..."

Tripp presses the button again; they can hear the chimes going off. Tripp presses it again, then beats on the door. They can hear the muffled sounds of a man yelling profanities. There are sounds of the lock mechanism being unlatched. Doug uses his arm to move Alice behind him and Tripp.

Tryone opens the door, looking pissed, "What the fuck?"

"Hey!" Doug exclaims. "We're here for the Bible study, hope we ain't late..."

"That is our friend's car. Jeff invited us!" Alice remarks, hiding behind Doug.

"Shit, you just missed him," Tyrone barks as he moves to close the door.

Doug places his foot against the door, Tripp steps forward, "His car is here, Snoop Dog. Can we talk to Jeff?"

"Snoop?" Tryone looks at Tripp like he is crazy. "What the fuck is a snoop dawg?"

"Ty, what is going on?" Geoff yells, coming around the corner. He freezes when he sees Tripp.

"See, there's Geoff. Tell this clown we are here for the bible study with Jeff!" Tripp yells.

"Damn Tripp, sorry man. He was uh...Jeff felt sick and I took him home," Goeff answers with suspicion.

"Hey Jeffy!" Tripp waves with sarcasm. "Mind if I use your phone...you know to call Jeff."

"G, what the fuck is this shit?" Tyrone barks, looking back at Geoff.

Geoff makes it to the doorway and folds his arms, "Jeff ain't here. You shouldn't be either, Tripp."

"No problem...say, can I use your bathroom?" Doug asks forcefully.

"Yeah, well piss off, shithead!" Geoff answers as he grabs the door to help close it.

In the livingroom, Jeff can hear some commotion near him. His mind is still in a fog. He struggles to open his eyes but cannot. His face feels numb. He is so confused. He begins to panic. Jeff thinks he cannot move, but he is not sure if his body just wasn't responding. The voices get louder. Jeff wants desperately to understand. His head hurts. He finally gets his eyes to open. It is blurry, but he can see a reflection in a mirror. He fights to be able to see.

He hears the voices again. He recognizes one of the voices. *Tripp Carson?* Jeff shakes his head. His vision starts to clear. The tingling and numbness fades–Jeff realizes he is tied to something. He struggles; the frame of the saw horse makes noise as Jeff moves. He can finally make out what he sees. He knows he only in his underwear–tied to something and in a very compromising position.

He hears the voice again. *Tripp,* Jeff tries to call out. It is difficult, his body is not doing what he wants. He tries again, *Tripp, please!* Still nothing. Jeff sums all the effort he can, knowing that his life depends on it.

"T-T-Tripp..." Jeff is able to say softly. His throat is dry and hurt.

Jeff isn't heard, he tries again, the fear driving him, "Tripp!" This time it is loud enough to be heard.

Tripp's eyes get big, he glances at Doug. Doug puts his hand on the door, glaring at Tyrone, "We just want our friend."

Tripp swallows hard. Tyrone rolls his shoulders forward, "Get lost, peckerwood"

"Geoff. Please. I just want my friend and we'll leave," Tripp pleads.

Doug motions at Alice," Al, run to the truck. If we don't walk back with Jeff in sixty seconds, lay on the horn until the whole neighborhood is awake!"

Alice takes off running through the rain, and Tyrone looks at Geoff. Tripp steps in front of him. Geoff flashes a sinister grin, "So I guess Jeff is the little tart you are in love with? Fuck you, you ain't nothing but a little tease. Get lost before I hurt you, **boy**. Tonight, Jeff is all mine!"

With as much force as Tripp can summon, he lunges into Goeff, knocking him backward. Doug quickly attacks with a jabbing punch into Tyrone's chest, causing the black man to cough.

"Oh, shit. Cracker's got some moves, huh? When I am done wiping the floor with your ass, I am going to kill you!" Tyrone barks, taking a swing at Doug.

Doug is able to block the first swing, but Tyrone makes contact with the next. Tyrone is surprised that it has no affect on the teen. Doug spins around and kicks Tyrone in the abdomen.

Goeff punches Tripp hard in the chest. Tripp slams his foot on top of Geoff's and then punches him in the nose.

Alice watches helplessly as the fight begins. "Shit!" she yells and slams both hands on the horn button of Doug's old truck. The loud response startles everyone.

Months ago, Robbie laughingly told Doug that he should install a train horn in the pickup as a joke. Doug is glad he followed up on that humorous suggestion. The intensely loud horn continues to blare as the lights in several houses begin to come on. Everyone in the county can hear it.

Geoff falls back, nursing the injury. Blood freely runs down Geoff's face. Undeterred, he flashes an evil smile while jumping at Tripp, screaming wildly as he moves. Tripp stumbles backward toward the fireplace. He shrieks out in pain as Geoff forces him into the wall, knocking the wind out of him. As the fight continues, Alice keeps the horn going. Several neighbors have exited their homes as more lights come on throughout the neighborhood.

Tyrone fights well, but Doug remains focused, countering every move. Doug lands a jab to the face. Then several punches to the gut as Tyrone yells out, pushing Doug away. Doug pivots and spins around; this time, his foot makes contact with the side of Tyrone's face. The force of the kick almost flips the large man over. Doug rapidly punches Tyrone as he loses balance and hits the ground. Doug stomps hard.

By this time, the neighbor across the street steps out on his porch. Still in his uniform, having left the station late, Corporal Nowak quickly assesses the situation. He does not recognize the caucasian male or the black adult male exchanging blows in the front yard. He can see the terrified girl sitting in the pickup is the source of the ear-piercing sound.

"Margie, hustle up and dial the station! We got a 10-103, multiple suspects, officer needs assistance. Do it now!" Jakup yells over his shoulder as he runs across the yard. **"NOW!"**

Alice spots the police officer running out of the home across the street. She stops pressing the horn button and frantically points towards the house where her friends are fighting for their lives. The policeman heads to the first two people fighting.

"Police!" Nowak commands, "On the ground! NOW!"

Doug raises his hands in surrender and quickly gets onto the ground. Tryone is holding his chest, rolling around from the pain. He coughs, and some blood appears on Tyrone's lips. His fight is over.

Nowark commands, "Police! Freeze!"

From inside the house, a familiar voice cries out. Tripp pleads, "Geoff, stop it!"

Geoff punches Tripp hard in the stomach, and he doubles over. Tripp catches a glimpse of something by the fireplace. He grabs the poker and moves quickly, swinging the iron rod at Goeff's leg. Geoff is knocked off balance. Tripp swings again, hitting behind the knee, forcing Geoffrey to the floor. Geoff screams out in pain, holding his injured leg.

Alice pushes herself out the window and yells, "Officer. Inside! Please hurry!"

Nowak moves to Doug and Tyrone, He swiftly removes his handcuffs. The seasoned police officer secures the two subjects to each other. Jakup operates on instinct and muscle memory. Years of training and dedicated service have taught him well. He is no stranger to deadly altercations.

"Help Jeff!" Doug screams, not resisting the policeman.

Officer Nowak unholsters his revolver and dashes to the door, "Police!"

He quickly checks the entryway, then proceeds in. He kicks open the kitchen door and assesses whether there is a threat. He moves forward into the room, only to be redirected when he hears someone calling out. It is a voice he recognizes.

"In here!" Tripp yells out as he gets onto his knees.

Nowak advances to the corner aiming at Tripp and Geoff. Tripp quickly places both hands on top of his head. Jakup spots another boy bound up on something in the corner.

"Tripp!" Corporal Nowak recognizes him. "Face down, on the ground, kid!"

"Help Jeff!" Tripp answers as he lies face down. Geoffrey, still holding his knee, curses under his breath while rocking back and forth, wincing in pain.

Nowak steps over to the corner. He can see the boy struggling. The ropes are arranged elaborately, securing him by his arms and legs. The subject is tied up too well for him to escape. The sounds of multiple police sirens can now be heard approaching. Tripp sighs in relief. Officer Nowak knows his backup is near, but he isn't out of the woods yet.

Nowak commands in a loud voice, "Cut the struggle, kid. I'm a cop, here to help. But you gotta stop moving, you hear?"

"Please! Help...help me!" Terror flows through his mind, Jeff cries out, still trying to free himself.

"It's all right, kid...just relax," Corporal Nowak lowers his voice and holsters his weapon.

Jeff can see clearly now. In the mirrors, he can see that it is Tripp Carson that he had heard. Jeff begins to cry quietly, the tears flowing down his face. Geoff moans, obviously injured. Jeff cannot help but feel glad; he trusted Geoff. He closes his eyes, thankful for Tripp Carson. Jeff opens his eyes and sees the policeman. He overcomes his fear and stops moving.

"I'm getting your legs first. Don't move, kid," Nowak instructs as he moves slowly so the boy could see.

Jeff nods. Nowak kneels, untying the ropes on the boy's legs. Tripp notices movement beside him. Geoff has rolled onto his knees and is trying to stand up.

"Jakup! Behind you!" Tripp warns.

Reacting from years of training, Jakup Nowak spins around as he removes the Billy club from his belt. Geoff tries to stand, but Officer Nowak strikes several blows to subdue him. Geoff grunts in pain, falling back down. Corporal Nowak remains steadfast. The sirens stop, having arrived on the scene. Two officers yell out that they are entering the house.

"Back here!" Nowak replies loudly.

The officers enter the room with their weapons drawn. They see that the corporal has everything in hand. The older officer nods to the hall. One officer goes to check the other rooms. The second cop moves to handcuff the two subjects, one teen and one adult male. Another cop brings in Doug, still handcuffed. Doug lets out a gasp as he sees Jeff. The cop pulls Doug over by Tripp and Geoff.

Jakup Nowak returns to the bound-up subject to remove the ropes securing his arms. He can see the boy trembling from fear. Nowak looks over his shoulder at Tripp. Tripp smiles and mouths, "Thank you." Nowak nods. He moves to the other side. He can see the endless stream of tears on the frightened boy's face.

"Tripp?" Jeff calls out, half with joy and half with fear.

"It's gonna be OK, Jeff. He's here to help," Tripp yells back, not moving until the cops instruct him otherwise.

"All right, Jeff, hold your horses. Once I loosen these ropes, let me get up first. Got it?" Nowak commands in a calm and steady tone.

Jeff nods, "Yes...uh, yes sir..."

Corporal Nowak unfastens the last rope. He stands up and taps Jeff on the back, "Take it easy, Jeff. Can you stand up, nice and slow?"

"I'll try... but my legs still feel funny," Jeff tries to say as he sniffles.

Corporal Nowak cups his hand under Jeff's arm to help him stand. Jeff's legs are weak, and he is losing balance. Jeff moans as his legs cry out in pain. Nowak steadies Jeff until he can stand up straight. His leg muscles are spasming. He places his hand on the cop's forearm. Nowak smiles, reassuring Jeff he is safe.

"You need a hand getting dressed again, kid?"

"I never... I never want those clothes back," Jeff replies without emotion.

"I get it, kid." Nowak nods and motions for one of the other officers to grab a blanket.

"Yo, Tripp, mind filling me in on what went down here?" Jakup asks as he helps Jeff over to the sofa to sit.

The second cop helps Tripp to his feet and walks him over to the corporal, "Yes, sir. Uh, well, Doug and I came to help Jeff..."

Nowak nods toward Geoff, "Is that the dude you were talkin' 'bout the other night?"

Tripp just nods, feeling embarrassed. Nowak shakes his head; glad that helped Tripp that night. Evidently, he was right about the man being a pedophile. Nowak wants nothing more than to have about five minutes with the dirtbag in private.

"Hey, Corporal!" the cop exits one of the bedrooms and yells. "Wanna come check this out?"

Nowak holds up one finger at Tripp and heads to the hallway. He follows the junior officer into the small bedroom. There are heat lamps over a small planter full of marijuana plants. On a workbench is a small oven. In front of the oven is a glass casserole dish. It has a layer of blue liquid in it. Spread out in the dish are over a dozen joints. Each with a varying degree of saturation of the blue liquid. The rookie holds up the satchel that Tyrone brought.

"Sir, I think this is the contraband from Texas; it has that particular smell to it," the rookie explains, showing the contents to the corporal.

"Check out the size of that bag. Looks like we got a couple of felonies we can nail 'em with. Nice work," Corporal Nowak praises his subordinate.

"What the hell do ya think that is, sir?" the rookie asks, pointing at the casserole dish.

Then Nowak notices the large container of cleaning solvent—a commercial-grade product available to anyone. He makes an angry grunt, "DMR..."

The confused rookie asks, "What?"

Corporal Nowak answers with disgust. "Dihydrogen Monoxide Ribotoxin. It's a non-toxic water based solvent with an interesting side effect."

"Sounds complicated..." The young officer shrugs.

"My cousin out in Philly, he's Vice," Nowak explains. "They've been clocking this freaky trend. This cleaning solvent, DMR, creeps are using it as a date rape drug. Nasty stuff, real effective, and tough to trace."

"Never heard of it," The young cop answers with a shake of his head.

"Yeah, well, it **was** unique to Philly..." Nowak shares more details. "It renders the victim unconscious and possibly suggestable when the awaken. It's water based, safe but untraceable."

"Guess not anymore, sir," he said with sadness.

"Corporal!" someone calls out from the living room.

"Good work," Nowark instructs. "Best collect this evidence. Make sure they photograph everything."

Corporal Nowak enters the living room. He can see that Jeff is shivering on the couch. The small blanket is not sufficient to cover the teenage boy, One of the officers from the front yard is looking at a box lying on the recliner seat. He looks up and motions for the corporal to come look.

"Hey, corporal, I am taking Tyrone Bascome to the ambulance for treatment." An officer updates him from the hallway.

"OK," He answers as he looks in the box. Jakup's face turns white as ash from what he sees. "Jesus, Mary, and Joseph! This scumbag's been pulling this crap for way too long!"

Tripp's interest is piqued, and he wonders what that means. The other cop joins Nowak as they investigate the box. The corporal reaches in and removes dozens of Polaroid pictures. Tripp can't see what was in the pictures, but there are a handful. The second cop glances over at the set-up in the corner.

"Fuckin' hell!" He mutters angrily. "How are we going to proceed?"

Nowak shrugs his shoulders and motions for Tripp to come over to him. Tripp looks at the cop standing beside him. With an approving nod, he moves towards Nowak. Doug can see that Jeff is cold and scared.

"Uh, officer. Sir, is... is it OK if I grab some sweatpants from my truck for Jeff?" Doug politely asks.

Nowak looks to the rookie, then at Doug, "All right, let's hold tight for now. Where you got those sweatpants stashed in your truck? I'll send someone to grab 'em."

"Duffle bag in the bed, sir," Doug replies.

The rookie leaves the room. Tripp patiently stands beside Corporal Nowak. He is nervous. Now that time has passed, and the adrenalin is gone, Tripp can't help but worry about what this will mean. He would have never guessed that this is how his night was going to end.

"Corporal, yes...sir, do you need me?" Tripp acknowledges.

Jakup Nowak leans close and whispered, "There's enough evidence here to throw the book at that scumbag and his dealer. I'll try to keep you and your buddies outta the reports. But you gotta know, this could draw a lot of eyes. Capisce?"

"Yes, sir. If you need a name, can you just use mine? I kinda feel responsible..." Tripp admitts reluctantly.

Still whispering, Nowak looks him in the eyes, "Tripp, keep in mind everything I laid out about that guy. Seems he's been pulling this scam time and again. You couldn't have seen it coming or done a damn thing about it. But what you and your friend did here tonight, that's some real heroic stuff."

"Sir?"

"Fuckin' heroic," Corporal Nowak said, patting Tripp on the shoulder. "Perkins, these two and the girl by the pickup truck, we can cut 'em loose. I got all the info I need from 'em."

"Yes, sir," Perkins answers pulling his handcuff key from his pocket and unlocks Doug.

Tripp smiles, grateful for the mercy he has received, he whispers back, "Jakup, I meant what I said. I will stand up if you need me to..."

"I know kid, see ya round," Jakub Nowak replies as he pulls his key out.

Perkins helps Jeff get dressed. Doug's sweat pants are for a tall individual and fully consume Jeff. He looks like a kid, dressed up in his father's clothes. But, Jeff does not care. He wants to get away from this house. As far away as possible. After Nowak uncuffs, Tripp, Jeff runs over and hugs him.

"Jeff, you ready?" Doug asks quietly.

"You wanna go home, Jeff?" Tripp motions for Jeff to leave.

"No...can I just stay with you for a while?" Jeff answers not letting go.

"We can do whatever you want, Jeff. Feel up to going to Lauren Master's party?" Doug asks softly. "Maybe some music and fun will help?"

Jeff smiles with a nod. He looks at Doug then Tripp. He couldn't think of what may have happened had they not shown up. Jeff no longer cares. He is surrounded by friends.

Corporal Nowak steps over, tapping Tripp on the shoulder. He gives Tripp car keys and a wallet that he retrieved from the discarded pants.

Jakup Nowak smiles, "He might need these, Tripp. Give me a buzz if you need anything. He might just need someone to talk to, you know?"

"Yes sir. I don't know how to repay you," Tripp replies, knowing that Jakup would not ask.

Doug and Jeff start heading out the door. Tripp offers a handshake to their benefactor. Jakup Nowak smiles and returns the handshake. He pulled out another one of his business cards and tries slipping it into Tripp's shirt pocket, but the pocket is torn. Accepting the card, Tripp nods with a smile and heads out the door.

Alice is mothering Jeff beside the truck. Doug looks lost, but happy that Jeff isn't hurt. Tripp sprints over to the truck. He can see the neighbors still in their yards, watching these events unfold.

Tripp holds up the keys, "Who wants to drive the Pinto Bomb?"

"Oh, I love danger!" Alice laughs, "Gimme the keys, I can handle that. Just take care of my Jeff."

Doug gets in and cranks up the truck. Tripp opens the passenger door and helps Jeff into the truck. Tripp turns–taking one last look at Geoff's home. A house of horrors.

How many unsuspecting guys fell prey to this piece of garbage? He takes a deep breath. He has to believe that he was here for a reason...

A Mix of the Truth

D oug finds his way back to Maplewood. No one has said anything since leaving. Jeff rests his head on Tripp's shoulder. He has his arm around Jeff. Tripp remembers his training from when he volunteered. He knows that Jeff will need some level of therapy. But it was rare to get that kind of help in the 80's, especially for homosexuals. Right now, it is just a matter of feeling secure. Tripp pulls Jeff close.

Doug watches from the corner of his eye. Now that the world has slowed to a speed he can comprehend, he wonders how this is possible. He hates himself for not listening to Alice sooner. She suspected something terrible when Jeff first mentioned the guy was interested in him. But this is not the main thought in his mind.

How did Mike know? There seems to be more going on than it appears. For a moment, Doug wonders if it should remain a secret.

"Uh, Jeff. I'm sorry," Doug offers, his voice uncertain. "I really should've listened to Alice."

"Doug, you came to help...that is all that mattered," Jeff looks at Doug and then Tripp. "You saved me. Both of you..."

Tripp is unsure how to respond: "I guess I'm sorry too, Jeff. I should have asked more that night at the river."

"Shh," Jeff replies, resting his head on Tripp's shoulder. "You were doing what a good friend should."

Tripp nods. Doug switches lanes and passes a slower truck. He keeps glancing over to Jeff. Doug has known Jeff almost as long as he has known Rob Davis, maybe longer. As kids, they played together. Doug glances at Tripp, fixating on the bright yellow shirt.

Doug remembers it was a gift from Stephanie Davis. He knows Robbie's sister never did anything without a reason. He thinks about all the changes Tripp Carson has made in the past few months. He worries that he recognizes what may have triggered that change. *Since the jump-start, I have learned so much about Mike; I should leave this alone...*

"Hey, Mike?" Doug asks, taking a deep breath.

"Yeah, Doug?" Tripp answers, leaning forward.

"I need to ask you something...it's uh, personal," Doug hesitating as he looks at Tripp.

"Doug, I'd like to think we are close friends now. You followed me blindly tonight. I know I can trust you," Tripp confides to Doug.

"Yeah, I did...and I will. You have my word. Are you," Doug pauses and stares at Tripp. "Are you in love with Lauren?"

"Betty made a thing about me and Lauren too," Tripp says with a smile. "Yes, I do love her—but like a sister. A sister, Doug. She's been my confidant while I figured out how to apologize to everyone I hurt."

"Like me?" Jeff asks enthusiastically, looking Tripp in the eyes.

"Yes...Jeff, I am sorry I didn't apologize the day I first arrived," Tripp answers with a smile.

"Arrived?" Doug and Jeff inquire in confusion and they wait for Tripp to reply.

"Yeah, uh...arrived at the conclusion I needed to be a better person. I guess fate had its reasons for picking that date," Tripp looks to his feet and takes a deep breath. "Things could have been worse. So much worse. Just gotta have faith."

Jeff smiles, hugging Tripp tight. Doug thinks about the answer. He remembers the party earlier and runs through every minute he has spent with Tripp Carson. *There are no other possibilities.* Despite his reservations, Doug has to know.

"Uh, Tripp...I need to ask," Doug begins reluctantly. "You can tell me to pound sand, but how did *you* know?"

"Know what?" Jeff asks, confused by the question.

"About your... your date," Doug says, glancing at him. "How'd you know something was wrong?"

Tripp gazes at Doug. *Does he know? Will it even matter if I tell them the truth?* Tripp sighs. Jeff turns and looks at Tripp. They're putting him on the spot. There is no way to avoid . He needs to say something. *Maybe a mix of the truth?* Tripp clears his throat.

"I've been going to that music store for a while, just to buy albums, plus there is a woman that I kinda like. Uh, she's 19. Rose, she works there. So does Geoffrey. Sometimes, I would show up and that guy tried to flirt with me. I didn't think anything about it but he kept flirting," Tripp explains.

Doug silently listens.

"Rose stopped by Maddox a few days ago. She told me some things that I didn't understand until you and Alice talked to me at the party."

"I'm glad you knew, Tripp. I'd be lost without you," Jeff interjects, resting his head on Tripp's shoulder. Tripp smiles, believing he dodged the issue.

Doug grunts, offering a skeptical nod. He isn't 100% certain, but Doug has the answer he wants. The altercation with Geoff occurred quickly – it has been a whirlwind night so far. So many things have happened, too many secrets exposed. Doug is glad that he and Tripp have become friends.

Tripp was right about fate. Doug reaches for the radio and cuts it on. The music fills the silence between them, knowing he has to stop talking. But that awareness does not stop the flood of thoughts in his mind. Doug asks himself, *Now, I just need to decide:*

Am I telling Rob?

Wait—this isn't the end.

The story of Michael Willis Carson continues.

Twice in One Lifetime set the stage for an unforgettable journey: one boy, two lifetimes, and countless second chances. But Tripp's story is far from over. Continue with the next chapters in his incredible journey to fix the past, help those he loves, and discover a love that just might last a lifetime.

Book Two – *The Price of Living Twice*

Tripp Carson fights to reshape his identity while avoiding the shadows of the life he left behind. As his mission to make things right leads him to Jeff Tyler, he begins to understand that redemption comes with a cost.

Book Three – *This Lifetime's Truth*

At a crossroads, Tripp and Robbie must navigate the fallout of hidden truths and difficult choices. As pressure mounts and hearts are tested, Tripp finds himself asking the hardest question of all: Can love truly last a lifetime?

www.ingramcontent.com/pod-product-compliance
Lightning Source LLC
Chambersburg PA
CBHW030757260626
47169CB00001B/86